THE SEVENTH
SACRAMENT

DAVID
HEWSON
THE SEVENTH
SACRAMENT

MACMILLAN

First published 2007 by Macmillan
an imprint of Pan Macmillan Ltd
Pan Macmillan, 20 New Wharf Road, London N1 9RR
Basingstoke and Oxford
Associated companies throughout the world
www.panmacmillan.com

ISBN 978-1-4050-5022-7 HB
ISBN 978-1-4050-9240-1 TPB

1 3 5 7 9 8 6 4 2

A CIP catalogue record for this book is available from
the British Library.

Typeset by Intype Libra Ltd
Printed and bound in Great Britain by
Mackays of Chatham plc, Chatham, Kent

Visit **www.panmacmillan.com** to read more about all our books
and to buy them. You will also find features, author interviews and
news of any author events, and you can sign up for e-newsletters
so that you're always first to hear about our new releases.

THE SEVENTH SACRAMENT

Principal Characters

THE PAST

Alessio Bramante – a schoolboy
Giorgio Bramante – his father, an archaeologist
Leo Falcone – a police *sovrintendente*
Arturo Messina – police commissario over Leo Falcone
Ludo Torchia, Toni LaMarca, Dino Abati, Sandro Vignola, Raul Bellucci, Andrea Guerino – students under Giorgio Bramante

THE PRESENT

Dino Abati – a homeless man
Raffaela Arcangelo – Leo Falcone's partner
Ornella Di Benedetto – warden of the church of Santa Maria dell'Assunta

Beatrice Bramante – former wife of Giorgio, mother of Alessio
Silvio Di Capua – Teresa Lupo's deputy
Nic Costa – an *agente* in the Rome Questura
Cristiano – a biologist specializing in worms
Emily Deacon – Costa's partner
Leo Falcone – Costa and Peroni's inspector
Pino Gabrielli – warden of the Piccolo Museo del Purgatorio
Lorenzo Lotto – a left-wing aristocrat and magazine owner
Teresa Lupo – chief pathologist
Arturo Messina – Bruno's father, now retired from the police in
    disgrace
Bruno Messina – police commissario over Leo Falcone
Gianni Peroni – a fellow *agente*
Rosa Prabakaran – a junior police *agente*
Prinzivalli – a police *sovrintendente*
Judith Turnhouse – an archaeologist
Enzo Uccello – a criminal on release

Mithras, God of the Midnight, here where the great bull dies,
Look on thy children in darkness. Oh take our sacrifice!
Many roads thou hast fashioned – all of them lead to the Light,
Mithras, also a soldier, teach us to die aright!

A Song to Mithras (Hymn of the XXX Legion: circa 350 AD),
Rudyard Kipling

Part 1

A CHILD IN DARKNESS

- 1 -

The boy stood where he usually did at that time of the morning. In the Piazza dei Cavalieri di Malta, on the summit of the Aventino hill, not far from home. Alessio Bramante was wearing the novelty glasses from his birthday party the day before, peering through them into the secret keyhole, trying to make sense of what he saw.

The square was only two minutes' walk from his front door, and the same from the entrance to the Scuola Elementare di Santa Cecilia, so this was a journey he made every day, always with his father, a precise and serious man who would retrace his steps from the school gates, then enter the outpost of the university in the square which acted as his office. This routine was now so familiar Alessio knew he could cover the route with his eyes closed.

He adored the piazza, which had always seemed to him as if it belonged in a fairy-tale palace, not on the Aventino, a hill for ordinary, everyday men and women.

Palms and great conifers, like Christmas trees, fringed the white walls which ran around three sides of the piazza, adorned at precise intervals with needle-like Egyptian obelisks and the crests of great families. They were the work, his father said, of a famous artist called Piranesi who, like all his kind in the Rome of the past, was as skilled an architect as he was a draftsman.

Alessio wished he could have met Piranesi. He had a precise mental image of him: a thin man, always thinking, with dark skin, piercing

3

eyes and a slender, waxy moustache which sat above his upper lip looking as if it had been painted there. He was an entertainer, a clown who made you laugh by playing with the way things looked. When he grew up Alessio would organize events in the piazza, directing them himself, dressed in a severe dark suit, like his father. There would be elephants, he thought, and small parades with dancers and men in commedia dell'arte costumes juggling balls and pins to the bright music of a small brass band.

All this would come, at some stage in that grey place called the future, which revealed itself a little day by day, like a shape emerging from one of the all-consuming mists that sometimes enshrouded the Aventino in winter, making it a ghostly world, unfamiliar to him, full of hidden, furtive noises, and unseen creatures.

An elephant could hide in that kind of fog, he thought. Or a tiger, or some kind of beast no one, except Piranesi in his gloomiest moments, could imagine. Then he reminded himself of what his father had said only a few days before, not quite cross, not quite.

No one gains from an overactive imagination.

No one needed such a thing on a day like this either. It was the middle of June, a beautiful, warm, sunny morning, with no hint of the fierce inferno that would fall from the bright blue sky well before the onset of August. At that moment he had room in his head for just a single wonder, one he insisted on seeing before he went to Santa Cecilia and began the day.

'Alessio,' Giorgio Bramante said again, a little brusquely.

He knew what his father was thinking. At seven, tall and strong for his age, he was too old for these games. A little – what was the word he'd heard him use once? – headstrong too.

Alessio was unsure how old he was when his father first introduced him to the keyhole. He had soon realized that it was a secret shared. From time to time others would walk up to the green door and take a peek. Occasionally taxis would stop in the square, release a few baffled tourists for a moment, which seemed a sin. This was a private ritual to be kept among the few, those who lived on the Aventino hill, he thought. Not handed out to anyone.

*

It was to be found on the river side of the piazza, at the centre of a white marble gatehouse, ornate and amusing, one of the favourite designs, he had no doubt, of that man with the moustache who still lived in his head. The upper part of the structure was fringed with ivy that fell over what looked like four windows, although they were filled in with stone – 'blind' was the word Giorgio Bramante, who was fond of architecture and building techniques, used. Now he was older Alessio realized the style was not unlike one of the mausoleums his father had shown him when they went together to excavations and exhibitions around the city. The difference was that it possessed, in the centre, a heavy, two-piece door, old and solid and clearly well used, a structure that whispered, in a low, firm voice: keep out.

Mausoleums were for dead people, who had no need of doors that opened and closed much. This place, his father had explained all those years ago, was the entrance to the garden of the mansion of the Grand Master of the Knights of Malta, leader of an ancient and honourable order, with members around the world, some of whom were fortunate enough, from time to time, to make a pilgrimage to this very spot.

He could still remember first hearing that there were knights living nearby. He'd lain awake in bed that evening wondering if he'd hear their horses neighing in the warm summer breeze, or the clash of their swords on armour as they jousted in the secret garden beyond Piranesi's square. Did they take young boys as pages, knights in the making? Was there a round table? Some blood oath which swore them to silent, enduring brotherhood? A book where their good deeds were recorded in a hidden language, impenetrable to anyone outside the order?

Even now Alessio had no idea. Hardly anyone came or went from the place. He'd given up watching. Perhaps they only emerged in the dark, when he was in bed, wide awake, wondering what he'd done to be expelled from the living world for no good reason.

A Carabinieri car sat by the gatehouse most of the time, two bored-looking officers ostentatiously eyeing up visitors to make sure no one became too curious. That rather killed the glamour of the Knights of Malta. It was hard to imagine an order of true gallantry would need men in uniforms, with conspicuous guns, to watch the door to its grand mansion.

But there was a miracle there, one he felt he'd grown up with. He could still remember the days when his father used to pick him up, firm arms beneath his weak ones, lifting gently, until his eye reached the keyhole, old green paint chipped away over the centuries to reveal something like lead or dull silver beneath.

Piranesi – it must have been him, no one else would have had the wit or the talent – had performed one last trick in the square. Somehow he'd managed to align the keyhole of the Knights' mansion directly with the basilica of St Peter's which lay a couple of kilometres away beyond the Tiber. Peering through the tiny gap in the door produced an image that was just like a painting itself. The gravel path pointed straight across the river to its subject, shrouded on both sides by a tunnel of thick cypresses, dark green exclamation marks so high they stretched beyond the scope of the keyhole, forming a hidden canopy above everything he could see. At the end of this natural passageway, framed, on a fine day, in a bright, upright rectangle of light, stood the great church dome, which seemed suspended in the air, as if by magic.

He knew about artists. The dome was the work of Michelangelo. Perhaps he and Piranesi had met some time and made a pact: you build your church, I'll make my keyhole, and one day someone will spot the trick.

Alessio could imagine Piranesi twirling his moustache at that idea. He could imagine, too, that there were other riddles, other secrets, undiscovered across the centuries, waiting for him to be born and start on their trail.

Can you see it?

This was a ritual, a small but important one that began every school day, every weekend walk that passed through Piranesi's square. When Alessio peered through the keyhole of the mansion of the Knights of Malta what he saw through the lines of trees, magnificent across the river, was proof that the world was whole, that life went on. What Alessio had only come to realize of late was that his father required this reassurance as much as he did himself. With this small daily ceremony the bond between them was renewed.

Yes. It's still there.

The day could begin. School and singing and games. The safe routine of family life. And other rituals too. His birthday celebration was a kind of ceremony. His entry into the special age – seven, the magical number – disguised as a party for infants. One where his father had picked out the stupid present from the lucky dip, something that seemed interesting when Alessio read the packaging, but just puzzled him now he tried it out.

The 'fly-eye glasses' were flimsy plastic toy spectacles, large and cumbersome, badly made too, with arms so weak they flopped around his ears as he tucked the ends carefully beneath his long jet-black hair in an effort to keep them firm on his face. The toy was supposed to let you witness reality the way a fly did. Their multifaceted eyes had lenses which were, in turn, hosts to many more lenses, hundreds perhaps, like kaleidoscopes without the flakes of coloured paper to get in the way, producing a universe of associated views of the same scene, all the same, all different, all linked, all separate. Each thinking it was real and its neighbour imaginary, each, perhaps, living under the ultimate illusion, because Alessio Bramante was, he said to himself, no fool. Everything he saw could be unreal, every flower he touched, every breath he took, nothing more than a tiny fragment tumbling from someone else's ever-changing dreams.

Crouched hard against the door, trying to ignore the firm, impatient voice of his father, he was aware of another adult thought, one of many that kept popping into his head of late. This wasn't just the fly's view. It was that of God too. A distant, impersonal God, somewhere up in the sky, who could shift his line of vision just a millimetre, close one great eye, squint through another, and see his creations a myriad different ways, trying better to understand them.

Alessio peered more intently and wondered: is this one world divided into many, or do we possess our own special vision, a faculty that, for reasons of kindness or convenience, he was unsure which, simplified the multitude into one?

Fanciful thoughts from an over-imaginative child.

He could hear his father repeating those words though they never slipped from his lips. Instead, Giorgio Bramante was saying something entirely different.

'Alessio,' he complained, half ordering, half pleading. 'We have to go. Now.'

'Why?'

What did it matter if you were late? School went on forever. What were a few lost minutes when you were peering through a knights' keyhole searching for the dome of St Peter's, trying to work out who was right, the humans or the flies?

'Because today's not an ordinary day!'

He took his face away from the keyhole then, carefully, unwound the flimsy glasses and stuffed them into the pocket of his trousers.

'It isn't?'

His father snatched a glance at his watch, which seemed unnecessary. Giorgio Bramante always knew the time. The minutes and seconds seemed to tick by in his head, always making their mark.

'There's a meeting at the school. You can't go in until ten thirty . . .'

'But . . .'

He could have stayed home and read and dreamed.

'But nothing!'

His father was a little tense and uncomfortable, with himself, not his son.

'So what are we going to do?'

Giorgio Bramante smiled.

'Something new,' he said, smiling at a thought he had yet to share. 'Something fun.'

He was quiet, waiting.

'You do keep asking,' his father continued. 'About the place I found.'

The boy's breathing stopped for a moment. This was a secret. Bigger than anything seen through a keyhole. He'd heard his father speaking in a whispered voice on the phone, noticed how many visitors kept coming to the house, and the way he was ushered from the room the moment the grown-up talk began.

'Yes.' He paused, wondering what this all meant. 'Please.'

'Well.' Giorgio Bramante hesitated, with a casual shrug, laughing at him in the way they both knew and recognized. 'I can't tell you.'

'*Please!*'

'No.'

He shook his head firmly.

'It's too . . . important to tell. You have to see!'

He leaned down, grinning, tousling Alessio's hair.

'Really?' the boy asked, when he could get a word out of his mouth.

'Really. And' – he tapped his superfluous watch – 'now.'

'Oh,' Alessio whispered, all thoughts of Piranesi and his undiscovered tricks fleeing his head.

Giorgio Bramante leaned down further and kissed him on the head, an unusual, unexpected gesture.

'Is it still there?' he asked idly, not really looking for an answer, taking Alessio's small, strong arm, a man in a hurry, his son could see that straight away.

'No,' he said, not that his father was really listening any more.

It simply didn't exist, not in any of the hundreds of tiny, changing worlds he'd seen that morning. Michelangelo's dome was hiding, lost somewhere in the mist across the river.

- 2 -

Pino Gabrielli wasn't sure he believed in Purgatory but at least he knew where it was meant to be. Somewhere between Heaven and Hell, a middle place for tortured souls, lurking, waiting for someone living, someone they probably knew, to perform the appropriate feat, flick the right switch to send them on their way. And somewhere else too, much closer. On the wall of a side room in his beloved Sacro Cuore del Suffragio, the church that had become Gabrielli's principal pastime since he retired from the architecture department of La Sapienza university almost a decade before.

Not that it was much of a secret any more. On that chill February morning, with wisps of mist hanging in the icy air over the Tiber, Pino Gabrielli saw there was a visitor already, at 7.20 a.m., ten minutes before he opened the doors. A man was standing in the doorway beneath the small rose window, stamping his feet against the cold. As Gabrielli cast one last glance at the river, where a lone cormorant skimmed lazily in and out of the grey haze, he wondered what brought someone there at that time, a middle-aged nondescript type, not the usual young sensation-seeker by the looks of things, though it was difficult to tell since the man was wrapped up tightly in a heavy black coat, with a woollen hat pulled low over his ears.

Gabrielli dodged through the heavy slew of rush-hour traffic, marched up to the church, put on his best welcome smile, and threw a rapid '*Buon giorno*' in the direction of his visitor. Something got muttered in return; he sounded Italian anyway, though the words came through a thick scarf pulled high up to his nose. Perhaps that explained the early start, and the sensitivity to the cold, though it was not as bad as some February mornings Gabrielli had known.

Then, straight away, the visitor asked the usual question – 'Is it still there?' – and Gabrielli's spirits fell. In spite of appearances, he was just another rubbernecker looking for something, anything, to chill the spine.

The warden suppressed a grumble, took out the old key that opened the main door, let the man in and pointed the way through the nave, half-lit by the persistent morning light. He watched him go then went to his small office, warmed his fingers around a paper cup of cappuccino, and devoured a single *cornetto*, filled with jam, as his diet allowed, feeling a little uneasy. He was used to a good hour on his own before anyone came, a time for reading and thinking, wandering around a church he'd come to regard as his own small universe for a few hours at a time.

Gabrielli picked up a pamphlet and wondered whether to go and offer it. The documents were a good twenty years old now and a little musty-smelling from the damp cupboard in the office where they lived, pile upon pile. When he held one out people always shook their heads and said, 'No'. But it wasn't the money he wanted. Gabrielli was happy to give them away for free. He'd just feel happier if more people appreciated the church in his charge for what it was, instead of rushing off to see a display that was mostly, he guessed, old junk.

In a city overloaded with the baroque and the classical, Sacro Cuore was a small, bright, sharp-featured beacon of northern neo-Gothic. The church was barely noticed by the masses as they cursed and sighed their way past it in the traffic crawl along the busy riverside road running west from the Castel Sant'Angelo. But Gabrielli knew every inch of the building, every ornate pillar and column, every last curve of the elegant vaulted ceiling, and understood, both as an architect and a lay, semi-enthusiastic churchman, how precious it was.

Those who could speak Italian might read in the guide how a Bolognese architect, Giuseppe Gualandi, had constructed a perfect pocket-sized cathedral on the orders of a French priest keen on giving Rome a Chartres in miniature, though with rather less expensive stained glass, and in a decidedly urban location. How, too, that same French priest, inspired by a strange incident in the church itself, had set up a small exhibition, just two glass cases on the wall, one large, one small, stocked with a modest collection of exhibits.

For some reason – Gabrielli didn't know and didn't much care – this small exhibition had come to be known as Il Piccolo Museo del Purgatorio, the Little Museum of Purgatory. It had existed in the side room, largely unvisited, for decades. But in the modern age more and more sought targets beyond the customary sights of the Colosseum and St Peter's. At some unforeseen point along the years Sacro Cuore had emerged from dusty obscurity and made its way onto the lists of arcane Roman spectacles exchanged among the knowing.

Gabrielli's four days a week as voluntary guardian in Sacro Cuore were once a time for meditation and solitary exploration of the dark corners of Gualandi's creation. Now a steady trickle of visitors arrived in ever greater numbers with each passing year, as the curious, mostly young, mostly agnostic, he imagined, came looking for a sight they hoped would send a shiver down the spine, make them believe, perhaps, that, in a world of such pressing and trite routine, where everything was capable of explanation if one turned on a computer, something, some whispered cry from elsewhere, existed that said: there is more, if you only knew.

Most were disappointed. They thought Purgatory and Hell were synonymous and were expecting something out of Hieronymus Bosch: real demons, real pits, places to convince the sceptical that the Devil still roamed the earth trying to find a crack, between the bus ride home and the TV, through which to work his way into the lives of the innocent. In truth, there was nothing lurid to see at all. Gabrielli, a man with a taste for foreign fiction, frequently tried to put it this way: the Little Museum was more M.R. James than Stephen King.

All he could show them – discreetly turning away in order to avoid witnessing their disappointment – was what had been there for dec-ades, unchanged: two glass cases and the eleven small items they contained, mundane objects deemed to provide evidence that there were indeed souls in torment, elemental creatures who could, on occasion, penetrate the world of the living and pass on a message.

There was one more item. But, given the chance, Gabrielli always stood with his back to that. The small case at the end of the little room was easily missed. It contained the only exhibit of modern origin, a diminutive T-shirt, with the insignia of an elementary school on the chest. It was an unusual image for a child's uniform, one that was also beginning to fade now, after fourteen years on the wall, behind the glass of the cabinet, beneath the persistent glare of the fluorescent tubes. Still, it was easy to see what was once represented on the cheap, white cotton: a seven-pointed star outlined in black, set inside a dark blue circle containing curious red symbols in its border, with seven smaller dark stars set at equal points around the outer ring.

For a while he had tried to decode this curious image until something – a nagging feeling of over-zealous inquisitiveness, perhaps – stopped him. That and the sure knowledge that, whatever the symbol's origin, it was most certainly not Christian, as befitted any modern school in Rome, even in a secular age.

The characters in the border of the circle were alchemical symbols for the months of the year. The outer stars represented, he had come to believe, the seven planets of the ancients: Mercury, Venus, Jupiter, Mars, Saturn, the Sun and the Moon. The inner star was the Earth itself perhaps, although he was unable to find any firm reference material to support this idea and the academic in him, though retired, found this hypothesis difficult. Whatever it represented, the symbol was pre-Christian. Gabrielli felt the inner star signified the soul, the essence of an individual's being, trying to find its place among the eternal, celestial certainties.

But by the time he had begun poring over that possibility he had come to realize the object in the case was becoming more than a little discomforting. Everything else belonged to the long-dead. This was recent. He'd even met the boy on a few occasions, when his father took him into the nearby archaeology department in La Sapienza where he worked and let him roam around the offices, charming everyone he met. Alessio Bramante was a beautiful child, slender and tall for his age, always curious, if a little shy around his father, a man who dominated even his more senior colleagues. Gabrielli found to his distress that he could still summon up the visual memory of him very easily. In his mind the boy still stood there in his office, quite serious and composed, asking slow, intelligent questions about Gabrielli's work. He had long, shining black hair, lively brown eyes that were forever wide open, and his mother's looks, a quiet, unhurried beauty of the kind that, centuries ago, had found its way into paintings when the artist sought a face that could silence the most troubled of watchers with a single, calming glance, one that said: I know, but that is how things are.

This personal connection changed things, so much that, in the end, he'd stayed away from the last exhibit as much as possible. It was unhealthy to become obsessed by the cast-off garment of Alessio Bramante, a dead schoolchild, victim of a tragedy no one could begin to comprehend. There were times he regretted his own personal involvement in having the shirt placed in the Piccolo Museo in the first place.

And there was another cause for concern too, one that bothered him much more when he cared to think about it.

There was the blood.

Beatrice Bramante said she had discovered Alessio's T-shirt while searching her son's room just after his disappearance. Over the lower-most star she found something inexplicable: a red mark, fresh and ragged at the edges, as if it had occurred only minutes before. Nothing could explain its presence. The garment had been newly washed shortly before the tragedy and left in a cupboard, untouched during the days of torment that had preceded its discovery.

The mother had approached him and asked if it would be appropriate for the item to be added to the collection of the Little Museum, contemporary proof that those departed in tragedy could still send a message to the living.

There had been doubts. Gabrielli believed it should have been sent to the police, though others deemed that the plight of the boy's father now made that inappropriate. The priest of the time had little affection for the strange assortment of curios he had inherited. Yet even he relented when faced by Beatrice Bramante, who was both distraught and determined to the utmost degree. Then there was the simple truth: a bloodstain had appeared on a seven-year-old's white T-shirt while it was folded, clean and neat, in a cupboard in his home. All at a time when he was gone from sight, presumed, by everyone, dead.

So they had relented, and before long come to regret the decision. Three years after the T-shirt went on the wall of the Little Museum it had acquired another bloodstain. Then, in subsequent years, two more. Each was sufficiently modest to prevent it attracting those unfamiliar with the object. The fact was acknowledged quietly by those more observant among the church hierarchy, the case withdrawn from view until the stain faded, losing its freshness, then returned to the wall, its metamorphosis never mentioned again for fear of unwanted publicity.

Gabrielli, who had been a party to this subterfuge, always knew a reckoning would come. If one accepted the premise of Purgatory, it was clear what was happening. The stains were a message. They would continue until someone listened, someone saw fit to act. The rational part of his mind told him this was impossible, ludicrous. Wherever the shade of the hapless Alessio – just repeating the name to himself brought back a memory of the boy, stiff and upright in his office – had departed, it could not be capable of making its mark on a simple object in a glass case on the wall of a curious church by the side of the noisy and traffic-choked Lungotevere Prati. The mundane and the unworldly were not supposed to meet like this.

For some reason these thoughts haunted him more than usual as he sipped his coffee and picked at the pastry. He knew why too. It was the man next door, hidden behind his hat and scarf, yet – and Gabrielli knew this was ridiculous – familiar somehow. There was also his eagerness to be in that confounded room. The visitor hadn't even asked a single question, it now occurred to him, except: *Is it still there?*

It was almost as if he'd been there before, and that was another thought that Gabrielli found disturbing.

Reluctantly – a part of him was coming to hate that little room – he got up and, with all the unenthusiastic speed a sixty-seven-year-old man could muster, crossed the passage and stood by the door to the familiar place. The too-bright lights of the passageway dazzled him. At first he fooled himself the visitor was gone, without a word of thanks or so much as a departing footstep. There wasn't a human sound from anywhere, save for his own laboured breathing, the gift of a lifetime's addiction to strong cigarettes. All Pino Gabrielli could hear was the repetitive, mechanical roar of the traffic, a constant tide of sound so familiar and predictable he rarely noticed it, though today it seemed louder than ever, seemed to enter his head and rebound inside his rising imagination.

Then he stepped into the narrow, claustrophobic room, knowing as he did so that he entered a place that was wrong, out of kilter with the world he liked to inhabit.

He didn't believe in Purgatory. Not really. But at that moment, with his heart beating a compound rhythm deep beneath his tight waistcoat, his throat dry with fear, Pino Gabrielli was aware that even a man like he, a former professor of architecture, well read, well travelled, with an open, inquisitive mind, sometimes knew very little at all.

The figure in black was busy in the pool of hard shadow at the far wall where Alessio Bramante's T-shirt was kept. The item was no longer in its case but pinned to the old pale plaster by the intruder's left hand. His right fist held some kind of grubby cloth, dripping with a dark viscous liquid. Gabrielli watched, unable to move, as the man stabbed at the boy's shirt four times, enlarging each old stain with a new one that was bright and shiny with fresh blood. Finally he added an extra mark, a thick, sanguineous blotch on a previously unblemished star to the upper left.

One more message, the petrified warden thought, to add to four that had already gone unheard.

Perhaps Gabrielli uttered some noise. Perhaps it was simply his difficult, arrhythmic breathing. He was aware his presence was known. The man placed the shirt back in its case with some slow, ponderous care, and pushed the glass back into position, leaving gory, sticky marks on the surface. Then he dragged off the heavy woollen hat and turned round.

'You . . .' Gabrielli murmured, astonished by what he saw.

Pino Gabrielli closed his eyes, felt his bladder go weak, his mind go blank, ashamed that, in extremis, he found it impossible to pray.

When he recovered the courage to look around him again he was alone. Gabrielli stumbled to the nave and fell into a hard wooden pew there, shaking.

Sacro Cuore was dear to him. He knew the rules, the protocols that bound its governance, and that of any church in Rome. By rights he should have called the priest and members of the parochial council before anyone. Just as he had done before.

And still the messages kept coming, this time with the messenger.

Enough was enough. With a trembling hand, Pino Gabrielli withdrew his phone from his pocket, waited for his fingers to stop shaking, and wondered who to dial in such circumstances: 112 for the Carabinieri or 113 for the police. There was no easy number for God. That was why men built churches in the first place.

He tried not to think about the face of the man he'd seen either. Someone he had once known, almost to the point of friendship. Someone who now had cold black eyes and skin that was the dry, desiccated pallor of a corpse.

The Carabinieri were more Gabrielli's kind. Middle class. Well dressed. Polite. More sophisticated.

Only half understanding why, he wandered back into the little room as he struggled with his phone, smelling the blood, dimly aware there was something else, something he should have seen. His shuddering finger fought for the buttons, fell all over the place and got the wrong ones anyway. Perhaps, he thought, it was just fate. Most things were.

Too late; he heard a hard female voice on the line, demanding an answer.

He looked at the Little Museum of Purgatory, properly this time, not fearful for his life because of some dark familiar stranger who stank of blood.

His intuition had been right. There was something new. A direct message, written in a way he'd never forget.

It was a moment before Gabrielli could speak. And when he did a single word escaped his lips.

'Bramante . . .' he murmured, unable to take his eyes off the line of bloody writing on the wall, a crooked, continuous script, with deliberate lettering, the handiwork of someone or something determined to make a point, in just a few words.

Ca' d'Ossi.

The House of Bones.

- 3 -

It had been a good winter, the best Nic Costa could remember in years. There were just two cases left of the *vino novello* they'd made the previous autumn. Costa was surprised to find the modest, home-grown vintage, the first the little estate had produced since the death of his father, met with Leo Falcone's approval too. Either it was good or the old inspector was mellowing as he adjusted to an unaccustomed frailty.

Or both. The world was, Costa had come to realize over the past few months, occasionally ripe with surprises.

That lunchtime they'd taken a few bottles over to the new home Falcone was sharing with Raffaela Arcangelo, a ground-floor apartment in a quiet back street in Monti, rented on a temporary basis until he became more mobile. The injuries the inspector had suffered the previous summer were slow to heal, and he was slow to adapt to them. The meal was, they knew without saying, a kind of staging point for them all, Costa and Emily Deacon, Peroni and Teresa Lupo, Falcone and Raffaela, a way of setting the past aside and fixing some kind of firm commitment for the future.

The previous twelve months had been hard and decisive. Their last investigation as a team, exiled to Venice, almost resulted in Falcone's death. Peroni and Teresa had emerged unscathed, perhaps stronger than ever once the dust settled. While she returned to the police morgue, Peroni became a plain-clothes *agente* again, walking the streets of Rome, on this occasion in charge of a new recruit, a woman who, as he was only too keen to tell anyone in earshot, drove him to distraction with her boundless enthusiasm and naivety.

Costa had pulled the best prize of all out of the bag: a winter spent organizing security for a vast art exhibition set around the works of Caravaggio, one that had played to full audiences in the Palazzo Ruspoli from its opening in November to its much-mourned closure two weeks earlier. There had been some last work to be done, most important of all a final round of security meetings for the return shipping of exhibits, and one long trip to London to liaise with the National Gallery. Then finally, two days before, nothing. No meetings. No deadlines. No phone calls. Only the realization that this extraordinary period of his life, one which had opened up so many new avenues, was now over. After a week's holiday he, too, would be back in the job, an *agente* working the *centro storico* of Rome, unclear of his future. No one had told him if he'd be reunited with Peroni. No one had hinted when Falcone might be back in harness. Only one piece of advice had been handed down to him from on high by Commissario Messina, an ambitious character, not a decade older than himself. It was time, Messina said one evening on the way out, for a man of Costa's age to start thinking about his future. The exams for promotion were being scheduled. Soon, he ought to consider trying to take one step up the ladder, from *agente* to *sovrintendente*.

Emily had looked at him sceptically when he passed on this information and said, simply, 'I'm not sure I can imagine you as a sergeant. You're either up there with Falcone or out on the street with Gianni. Although I suppose we could use the money.'

There were always decisions to be made, ones that conflicted with his own personal desires in the perpetual dilemma faced by any police officer with enthusiasm, ambition and a conscience. How much of a man's life was owed to his profession? And how much to those he loved?

Costa had found the answer to that eight weeks before when Emily had joined him in an expensive restaurant in London, after his final meeting at the Gallery in Trafalgar Square. She had been living in his house on the outskirts of Rome for a year now. Come the summer she would possess sufficient qualifications to seek work as a junior architect.

When he looked into her face that night in the West End, over some of the most costly bad food he'd ever eaten, Nic Costa knew, finally. For once, he wasn't hesitant. Too many times she'd reprimanded him with an amused look and the words, 'Are you sure you're Italian?'

Some time that summer, in June possibly, or the early part of July, depending on how many relatives of Emily's wanted to make the journey from the US, there would be a wedding, a civil affair, followed by a reception in the grounds of the house on the Via Appia. Some time in late July – around the 24th if the doctors were right – they would have a child. Emily was now seven or eight weeks pregnant, enough for them to tell others of their plans, which had formed slowly, growing like the infant curled in a tight, hidden ball inside her still flat stomach, taking shape, to become something both simple and infinitely complex, mundane and magical. And when they were parents, Nic Costa said to himself, life surely began in earnest, something he was about to say to the four of them in Leo Falcone's living room, after he and Emily had made their two announcements, only to find his words drowned out in the clamour of noise around them.

Falcone hobbled off to the kitchen talking excitedly of the bottle of vintage champagne – real champagne, not just good *prosecco* – he'd been keeping for such an occasion. Raffaela was busy fussing over him, while hunting for even more food to pile on the table. Teresa Lupo was piling kisses on the pair of them, looking worryingly close to tears or hysteria or both, before dashing to help Raffaela with the glasses.

And Gianni Peroni just stood there, a big smirk over his battered face, one aimed in the disappearing Teresa's direction, saying: *I told you so.*

Emily, still next to Costa, a little amazed by the histrionics, leaned her head onto his shoulder, and whispered, 'Haven't they had any weddings in this country for a while?'

'It seems not,' he answered softly then, theatrically, took her in his arms and kissed her.

She broke away, laughing as they were both confronted by a forest of waving arms bearing glasses and plates of food.

'Is it going to be like this forever from now on?' she stuttered, avoiding the wine, reaching for a glass of mineral water.

'Forever,' Gianni Peroni repeated, and began to make a toast so eloquent, touching and funny that Costa found it hard to believe he hadn't rehearsed it many times before.

– 4 –

Pino Gabrielli wasn't the only church warden in Rome to receive a surprise that morning. Half an hour after he opened the doors of the small white church in Prati, Ornella Di Benedetto found herself facing the padlocked chains on the shuttered, abandoned wreck that was once Santa Maria dell'Assunta, wondering what looked different. The logical answer – someone had gone inside – seemed too ridiculous for words.

Rome had many churches. Too many to cater for a population that grew more secular by the year. Santa Maria dell'Assunta, set on the south-eastern side of the Aventino hill, not far from the Piazza Albania, had little to keep it in business. The historians said it stood on the site of one of the oldest churches in Rome, dating back to the earliest times, when Christianity was one religion among many, some-times persecuted, sometimes tolerated, occasionally encouraged. Not a trace remained of the original. Over the centuries it had been rebuilt on at least five occasions, burned to the ground more than once, then, in the sixteenth century, handed over to an order of Capuchin monks. The tiny, unremarkable building that survived lasted a further three centuries as a consecrated property then, under Napoleon's anti-clerical hand, fell into disuse, and was later converted into municipal offices. At the beginning of the twentieth century it became, briefly, a private residence occupied by an elderly British writer of arcane and macabre tastes. After his death it fell steadily into ruin, maintained only by a small grant from the city and a local diocese still somewhat guilty over its abandonment. The mishmash of architectural styles and the absence of a single important painting or sculpture meant that the middle-aged woman who kept an eye on the place was, for months on end, the only person to set foot beyond the dusty, rotting oak doors, in the narrow cul-de-sac just a few metres from the bustle of the Viale Aventino.

Even so, it had one esoteric feature, hidden away in a crypt reachable only by a narrow, damp and winding corridor cut into the hill's soft rock. The same Capuchin monks who maintained the church for a while continued to own a greater property in Rome, Santa Maria della Concezione in the Via Veneto, just a little way up from the American Embassy. Here they had created a curiosity too: a crypt much larger than that of Santa Maria dell'Assunta, decorated – there was no other way to put it – with the bones of some 4,000 of their fellows, deposited there until the late nineteenth century, when the practice was deemed a little too grisly for modern tastes.

Ornella Di Benedetto knew that place well and had compared it in detail with the one in her own charge, hoping one day to be able to impress visitors with her erudition. The charnel house in the Via Veneto was undoubtedly impressive. She wished her own dead monks had provided a similar quotable motto for the inscription over their tomb on the Aventino.

'*Quello che voi siete noi eravamo, quello che noi siamo voi sarete,*' read their epitaph.

What you are we were, what we are you will be.

But her smaller version was, she felt, more tasteful, more in keeping with the original purpose. It had none of the theatrical touches of Concezione: skeletons still in their monastic robes, cowls drawn around their skulls, patterns of vertebrae and jawbones arranged like some ghastly frieze, mocking the spectator, seeming, to her, to deny that anything of value existed in their worldly lives.

Santa Maria dell'Assunta was, simply, an underground public tomb, a place where a hundred monks – no more, no less – decided that their remains should stay visible for anyone who wished to see them. After a suitable time in the Capuchin cemetery in San Giovanni

– she had researched this thoroughly for her imaginary visitors – they would be exhumed and taken to the crypt. There each corpse was arrayed tidily on the bare earth, five rows, twenty in each, skeletal arms neatly folded over skeletal chests, patiently awaiting resurrection.

The late English writer had installed some weak electrical lighting so that his visitors would enjoy the spectacle. Rumour had it that his will had demanded he be laid among them too, an idea the city authorities quashed on health grounds, though only when he was in no condition to object. The man had lived in Venice for several years, in a small palazzo adjoining the Ca' d'Oro on the Grand Canal, before moving to Rome. That had, apparently, been the inspiration for him to give the place the nickname by which it continued to be known in the neighbourhood: Ca' d'Ossi. Not that it was a soubriquet she would ever use.

The Capuchins of Santa Maria dell'Assunta had, she believed, bequeathed to future generations a humane and instructive exhibition, with none of the tourist-seeking histrionics of the place on the Via Veneto. It deserved to be better known, and perhaps receive a little restoration money, some of which would, naturally, find its way into the pocket of its lone custodian over the years.

Nor – and she had to explain this point repeatedly to friends and relatives over the years – had Santa Maria dell'Assunta ever scared her. Death, for Ornella Di Benedetto, was an ordinary, unremarkable figure who walked through the world like everyone else, trying to get on with the job fate had given him. Some days, she imagined, he would hop onto the Number 3 tram that ran through Testaccio across the river to Trastevere, and back into the city in the opposite direction, watching the faces of his fellow travellers, trying to decide which among them was deserving of another journey altogether. Then, when his work was done, he would sit by the Tiber for a while, letting the traffic roar drown out his thoughts.

Ornella Di Benedetto was never in fear of the corpses in her care, which made it all the more inexplicable that she was reluctant to enter the church that morning. The padlock and chain had been broken. It had happened before, a long time ago. Some youngsters had entered the building, looking for somewhere to sleep, something to steal. They would be disappointed on both counts. The place was cold and fusty, populated by rats, for which she left poison. Not an item of value remained, not even decent furniture. In the small nave, which the Englishman had used as a general hall and dining room, only a few worthless pews and a shattered pulpit remained.

Another time, twenty years ago, a drunk had found his way into the cellar, turned on the lights then run out into the street screaming. That amused her. It was nothing less than the idiot deserved.

No serious criminal would give Santa Maria dell'Assunta a second look. No thrill-seeking teenager could possibly think it was worth breaking into; there were much more atmospheric underground caverns scattered throughout Rome if that was what they wanted.

Still, she stood there for a good two minutes, the bag with fresh rat poison in it hanging on her arm. It was ridiculous.

With a brief curse at her own timidity, Ornella Di Benedetto threw the shattered chain and padlock out of the way, mentally making a note that she would have to charge someone, city or diocese, for a replacement, and pulled open the oak door.

- 5 -

They were fifty metres beneath the red earth of the Aventino hill, slowly making their way along a narrow, meandering passageway cut into the soft rock almost twenty centuries before. The air was stale and noxious, heavy with damp and mould and the feral stink of unseen animals or birds. Even with their pocket torches and the extra shoulder lanterns stolen from the storeroom, it was hard to see much ahead.

Ludo Torchia trembled a little. That was, he knew, simply because it was cold, a good ten degrees or more chillier below the surface, where, on that same warm June day, unknown to him, Alessio Bramante and his father now stood at the gate of the mansion of the Cavalieri di Malta, not half a kilometre away through the rock and soil above them.

He should have expected the change in temperature. Dino Abati had. The young student from Turin wore the right clothes – a thick, waterproof, bright-red caving suit that clashed with his full head of curly ginger hair, heavy boots, ropes and equipment attached to his jacket – and now looked entirely at home in this manmade vein tunnelled by hand, every last, tortuous metre. The rest of them were beginners, in jeans and jackets, a couple even wearing trainers. Abati had scowled at them on the surface, before they started work on the locks of the flimsy iron entrance gates.

Now, just twenty minutes in, their eyes still trying to acclimatize to the dark, Toni LaMarca was already starting to moan, whining in his high-pitched voice, its trilling notes rebounding off the roughly hacked stone walls just visible in their lights.

'Be quiet, Toni,' Torchia snapped at him.

'Remind me. Why exactly are we doing this?' LaMarca complained. 'I'm freezing my nuts off already. What if we get caught? What about that, huh?'

'I told you! We won't get caught,' Torchia replied. 'I checked the rosters. No one's coming down here today. Not today. Not tomorrow.'

'So why?'

'So we can leave you down here to rot, you moron,' someone said from the back, Andrea Guerino, judging by the gruff, northern voice, and he was only half joking.

Ludo Torchia stopped. So did the rest of the group. That much of his superiority, his leadership, he'd established already.

'What did we say last night?' he demanded.

'Search me. I was out of my head,' LaMarca replied, looking at each of them in turn, searching for confirmation. 'Weren't we all?'

It had been a long night in the bar in the Viale Aventino. They'd all spent too much money. They all, Dino Abati excepted, had smoked themselves stupid when they got back to the dingy house they shared near the old Testaccio slaughterhouse, the one with the statue. The abattoir was surmounted by the struggling figure of a winged man fighting to wrestle a bull to the ground, amid a sea of bones, animal and human. Mithras lived, Torchia thought. He was simply invisible to the masses.

'We said we would finish this,' Torchia insisted.

He held out his wrist, showed them the small wound each of them shared, from the blunt razor blade he'd found in the bathroom, late that night.

'We said we would do this together. In secret. As brothers.'

They were all drones really. He didn't like a single one of them. Didn't like anyone in Giorgio Bramante's archaeology class, if he was being honest. Except Bramante himself. That man had class and knowledge and imagination, three qualities Torchia judged to be supremely important. The rest were marionettes, ready to be manipulated by anyone who cared for the job, though these five he'd picked with care and reason.

LaMarca, the skinny offspring of some minor hood from Naples, dark-skinned, with an untrustworthy face that never looked anyone in the eye, was quick and crooked and could surely help if things went wrong. Guerino, a none-too-bright farmer's son from Abruzzo, was big enough and tough enough to keep everyone in line. Sandro Vignola, the sick-looking kid from Bologna, short and geeky behind thick glasses, knew Latin so well he could hold rapid, fluent conversations with Isabella Amato, the plain, bright, fat girl Vignola adored so much he blushed whenever they spoke, and still didn't dare ask her out. Raul Bellucci, always on the edge of terror, had a lawyer for a father, one who'd recently won himself a seat in the Senate, the kind of man who would always turn out to help his son, should the sort of influence LaMarca possessed fail to do the trick. And Dino Abati was there to keep them all alive, the class cave-freak, fit, knowing, shorter than Guerino, but just as powerfully built.

Abati didn't say much. Torchia half suspected he didn't believe in what they were doing at all, and was just looking to extend his knowledge, to pierce yet another mystery in the vast, unknown territory that was subterranean Rome. But he knew more of this strange and dangerous landscape than any of them. Abati had led the team that found the trapdoor in an ancient pavement, close to Trajan's Markets, which had revealed an underground cavern housing a hidden room and tomb dating from the second century, rich with paintings and inscriptions. His idea of weekend leisure was to spend long hours in a wetsuit, waist-high in water and worse, walking the length of the Cloaca Maxima, the ancient sewer that still ran through the city, beneath the Forum, on to the Tiber and, as Torchia had discovered the one time he went down there, continued to take foul matter from unknown pipes and flush it towards anything that sought to penetrate its secrets.

Most important of all, though, and the reason Torchia had entangled him in this scheme, Abati knew caves, was comfortable with ropes and lights, knots and pulleys, and understood, too, how to respond in an emergency: a broken leg, a sudden flood, the collapse of a corridor or roof.

For some reason – jealousy, Torchia guessed, since Abati was clearly going to be a professional archaeologist one day – the professor had kept him out of this last part of the dig. Torchia himself had only found out about the discovery by accident, overhearing Bramante and the American post grad student, Judith Turnhouse, discussing it quietly in the corridor of the school after classes. After that he'd stolen a set of keys from the admin department, copied every last one, tried his versions until they worked, letting him get further and further into the labyrinthine warren Giorgio Bramante was progressively penetrating, with Turnhouse and just a coterie of other trusted members of the department. It was easy to keep a secret too. From the surface, nothing was visible except the kind of iron gate most Roman subterranean workings possessed, principally for reasons of security, to keep out kids and vandals and party-goers. Nothing on the outside hinted at what lay in the soft rock beneath the red earth just a little way along from the archaeology department office, beside the church of Santa Sabina, beneath the little park, with its lovers and old men and dogs, which the locals insisted on calling, to Torchia's annoyance, 'the Orange Garden'.

Its real name, as he and Bramante knew well, was the Parco Savello, from the ancient Roman street, the Clivo di Rocca Savella, which led up from the choking modern road by the Tiber below, still a narrow cobbled path cut into the rock, now strewn with rubbish, the occasional burned-out Lambretta, spent syringes and used condoms.

There'd been a garrison at the summit of this hill once. Battalions of men had marched down that road, one of the first to be paved in Rome, defending the empire or expanding it, whatever their masters demanded. And beneath their barracks they'd created a magical legacy. Torchia was unsure of its precise date. Mithraism came from Persia to Rome in the first century AD, the favoured religion of the military. Somewhere short of 2,000 years before, those soldiers must have started digging secretly beneath their barracks, creating a labyrinth with one purpose: to bring them closer to their God, then, through a series of trials and ceremonies, to bind each of them together in a tight, unbreakable bond, a chain of command and obedience they would take to the grave.

He'd only appreciated a part of this before. When he stole the keys and discovered, with a growing amazement, what lay in the warren of tufa corridors and caverns, he began, finally, to understand, as they would surely too. In the final hall, the holiest of holies, desecrated, stomped on by some brutish, all-conquering might, came the revelation, an epiphany that had left him breathless and giddy, holding onto the damp stone walls for support.

His mind ground to a halt. The passageway was so low here they had to crouch, bumping into one another, getting closer and closer. He wished he'd managed to find Giorgio Bramante's cavern map, for one surely existed. They had to be almost there. He'd passed several of the anterooms without showing them in. There wasn't enough time. He needed to maintain their attention.

Then, without warning, Toni LaMarca was screaming, sounding like a girl more than ever, his falsetto yells bouncing up and down the corridor, forwards, backwards, like a virus trapped in some empty stone artery, looking for a way out.

'What is it?' Torchia demanded, realizing that LaMarca was starting to get to him.

He ran the big torch over the idiot, who seemed frozen to the craggy, rough wall. LaMarca was staring in horror at his right hand, which he'd just lifted off the stone. It had made contact with something there, something living. It was about fifteen centimetres long, as fat as a finger and about the same colour too. As they watched, it moved a little, wriggling its smooth, lean body as if it hated the touch of Toni LaMarca as much as he loathed it in return.

Dino Abati cast his own beam on the creature and took a closer look.

'Flatworm,' he announced. 'You get them down here. Though' – he took a closer look – 'I've never seen one quite like that before.'

'Make the most of it,' LaMarca grumbled, then flipped the worm off the wall with one quick finger and ground his right trainer into the thing until it was just mush on the floor.

'Oh my,' Abati said with heavy sarcasm, when LaMarca was done. 'You've stomped a worm. That was so impressive.'

'To hell with it!' the idiot yelled back. 'I've had enough. I'm gone. Now.'

'Even for a *babbo* like you,' Abati replied, as cool as could be, 'premature withdrawal seems excessively stupid in the circumstances. Remember your geology, Toni. This is tufa we're in. Valuable rock. These corridors aren't natural, formed by water or anything. They were worked. Part of a quarry some time probably. Or . . .'

Abati's confidence dropped for a moment.

'Something else I don't know.'

'So?' the kid asked, with a dumb, petulant aggression.

'So manmade workings come to an end,' Abati said wearily. 'It can't be much further either. I've never seen an offshoot of a tufa quarry this big in my life.'

Torchia nodded into the deep velvet blackness ahead of them.

'You haven't seen anything. Not yet.'

- 6 -

The lights were still on in the internal portico. Ornella Di Benedetto turned them off. Then she walked into the diminutive nave, where a little thin winter sun was streaming through the cracked stained glass on the western end of the building.

To her dismay the door to the crypt was open. There was a light in there too, the familiar weak yellow haze creeping up from the underground cavern.

The sight made her furious. She hated waste. Electricity was more expensive than ever. But she needed to try to understand what had happened. To work out whether it was worth calling the police.

It was possible, just, that someone was still down there, hidden with her familiar skeletons, up to no good. That thought hadn't occurred to her until her fingers touched the old, damp powdery plaster of the corridor wall.

Still, why would anyone break into an empty, deconsecrated church? It was ridiculous, she reminded herself, then became aware of the smell, elusive at first, but soon familiar. It was the smell of the market in Testaccio, the little, local one off Mastro Giorgio, where every morning she bought that day's food: salad and vegetables, and a little meat from one of the many stalls with their vivid red displays of pork and beef, rabbit and lamb. Even, in one little-visited corner, horse, which only the old people ate these days.

She didn't turn off the lights. Something about the smell made that impossible. Instead Ornella Di Benedetto took three steps down the narrow, worn stone stairs, just far enough to see into the crypt, with its serried rows of grey, tidy bones.

And something else among them too. Something gleaming under the bulbs, a half-familiar shape transformed somehow, metamorphosed into the source of that rank, permeating stench that wouldn't quit her nostrils.

When she finally reached the street, babbling like a madwoman, trying to catch the attention of passers-by who ignored her shrieking implications, she'd no idea how long she'd spent in that place, or what, in truth, she'd done there.

They stared at her. All of them. Every shopper in the market. Every stallholder. Everyone.

I am not insane, she wanted to scream at them. *I am not!*

Even though she couldn't recall how she made her way from the Piazza Albania into Testaccio in order to find the market, or how long it had taken. An hour at least, or so it seemed from the market clock which now stood at five past eleven. Somewhere along the way, she thought, she'd sat down and passed out for a while, like some neighbourhood drunk, stunned by cheap grappa.

Her eyes worked their way across the hall, to the lines of butchers' stalls where the meat hung, fresh and livid, on the hook, scarlet flesh, waxy white fat, veins and organs, limbs and carcasses, entrails and the occasional small pig's head.

Since she was a child the market had been a place of delight. The aroma of flowers mingled with the fresh salt tang of the fish stalls. Oranges from Sicily sat next to stands selling fresh white buffalo mozzarella at prices even ordinary people could afford.

She'd never really thought about the meat stalls until then, when the sight and the smell of the crypt came back to her. Ornella Di Benedetto turned her head away from the butchers' stands, tried to stop the fleshy, organic stink of them creeping into her mouth and nostrils, breathed deeply once, gasping down a lungful of the market's now vile and rotting aroma, wondering whether she was about to be sick.

It was an unconscionable time before anyone listened and that was the closest human being she could think of who knew her: the kindly young girl on the farm vegetable stall in the market, who listened to her ragged, incoherent story then sat her down with a stiff *caffè corretto* before calling the police.

When she looked up, still fighting the urge, she found a dark-skinned woman, Indian perhaps, staring thoughtfully into her face, her eyes full of concern and curiosity.

'My name is Rosa Prabakaran,' the woman said. 'I'm a police officer.'

'The church . . .' she murmured, wondering where to begin.

The young policewoman nodded, confidently, in a way that made Ornella Di Benedetto feel a little better.

'We know, Signora,' she said, glancing around the hall, not looking too hard at the meat stands either. 'I just came from there.'

– 7 –

There was an entire community of cafés in the Via degli Zingari, the narrow street round the corner that wound down the hill towards the Forum. When Falcone's bottle of champagne was done he suggested a walk for some proper coffee. That bachelor habit had yet to disappear; the inspector still resolutely refused to believe it was possible to make a decent *macchiato* at home.

Half an hour later they were ambling in a ragged, animated fashion towards Falcone's preferred destination, enjoying the meagre warmth that had arrived with the disappearance of the morning murk. The wedding arrangements and the pregnancy had been dealt with, in a flurry of frantic questions, hugs and no small amount of tears on Teresa's part. Then, as so often happened with such dramatic personal news, they'd found the need to move on to other matters. For Costa, it didn't get much better than this. Emily, friends, Rome, his home city, a few days off. And both Peroni and Teresa in garrulous, postprandial mood, she reminiscing about work, Peroni fixated with its avoidance.

After one brief and inconclusive argument, the pathologist caught up with them, fat arms pumping with delight, pointed across the square, towards the Via dei Serpenti, tugged on Emily's shirt sleeve, and exclaimed, in her gruff Roman tones, 'Look! Look! I had this wonderful customer down there once. Some dreadful accountant skewered with a sword. It was . . .'

'It was horrible,' Peroni complained.

'Oh,' Teresa replied, brightly surprised. 'We're getting discriminating in our old age, are we? I suppose this new female companion of yours puts these crazy notions into your head.'

'Don't rub it in.'

This wasn't a popular subject between them.

'Who is she?' Emily asked.

'Indian girl,' Teresa cut in. 'Quite pretty too. God knows why she's in the police.'

The big man grumbled, 'Rosa – which does not sound a very Indian name to me at all – was born in some public housing block in Monte Sacro. As I have told you a million times, being of Indian extraction and being Indian aren't the same thing.'

Teresa didn't look convinced.

'Now you're being unreconstructed. Of course she's Indian. Her dad's from Cochin. He sells umbrellas and lighters and all that junk on some street stall in Tritone. So what? She's got India in her genes. You can tell that just from talking to her. She doesn't get mad about anything, not on the surface anyway. I guess it's karma or whatever.'

Peroni waved a finger in her direction.

'She's a Catholic, for God's sake!'

'That doesn't make her an Italian,' Costa interjected. 'Not even an honorary one, these days.'

'Quite,' Teresa went on. 'And her old man's a Catholic too. He was one back in India long before he came here. Did you know that?'

Peroni muttered a low curse. Then, grumpily, 'No . . .'

'You should talk to her more,' she went on. 'Rosa is a sweet, serious, responsible human being. Which brings me back to my original point. Why the hell is she in the police? What's going to happen if she's left hanging around people like you for long? You, with all these special talents? I mean it.' This last point was aimed at Emily. 'I've worked in that morgue for a decade and when they're gone it can be just plain boring. You miss the quality customers. No rubbish from these boys. No time-wasting. Just . . .'

She sighed, a beatific expression on her face.

'. . . the goods.'

Peroni shook his head and sighed.

'Goods like that I can do without.'

'Goods like that put food and drink on our tables, Gianni. Some-one's got to deal with them. Unless you were thinking of moving over to traffic,' she added slyly. 'Or still fantasizing about . . . what was it?'

'OK, OK,' he conceded. 'We don't need to be reminded.'

'Pig farming,' Teresa went on. 'Back home in Tuscany. With me working as some local doctor. Stitching up the bucolics after their Saturday night fights. Ministering to fat pregnant housewives.'

She slapped him on the arm, quite hard.

'What were you thinking about?'

'What were *we* thinking about?' he asked quietly.

'Running away,' she answered, serious in an instant. 'Believing you can dump your problems in the gutter and walk on to some new place and forget about them. I've been doing that most of my life. In the end it just gets downright tedious. What's more, the little bastards have a habit of picking themselves out of the gutter and following you in any case, whining, "Look at me! Look at me!".'

'I would have made a good pig farmer! A great one.'

'You would,' she said, full of genuine sympathy. 'Until the moment you had to drive them off to the slaughterhouse. What then, my Tuscan hulk? Would you sit outside munching on your *panino* and *porchetta*, listening to the squeals?'

Peroni didn't say anything, just looked at the cobbled pavements, worn down by generations of feet.

Then Teresa stopped, aware that someone was missing.

'I didn't realize Leo was walking so slowly,' she said. 'He's not as bad as that, is he?'

They'd turned a corner a little way back. When Costa looked behind there wasn't a soul in the street. It wasn't right. Leo was making slow but steady progress in his return to health. Soon, Costa thought, he'd be back on the job, forcing their new boss, Commissario Messina, to make a tough decision. Did he put them back together, or keep them apart?

'Nic . . .?' Emily said softly, a note of concern in her voice.

He was turning to retrace his steps, Peroni starting to follow, when, from somewhere close by, in the direction of the neighbouring broad main street of Cavour, came the familiar sound of a police siren, followed by another, then a third, and the honking of angry horns.

'I think . . .' Teresa began to say, then stopped.

Nearby, someone was screaming and, in that curious way the human mind worked, Nic Costa understood that, wordless and panic-driven as the noises were, they came from a terrified Raffaela Arcangelo, out of sight, and for a few desperate moments out of reach too.

Then two figures stumbled into view: Leo Falcone in the arms of a strong, powerful individual whose head was obscured by a black woollen hat pulled down low over his ears.

A man who held a gun tight to Falcone's neck, jabbing it, shouting something Costa couldn't quite hear.

– 8 –

After a minute or so – it was difficult for Ludo Torchia to judge time in this half-lit world where the dimensions seemed unnatural, impossible to gauge – a low opening emerged to his left. It looked familiar. This had to be the place.

To his amazement LaMarca was starting to moan again.

'You said . . .' he mumbled.

'I said what?'

'You said there *had* to be seven.'

'There would have been seven. If that shit Vincenzo hadn't turned chicken.'

'You said there had to be seven. Otherwise it didn't work. You—'

Furious, Torchia turned and grabbed LaMarca's jacket, took hold of him hard, swung him past his shoulder, and sent him head first down the rough steps, into the cavern that now opened to their left.

Then he took all the big lamps off the others, who stood mute, a little scared, and placed them in a line on the floor, shining inwards.

As their eyes adjusted, the room in front of them emerged from the gloom. A shocked silence fell on everyone for a few moments. Even Torchia couldn't believe his eyes. With better illumination the place was more wonderful than he could ever have hoped.

'What the hell is this, Ludo?' Abati asked. There was now a note of grateful amazement in his voice.

With more lamps he could appreciate the detail: the paintings on the seven walls, still with the distinct shades of their original colours, ochre, red and blue, all a little muted by the years. The two ranks of low stone benches in precise order in front of each of the chamber's facings. And at their focus, in the wall facing the main entrance door, the altar, with its dominating statue of Mithras slaying the sacrificial bull, a study so characteristic of the cult it could have come from a textbook. Torchia had spent an hour staring at the statue when he first sneaked in here, touching the ghostly white marble, feeling the precise, human contours of its players. He felt now as he did then: that he was born to be part of the place somehow, created in order to belong to what it represented.

He picked up two big lamps and approached the flat white slab set before the statue. The figures seemed alive: the human Mithras, taut and powerful, standing, legs apart, over the crouched, terrified bull in its death agony. The god wore a winged, high-peaked Phrygian cap and held the beast's head upright with his right hand, thrusting a short sword into its throat with his left. A scorpion rose from the carved grass below to feed greedily from the tip of the bull's sagging, extended penis. A muscular, excited dog and a writhing snake clung to the animal's shoulder, sipping the blood from its wound.

'At a guess,' Torchia said, answering Abati's question in his own good time, 'I'd suggest we're in what could be the largest and most important temple of Mithras anyone's ever seen. In Rome anyway.'

He walked up to the altar table then ran a finger across the surface, noticing the way it cut through both the dust and the colour. He'd been right the first time. The stains there, like old rust, weren't marks of the stone at all.

'Until the butchers came and put an end to it all. Am I wrong?'

They had followed in silence. Abati was gazing around the chamber, wide-eyed.

'What happened here, Ludo?' he asked.

'See for yourself. You tell me.'

Abati walked to one side and picked up some shards of pottery on the floor. They'd been shattered by some kind of heavy blow. Then he looked at the wall painting close by: an idyllic country scene, with the god in the midst of a crowd of fervent devotees. Axe marks scored the paint in deep, symmetrical lines. The god's face had been hacked out from the stone and was now little more than mould and dust.

'It's been desecrated,' Abati said. 'And not by a couple of grave-robbers, either.'

Torchia picked up some more fragments of pottery, from what looked like a ceremonial jug.

'It was Constantine.'

This was clear in his own mind now. What they stood amidst was the precursor, the template for everything to follow, from the Crusades to Bosnia, from Christian slaughtering Christian in the sacking of Constantinople, to Catholics murdering Aztecs with the blessing of the priests who watched on, unmoved. This was the moment, hours after Rome fell to Constantine's troops, where the Christian blade sought the blood of another religion, not on the battlefield but in the holiest of holies. October 28th, AD 312, had changed the shape of history, and in this underground chamber, perhaps just a few brief hours after the crossing at the Milvian Bridge, the oppressed had turned into the oppressors, and sought a savage, final vengeance on everything that went before.

Abati laughed.

'You can't know that. It must have been early. But . . .'

Abati was both amazed and baffled by what he saw. This pleased Ludo Torchia.

'It was the same day Constantine entered Rome. Or perhaps the day after. There's no other explanation. I'll show you . . .'

He led Abati to a low doorway off to the left. Torchia carried the largest torch in his hand. He was glad of company. This discovery had shaken him when he came across it alone, that first time.

'After you,' he said, ushering Abati and the others through. Then he turned the light full onto what lay in front of them, a sea of human bones: ribs and skulls, shattered legs and arms, like the cast-off props of some ancient horror movie, thrown into a heap when they were no longer needed.

Abati moaned, 'Sweet Jesus.'

LaMarca, behind, began to whinny in fear.

'What the hell is this?' Abati asked.

'It's where they killed them,' Torchia said without emotion. 'Look if you like. I'd say there's more than a hundred, maybe lots more. I'm no expert but I think they're mainly men, though I think there are some children here too. They were probably cut down naked.'

He shifted the beam into the far corner.

'If you look there, you can see their clothes. I couldn't find any uniforms or weapons. They weren't looking to fight, not any more. They were made to strip. Then they were cut down. You can see the marks on their bones if you want to look closely. It was a massacre.'

The kid from Naples was shaking again, half curious, half terrified. LaMarca liked violence, Torchia guessed. But only from a safe distance.

'I don't want to see any more of this,' LaMarca muttered then crept back into the main chamber, chastened. Abati felt the same way. He took one last look at the scattered bones on the stone floor then followed.

'Professor Bramante knows about all this?' he asked when they were back by the altar. 'And he never told anyone?'

Torchia had his own theories on that.

'What do you say? You've found the greatest Mithraic temple in existence? Oh, and a few hundred followers cut to pieces by the Christians? How do you handle the publicity on that just now?'

'I can't believe . . .' Abati began, then went quiet.

Ludo Torchia had been through this argument in his own head already. Giorgio Bramante had uncovered one of the world's greatest archaeological finds, and one of its earliest examples of religious genocide. Those were real bones, the remains of real people in the next room, a shocking display of shattered skulls and limbs thrown together like some grisly precursor of a scene from Belsen. Or the thousands in Srebrenica who'd been handed over by 'peacekeepers' to the Serbs, then routinely, efficiently slaughtered when a different group of Christians decided to cleanse the gene pool. That story still made headlines. There was shame throughout Europe that such acts could still happen just a few miles away from the beaches where contented, middle-class holidaymakers were sunning themselves. So perhaps Bramante was waiting for the right moment, the right words, or some other find that would soften the blow. Perhaps he didn't have the courage at all, and hoped to keep this very large secret to himself forever, which would, in Torchia's eyes, be a crime in itself.

Something in Abati's face told Torchia he was beginning to see the true picture now.

'Why do you think they came here?' he asked. 'To make some kind of last stand?'

'No,' Torchia insisted. 'This was a temple, a holy place. Not somewhere for human blood. Do you think the Pope would have fought in front of the altar in St Peter's? These men were soldiers. If they wanted to fight, they would have made a stand outside. They came here . . .' He scanned the room. '. . . to worship one last time.'

In his mind's eye he could see them all now, not afraid, knowing the end was close, determined to complete one last obeisance to the god whose strength slaughtered the bull and gave life to the world.

He bent down and turned the light onto the floor. There was a crude wooden cage there, and inside it bones that must have been those of a chicken, now looking like the dusty remains of some miniature dinosaur, legs folded beneath the carcass, beaked head still recognizable. The temple followers never had time to finish the sacrifice before the Christian soldiers arrived, racing into the holiest chamber en masse, Constantine's symbol, the *Chi-Rho* symbol, for *Christos*, on their shields, screaming for more deaths on a day when the city must have already run red with slaughter.

'They came here to make a final sacrifice,' he said. 'Before the light went out on their god, forever. And they weren't even allowed to finish that.'

Ludo Torchia slung the rucksack off his shoulder onto the floor then unzipped the top. Two sharp eyes gleamed back at him. The cockerel was shiny black with an erect, mobile red comb. It had cost him €30 early that morning in the busy local market in Testaccio, close by the Via Marmorata down the hill.

The bird was still and silent as he lifted the cage out of the bag.

'Wow . . .' LaMarca whispered excitedly into the dark. 'What now?'

There was plenty of reference material in the standard Latin texts about how to offer a sacrifice correctly. It wasn't hard. Torchia could do it just the way an emperor used to.

Something continued to bug him, though. Toni LaMarca was right. Seven was the magic number. And they fell one short.

- 9 -

He didn't have a weapon.

That thought struck Costa as he raced up the street, trying to analyse what was happening in front of him. It had been months since he'd touched a gun. Months since he'd given firearms a passing thought. It couldn't be that important. They were in the centre of Rome, in a highly public area. The worst anyone encountered hereabouts was some lowlife bag-snatcher, nothing more serious than that, though something in Raffaela's desperate voice had told Costa to bark at the women to stay behind, just in case. Gianni Peroni was following, as fast as he could. But Costa was twenty years younger than his partner. When he rounded the corner into the narrow side street where Falcone's attacker had dragged the old inspector he was, he knew, on his own, unarmed, reliant only on his own wits to deal with whatever he found.

The sirens were getting louder in Cavour, the nearest main road. That didn't make things any easier. Costa turned left into the narrow thoroughfare, little more than an alley, dark from the high-walled houses that blocked the afternoon sunlight.

There was a small white van, parked at an awkward angle, cut across the cobbles to block the road to other cars. Raffaela Arcangelo was on the ground a short distance away, screaming, looking as if she'd been hit. Leo Falcone struggled feebly in the arms of an attacker, who held a gun tight to his left temple and was dragging the stricken inspector back towards the open doors of the van.

Peroni reached the junction sweating, gasping for breath.

'Leave this to me,' Costa ordered, waving a hand in his direction. 'Don't let the women come close. There's a weapon. Numbers don't count.'

'Nic!' Emily yelled at him angrily.

He turned and looked at her. The pregnancy had made her pale. That morning he'd found her throwing up in the bathroom. Noisily, a little angry and shocked by the way something inside her, something she would grow to love, could inflict such a base, physical humiliation out of the blue.

'Please,' he said firmly. 'Nothing's going to happen. Just stay where you are.'

Easy words, stupid words. They'd work for a minute or so, though.

He walked calmly forward, ignoring the stricken woman on the ground. Costa was trying to see into the eyes of the man in the black jacket, work out what might be going on in his mind. He looked more determined than confident. They'd all done anti-terrorist training in the Questura. They knew how a professional hitman or kidnapper was supposed to behave, what grips, what tactics they used to get the victim they wanted. What he saw here didn't match the profile. This was an amateur, improvising along the way.

Costa took a close look again. He was a good amateur, unruffled, determined.

Peroni had his breath back and was marching into the light at the street junction – the firing zone – Costa couldn't think of it any other way.

'Back! I told you!' he yelled, angry at his partner this time. There wasn't space for confusion. This situation was delicate enough as it was. He was relieved to see the older man halt in his tracks, a dark expression on his face.

Then he looked at Leo Falcone and felt the stirrings of anger inside him. There was blood on the inspector's mouth. Worse than that, something strange, foreign, in his eyes, a resigned, baffled kind of acceptance that didn't fit in with what he knew of Falcone's character at all.

A stray sentence entered Costa's head.

You look like you've seen a ghost, Leo, he thought.

– 10 –

The birthday party had taken place in their family garden, beneath the shade of the dusty vine trellises, on the terrace with its uninterrupted view down the Aventino towards the elongated green open space of the Circus Maximus. There were nine classmates there, invited by his mother.

But as far as numbers were concerned, only one mattered, and that wasn't simply because it represented his age. His father had taken him to one side and talked of it a little, before the other children came.

Seven was the magic number.

There were seven hills in imperial Rome; the Bramantes still lived on one that, in parts, was not that much changed over the centuries.

Seven were the planets known to the ancients, the wonders of the world, the primary colours, the heavens deemed to exist somewhere in the sky, hidden from the view of the living.

These were, Giorgio Bramante said, universal ideas, ones that crossed continents, peoples, religions, appearing in identical guises in situations where the obvious explanation – a Venetian told a Chinaman who told an Aztec chief – made no sense. Seven happened outside mankind, entered the existence of human beings of its own accord. The Masons, who were friends of the Knights of Malta, believed seven celestial creatures called the Mighty Elohim created the universe and everything in it. The Jews and the Christians thought God created the world in six days and rested on the seventh. For the Hindus, the earth was a land bounded entirely by seven peninsulas.

Jesus spoke just seven times on the Cross, and then died. Seven ran throughout the Bible, his father said, during that private time they had before the balloons and cake and the stupid, pointless singing. In something called Proverbs – a word Alessio liked, and decided to remember – there was a saying his father recalled precisely, though they were a family that never went to church.

' "For the just man falls seven times and rises again, but the wicked stumbles to ruin." '

At that moment Alessio asked what the saying meant. The Bible puzzled him. Perhaps it puzzled his father too.

'It means a good person may do the wrong thing time and time again, but in the end he, or she, can still make it right. While the bad person . . .'

He'd waited, wishing the hated party would begin soon, and quickly end. He wouldn't eat the cake. He wouldn't be happy till he was left alone with his imagination again, his father back deep in his books, his mother in the studio upstairs, messing with her smelly paints and unfinished canvases. Some of the others in the school said it was bad to be an only child. From what he understood of his parents' whispered conversations, which grew heated when they thought he was out of earshot, it wasn't a matter of choice.

'The bad person stays that way forever, whatever they do?' Alessio suggested.

'Forever,' Giorgio Bramante agreed, nodding his head in that wise, grave fashion Alessio liked so much he imitated it from time to time. This gesture, knowing and powerful, established what his father was: a professor. A man of learning and secret knowledge, there to be imparted slowly over the years.

Forever seemed unfair. A harsh judgement, not the kind someone like Jesus, who surely believed in forgiveness, would make.

That thought returned to him the next day when, in the hill beneath the park with the orange trees, he listened to more secrets, bigger, wilder ones than he could ever have imagined. Alessio Bramante and his father were in a small, brightly lit underground chamber only a very short distance from the iron gate in an out-of-the-way channel at the riverside edge of the park near the school. A gate Giorgio, to his obvious surprise, had found unlocked when he arrived, though the fact didn't seem to bother him much.

Seven.

He looked around the room. It smelled of damp and stale cigarette smoke. There were signs of frequent and recent occupation: a forest of very bright electric lights, fed by black cables snaking to the doorway; charts and maps and large pieces of paper on the walls; and a single low table with four cheap chairs, all situated beneath the yellow bulbs hanging from the rock ceiling.

Alessio sat opposite his father in one of the flimsy seats and listened in awe, turning his head as he told of what they'd found, and what greater secrets might lie elsewhere, in this labyrinth beneath the hill.

Seven passageways, just visible in the sudden gloom at the edge of the illumination given off by the lights, ran off the room, each a black hole, leading to something he could only guess at.

'Mithras liked the number seven,' Giorgio said confidently, as if he were talking about a close friend.

'Everyone likes the number of seven,' Alessio commented.

'If you wanted to follow him,' Giorgio Bramante continued, ignoring the remark, 'you had to obey the rules. Each one of those corridors would have led to some kind of . . . experience.'

'A nice one?'

His father hesitated.

'The men who gathered here came with an idea in mind, Alessio. They wanted something. To be part of their god. A little discomfort along the way was part of the price they were willing to pay. They wanted to receive some sacrament, at each stage along their journey through the ranks, in order to attain what they sought. Knowledge. Betterment. Power.'

Alessio wondered what kind of gift could be that powerful. All the more so when his father said that the sacrament had to be repeated, perhaps made greater, through each of the seven different ranks of the order, rising in importance . . .

Corax, the Raven, the lowliest beginner, who died and then was reborn when he entered the service of the god.

Nymphus, the bridegroom, married to Mithras, an idea Alessio found puzzling.

Miles, the soldier, led blindfold and bound to the altar, and only released when he made some penance that was lost to the modern world.

Leo, the lion, a bloodthirsty creature, who sacrificed the animals killed in Mithras' name.

Perses, the Persian, bringer of a secret knowledge to the upper orders.

Heliodromus, the Runner of the Sun, closest to the god's human representative on earth, the man who sat at the pinnacle of the cult, his shadow and protector.

He waited. When Giorgio didn't give the final name he asked. 'Who was the last one?'

'The leader was called Pater. Father.'

He screwed up his face, trying to work out what that meant.

'He was their father?'

'In a way. He was the man who promised he'd always look after them. For as long as he lived. I say that to you because I'm your real father. But if you were Pater here you were a great man. You were responsible, ultimately, for everyone. The men in the cult. Their wives. Their families. You were a kind of greater father, with a larger family, children who weren't your real children, though you still cared for them.'

He knew what kind of being that was supposed to be.

'You mean a god?'

'A god living inside a man, perhaps.'

'What kind of sacrament do you need,' he asked, 'to become like that?'

Giorgio Bramante pulled a puzzled face.

'We don't know. We don't know so much. Perhaps one day . . .' He looked around him. Disappointment showed in his features at that moment. 'If we get the money. The permission. You could help me find those secrets. When you grow up.'

'I could help now!' the boy said eagerly, certain that was what his father wanted to hear.

All the same, he wasn't so sure. There was so much that was unseen in this place, lurking at the edge of the flood of yellow light bulbs above them. And the smell . . . it reminded him of when something went off in the refrigerator, sat there growing a furry mould, dead in itself, with something new, something alive, growing from within.

'You do know some of the gifts they gave,' Alessio pressed. 'You said. About Miles and the lion.'

'We're familiar with a few. We know what Corax had to undergo . . .'

He hesitated. Alessio knew he'd say what was on his mind in the end.

'Corax had to be left on his own. Probably somewhere down one of those long, dark corridors. He had to be left until he became so frightened he thought no one would come for him. Ever. That he'd die.'

'That's cruel!'

'He wanted to be a man!' his father replied, his voice rising. 'A man's made. Not born. You're a child. You're too young to understand.'

'Tell me.'

'In a cruel world a man must sometimes do cruel things. This is part of growing up. A man's there to carry that burden. Out of love. Out of practicality. Do you think it's kind to be weak?'

His face creased in distaste when he said that last word. Weakness was, Alessio Bramante realized, some kind of sin.

'No,' he answered quietly.

His father calmed down somewhat.

'Cruelty can be relative, Alessio. Is a doctor cruel if he cuts off a diseased limb that could kill you?'

Alessio Bramante had never thought of doctors this way. It left him uneasy.

'No,' he replied, guessing this was the right answer.

'Of course not. Men are here to make those kinds of decisions. I learned this. You will too. What hurts us can also make us strong.'

Giorgio Bramante had his head cocked to one side, like a blackbird listening for worms in the garden.

'Did you hear that?' he asked.

'No . . .'

'I heard something,' he said, getting up, looking at the dark entrances of the corridors. Seven of them. Wondering which to choose.

'It's safe here, Alessio. Just stay in your chair. Wait for me. I have something to do. Be patient.'

Alessio shivered and stared at the old surface of the cheap table, trying not to think. Giorgio had brought a thick jacket with him. It occurred to his son that his father had known all along that they would end up in this cold, damp chamber beneath the ground, and had said nothing to him. Alessio wore just a pair of thin cotton school trousers and his white T-shirt, a clean one that morning, with the symbol his mother had designed for the school outlined in clear colours on the front: a star inside a dark blue circle, with a set of equidistant smaller stars set around them.

Seven stars. Seven points.

'I will,' he promised.

- 11 -

Leo Falcone could cope with almost anything life could throw at him. Even a bullet in the head that had disrupted, temporarily, the doctors all said, the neural connections between his brain and his limbs. But what was happening to him now was outside his realm of expectation. There was real fear on the inspector's face, and it made him look old and weak and vulnerable.

Tyres squealed at the end of the street, down on Cavour. Three blue police cars had fought their way onto the busy pavement and screeched to a halt at the concrete blocks placed there to impede traffic. Uniformed officers were scrambling out of them, looking up the narrow alley in the direction of the two men by the car and Costa, exposed in the wan spring sunlight at the junction.

That's just what you do in a situation like this, Costa thought with a rising dismay. Turn up the heat.

He moved closer, until he was no more than a couple of metres away from Falcone and his assailant, his arms held high, hands open, fingers spread wide, talking calmly, not angry, not engaged, as cool as he could make it in the circumstances.

'No one's going to get hurt,' Costa said. 'Let's just do this simply. You put the gun down. We talk this through.'

'Nic . . .' Falcone growled, held tight in that painful position, still with enough venom left to make his point. Costa knew that low, embittered tone of voice. It said: *leave this to me.*

He glanced behind him. A large police van, too big for the narrow streets, was blocking the opposite end of the alley. It sounded as if more cars were screaming up either side of the Via degli Zingari, determined to close every exit.

Costa took a good look into those smart dark eyes. The man wasn't working Leo so hard now. Just holding him tight, one arm round his neck, the other keeping the gun, a large black revolver, something ex-military, Costa guessed, at an uncommitted angle, one that could go anywhere, forward, back, where he liked, in an instant.

In training they taught you two things about a situation like this. First, that a man was always most dangerous when he was cornered. And second, that it was so easy to let your emotions get the better of you, and forget that nothing much mattered except getting the victim out alive.

'Nowhere to go . . .' Costa began saying, then found his voice drowned out by a familiar sound.

The high-pitched screech of a small, overworked scooter engine, a mechanical, too-loud bee buzz, rose up from Cavour, getting more vocal, more angry, all the time.

To his astonishment, the bike had crossed the stone barriers, worked its way through the officers and marked cars, and was now accelerating up the hill. The middle-aged man at the controls gunned the little engine and dropped another gear to get some speed, turning to shake his fist at the cops, a little unsteadily, and maybe not through mere gravity either.

He recognized the model. It was a scarlet Piaggio Vespa ET4, a retro machine clothed in 1960s styling to give it the look of the original from some old black and white movie in the old Rome of Fellini and Rossellini.

This incongruous sight silenced them all: Falcone and his captor, the baffled and irate uniforms who let it slip past them.

The figure in black watched the Vespa approach, then picked up Falcone by the scruff of his overcoat and saw something, an opportunity perhaps.

Costa assessed the situation around him. A good dozen officers, at least six vehicles, all with four wheels. A perfect close-down for a man on foot or in a car. But with some fake sixties Vespa . . .

He took one step forward and found himself facing the weapon.

'Don't do anything stupid,' Costa said quietly.

Falcone found his voice. He turned his head as best as he could, looked the man straight in the face and said, a little of his old self surfacing, 'This is Giorgio Bramante. He only ever did one stupid thing in his entire life, as far as I'm aware. I thought he was still paying for it.'

'You thought right,' the man said, and placed the barrel of the gun tight against Falcone's temple.

Raffaela was screaming again. The rattle of the bike got louder. Costa weighed his chances: next to nothing. It didn't make a difference. He had to try.

Then something extraordinary occurred. Bramante leaned close to Leo Falcone's ear and whispered something, his eyes never leaving Costa, always ready for the attack. The weapon flashed hard against Leo's head. Bramante released his grip. The inspector went down, clutching his skull.

The fake Vespa reached them then, lurching over the cobbles, slowing out of curiosity, the drunk at the handlebars mouthing something faintly obscene. Bramante timed what came next perfectly, before Costa could begin to intervene, leaping out in front of the scooter, waving the gun at the rider until he stopped, punching the idiot out of the saddle, then picking the light machine off the ground, revving that high-pitched engine up into the red, and leaping up the hill, front wheel rising.

The two officers from the Fiat across the junction had their weapons out already. The man was jinking to the right, trying to head past them, into the skein of alleyways that got narrower and narrower into the heart of Monti, an area where no car stood a chance against a man on a fast, agile bike.

'No guns!' Falcone yelled, clawing himself to his feet on unsteady, wavering legs. 'There are civilians here, dammit!'

No one argued with the old inspector when he sounded like that. The uniforms let their weapons drop.

Costa walked over and offered Falcone his arm. He took it, furious, then hobbled, in obvious pain, to the crossroads, staring at the fumes of the departing scooter as it disappeared down a turning ahead.

'You're bleeding,' Costa said, and held out a clean white handkerchief. It wasn't necessary. Raffaela Arcangelo was at Falcone's side, distraught, wiping his face, checking the damage, which was minor. A cut lip. A bruise starting to form a shade on his temple where Bramante's weapon had struck.

Falcone let her fuss over him, scowling all the while in the direction of the vanished bike.

'There's nothing wrong with me, Raffaela,' he said curtly. 'Please. This is too much fuss.'

Another large police van had navigated the bystanders in the Via degli Zingari. It was now stationary behind Peroni, Emily and Teresa Lupo, none of whom knew quite what to do next.

A stout, powerful-looking man got out. He was in his thirties, wearing a black woollen overcoat and the disdain that went with rank. Nic Costa had already decided, for no good reason, he didn't much like Commissario Bruno Messina.

Falcone watched the newcomer approach.

'You know, Leo,' he said, shaking his head, as if dealing with amateurs. 'It would be nice if, just this once, you were where you were supposed to be. Home.'

Falcone said nothing, just nodded with that brief smile that was too professional to be classed as insolence.

'Did he say much?' Messina asked. 'An explanation? Anything?'

Costa thought of that last whispered message. Bramante meant it to have some private significance, he thought.

'He said,' Falcone replied, looking a little slow, a little baffled, 'that he was sorry, but I'd have to be the last now. Number seven.'

Commissario Messina listened and then, to Costa's disgust, burst out laughing.

'I want everyone in the van,' Messina ordered when his private amusement had receded. He pointed to Falcone, Costa, Peroni and Teresa Lupo. 'You four are back on duty, as of this moment.'

Raffaela was squawking a protest already, about Falcone's sick leave, his injuries, his physical difficulties.

'You,' Messina interrupted her, 'and Agente Costa's girlfriend here are in protective custody. One of the cars will take you to the Questura. You can wait there.'

'And where,' Teresa Lupo interjected, just loud enough to overcome the shrieks of protest from Emily and Raffaela, 'are we going, might I ask?'

Bruno Messina smiled.

'To see number five.'

- 12 -

It began, Torchia knew, with Giorgio's lecture the previous month, three hours of a long, warm afternoon in the airless *aula* in the Piazza dei Cavalieri di Malta, one he'd never forget. Bramante was on his finest form: brilliant, electrifying, incisive. The subject, nominally, was what little was known about the philosophy of the Roman military Mithraic sects. But it was about much more than that, though Ludo Torchia suspected he was the only one who knew it. What Bramante was really talking about was life itself, the passage from child to man, the acceptance of duty and deference to those above, and the need, absolute, unquestionable, for obedience, trust and secrecy within the tight, closed ranks of the social group to which an individual belonged.

He'd listened, rigid in his seat, unable to take his eyes off Giorgio, who sat on his desk, fit and muscular in a tight T-shirt and Gucci jeans, a leader at ease with his flock.

One part came back to Torchia now. Bramante had been discussing the seven-ranked hierarchy. Vignola had asked a question that seemed, on the face of things, sensible. How did structures like this begin? At what point, in the nascent stage of Mithraism's emergence, did someone dictate that there would be seven ranks, with set rituals for the progression from one to the next? Where, he wondered, did it all come from?

Bramante had smiled at them, an attractive, knowing smile, like a father indulging a son.

'They didn't need to ask that question, Sandro,' he said in his measured, powerful Roman voice. 'They knew the answer already. Their religion came from their god.'

'Yes, but . . . in real life,' Vignola objected. 'I mean, it didn't happen that way. It couldn't.'

'How do you know?' Bramante had asked.

'Because it couldn't! If Mithras was real, where did he go?'

'They murdered him,' Torchia said without thinking, and was both pleased, and a little disturbed, by Giorgio's reaction to his answer. Bramante was staring at him, an expression of surprise and admiration on his handsome face.

'Constantine murdered him,' Giorgio agreed. 'Constantine and his bishops. Just as they murdered all the old gods. If you talk to the theologians they'll give you other answers. But I'm not a theologian, nor is this a theology class. We're historians. We look at facts and deduce what we can from them. The facts state that much of the Roman army followed Mithras for the best part of three centuries. Then, with Christianity, Mithras died, and with him the beliefs of those who followed him. Whether you view that literally or not, that is, inescapably, what happened. If you want more complicated answers, you're in the wrong department.'

'It must have been terrible,' Torchia said, unable to take his eyes off his professor.

'What?' Bramante asked.

'To have lost your religion. To have watched it ripped from you.'

'The Christians had to put up with that for three centuries,' Bramante pointed out.

'The Christians *won*.'

There was a flicker of something, knowledge, perhaps even self-doubt, in Giorgio Bramante's eyes at that moment. Torchia couldn't stop looking at it. Giorgio was a patient, knowledgeable professor, but he led them like a general led his troops. What he sought was their comprehension, not their approval. Torchia understood this implicitly, and understood, too, that the rest of them were still just kids really, and he knew what to expect from kids. Fear, interest, then the onset of boredom before, with the right leader, in the correct, ritual circumstances, comprehension.

'What would have been truly terrible, I think,' Giorgio continued, 'would have been if one were denied a final chance to make peace with what one was losing. A Christian would hope to confess before dying. To have that last comfort snatched from your hands . . .'

He said nothing else. It would be two weeks before Ludo Torchia finally understood the misty, almost guilty look in his eyes at that moment.

So he hadn't just brought the live cockerel from the market in Testaccio. While he was there he'd visited a dealer in one of the tenement blocks, purchased, on long credit, two ready-rolled smokes, harsh black Afghan mixed with cheap cigarette tobacco. From what he'd read there'd been some kind of drug down here in the beginning. The Romans knew hemp. They introduced the drug, with much else, from the colonies they'd absorbed over the years. They knew alcohol too. Many of the Mithraic rites had been stolen and incorporated into Christianity. For the winter solstice, celebrated around 25 December each year, they drank wine and ate bread together, a symbolic feast upon the blood and the body of the sacrificial bull. He wondered how many good Catholics knew that when they were on their knees taking Holy Communion under the candles.

Toni LaMarca fell greedily on a joint straight away and stole into the shadows like the fool he was. Raul Bellucci and the Guerino oaf were now choking on the second, giggling, alive with that childish pleasure of being an illicit visitor in a strange and forbidden place. Torchia hadn't any intention of joining them. There was too much to think about in this magic place. Nor was the arch-geek midget Sandro Vignola much interested either. He'd been goggle-eyed since they entered the temple and was now down on his little hands and knees in front of a slab next to the altar, looking for all the world like some overweight choirboy come to do homage to the god who stood above him, sword in hand, straddling the bull, blade in its writhing neck.

Torchia watched Vignola mouthing the Latin inscription on the stonework, set beneath a cut-out half moon, and wished he was better at languages himself. He nodded at the slab.

'What does it say?'

Latin was rarely simple, old words for new. It was a tongue from another era, close yet unknown too, a code, a collection of symbolic letters, each with a meaning obvious only to the initiated.

He shone his torch on the carving in the dusty white stone.

DEO INV M
L ANTONIUS
PROCULUS
PRAEF COH III P
ET PATER
V · S · L · M

'What does it say?' Torchia asked again, more loudly this time after Vignola had ignored him.

'"Deo Invicto Mithrae, Lucius Antonius Proculus, Praefectus Cohors Tertiae Praetoria, et Pater, votum solvit libens merito."'

The bright round eyes stared at him from behind the oversized spectacles.

'"To the invincible god Mithras, Lucius Antonius Proculus, Prae- fect of the Third Cohort of the Praetorian Guard, and Father, willingly and deservedly fulfilled his vow." I can't believe you don't understand that.'

'I don't read Latin well.'

Dino Abati was there. He'd been poking about in the corners with his gear, bright ginger hair bouncing around, in places he didn't belong.

'You should still know the name. We did it in class. Lucius Antonius Proculus was with the Praetorian Guard for the Battle of the Milvian Bridge. The Praetorian backed Maxentius. The one who lost. Remember?'

Torchia didn't like being treated like a moron.

'I don't waste time on old names,' he murmured. 'So you think he was here?'

Abati shot a glance towards the anteroom, where the dead were.

'Perhaps he still is,' he suggested. 'Constantine wiped out the

Praetorian Guard completely after he entered Rome. They'd backed the wrong side. He felt he couldn't trust them. So he razed that headquarters of theirs . . . what was it?'

'The Castra Praetoria,' Vignola answered.

'Wiped it out completely. And here too, I guess,' Abati added. 'It's creepy, really. Did anyone know about this place until Giorgio came along?'

'Of course not!' Vignola squealed. 'Don't you think it would be in the books? This is the best Mithraeum in Rome. Perhaps the best in the world.'

Abati thought about this.

'And Giorgio's in two minds about whether he dare tell people? It's crazy. He can't keep it hidden forever.'

Vignola shook his head, dragged himself off the floor and rubbed the grime off his hands.

'He can keep it hidden for as long as he likes. The department has charge of this entire excavation. He can just carry on as he is now, working quietly with Judith Turnhouse and whoever else is in on the secret. Then some day, when the time's right, he calls up the right people and says, "Look what we found." Behold, Giorgio the hero. The discoverer of unknown wonders. Schliemann, Howard Carter, all rolled into one. Wouldn't he love that?'

'This is holy ground,' Torchia said suddenly, without thinking.

'So what are we supposed to do, Ludo?' Abati asked in that infuriating slow drawl of his. 'Sing a few songs? Kill the cockerel? Bow before the god or something then go home and complete our assignments? You shouldn't take this Mithras thing too seriously. It was all just a bunch of us messing round. Hey! *Hey!*'

He was shouting now, abruptly animated and angry. He flew across the dimly lit room and took hold of Toni LaMarca who was about to stumble down a small rectangular exit on the far side, behind the altar and its figures.

'What the hell do you think you're doing?' Abati yelled.

'Looking . . .' LaMarca replied, his voice thick with dope.

'Don't . . .'

'But . . .'

Something in Abati's face silenced him. Then the figure in the red caving suit, who looked so much at home here, picked up a rock from the ground and threw it into the black hole ahead of them, where LaMarca had been about to enter. There was no sound. Nothing at all. Until, eventually, a distant echo of a hard, lost object falling into water.

Dino Abati gave each of them a filthy look in turn.

'This is not a playground, children,' he said with venom. 'There's a reason you should be afraid of the dark.'

– 13 –

Giorgio Bramante had been a model prisoner. Commissario Messina possessed the man's full prison records in his large, black briefcase that morning, running carefully through them as the control van navigated the traffic from Monti to the Aventino. Bramante had spent fourteen unremarkable years in jail after being found guilty of murder in a trial that had triggered many conflicting emotions at the time. No one liked unfinished stories about missing children. No one was happy when an investigation went bad because the police fouled up, and on this occasion in the most unexpected of ways, one in which the wronged party, Bramante, went to prison while the guilty, the students who had apparently kidnapped his son and refused to disclose his fate, went free.

Five of them, anyway.

As Costa listened to Bruno Messina, reading the expression on Falcone's attentive face along the way, he began to realize the Bramante case was still alive, for both of these men. Falcone had been on the brink of promotion to inspector at the time, a promising *sovrintendente* underneath Messina's commissario father, who had retired from the force in disgrace not long after the case against the students had collapsed. Messina senior had seen his career torn apart by what happened in the wake of Alessio Bramante's disappearance. That fact clearly caused his son pain to this day. They were, as the entire Questura knew, a police family going back several generations. The uniform ran in the blood. There were professional reasons for Messina, and his father, to be dissatisfied too, ones Falcone surely shared. Cases that involved missing children demanded resolution more than most. For both parents, since Beatrice Bramante, though she had divorced her husband while he was in jail, was still alive and living in Rome. And for the officers involved.

Peroni, always one to come straight to the point, waited for the control van to circumnavigate the round of traffic at the Colosseum then asked, 'Remind me again. Why exactly didn't these scum go to jail?'

'Because of the lawyers,' Messina said scornfully. 'They said it wasn't possible.'

Falcone stroked his silver goatee then emitted a long, pained sigh.

'It's important we have this conversation, Commissario, so that both of us are sure where we stand. Unlike you, I was there . . .'

'And don't I know it?' Messina replied, his face a black scowl.

Falcone didn't bat an eyelid. Costa had seen him deal with much worse than this young, over-ambitious commissario with just a few months in the job.

'Good. Then let me explain. There are two reasons why no charges were pursued against any of Bramante's students. Firstly, we had no evidence. They provided none. Forensic provided none. We had no body. No clue as to where the child had gone or what had happened to him. Only suspicions, created principally by the unwillingness of the students to do much to help themselves. There was nothing there on which we could base a prosecution . . .'

Bruno Messina was a thickset man, with a head of fulsome black hair and an expression that could turn from polite to malevolent in an instant.

'I could have got it out of them,' he said, with no small hint of menace.

'That's what your father thought. But he failed. Then he left the ringleader alone with Giorgio Bramante for an hour in a quiet little cell at the far end of the holding block in the basement we all know so well. Which brings me to the second reason why no one ever faced any charges over Alessio Bramante's disappearance. I hate to remind you of this but during that hour Bramante beat the unfortunate youth senseless. Ludo Torchia died in the ambulance, while I watched, on the way to hospital. After that we were knee-deep in civil rights lawyers who made sure that the other suspects, if they weren't aware of the fact already, could get away without saying a damn thing to anyone because we'd already allowed one of their number to be, in all but name, murdered before our very eyes.'

He gave Messina the kind of look Falcone normally reserved for impudent, uncomprehending juniors.

'Case closed,' the inspector observed without emotion.

Peroni glowered at him.

'I've got to say, I remember what was in the newspapers back then. It wasn't quite that clear cut. You don't have kids. I do. If I thought one of mine might be alive, if there was the slightest chance of that, I'd have beaten the living daylights out of those students too.'

Falcone shrugged.

'The significance of this being what, exactly?'

Peroni tautened, taken aback by the nonchalant tone in Falcone's voice. Costa watched Bruno Messina recoil from his partner's visible anger, and reminded himself that those relatively new to the Questura still found Peroni's physical presence – the large, scarred face, the corpulent, powerful thug's body – intimidating.

'That any father would have felt that way!' Peroni objected.

'I hate having to repeat myself but this seems unavoidable. I was there. I walked into that cell because I was sick of hearing the screaming, over and over again. I was the one' – Falcone glowered at Messina – 'who made sure it went to a higher authority than your father. This wasn't difficult since he had, as I recall, decided to attend a management meeting the moment he left Bramante alone with the youth.'

'He was commissario,' Messina objected. 'He was desperate.'

'And I was just the *sovrintendente*, the junior meant to clean up afterwards. It was quite a mess, too. Look up the photographs. They'll still be in the records. That cell was covered in blood. I've never seen anything like it, before or since. Giorgio Bramante took Torchia apart.

He was barely breathing when I got in there. An hour later he was gone.'

Peroni said again, 'He thought the child was alive, Leo!'

'It was more than that,' Messina continued. 'He thought that if you'd not burst in there stopping him when you did, he could have beaten the truth out of that bastard. Perhaps he was right and we could have found the boy. Who knows?'

'No one!' Falcone replied with a degree of heat Costa hadn't witnessed in a long time. 'Not you. Not me. In situations like that we deal with certainties, not guesswork. Ludo Torchia was brutally assaulted, in a cell in our own Questura, and then died. How are we supposed to ignore that? The law's the law. We don't pick and choose to whom it applies or when.'

Teresa Lupo raised her large hand in objection. Costa observed the interest in her pale, loose features. She was never far away from the front of a case, particularly a difficult one like this.

'But if Bramante thought . . .'

'None of us knows what he was thinking!' Falcone insisted. 'I was there when he was interviewed afterwards. I told him Ludo Torchia was dead. I told him that the doctor in the ambulance said he'd several broken ribs. It was as bad a beating as I've seen in my life, all done slowly, deliberately. And Giorgio Bramante? He acted as if it was just an everyday event. I have no idea what he thought. He scarcely said a word afterwards. Not to us. Not to his wife. To the press. To anyone. Yes, yes, I know what you're about to say. It was grief. Perhaps. But we still don't understand what happened, and that's a fact.'

Messina leaned forward and tapped Falcone on the knee.

'I'll tell you what happened. You made inspector. My father got kicked out of the force. After thirty years. We'll leave that to one side for now. Just don't fool yourself. Those morons were responsible for that boy's death somehow. Not my father. Not Giorgio Bramante. Ludo Torchia apart, they walked away scot-free. Changed their names, most of them. Grew up and found themselves different lives, mostly in places where no one knew who they were. They thought it was over, like a bad dream that scares the shit out of you at night and just fades away the next morning.'

'As far as they are concerned it *is* over,' Falcone replied. 'That's the law.'

Messina pulled a set of folders out of his capacious briefcase.

'Not for Giorgio Bramante it isn't.'

– 14 –

Bruno Messina seemed to know Bramante's entire history from the moment he went to jail.

'He helped other prisoners with their work. He taught them to read and write. Counselled them on giving up drugs. Ran up every credit he could. The perfect prisoner. After three years he was getting early day release and he didn't ever go running to the press. There was nothing to suggest he was anything else but an unfortunate man who lost his temper and paid a heavy price for it, in circumstances where most people would feel sympathetic.'

'And?' Falcone asked, interested now.

'There were six students in those caves when Alessio went missing. Torchia died that day. Another, Sandro Vignola, moved to Puglia then, three years after the case, came back to Rome for the day. We don't know why. He was never seen again. Of the remaining four . . .'

He spread out some papers from the files and went through them.

'Andrea Guerino. Farmer's son. Changed his name. Moved to near Verona where he ran a small fruit farm. Found dead of shotgun wounds out in the fields, June, three years ago. The local police say his wife went missing the day before. She turns up alive. He gets half his head blown off, and she's too scared to say a word about where she's been, who with, anything. The local force put it down to some kind of affair gone wrong and never get to charge a soul.

'Fifteen months ago, Raul Bellucci. He was working as a cab driver

71

in Florence, again under an assumed name. He gets a call at home. Someone's kidnapped his daughter and wants a ransom or she's gone. The idiot doesn't go to us, of course. I imagine he's worried we'd find out who he really is. The following day he's dead on some industrial park used by hookers on the edge of town. The police' – the venom in Messina's voice was unmistakable – 'decide that, since his throat's been cut from ear to ear and his genitals have been removed, this is the work of some African gang. Most of the hookers thereabouts are Nigerian.'

'And today?' Teresa looked interested. She'd been complaining about the lack of challenging work.

'Today, or rather last night from what we've seen, was the turn of Toni LaMarca, the only one who stayed in Rome. He was some hoodlum's kid from Naples. Perhaps he thought that made a difference. Bad piece of work. Involved in some dope and prostitution rings around Termini. Not a man to mourn. It was the same story. Well, similar. LaMarca's teenage boyfriend got kidnapped on the way home from the cinema. He managed to claw his way out of some lock-up near Clodio this morning and went straight to us. Not much else to say on his part. It doesn't take a genius to work out what happened. Someone had called LaMarca. A ransom perhaps. He went out . . .'

'Commissario,' Peroni pointed out. 'I thought you said Bramante was in jail until three months ago. Maybe he could have kidnapped this kid and killed LaMarca. But the rest?'

Messina pulled out a prison file and thrust it in front of them.

'I told you. Giorgio Bramante was a model prisoner. He had all the parole he wanted. They even let him out to do odd jobs for people from time to time. Nothing illegal. Nothing that didn't get recorded. When Vignola disappeared, Bramante was on emotional leave to see his sick mother. Here in Rome. When Guerino died, he was on a free weekend. Plenty of time to do what he did. Same with Raul Bellucci.'

'These people had changed their names?' Teresa pointed out. 'How the hell would he know how to find them?'

'That's for you to discover,' Messina answered, then stuffed the pages back into the briefcase and passed it over to Falcone. 'One more thing. The boy's mother gave a school T-shirt to some weird little church in Prati. They have a collection of memorabilia that appeals to psychics. She told them that soon after Alessio went missing, and Ludo Torchia was pronounced dead, she found it at home. With a fresh bloodstain on the chest. As if the two events were connected. The Church likes that kind of thing, apparently.'

Teresa scowled.

'Leave me out of this. I'm a scientist. I don't do witchcraft. What if someone had a nosebleed?'

'They didn't,' Messina said. 'This T-shirt has gained a few more bloodstains over the years, not that we found out until this morning. The church warden tried to keep it all quiet. But he's a precise man. He kept the dates. Any guesses?'

They looked at one another and stayed silent.

'The first happened just after Sandro Vignola went missing. Then, following each death, a day, two at the most, the warden finds another stain on Alessio Bramante's shirt. It's no big deal. The place scarcely has any security. Anyone could get in there, open the case, and pour something on the shirt. It doesn't take magic. This morning . . .'

He paused to look out of the window. They were moving into the Viale Aventino at last. It couldn't be far away.

'. . . the church had a visitor. A man on his own, with a physical description that matches Bramante. This was around seven thirty. Afterwards there was several fresh stains. *Big* stains this time, ones they couldn't keep quiet. And some writing. It took a little while to work out what it meant but eventually it brought us here. Not, unfortunately, before the caretaker had got in there first. Rosa Prabakaran is talking to her.'

Peroni's face lit up with fury.

'You've got a junior officer straight out of school on something like this? Aren't there any grown-ups around?'

Messina gave him a cold managerial stare. He didn't appreciate the interruption.

'She's got nothing to worry about. You people, however . . .'

Even Falcone looked lost for a clue at that moment.

'He's got two left on his list,' Messina continued. 'Dino Abati. God knows what he calls himself or where he's living these days. Then the police officer he blames for stopping him beating the truth out of Ludo Torchia fourteen years ago. I hope you like the emergency quarters in the Questura, by the way, Leo. You'll be staying there, all four of you, until this is over.'

'Oh no,' Peroni declared, waving his hand. 'I'm just a man on the street these days. Don't lay this at my door.'

'It's already there,' Messina snapped. 'Don't you get it? Bramante isn't just killing these people one by one to get his revenge. He's taking someone they're close to beforehand, holding them ransom, trying to . . .' The commissario struggled for the words.

'He wants to put them through exactly the same nightmare he experienced,' Falcone said calmly. 'But what makes you think he wants me?'

'After we worked out what was going on here I sent a team round to the apartment Bramante had been using since he got out of jail. He was long gone. But he's been busy. Too busy to take everything with him. Take a look at these.'

He withdrew three packs of photographic prints out of the brief-case, checked the labels, and passed one to each man. They began sifting through the contents in silence.

Nic Costa was halfway through his own when he stopped, unable to imagine how any of this had come about.

He was looking at a photograph of himself and Emily, walking out of the Palazzo Ruspoli, happy, smiling, arm-in-arm. He recognized the new red coat she was wearing. The picture had been taken two days before. They'd seen the doctor that morning, had the standard talk about what to do, what to expect, during the coming months of impending parenthood.

'What's this lunatic doing taking photographs of me?' Teresa demanded, pointing at the pack in Peroni's hand.

Costa glanced at them, then at Falcone's set. Raffaela was there, shopping in the Via degli Zingari. Something didn't ring true.

'He didn't try and seize any of us today,' Costa said, still trying to work out what to make of the photo of them together, unable to take his eyes off Emily's tired, strained face. 'He went straight for Leo.'

Messina scowled at the familiarity.

'I know. Perhaps he just saw an opportunity. He's intelligent enough to improvise, isn't he?'

'He's intelligent enough to get what he wants first time round,' Falcone answered, giving Costa an interested look.

The commissario looked pleased by this response.

'I'm glad you find this worthy of your attention, Leo. It's your case now. As I said, sick leave ends today. Costa here is done playing museum curator. Peroni's off the beat. Head this up or sit inside the Questura trying to remember how to play chess. It's up to you.'

Some choice, Costa thought. The avid look in Falcone's eyes told him it was already made. A part of him was glad to see the old inspector fired up by something outside himself for a change. Another part wanted, more than anything, to see Emily, to take her away from this new threat, let her sit down, rest, recover some of the strength she seemed to have lost, without his noticing, in recent weeks.

'And the ladies?' Peroni asked.

Messina smiled.

'Yes. The ladies. We have a family villa near Orvieto. It's beautiful. Big, secluded and hard to find. A car will take them straight from the Questura. My father's there. Giorgio Bramante isn't looking for him. So they'll be safe. Call it a surprise vacation. I don't want the complication of having them around in Rome.'

'That's their decision,' Costa complained.

'No,' Messina replied. 'It's not.'

Teresa Lupo leaned forward and tapped the commissario hard on the knee.

'Excuse me for pointing this out, but I'm a lady too. Maybe I could use that vacation.'

'You're a pathologist,' he replied. 'And I want to introduce you to Tony LaMarca. What's left of him.'

– 15 –

'Basic caving technique,' Abati said, and pushed LaMarca back into the centre of the room. 'Know the place you're in and what's around it. This wasn't always a temple. I told you. These were tufa workings. Someone put the temple in here later, when they were finished digging out the stone. This is an underground quarry. Half those things you think of as corridors either lead nowhere or just meet up with some fissure or fault in the rock.'

'I heard water,' Vignola said, puzzled.

'This is Rome!' Abati declared. 'There are springs. Fault lines. Unfinished workings that lead nowhere. There must be channels that go all the way down to the river. It could link up with the Cloaca Maxima itself somehow. If I had the equipment . . .'

He gave them that condescending look Torchia was beginning to resent.

'. . . and the people. I could find out. But I don't think any of you quite fit the bill. So don't walk anywhere I can't see you. I really don't feel in the mood for rescue work.'

In his head, Ludo Torchia had allotted each of them a role. Abati was Heliodromus, protector of the leader. Vignola was Perses, clever, quick and not always willing to reveal what he knew. Big, stupid Andrea Guerino made a good foot soldier as Miles. Raul Bellucci, an underling who always did what he was told, could pass as Leo, the mechanism for the sacrifice. And for Nymphus, the bridegroom, some kind of creature who was both male and female in the same body, the slim, annoying creep who was Toni LaMarca, a kid whose sexuality seemed as yet undefined.

There could be only one Pater. Torchia understood exactly what that meant. Pater involved leadership, not blood relationship, certainly not love. He'd watched the way his own father had behaved, the simple, blunt dictatorial attitude that said: *here in my own house I am a kind of god too.* From obedience came knowledge and security. It had been that way for Ludo Torchia right up to the age of nine when his father went down to work at the docks in Genoa one day and never came back. A year later, when his weak, incapable mother thought he was over everything, Torchia had stolen into the jetty where the accident occurred, stared at the giant black crane, its head like that of some stupid black crow, trying to imagine what had happened, how it would feel to have that mass of evil steel tumble over towards you, hungry for something to destroy.

Ludo loathed the Church from that moment forward, watching his mother cling to the Bible each night, trying to find some solace in a religion that, the young Ludo Torchia knew, had failed them by allowing the crane to topple in the first place.

When he came to La Sapienza and began, under the careful tute-lage of the knowledgeable Giorgio Bramante, to study Mithraism, he understood what his life had lacked, and how that gaping hole could be filled. By duty, responsibility, leadership. Some clear declaration of his own identity, one that set him apart from the drones. He would be Pater some time too, part of the old religion, one that kept its secrets beneath ground, not sharing them with the masses in vast golden palaces. Here, in the temple that Bramante had uncovered, all the pieces should have been in place, and he could begin by finishing the task those long-dead soldiers had begun almost eighteen centuries before.

Except one detail was missing. The cowardly Vincenzo had failed them, failed his destiny, to be Corax, the initiate, the beginner, a child even, if the old books had it right.

'Also,' Abati added quickly, marching towards the altar again, intent on something Torchia couldn't predict, 'I am not countenancing any of this nonsense.'

To Torchia's astonishment, Abati now had the bird's cage in his hands, was lifting it high, opening the lid. The shining black cockerel flapped its wings and made a low, aggressive crowing noise.

'Don't touch that,' Torchia ordered. 'I said . . .'

Dino Abati was working on the cage.

'Ludo. Think about it. We're in trouble enough without these stupid games.'

'Andrea,' Torchia yelled. 'Stop him.'

Guerino had the joint in his mouth. The big farmer's son looked half stoned already.

'What . . .?' he mumbled.

None of them understood. Bramante's words kept ringing in Ludo Torchia's ears. How terrible must it have been to have lost your religion? To have seen it snatched from your hands, just before death, denied the final sacrament, the last opportunity you would have on this earth to make peace with your god?

Abati had the cage open, was turning it sideways, trying to shake the cockerel out into the damp, dark air.

'Don't do that,' Torchia said, walking over towards the red-suited figure.

Heliodromus always wore red. He coveted the position of Pater. Had to. Until Pater died there was nowhere for him to go.

Ludo Torchia surreptitiously retrieved a fist-sized rock from one of the stone benches as he moved, held it low and hidden in his right hand.

'I said—' he began to murmur, then stopped, found he was waving away a cloud of stinking black feathers, flapping furiously around his face.

Maybe he screamed. He wasn't sure. Someone laughed. Toni LaMarca, by the sound of it. Terrified, screeching with fear and rage, the cockerel dug its claws into Ludo Torchia's scalp then launched itself over him, towards the exit, flapping manically, its cawing metallic voice echoing around the stone chamber that enclosed them like a tomb.

He didn't know why he'd picked a bird that was black. Like a crow, its wings and limbs extended. Like some miniature mocking imitation of a crane.

Sometimes Ludo Torchia didn't know why he did things at all. When he'd caught his breath again he found he was on his knees, looking at the bloodied head of Dino Abati, pinning the figure in the red caving suit to the ground.

Not that it was necessary. Abati's eyes were glassy and dead-looking. His mouth flapped open, slack-jawed, motionless. He didn't actually remember hitting Abati, which meant, Torchia realized, he could have piled the big, jagged rock that was still in his hand deep into his skull time and time again.

The rest were crowded round the two of them now. No one seemed much keen on speaking. The room stank. Of dope and the bird and their mutual sweat and fear too.

'Oh Christ, Ludo,' Toni LaMarca – it had to be Toni LaMarca – said eventually. 'I think you killed him.'

He looked at Abati. There was blood seeping from his nostrils. It rose then subsided as he watched. He was breathing. Abati was probably just knocked out. That was all. Still, he'd made a point. He'd established himself, the way the Pater had to.

Torchia turned and looked at all of them, and kept gripping the rock in his hand. The Pater had to rule. That was how it worked.

'Listen. All of you.'

He realized he was speaking in a different kind of voice already. Older. A voice with an authority he hadn't quite found inside himself before.

'If you try and say this was just me no one will believe you. I'll tell them we did this between us. Everything.'

'Ludo,' Guerino moaned in his stupid, country-boy whine. 'That's not fair.'

'Just do what I tell you,' Torchia ordered, voice rising, with a commanding tone inside it he hoped was copied from Giorgio Bramante. 'Is that so hard? If you stick with me, everything works out fine. If you don't . . .'

This was the moment on which everything turned. They outnumbered him. They could walk out, go bleating to the college people. To Giorgio Bramante, and that thought sparked both fear and some deep, interior delight of anticipation in Ludo Torchia's head.

Dino Abati groaned beneath him, his eyes flickering open.

Torchia held up the rock again, noting the blood on its surface, and pulled back his arm, as if to strike Abati's head once more.

'It's your choice,' he said calmly.

They looked at one another. Then Sandro Vignola, the smallest, brightest intellectually, but just another dumb, scared teenager in his head, plucked up the courage to speak.

'Let's just keep this among ourselves, Ludo. We can clean Dino up. It was an accident, really. Let's do what has to be done. Then get out of here.'

Vignola was always the smart one. Perses. Number three behind Abati and himself.

Torchia looked at Andrea Guerino, aware that some new spirit of authority now lived inside his own head.

'Hey. Farm boy. Fetch the bird.'

Then, audible to each of them, came a brief high sound, unintelligible, half frightened, half excited.

It could have been a child, trying to say something that was lost in the shadows.

'Fetch me that too,' someone ordered and Ludo Torchia was surprised to find it was him.

– 16 –

None of them wanted to stay long in the old crypt beneath the abandoned church of Santa Maria dell'Assunta, not when they saw what was down there. They left that to Teresa Lupo and her assistant, Silvio Di Capua, who worked away under the arc lights they'd brought, aided by a team of goggle-eyed morgue monkeys. This was an unusual one, even for them.

Bruno Messina went back to the Questura, having handed over his responsibility. Falcone began to assemble his team, slowly at first, but with a rapidly growing confidence. Officers were despatched to bring in the latest news on the hunt for Dino Abati. Two more were sent back to the old church in Prati to take a look at the blood-stained T-shirt. Falcone insisted it stay on the wall there so that a surveillance officer could be placed on stake-out duty day and night to see if Bramante returned. Whatever forensic it contained seemed, to Falcone, irrelevant. They already knew the man they were seeking. The abandoned church on the Aventino would provide enough for Teresa Lupo's team to work on for the foreseeable future.

Once that team had gone, Falcone, Costa and Peroni sat down in the control van and listened to Rosa Prabakaran's description of her interview with the woman who'd found the body in the crypt.

Costa had seen the junior officer in the Questura before, a distant, quiet individual in her early twenties who kept herself apart, and not just because of her background. She had ambition written all over her, that careful, reticent attitude he'd come to recognize among those who kept looking for the way to the up escalator the moment they arrived. She'd been in the force just six months, joining after completing a master's degree in philosophy in Milan the previous summer. Young, educated, smart, keen and with an ethnic background . . . she had just about every last qualification the force was looking for in its next generation of officers.

Except, perhaps, some harsh collision with the real world. He'd spoken to Peroni about this briefly, as he accompanied the big man out of the crime scene deep beneath the earth, making sure his partner didn't go round the corner and buy a pack of cigarettes, falling back into bad habits. Rosa's experience on the force had been routine and perhaps even a little privileged. But now she was on the Bramante case, and had been for a good half day before it engulfed them. She was the one who had gone to the church in Prati, talked to the caretaker and worked out where the message on the wall was pointing them. Early that morning, while they were preparing for a sociable lunch and the news of a wedding to come, a pleasurable moment which already seemed long distant, she'd walked into the crypt, seen the fresh new corpse there. Then, after interviewing the woman caretaker, she'd set about assembling all the data available on Giorgio Bramante, which she had requested from Pino Gabrielli's identification of the intruder in his little church. It was she who'd managed to link the dates of the attacks with the bloodstains in Sacro Cuore del Suffragio, more rapidly than most old hands on the force could have hoped for. It was clear to Costa from listening to the fluent, concise way she managed to sum up what they already knew about Bramante and his movements after leaving prison that Rosa Prabakaran could, one day, make a formidable officer. Only one thing bothered him. It all seemed to be a touch unreal to her, a kind of cerebral puzzle, like the arguments she might juggle in an academic dissertation. That sort of self-detachment could, in his view, be dangerous, both for her and the outcome of any investigation. If there was one thing he'd learned in his short career it was this: results came from engagement, however painful that sometimes proved to be.

Costa forced himself to put aside his concerns about Rosa Prabakaran, which probably stemmed from nothing more than her inexperi-ence, and got back into the conversation.

'They offered him his old job back?' Peroni asked, amazed.

'Academics . . .' Falcone said with a grimace.

According to Rosa, Bramante had walked out of jail after serving fourteen years of a life sentence for murder and found himself immedi-ately faced with the gift of a professorship back at La Sapienza, on an index-linked salary, with university tenure, effectively a job for life. And he'd turned it down.

'Why the hell would he say no?' Peroni demanded.

To Costa it was obvious.

'Because he had a job to do, Gianni. He'd already started on it while he was in jail. Bramante felt he had a . . .'

'Higher calling?' Falcone suggested wryly.

'Exactly. He wasn't going to be deflected from that for anything. Besides . . .'

A man who spent years in jail, carefully plotting the elaborate deaths of those he blamed for the loss of his son, was someone capable of powerful emotions.

'Perhaps he'd feel guilty too,' Costa went on. 'If he got his old life back, and nothing had changed.'

Falcone stared at Rosa.

'Do you agree?'

She shrugged, with the dismissive confidence of the young.

'Why complicate matters by trying to think yourself into his head? What does it matter?'

Costa couldn't stop himself flashing a look of disappointment in her direction. He'd felt much the same way at her age, believing that cases came down to facts and procedures. It was only with age and practice that a more subtle truth emerged: motivation and personality were important issues too, and, in the absence of hard forensic, were often the only trails an investigation team could follow.

'I'm sorry,' she said testily. 'It seems obvious. He knew what he was planning to do. He wasn't going to let anything get in the way. Why else would he have taken the job he did?'

'Which was?' Peroni asked.

'The one he had part-time in jail,' she replied. 'Working in a slaughterhouse. For one of the butchers in the market here.'

She let that sink in.

'A horse butcher,' she added. 'I'd sort of forgotten they even existed.'

But this was Testaccio, Costa thought. One of the oldest central working-class communities in Rome. Less than a kilometre away from where they were stood the old slaughterhouse, a vast complex now being turned over to the arts after years of dereliction. The killing had moved elsewhere, out to the hidden suburbs. The shops still remained though, in the quarter's narrow streets, and the busy market where Rosa Prabakaran had found the caretaker of Santa Maria dell'Assunta that morning. Bramante's cheap little apartment had been close by. It was now being swept clean for less obvious clues than a set of snatched photographs of men and women who could lead him to Leo Falcone. Not, it seemed to Costa, that there would be much there to help. Bramante was gone, to a hiding place he'd doubtless prepared in advance. He was an intelligent, organized, careful individual. That much was clear already. The kind of man who was unlikely to reveal himself easily.

'Where does the wife live?' he asked.

She looked nervous for a moment.

'Three blocks away. And that's ex-wife. They divorced not long after he went to jail.'

'Clever as Bramante is,' Costa pointed out, 'it's still hard to believe he could do all of this on his own. When he's out of jail, maybe. But to kill those people while he was on parole he'd need transport, money, information.'

'It wasn't his wife,' she insisted. 'I talked to Beatrice Bramante this morning. After I saw the old lady home. Just five minutes. It was enough.'

Falcone's grey eyebrows rose. He said nothing.

'She saw Giorgio once in the street after he was released about two months ago. She followed him home to his apartment and tried to talk to him. It didn't go anywhere. The woman's lost everything. Her husband. Her child. Her money. She's living in some one-room dump in a public housing block, not much better than his. There's nothing for us there.'

The three men exchanged glances. Rosa Prabakaran's ambitions were, Costa thought, getting the better of her.

'Agente,' Falcone said quietly. 'When you interview potential suspects you do so in company. With an experienced officer. And at my command. Is that understood?'

Her brown eyes widened with anger.

'You weren't even on the case when I saw Beatrice Bramante.'

'I am now,' Falcone snapped. 'Interview rules are interview rules. If the mother had told you anything incriminating it would have been inadmissible as evidence. Do you understand that?'

She pointed towards the yellow barriers outside the church.

'I'd just seen what happened in there! I was trying to help.' Her brown eyes looked glassy, misting over with the sudden hint of tears.

'When you work for me you work as part of a team. Either that or you don't work at all.'

She didn't burst into tears. Not quite. Then Peroni's broad, ugly smile broke the chill.

'Youthful enthusiasm, Inspector,' he declared. 'We all had it once. Even you.'

Falcone glowered at him.

'Someone's going to have to go back and see her. Properly this time. Find out what Bramante was up to when he wasn't working.'

'Caving,' she said. 'He wouldn't let her into his apartment because it was full of things he needed. She saw lots of equipment through the door. Ropes. Torches. Clothing.'

'So she *did* tell you something!' Falcone declared. 'Let's hope to God I don't have to try to introduce that into court some time soon.'

Rosa Prabakaran went silent, mute with fury and perhaps a little shame. Falcone was busy flicking through Bruno Messina's papers again, engrossed.

'Your shift ends in two hours,' he said to her, staring at a photo of Raffaela Arcangelo, bags in hand, lugging shopping back to their apartment in Monti. 'It's been an eventful day. Go home now. I'll get you reassigned to something more suitable in the morning.'

'Reassigned?'

'You heard me.'

'I worked out what that message on the wall meant. I found that body. I tracked down the woman who discovered it. I—'

'You did what you were paid to do,' Falcone interrupted. 'Now leave us.'

- 17 -

Incandescent, breath coming in short gasps, aware that their attention had gone elsewhere the moment she walked out of the control van, Rosa Prabakaran stood between the vehicle and the old abandoned church, wondering what to do next. The three of them made her feel like an intruder, someone who had walked in on a private gathering. She had been on the force long enough now to understand there was a strong, unusual relationship between these men, one other officers talked about with more than a little suspicion.

She was, she suddenly realized, jealous.

The woman pathologist was outside, standing by the yellow lines, gazing up at the weak winter sun, a large, amiable figure whose bright, intelligent eyes never seemed to be still. She ambled over, smiled and held out a hand.

'Rosa?' she said.

Another searching glance from an intimate in Falcone's team.

'Did I hear,' the woman asked, 'the much-missed sound of our beloved inspector losing his cool?'

'Is it that common?'

'It used to be. I haven't experienced it in a while. You'll find this strange but it's rather heartening to hear him bawling someone out again. It means we stand a chance of getting the old Leo back.' She paused. 'He nearly died last year. Remember that.'

'I know. Still, it doesn't give him the right to be downright rude.'

Teresa Lupo frowned.

'I've known Leo for a long time. He's . . . fixated. It's nothing personal.'

'It sounded personal.'

'That's one of Leo's habit's, I'm afraid. It always does. Did you, um,' she smiled slyly, 'deserve it by any chance?'

Rosa Prabakaran didn't answer that.

'Ah.'

Teresa Lupo looked at the blue van and the three heads visible through the still-open door.

'Being right is another of Leo's annoying traits. You'd best live with it. You could learn a lot from him. Besides, there are plenty of mediocrities around who'll bawl you out too. Best get the treatment from one who can teach you something. You, of all people, should bear that in mind. There are still some . . . old-fashioned ideas around in corners of the Questura.'

They'd covered the colour question once before, got it out of the way in the little café around the Questura a few months back after Teresa had taken her to one side and quietly passed on a few tips about how to handle Gianni Peroni. It didn't take long. Rosa Prabakaran never once felt the issue of her skin posed much of a problem for the people she worked with. Rome was a multicultural, multicoloured society. It wasn't a big deal. She was more likely to feel out of place because of her sex.

'I will not screw up again,' Rosa said with feeling.

'Of course you will. We all do.'

The pathologist was thinking. She didn't look much as if she ever stopped.

'Tell me again. What did this man we're looking for actually do?'

'He was a university professor. An archaeologist.'

Teresa Lupo's pale, flabby face screwed up with dissatisfaction. She was, Rosa thought, remarkably like Peroni in some ways.

'That was years ago.'

She sighed. Another dissatisfied customer.

'That's what he did. OK?'

'No, what did Giorgio Bramante *do*?' Teresa insisted. 'In prison.

After prison. When he wasn't being a university professor? Forget about the way you want to think of him. As some nice, middle-class individual gone wrong. Give me what you know about him after he lost his son.'

'In prison he worked in a slaughterhouse. When he was out he went and did the same job. With some Testaccio butcher's shop that had a slaughterhouse somewhere else. A horse butcher, would you believe?'

The pathologist thought about this then smiled again, a broad, confident, happy smile.

'Odd that, don't you think? A smart man could have got a better job, surely.'

'I've been through this with Falcone. He had other things on his mind.' She'd hoped the picture of what she'd seen in the crypt wouldn't come back. The presence of this inquisitive, infuriating pathologist, who understood so much more than she was going to say, made that impossible. With the memory came the inevitable question.

'What kind of gun does that?' she asked. 'I've seen photos of wounds before. None of them . . .'

The sight of the man remained in her head, a lurid spectacle lit by her bright police torch. And the smell was still there too. The stench of meat and the iron tang of blood.

'What did you see?'

'You know what I saw!'

'Of course I don't. Tell me. This is important.'

She wanted to go home. Her real home, not the plain little apartment she'd insisted on renting in order to make a point. She wanted to talk to her father, sit down with him and have a quiet meal, watch TV, look at her old law books and wonder why she didn't take his advice and go for a comfy, well-paid job convicting criminals instead of a difficult, poorly paid one trying to sort them out from the rest of society.

'I saw a naked man, quite deliberately placed on the ground, as if he were a corpse in some kind of ritual. He was in a crypt full of skeletons. Old ones, all in a line. The odd one out. All to himself. At the front.'

'Good. And?'

'Something . . . a shotgun, I don't know, had blown a hole in his chest. I could see . . .' She shook her head. 'What's the point?'

'The point,' Teresa Lupo said severely, 'is that you're supposed to be a police officer. Either look or don't look. Just don't half look.'

Rosa could feel her temper rising again, ready to snap.

'I *did* look.'

'No, you didn't. Was he killed in that room?'

'I don't know . . . No. I don't remember seeing much blood. I would have thought there'd be lots. When you shoot someone.'

'There is when you shoot someone, at least with something that could cause a wound that big. But he wasn't shot.'

'I saw!'

'You saw a wound on his chest. Then you jumped to easy, quick conclusions. Don't be too hard on yourself. Most people would have done the same. But if you want to work around Leo Falcone you need to drag yourself out of the category of "most people". Actually, include me in that too.'

'I saw . . .' She tried to think again, painful as it was. The man's chest was a mess, worse than anything she'd seen in any photos of a car accident or a murder.

Teresa Lupo was waiting.

Finally, Rosa said, 'I saw bone. Not broken bone. Part of a ribcage. It wasn't damaged. It looked like all those others skeletons in there. Except it was white. Very white.'

The pathologist nodded and looked pleased.

'Good. Next time I'd prefer not to have to drag it out of you. Now, let me tell you something I saw when I took a close look at him. On his back, beneath the scapula, the shoulder, was another wound. It was made by some sharp spiked metallic object, one that had gone through the flesh and under the bone, causing some very extensive bruising. As if whatever caused the wound had carried the dead man's weight too, for a while anyway.'

She tried to think this through.

'So he was stabbed in the back? With a spike?'

Teresa Lupo screwed up her nose with disappointment.

'You're being literal again. What if the spike was stationary and he was put on it?'

She wanted to scream. This wasn't how they told her to work at the training college at all. This was imagination, not the slow, methodical technique she'd believed was the way to proceed with most criminal investigations.

'That's ridiculous,' she said finally. 'It doesn't make sense.'

The expression of amused exasperation on Teresa Lupo's face worried her. Rosa Prabakaran was aware that she was developing a force-ten headache.

'Oh my God,' she blurted out, shocked, baffled by not knowing what thought process had tied those two disparate threads of knowledge together. 'He worked in a slaughterhouse.'

'Great place to kill people if you think about it,' Teresa said with a grin. 'And full of hooks. Now, by way of thanks, do you want me to talk you back into this case or not?'

- 18 -

Twenty minutes later a plain blue Fiat saloon was speeding past the ageing concrete facade of the film studios at Cinecittà, out to the nondescript modern suburb of Anagnina. Peroni was driving. Teresa and her right-hand man, Silvio Di Capua, were in the back looking like five-year-olds on their way to a party, though one to which they had, for the moment, no invitation. There were no papers to guarantee entry to the slaughterhouse where Giorgio Bramante worked. Papers took time, and preparation. They were hoping to circumvent both. Somehow . . .

Costa glanced out of the right-hand window. Little more than a kilometre away was his home. When he and Emily left the farmhouse that morning it was to spend a pleasant, lazy day in the city with friends. Suddenly the old job had intervened. He'd no idea when he'd be back, or would see her again. There'd been time to make a brief call to her before they left. She was in the car to Orvieto, as Messina had promised, just a few minutes from the villa owned by his father. She was a little puzzled, resigned to being out of the city for a while, accepting that there wasn't much alternative. Raffaela Arcangelo felt the same way, she'd said. Costa wondered whether Falcone had found the time to speak to her yet.

He watched the flat, dead lands of the modern suburbs flash past the window. He hadn't raised the subject of her health. He didn't know how. Not on a phone call from a police van outside a former church overrun with scene-of-crime officers trying to piece together a picture of a murder. That had to come later.

A hand came over from the back seat and tapped his shoulder.

'They kill horses on your doorstep,' Di Capua declared, with his customary tact. 'I bet you didn't know that.'

'Being a vegetarian,' Costa observed, 'I'm not sure it's any of my business. How do you carnivores feel?'

'About horse-eating?' Peroni asked, waving a large, pale hand at the window. 'Barbaric. Cows. Pigs. Lambs. That's what they're bred for. Horses . . . it just doesn't feel right.'

'Seconded,' Teresa agreed.

Silvio Di Capua said nothing, until what Costa took to be a jab in the ribs from his companion prompted him to speak.

'I haven't eaten horse in ages,' he complained. 'You hardly find it anywhere these days. Besides, it's dead already, isn't it?'

Teresa's hand swatted him loudly on the shoulder.

'If you didn't buy it, they wouldn't kill horses for you to eat in the first place, idiot.'

'In which case they wouldn't breed the things, would they? Except as ponies for rich kids, and' – he waved at the housing estates flashing past outside – 'I don't see much of a market for them around here. So instead of being dead they'd just be unalive. You're arguing that's an improvement?'

No one said anything for a while after that, until Peroni simply muttered 'barbaric' again, then turned the car onto a small industrial estate, cruised slowly along until he got the right number, and pulled up by a large iron security gate behind which lurked an anonymous low building, much like a factory unit anywhere. A sign on the gate said, simply: Calvi. Just the owner's name. Not a hint of what went on inside. Horse butchers didn't advertise their presence too loudly.

They got out, Peroni pressed the bell and the four of them waited.

'What kind of hours do you think a slaughterhouse works?' Teresa asked. 'I mean . . . I've no idea. I never met anyone who worked in one. I never thought about it . . .'

She fell silent. A short, elderly man with a pained gait, the kind that spoke of hip trouble, had left by a side door and was now hobbling towards them.

When he arrived and stared suspiciously through the iron bars of the gate Costa flashed his ID card and asked, 'Calvi?'

He had a thick walrus moustache and was wearing a heavy lumberjack shirt. Stained.

'The only one. This is about Giorgio, I guess.'

'What makes you say that?'

He sighed and unlocked the gate. It was a heavy mechanism. It wouldn't be easy to get inside without a key. Certainly not if you had a reluctant companion with you.

'The probation people phoned this morning. Said he hadn't called in or something. I don't get it. Either he's free. Or he's not. You tell me. Which is it?'

'You haven't been listening to the news?' Costa asked.

The lurid circumstances surrounding Toni LaMarca's death had already made it onto the hourly broadcasts. Costa didn't want to think what over-imaginative junk would fill the papers tomorrow. But the Questura was on form. Somehow Giorgio Bramante's name had been mentioned as prime suspect. Given the number of memories that were still fresh about the original case this had the makings of a story the media would love. He couldn't help but wonder whether Bruno Messina had realized that and called a few TV and newspaper friends directly, just to stir things a little. Fourteen years before all the sympathy had run one way. For Bramante and, by implication, Messina's fired father. If the story was to get big – and that seemed inevitable – Messina was sufficient a political animal to make sure it came complete with the spin he wanted.

'Something's happened to Giorgio?' Calvi asked, with a sudden concern. 'Don't tell me that. The poor guy's been through enough as it is. Going to jail for what he did. Unbelievable.'

'We need to know where he is,' Costa replied carefully. 'Do you have any idea? When did you last see him?'

'He was on the morning shift here yesterday. Till three in the afternoon. Then he went home. Never came back. I don't know where else he spent his time. You should ask Enzo Uccello. They were in jail together. Got released around the same time. No, Enzo was a couple of months before Giorgio. Good men. Good workers. I don't mind giving them a break.'

Teresa caught Costa's eye. Here was the opening.

'Where do we find Enzo?' he asked nonchalantly.

Calvi nodded at the building.

'Working.'

'Do you mind if we come in?'

'It's a slaughterhouse,' Calvi reminded them. 'Just so you know. It's clean, as hygienic as the city people say it should be. We don't break the law. We do a good job, as kindly as we can. But I'm warning you . . .'

'Thanks,' she said, smiling. 'After you.'

Calvi led the way, the rest of them a little way behind.

She'd told them the problem in the car. At first examination – and Teresa's preliminary opinions were rarely wrong – Toni LaMarca had suffered two significant injuries. The spike through the back, beneath the shoulder blade, which would have been extraordinarily painful, but not fatal. She had an idea about that already. Then – and this must have occurred afterwards – some massive, so far unexplained, trauma to his chest, directly over his heart. A trauma that removed a substantial amount of tissue, in a circular pattern some forty centimetres wide, clean down to the ribs, then continued on to penetrate to the heart beneath. Rosa Prabakaran could have been forgiven for thinking some close-up shotgun was to blame. But for the absence of powder and shot – and those bright clean unmarked ribs staring at her in the crypt – Teresa said she'd have felt much the same way at first glance. But what killed LaMarca was no ordinary weapon. Somehow, she told them, it had to do with the work Bramante had done in the slaughter-house. A knife. An implement. Something that lived in the bloody arena behind those closed doors, and didn't get mentioned much in the outside world.

The owner opened the door and straight away the smell and the light hit them. The place reeked of meat and blood and the over-whelming stench of urine. Ranks and ranks of bright spotlights, like batteries of miniature suns, ran across the ceiling. Once his sight had adjusted Costa found the slaughterhouse hall was empty, save for one lone individual at the far end, sweeping what looked like a grubby tide of brown water into a central, lowered drainage channel.

'You're lucky,' Calvi said. 'We're between consignments. But' – he made a deliberate show of staring at his watch – 'there's a truckload outside that has to come through in thirty minutes. I'm warning you. Now I have to do paperwork. You talk to Enzo on his own. These cons don't like it if the rest of us are around when they get reminded of things.'

He stopped. They all went quiet. Somewhere outside there was the sound of a horse, whinnying. It was a scared sound, high and loud, the cry of a creature pleading for comfort. Then a rattle of angry hooves on wood.

'You get used to it after a while,' Calvi added, then limped away, leaving them on their own.

– 19 –

The light was so bright it hurt. Alessio Bramante looked at the switches on the wall and knew he'd have to do something about them, that he couldn't sit on his own under this incandescent yellow sea much longer. It was like being beneath the eyes of some harsh, electric dragon. He was happy with the dark. Not the total darkness his father used to enter much of the time when he was working. Just the quiet half-light of dusk or early morning, an hour when there was room in the world for imagination. A time when he could think about the day ahead, and that walk down to the Piranesi's piazza, the moment when he would peer through the keyhole, locate the distant shining dome, and say to his father, for both of them, 'I see it. The world is still with us. Life can go on.'

He couldn't think straight now. And how long was he supposed to wait? He didn't wear the watch his grandmother, on his father's side, had given him the previous Christmas. It had a picture of Santa Claus on the face. Watches were hateful, intrusive things, unnecessary machines ticking away the minutes of a person's life without mercy, without feeling. The face with its red hat and snowy beard grinned back at him all the time.

He knows when you've been good or bad . . .

Santa Claus was an invention out of a fairy tale. A face on a dial. A spy on the wrist. Alessio didn't like the idea of someone watching him like that. It wasn't right.

Just as leaving him alone in the bare, bright chamber, in the red earth and grey rock wasn't right either. The place smelled of damp and decay. Not what he'd hoped for, the sharp citrus aroma of old fruit skins squashed under foot.

They're oranges on the surface only, he thought. Something else lies beneath. Bones and dead things, all the decay of the centuries.

He recalled staring through the stupid spectacles that morning, wondering who was right. The way he saw – or didn't see – things. Or the multiple worlds envisioned by a fly.

Alessio sat at the table and said, in a calm, unemotional voice, more for himself than anyone listening, 'Giorgio.'

Then again.

'Giorgio!'

He'd never used his father's first name like that before. There was a rule, a law, that forbade children from speaking out loud their parents' real names. Giorgio – he'd thought of him this way for months now – had told him stories about magical names. Of how the Jews had a word for God which no one but the highest priest could utter, and then only in special circumstances, deep inside the holiest of places. And now he knew about the followers of Mithras, with their secret rituals, too, enacted out in this underground labyrinth.

Seven orders of humanity. Seven trials. Seven sacraments. Precious rites, never shared with outsiders. Not until the moment of initiation, the point at which the blank, empty page of the novice gained a single scrawl, the birth of knowing.

The beginner became Corax.

After . . . what?

Giorgio had disappeared into the darkness some minutes before. Alessio thought he'd heard distant sounds from down one of the black corridors. A faraway voice. Perhaps more than one. Perhaps it was his father watching from the shadows, or an echo of his own voice, made deeper, made strange by the tunnels chasing off from those seven exits cut into the rock of the chamber in which he now sat, not afraid, just thinking, trying to work out what this was.

Games.

Giorgio played those sometimes. A few months before, his father had taken him into a warren of excavated houses on the Palatino, had found, through a labyrinth of ancient stone rooms, the kitchen of someone called Livia, wife to a famous emperor, Augustus, and a woman of fearsome reputation, cruel and controlling, determined to do the utmost for her clan. A kind of Pater, but in a dress.

He was gone when Alessio turned a corner and found himself in some dark rocky alcove, green with algae, alive with insects, centipedes and beetles, bristling with furry moss that clung like crude living skin on the damp stone walls, yellowing with the onset of decay.

He hadn't done what Giorgio had wanted. Broken down, cried, whined, kicked and yelled, hammered his new white trainers against the green, gunky stone until they were ruined.

Afterwards Giorgio had bought ice cream and, for Alessio, a toy he didn't want. All in return for a promise never to tell his mother, one he readily agreed to, because men needed secrets, bonds, just like those of Mithras, whispered in this place 2,000 years before. Secrets bound them together more tightly, made Giorgio tell him more stories, daring ones, frightening ones sometimes. About the darkness and the old things that lurked there.

He glanced at the seven doors. He hadn't looked to see which one Giorgio used when he left. He was mad at him. Giorgio hadn't wanted him to watch either, and he knew that without being told. But now . . . For a moment he wished he'd kept that watch. It would have provided some kind of marker by which to judge his father and the things he did.

There was another sound from the corridor and this time he was certain. It was a distant, low, male voice. Giorgio was there surely, waiting for him, wondering what he would do. This was the Palatino again, only more severe, a bigger test. Alessio stared down at his clean school clothes and wondered what his mother would say if he arrived home with them ruined.

Games.

There were so many when he thought hard. Theirs was an entire relationship based on play, because when Giorgio wasn't engaged in some obscure diversion he was somewhere else, inside a book, head bent deep over a computer, always avoiding what his mother called 'the real world'. Games joined them. Hide and seek. Show and tell. Games that collided with the past sometimes, and with the stories he told too.

Theseus and the Minotaur.

That was one of his favourites. A brave lost warrior, a stranger in a strange land, meets a beautiful princess and, in order to win her, must accept a challenge. A monster lurks in a lair, a hidden labyrinth of corridors beneath the ground. Half-man, half-bull, a dreadful, unnatural being that devours young men and women – seven of each, which, he thought, was one reason he remembered so clearly – as a tribute.

Theseus offers himself as a sacrament, enters the labyrinth, finds the monster and – this was clear in his memory too – beats the creature to death. Not a clean end, cut in two by a sword, but with some crude, bloody club, because this was a beast, not a man, and it deserved no better.

Or a half-beast, half-man. To Theseus there wasn't much difference.

The princess, Ariadne, helped him with a gift: a ball of twine which he unwound as he entered the caves, and used to find his way back home to safety, with those he rescued.

Alessio sat calmly at the table in the cave, remembering all this, trying to wonder what it meant. Giorgio had retold this story only a few days before. Alessio appreciated that his father was a man who rarely wasted anything, a breath, a sentence, the simplest of physical acts. Was that conversation, then, significant?

Mithras, the god his father knew well, killed a monster too. One that was all beast. He'd looked in Giorgio's desk once and seen a picture there, lurking like a secret waiting to be found. The bold, strong god, straddling the terrified animal, holding its head, thrusting a sword into its neck. He hadn't resorted to a club. But this was all-beast so perhaps that was different.

One more memory. Beneath the animal there were creatures, strange and familiar, doing things he didn't quite understand.

'A game,' he said quietly to himself. In the end, everything came down to this, whether it was seeking a monster in a cave to prove oneself worthy of respect, or peering through the keyhole of an order of ancient knights, looking for a familiar shape across the river, one whose presence would keep in balance the myriad worlds he saw through those stupid glasses.

A game was what Giorgio wanted. That was why they had come here in the first place. It was a challenge. Perhaps *the* challenge, one so large, so daunting, so difficult, like the Minotaur pitched against Theseus, that it would be his making. Giorgio Bramante was waiting for his son to understand, to rise and accept his fate, to find the courage to walk into the darkness and track down where he was lurking. And then . . .?

It came to him, instantly. This was the first sacrament, the striking of fear in the beginner. Afterwards he became Corax to Giorgio's Pater, part of the greater secret. The elusive relationship of family, the eternal trinity, father, mother and child, would be strengthened and one day made perfect by these changes, endured forever, never doubted, even in those dark moments, when he heard the two of them, Giorgio and her, screaming at each other, full of drink and fury, bellowing words he didn't quite understand.

Alessio Bramante looked around the room and laughed. Dark doorways didn't scare him, nor the sounds he thought he continued to hear echoing from some distant, hidden location.

He got up and walked past each of the seven exits, thinking, looking, listening. He imagined that somewhere in the unseen distance he could discern his father's voice, teasing in the dark.

Games involved two people. Both had to play.

He returned to the table and picked up the large torch his father had left there, deliberately, he now knew. It was big, almost half the length of Alessio's arm, encased in hard rubber, and let loose a long yellow beam when he turned it on.

The light painted the shape of a full moon on the wall nearest the entrance, which was now almost completely in shade, barely illuminated by the single bulb he'd left alive. Alessio placed two fingers in front of the lens and made an animal shape. A beast with horns. Theseus' Minotaur. The bull that Mithras sought.

There was a pile of tools near the exit he'd chosen. Pickaxes and shovels, iron spikes for marking things, spirit levels. And a large ball of twine, held at one end with what looked like a long knitting needle.

Alessio put down the torch and retrieved the twine, unpicking the iron object from the end. He tied the open loop of string to his belt and tugged. It came away easily and left a fresh end of the thread dangling in his hand. Alessio looked at the string again. Someone had tried to cut it once before, weakening it at the point before the loop. Quickly, he tied a second loop through his belt, tugged on that, made sure it was firm, then dropped the ball on the floor.

Then he retrieved the torch and turned to face the long corridor, wondering what, if anything, he – or his father – would dare tell his mother when they finally came home.

Nothing, he thought. These were secrets, never to be repeated. This was part of the great adventure, the journey from boy to man, from ignorance to knowledge. He walked forward, feeling the tickle of the unwinding string fall against his legs like the desiccated wings of some dying insect, tumbling down to the ancient dust at his feet.

- 20 -

The four of them watched as Calvi went inside a small office next to the door. It had one window looking out directly onto what Costa took to be the production line of the slaughtering floor; live animals came in at the far end, where Uccello was sweeping up, were stunned, killed, then hung on a moving chain and progressively butchered as the corpses travelled down the hall.

Teresa shaded her eyes against the burning lamps in the ceiling, looked up at the mechanism that moved the carcasses along, took hold of one of the big hooks and said, 'Exhibit number one, gentlemen. It was one of these that put that hole in Toni LaMarca's back.'

Peroni blinked at the long hallway.

'There's got to be a hundred of them at least. And . . .'

A series of smaller adjoining rooms, with the same white clinical look and burning lighting, ran off from the opposite wall. Sizeable sides of red and fatty marbled meat hung on them.

'. . . the rest. It's so bright in here.'

'When you're dealing with dead things you need to see what you're doing,' Di Capua muttered. 'I'm looking,' he added and walked across the hall, surreptitiously pulling on a pair of white plastic gloves.

The figure under the last set of lights stopped pushing the huge broom and glanced back at them, uncertain at their approach. The tide of grubby water at his feet swelled slowly round his boots then continued down to the channel at the centre of the hall.

'Enzo,' Peroni shouted. He nodded. They walked over. Costa showed the card again.

'First-name terms,' the man muttered. 'This must be bad.'

Enzo Uccello was a short, skinny man with a long, half-attractive face, prominent teeth and thoughtful eyes. He looked in his mid-thirties, and a little worn down by life.

'We need help,' Costa said. 'When did you last see Giorgio Bramante? And where were you last night?'

He muttered something under his breath. Then . . .

'Giorgio went off shift here yesterday at three. I haven't seen him since. Last night I stayed in, drank my one regulation beer – which is as much as I can afford – and watched TV. On my own, before you ask.'

Uccello had that easy, glib way of answering questions any cop recognized. He'd been here before.

Costa was getting interested.

'Where do you live, Enzo?'

'Testaccio. The same block as Giorgio. The prison people have some kind of deal.'

Teresa stared at him.

'And you didn't see him?'

'Signora,' Uccello sighed. 'Giorgio and I shared a cell the size of a dog kennel for the best part of eight years. I respect the man. He should never have been in jail. He never would have been if you people knew what you were doing. But after all that time together it's nice to spend a little while apart. Trust me.'

'I can see that,' Peroni agreed. 'Did he tell you he was still angry? Was he looking for some kind of payback?'

'What?'

Uccello had been working all day, Costa guessed. He hadn't heard.

'He killed someone last night. One of the students who was under suspicion over his son.'

'Oh no . . .' Uccello murmured.

'This wasn't the first, either,' Peroni went on. 'Are you sure he didn't mention anything?'

The ex-con threw down the broom. The grubby water splashed them all.

'No! Listen. I'm on conditional release. If I just fart at the wrong time they put me back in that stinking place. I know nothing about what Giorgio's been doing. That's his business. And yours, if you say so. Nothing to do with me. Nothing.'

They didn't press it. Uccello was sweating. Peroni had that look on his face Costa recognized; he didn't like pushing people, not unless there was a good reason. If it was an act, it was a good one. Uccello seemed like someone who seriously wanted to avoid going back to jail.

'What did you do?' Peroni asked. 'We can find out easily enough. I'd just like to hear it from you.'

Uccello spat on the floor then picked up the broom and moved it around aimlessly, not looking them in the face.

'I came home and found the neighbourhood loan shark screwing my wife. So I shot him.'

Peroni grimaced.

'Bad . . .'

'Yeah. Got worse when you people came round and found out I was also the neighbourhood dope dealer. So don't go feeling too sorry for me. Giorgio . . . he's different. He never belonged in that place. I was heading there all along. Now I'm out and staying here. Even if it means sweeping up blood and shit in here for the rest of my life. Any more questions? We've another bunch of animals to deal with soon.'

'There's just the two of you here? And Calvi?'

'It's a small business these days. We've got two more men on shift when it comes down to the butchering. But first . . .'

He didn't need to say it. Teresa cast a long, quizzical glance down the room.

'How do you kill them?'

'Same way you kill most big animals.'

He put a finger to his forehead.

'Captive bolt to the forehead. Bang . . .'

She looked unsure of his answer.

'What does that do?'

'Makes a hole through the skull into the brain.'

'And then it's dead?'

'No. Then it's unconscious. I have to stick it. Open a vein in its neck. Five minutes or so and then it's dead.'

'The bolt goes *through* the skull?' Teresa asked.

'Correct.'

She scanned the room again, unhappy.

'And the rest,' she continued, 'you just do with knives?'

'And saws. It's a process. Most people don't want to know about it. Is there something you're looking for?'

Teresa Lupo shook her head.

'Just a way of tearing a hole in a man's heart without doing the slightest damage to his ribcage. There has to be something else.'

Costa had watched Silvio Di Capua work his way through the three adjoining smaller halls, looking progressively more miserable as he passed through each.

'What happens in there, Enzo?'

'You start off with a live horse,' Uccello explained with mock patience. 'Then you get a dead one. Once it's hung for a while it moves down the line, and the further it goes, the smaller it gets. Over there we start packing it. Making it the kind of shape people can buy without thinking what it used to be. Is this useful?'

Costa tried to focus on something that was hovering at the edges of his memory.

'And the bones? What do you do with the bones?'

Uccello shrugged.

'Not our job. They just go. Someone takes them away. After . . .'

Something occurred to him.

'After what?' Costa prodded.

Uccello walked into the third room, the one Di Capua had just vacated. They followed. It seemed cleaner than the rest, washed down more recently. There was a small line of hooks in the ceiling, but this time they were fixed, not attached to some kind of production line.

'Have you ever heard of "mechanically recovered meat"?' Uccello asked.

'You know,' Peroni grumbled, 'if I hear much more of this I'm going vegetarian too.'

Uccello almost laughed.

'Don't worry. It doesn't go into humans. Not any more. It's for dog food, cat food. Animal meal. That kind of thing.'

' "Mechanically recovered meat"?' Teresa asked.

'We butcher them by hand, as much as we can. When that's done you'd think there wasn't much left on the carcass. There is. Sinew. Gristle. A little meat, even. You can't get it off with a knife. You need something more powerful.'

Silvio Di Capua was one step ahead of him. He'd gone to the wall. There were three long lances there, each with an accompanying pair of stained gloves, face mask and set of goggles. He took down the nearest one and played with the trigger.

'Don't mess with that . . .' Uccello was saying.

Some kind of device kicked in from outside, making a loud mechanical whirring noise. The lance leaped violently upwards in Di Capua's hand. A hard, thin stream of water shot out of the end of the device and flew straight to the opposite wall, a good eight metres away, with sufficient force to cover them all in a fine, cold spray.

'Water,' Teresa exclaimed, laughing. 'Water!'

'Yeah,' Uccello agreed. 'Water. We couldn't use this room this morning for some reason. The drain was blocked. It wasn't running away properly.'

She cackled again. Then, before Costa could say a thing she'd walked along the channel, found the sump where it ended, and was down on her knees, right sleeve rolled up, reaching down with her hand, deep into the gulley.

'As the man who shares your bed I would really prefer it if you wore gloves for that,' Peroni said quietly. He looked as white as a sheet.

So did Uccello when his boss stormed into the room. Calvi was incandescent.

'What the hell is this?' he yelled. 'I let you in to talk to one of my employees. Next thing I know you're messing around with the equipment. Get out of here! Enzo! What are you doing, man?'

'I just . . .'

There was fear on Uccello's face at that moment. Fear of Calvi. Fear of doing something that could end his fragile freedom.

'I want you people gone,' Calvi bellowed. 'You have no right. Out of here. Now!'

Teresa got up from the floor and came back to them, standing close to the slaughterhouse owner, so close he was flinching a little. She had something in her hand. Costa wished he didn't have to look at it too closely. Grey flesh. White tissue. Unmistakable hanks of dark, wet hide.

'What kind of horses do you kill here?' Teresa asked.

Calvi glowered at her.

'Whatever I get sent! Whatever you people feel like eating tomorrow.'

'Nobody's going to be eating anything that comes through here for a very long time,' she said. 'This is a murder scene. Silvio. Call in. Seal everything. I don't want any civilians in here until I'm done. No horses either.'

'What?' Calvi yelled. 'I'm struggling to make a living as it is. You can't do this? Why?'

She pulled a piece of tissue out from the morass of stuff in her fist, something white, very white, washed clean, as if it had been sitting in water for hours. It was a segment of skin, just big enough to fit in the palm of a hand. In the centre was the unmistakable brown circular shape of a human nipple.

'Because,' she went on calmly, 'some time last night Giorgio Bramante came back here with a man who'd rather have been any-where else in the world. He beat him about. He put him on one of those hooks up there then hoisted him off the floor. And after that, while he was still alive, he hosed his heart out.'

Calvi had turned the same colour as Peroni. Both of them looked ready to hurl.

'That,' Teresa added, 'is why.'

- 21 -

It was getting dark by the time Falcone was finished at Santa Maria dell'Assunta. Perhaps it was age or his convalescent state. Whatever the reason, Falcone found he had, for the first time, to make a conscious effort to list on a notepad what had to be done in order to make sure all the threads stayed in the head. There were many, some from the present, some from the past. And practical considerations, too. Falcone had sent an officer to his apartment to fetch some personal things for the enforced stay inside the Questura. Then he'd ordered copies of the most important Bramante files to be emailed to the Orvieto Questura, printed out, with a covering note he'd dictated, and sent to await the arrival of Emily Deacon at the house of Bruno Messina's father. Cold cases – and many aspects of this were cold – required an outside eye. She had the analytical mind of a former FBI agent, and no personal ties to what had happened almost a decade and a half before.

The one person who wouldn't be pleased was Nic Costa. Falcone felt he could live with that.

After despatching those commands, he'd made several careful walks around the crypt, mindful of his frail state, thinking about Giorgio Bramante, trying to remember the man in some detail, trying to begin to understand why he would return to this place, so close to his family home, to perform such a barbaric act.

Remembering wasn't easy. What he'd told Messina was true. Bramante had offered them nothing after his arrest, nothing except an immediate admission of guilt and a pair of hands held out for the cuffs, as if he were somehow the victim. The man never tried to find excuses, never sought some legal loophole to escape the charges, or have them reduced to some lesser degree.

It was almost as if he was in control throughout. Bramante was the one who called the police to the dig on the Aventino when his son went missing. He had readily acceded when Bruno Messina's father had allowed him the chance to talk to Ludo Torchia alone.

Falcone remembered most clearly the aftermath of that decision: the student's screams, getting louder and more desperate with every passing minute, as Bramante punched and kicked him around the little temporary cell, in a dark, deserted subterranean corner of the Questura, a place where only a man told to sit directly outside would hear. Those sounds would stay with Leo Falcone always, but the memory offered him nothing, no insight, no glimpse into Giorgio Bramante's head, whatsoever.

The man was an intelligent, cultured academic, someone respected internationally, as the support Bramante gained when he came to court demonstrated. Without an apparent second thought he had turned into a brutal animal, ready to bludgeon a fellow human being to death. Why?

Because he believed Ludo Torchia had killed his son. Or, more accurately, that Torchia knew where the seven-year-old Alessio was, possibly still alive, and refused, in spite of the beating, to tell.

Falcone thought of what Peroni said. *Any father would have felt that way.*

Falcone had listened to those screams for the best part of an hour. If he'd not intervened, they would have gone on until Torchia died in the cell. It wasn't a simple, sudden outburst of fury. Bramante had methodically pummelled Torchia into oblivion, with a deliberate, savage precision that defied comprehension.

A memory surfaced. After Torchia was pronounced dead, when the Questura was in an almighty panic, wondering how to cope, Falcone had found the presence to think about Giorgio Bramante's physical condition and asked to see his hands. His knuckles were bleeding, the flesh torn off by the force of the blows he'd rained down on Torchia. On a couple of fingers bone was visible. He'd needed stitches, serious and immediate treatment. Weeks later his lawyers had quite deliberately removed the bandages from his hands for each court appearance, replacing them with skin-coloured plasters, trying to make sure the public never saw another side to the man the papers were lauding, day in, day out. The father who did what any father would have done . . .

'I don't think so,' Falcone murmured.

'Sir?'

He'd forgotten the woman was still around, seated in a dark corner of the van, awaiting instructions. Rosa Prabakaran had, somewhat to his surprise, earned his approval after Teresa Lupo talked her back into the case. She was quick, had a good memory and didn't ask stupid questions. In the space of a couple of hours she'd touched base on several important points, most importantly in liaising with intelligence to see what else could be gleaned from existing records. There was little there. Dino Abati had left Italy altogether a month after Bramante went to jail, abandoning what had been a promising academic career. Perhaps Giorgio Bramante had tracked him down somewhere already, found him in the dark, done what he felt was right in the circumstances. Falcone wondered if they'd ever know.

Focus.

He'd lost count of how many times he'd said that word to a young officer struggling to come to terms with an overload of information, a succession of half-possibilities just visible in the shadows. Now Leo Falcone knew he needed to heed his own advice. He was out of practice. His head hadn't worked right since he was shot. Everything took time. And work, too, something he had, he now realized, been missing all along. The delightful presence of Raffaela Arcangelo had clouded his judgement, made him forget what kind of man he was. It was time to put matters right.

He looked at Rosa Prabakaran.

'Make sure intelligence keep looking. They've got to have more than this.'

She nodded.

'How do we find him?'

It was such an obvious question. The kind you got from beginners. Falcone felt oddly pleased to hear it.

'Probably we don't. He finds us. Giorgio Bramante is looking for something or someone. That makes him visible. When he's not looking, he's probably untouchable. He's too clever to have left any obvious tracks. To stay with people he knows.'

He thought about what she'd said earlier.

'If he's got all that equipment I rather imagine he's in a cave somewhere. Bramante knows subterranean Rome better than just about anyone in the city. He could be somewhere different every night and we wouldn't have a clue.'

'You mean there's nothing we can do? Except wait?'

'Not at all! We work harder to understand the information we have. We see what else we can find out there. We cover all the proper bases. But, to be honest, I don't see routine trapping a man like that. Routine works for ordinary criminals. Giorgio Bramante is anything but ordinary. The one consolation is that, as far as we know, there's no one else in the city on his list.'

'Except you,' she said, just remembering to add, 'sir.'

'So it would seem,' he agreed with a polite nod of the head.

- 22 -

Dino Abati was conscious again, leaning against the altarpiece, looking a little woozy. He'd got a handkerchief to his head. The blood was dying, matting his ginger hair against the pale skin of his forehead. He'd survive. Maybe, Torchia thought, he'd learn. That's what it was all about. The cult. The rituals. The processes that happened here. Men learned what it took to make them good in the eyes of their peers, to prepare them for the rigours of life. Obedience. Duty. Self-sacrifice. But obedience more than most. That came easy to some people. No one else in the temple had dared challenge him when he attacked Abati. No one questioned why they were here any more.

Not after he had told them, quite simply, but with a firmness that couldn't be misinterpreted, 'We find the bird. We kill it. We swear on its blood we never tell anyone else about what happened. Then it's done. We don't mention this again to anyone. Ever. Understood?'

Andrea Guerino was still out there, somewhere in the warren of corridors, trying to do his bidding. Abati would cause no more trouble. Sandro Vignola was back on his knees, peering at the inscriptions on the stonework, open-mouthed, looking idiotic, still aghast at what they'd found: an underground shrine to a long-lost god, one despoiled by Constantine's Christians at the moment of their victory.

And then there was that other voice.

'How are you going to kill the bird?' LaMarca asked, interested.

113

Torchia had checked this out, just to make sure. This was a ritual, for him, even if the rest were now just going along with what he wanted, out of fear, out of survival. Rituals had to be enacted correctly, with precision. Otherwise they could rebound on those who performed them. Make the god angry, not satisfied.

'I hold it over the altar and cut its throat.' He pulled out the penknife from his pocket. 'With this.'

LaMarca's eyes glistened under the light of the big lantern Abati had brought and placed on the ground, scattering its weak rays in all directions.

'We were on this farm in Sicily once. Out in nowhere. Everyone was everyone else's brother and sister, right? And one day I see this kid in the farmyard. No more than six or seven. They sent him out to get a chicken. He just chases one, picks it up by the legs' – LaMarca was doing the actions now, stooping and waving his arm beneath him – 'and he's swinging it like this. Around and around. Like it's a toy.'

'A toy?'

'Right. And you know what happens in the end?'

'Tell me.'

'The fucking head comes clean off! I'm not kidding you . . . He swings it so hard.'

Toni LaMarca couldn't handle drink or dope. He was utterly stoned, a fact Torchia registered in case this came in useful.

'One moment the chicken's going around and around, squawking like it's furious or something. Next, the head flies straight off and there's nothing there but a neck and it's . . .'

This must have been a real memory because something clouded over his face at the moment, some forgotten image that had been prodded out of its slumber by the drug.

'. . . pumping blood. Like a little fountain. Pumping away. Not for long. We had it for supper. *They* had it. I didn't feel so hungry.'

Ludo Torchia listened, wondering if there'd be more. There was nothing. Instead it was Dino Abati who spoke. He took away the cloth from his head and said, 'These caves are dangerous. We shouldn't be here.'

Toni LaMarca prodded him with his foot.

'When . . . the . . . chicken's . . . dead . . .' he said with the slow, difficult precision of the stoned, then began to giggle stupidly.

'Don't touch me, Toni,' Abati said calmly.

LaMarca backed away.

'We go,' Torchia repeated, 'when we're done.'

Abati shook his head and went back to dabbing it with the handkerchief.

'If Giorgio hears of this . . .'

'Leave him out of it,' Torchia snapped.

He thought he could hear footsteps coming down the corridor outside now, approaching. Something about the nature of the sound made him uneasy. The others went quiet too.

'Ludo . . .' Abati was beginning to say.

Then Bellucci marched in, grinning like a moron. He had the black cockerel tight in his arms, cuddling it like a pet. The bird turned its neck with a mechanical precision and let out a low, puzzled complaint.

Andrea Guerino was behind him, pushing a small child, a young boy Ludo Torchia recognized, though it took him a moment to remember how. It was the party the previous Christmas, when families were invited to meet staff and their students, in a garishly decorated room – he didn't believe Giorgio could be part of such crass Christian foolishness – in the building in the Piazza dei Cavalieri di Malta.

The young Alessio Bramante had been there, staring at them all resentfully, as if there was something in their age he envied.

'Jesus Christ,' Abati murmured, and clawed his way to his feet. 'That's it, Ludo. Time to go and meet the man.'

Torchia put a hand on Abati's shoulder. There was something in the child's face that made them all want to stop and see.

'What are you doing here?' the boy yelled at them angrily, struggling to get out of the strong arms that held him tight. 'This is a secret. When my father finds out . . .'

Guerino took hold of his long hair and pulled it until he stopped yammering.

'Where's your father, Alessio?' Torchia asked.

'Here.' Then, with an odd expression on his face. Furtive. One that stirred some memory, some idea in the child's head that brought the blood to his cheeks. 'Somewhere. Don't you know that?'

He was angry and confused, uncertain of himself, disturbed at being lost in these caves. He wasn't frightened, though.

'I know what this is,' Alessio added hesitantly, uncertain of himself. 'It's a . . . game.'

Then he jerked his hands peremptorily out of his trousers. An object came with them and fell to the floor. Ludo Torchia reached down and picked up a pair of toy glasses. The kid didn't complain. Torchia looked through them for a moment, saw the room, the people in it, multiplied many times over. There was something unnerving about the sight. He stuffed the glasses into his pocket.

'It's just a game,' Torchia agreed. 'But a very important one.'

They were all quiet, even Dino Abati. The scent of opportunity was in the air and even the most stupid of them surely understood that. Each knew what would happen if Bramante found them there. Suspension. Expulsion. Disgrace. The end of their time at La Sapienza. Ludo Torchia was probably the only one who didn't care.

'So what do we do now?' Dino Abati asked.

Torchia picked up one of the large lanterns and walked to the door. To the left the corridor ran slightly downhill, working its way further into the rock, further beneath the earth. There were more adjoining tunnels in the distance on either side. A labyrinth lay ahead of them, a spidery maze of possibilities among the narrow channels cut into the tufa. Very few of them, it occurred to Torchia, explored.

Alessio Bramante was by his side for some reason.

'We play,' Torchia said.

He grasped the boy's hand and tugged him down the corridor, down towards the darkness.

– 23 –

Falcone told Rosa Prabakaran to find a driver.

'I don't know drivers,' she confessed.

'See that big *sovrintendente* from uniform? The one looking as if he's ready to sneak off for a cigarette?'

'Taccone,' she said. 'I think.'

'Taccone. You're right. I thought you didn't know any drivers.'

'Sometimes I seem to know more than I remember at first.'

'I sympathize,' he said dryly.

'Sorry. You've got more reason. They said you nearly died.'

'They say all kinds of things about me. Tell Taccone to bring the car round. We're paying someone a visit.'

'Who?'

'Someone you've met already. Someone I last met years ago. Beatrice Bramante.'

He saw the expression of concern on her face.

'Don't worry,' Falcone said. 'I'll try to be gentle.'

She lived in one of the big tenement blocks in Mastro Giorgio, five minutes away. These apartments were part of the area's history, built about a century before, tiny homes set around central courtyards joined by hanging walkways, several hundred little boxes in which the population of an urban hamlet lived cheek by jowl. In the old days, when Testaccio was one of the poorest quarters of Rome, the places were so crowded some people slept on the walkways permanently. The area had come up in the world over the years, a little, anyway. There were no bodies under makeshift mattresses any more. Some of the properties were now in private ownership, and fetching rising prices on the extortionate Roman housing market. But most remained rented, home to a mixed population of locals, immigrants and students, all looking for a cheap place to stay.

He tried to recall the Bramantes' house on the Aventino. It was a substantial family villa, lived in, a little worn at the edges. But the property must have been worth a fortune even then, with its position on the hill, looking back towards the Circus Maximus, a sizeable garden, and an isolated aspect, a good fifty metres away from adjoining houses on both sides.

As his finger hovered over the bell on the door of the tiny apartment he was forced to appreciate how much Beatrice Bramante had come down in the world. Alessio Bramante's disappearance – the logical, police inspector's part of his mind refused to use the label 'death' without firm proof – was like every case involving a lost child he'd ever dealt with. The ripples, the effects, the subsidiary tragedies, took years to become wholly visible. Entire lifetimes, perhaps. Sometimes, Falcone thought, even they weren't long enough to allow the whole story, the full catalogue of pain and darkness, to run out into the light and dissipate into nothing.

The door opened. He didn't recognize the face there for a moment. She'd aged considerably. Beatrice Bramante's hair was as long as ever but now entirely grey. It hung lank and loose around her shoulders. She wore a threadbare blue cardigan pulled tight around her skinny frame, with long sleeves clutched into her palms. The intelligent, attractive face he remembered was now lined. Bitterness had taken the place of the grief-stricken bewilderment he remembered from fourteen years before.

It took her a moment to understand who he was. Then an unmistakable expression of hatred grew in her dark eyes.

'What do you want?' she asked through gritted teeth. 'I have nothing to say to you, Falcone. Nothing at all.'

'Your husband . . .'

'My former husband!'

He nodded.

'Your former husband killed someone yesterday. We're coming to believe he's killed before. This morning I think he may have made an attempt to murder me.'

It didn't cut the slightest ice with her.

'None of this is my business. None . . .'

She stared at the concrete walkway where the three police officers stood, a stiff, furious figure.

'Signora,' Rosa Prabakaran said suddenly. 'I'm sorry. This is all my fault. I should never have come here on my own this morning. It was wrong of me. Please. You must say what you have to say in the presence of these officers. Then we can go.'

The woman didn't move. Leo Falcone glanced behind her. The little room seemed full of canvases, large and small, on the walls, parked against cupboards, everywhere.

'You still paint?' he observed. 'I should have expected that.'

There was just one subject on every canvas he could see. A pretty young face with bright, shining eyes staring out from the painting, challenging everything he saw, asking some question the viewer could only guess at.

'I have to find Giorgio before he can do more harm,' he added. 'I would like to put Alessio's case to rest for good too. We couldn't do that before. There was too much . . .'

He hunted for the word.

'. . . noise. Much of it regrettable. Now I'd like to find out what happened to him, once and for all. With your permission . . .'

She said something Falcone couldn't catch, though perhaps it was simply a mumbled curse. Then she opened the door further, with what seemed to him a marked unwillingness.

'Thank you,' Falcone said and beckoned Rosa Prabakaran to go in first.

– 24 –

Beatrice Bramante excused herself and went to the bathroom. Falcone, Rosa Prabakaran and Taccone sat tightly together on the small, hard sofa next to a tiny dining table. They could see into the adjoining bedroom and the dark open courtyard beyond. The entire apartment was smaller than the living room Falcone recalled from the Bramantes' house on the Aventino.

'You never mentioned the paintings, Agente,' he said quietly, trying to stifle the note of reproach in his voice.

'They weren't here,' she replied, unable to take her eyes off the single face in front of them, multiplied over and over again, always with that same querulous expression.

'No,' she corrected herself. 'They were here. I saw some things piled up in the corner. They weren't out like that. I imagine I brought back some memories.'

Falcone sighed, exasperated at the way the young were so anxious to make up their minds. Then Beatrice Bramante returned. Carefully, with more tact than he would have possessed a decade and a half before, he led her through all the points she'd covered that morning with the over-zealous Rosa. The woman recounted everything without hesitation, unemotionally, with the same kind of matter-of-fact attitude Bramante himself had adopted after Alessio's disappearance. Falcone reminded himself that they had appeared to be a close couple at the time.

'What do you do these days?' he asked when she'd finished.

'I work part-time at a kindergarten. I paint a little. Just for me. Not for anyone else.'

He looked around the apartment.

'I'm sorry. I have to ask. Why are you living here? Why not the Aventino?'

'Lawyers cost,' she said flatly.

'But Giorgio pleaded guilty. There was no trial.'

'That was his choice. I tried to persuade him to argue. I spent most of the money I had on lawyers who thought they could change his mind. We had a lot of debt on that place anyway. Besides, with him gone, with Alessio gone . . .'

The dark eyes shone accusingly at him from underneath the silver mess of hair.

'It wasn't a home for a spinster.'

He nodded, appreciating that fact.

'And you divorced. Do you mind my asking . . . was that his idea or yours?'

'I mind but if it'll get you out of here more quickly you can have your answer. It was Giorgio's. I used to visit in prison, once a week, every Friday. It didn't seem to make much difference to him. One day, after a year or so, he told me there would be a divorce.'

'You agreed?' Rosa asked.

'You don't know Giorgio,' she answered, gripping the sleeves of her cardigan tightly. 'When his mind's made up . . .'

Falcone's eyes were fixed on the largest of the paintings. Some, it seemed to him, were recent. One, of the boy in his school uniform, with an odd emblem on his shirt, seemed to be painted from life. Unlike the rest it had no tragedy welling up beneath a sea of frozen, frenzied oils.

'You have some more paintings of Alessio,' he said, and it wasn't a question.

Her face tightened with anxiety.

'I do?'

'Well, you seem to prefer the one subject. Do you mind . . .?'

He walked into the tiny bedroom. It was a shambles. A set of canvases lay beneath the window, face to the wall. He turned over the first three then stopped. The first few were of Alessio. But as he would have been. When he was ten or twelve. One was much older than that. He was almost a man, with the same half-effeminate features but an expression on his face that was serious, almost cold. The same kind of look Falcone had seen in his father.

One curious point struck him. In most of the works, including the adult one, he was wearing a T-shirt of the kind found in the Piccolo Museo, one bearing the same logo: a seven-pointed star.

Falcone returned to the sofa. Beatrice hadn't moved.

'I never had children, never thought about it, to be honest,' he admitted. 'It's only natural in the circumstances to imagine how they would grow up.'

'Natural?'

She echoed his words with a hard, sarcastic edge.

'What's that symbol? The one with the stars. It seems important to you.'

She shrugged.

'Not really. Giorgio had me design it for the school. The stars come from Mithraism. Giorgio was a little . . . obsessed with his work sometimes. It spilled over into the rest of our lives.'

'Did he have affairs?' he asked abruptly, aware of the police-woman's sharp intake of breath next to him.

Beatrice Bramante stared at her hands and shook her head, saying nothing.

'Did you?'

Again, she was silent.

'I'm sorry,' Falcone went on. 'These are standard questions. We should have asked them when Alessio disappeared, but somehow the occasion never arose.'

She stared at him, her face creased with hate.

'So why ask them now? Do you enjoy torturing me?'

'I'm trying to understand.'

'We were an ordinary family until that day. No affairs. No secrets.'

'And yet he took Alessio down into that place,' he replied. 'You didn't know he'd done that. I know you never said that to us at the time. I didn't want to pursue it. You had enough to deal with. But you didn't know. It was obvious you didn't understand either. At least, that's what I thought.'

She shook her head.

'What is it you want from me? I ask myself that question every day. Every morning. Every night. What if I'd taken him to school instead? What if he'd been sick? Or gone in a different direction? When you lose a child, Falcone, a part of you never stops playing that awful game.'

The big *sovrintendente* shuffled next to Rosa, glanced at Falcone as if wondering whether he was allowed to intervene, then spoke anyway.

'And what if they'd turned the wrong corner and found some idiot drunk coming up the street, with his car on the wrong side of the road?' Taccone asked. 'We're police, Signora. We hear people going through that kind of agony every day. It doesn't get you anywhere. It's understandable. But it's pointless too.'

Falcone wished he had Costa and Peroni by his side, not this well-meaning pair, one raw and unobservant, one decent and unimaginative.

'No,' the inspector said quietly, 'it's not pointless at all. Alessio didn't disappear because of some drunk driver. His father took him to that strange place for some purpose. Perhaps what followed was an accident of a kind but the reason he was there to begin with is something I can't begin to comprehend. Can you?'

– 25 –

Police drivers possessed the same contempt for speed limits as the average civilian. So, to Emily Deacon's surprise, it took less than two hours to get from the centre of Rome to Arturo Messina's isolated villa on the outskirts of Orvieto.

Her bedroom, which was next to Raffaela's, on the third floor of the palatial home, had an extraordinary view, out over the rolling countryside of Umbria towards the rock face fronting the small, castellated city which gave the region its name. The Duomo, Orvieto's grandly elegant cathedral, stood proudly over the *città*, its single rose window staring out like a monocular eye, watching over everything in its care. But this was February. The light was gone too soon for them to enjoy much of the tour of the premises offered by Messina senior, a man of far more prepossessing character than his son. If Arturo felt any embarrassment about the circumstances of their visit – once he had acquainted them with the facts when they arrived she was acutely aware that the Bramante case had cost him his career – he didn't show it. He must have been in his early sixties but looked a decade younger, of medium height and stocky build, with a dark, handsome face, a small, neat moustache, and bright, twinkling brown eyes.

The house was far too large for one man. Messina, who had lost his wife to illness some five years before, told, without hesitation, how it had been handed down from generation to generation after his great-grandfather had acquired it some eighty years before. From the ornate entrance hall on the ground floor to the guest quarters and the small but impeccable garden at the rear, with its view to the Duomo, it was a perfect little palace. When Emily wondered, idly, what he did with his time Arturo regaled them both with stories of trips into the wild hills to hunt game, fishing on the local rivers, and long outings to distant restaurants with his friends from the Questura. Orvieto seemed a retirement ground for old cops. Two had called by that afternoon, one for coffee and, she thought, a look at his visitors, the second with a couple of pheasants for supper. Arturo Messina wasn't lonely. He wasn't bored. He wasn't resentful. This idyllic break from Rome seemed a little too good to be true, until he took her to one side and showed her the package Falcone had sent that afternoon.

She'd stared warily at the crest of the Rome Questura on the covering message. When she opened it, Messina stole one good look at the cover page, then went to a cupboard to find something which he retrieved and placed on the table. It took her straight back to training days in the FBI school in Langley, with an alacrity that was scary.

'That, Arturo,' Emily declared, 'is a conference phone.'

'Even an old man like me knows what century this is,' he replied cheerfully. 'I like to keep up with the times. Besides, if Leo Falcone is going to rope you into this case, I can surely come too. It did belong to me once, remember.'

'But . . .'

'But what?' The brown eyes gleamed at her. 'Oh, come. There's nothing personal here. Do I look like a man eaten up by resentment? Even if I was, isn't the case more important?'

'It's not really my decision, is it?'

'I'll talk to Leo when we're ready. Agreed?'

She said nothing. She wasn't even sure she wanted to agree herself.

'You are prepared for this, aren't you?' he asked kindly.

She didn't look ill. She didn't even look pregnant. It was just tiredness. Mainly. The physical symptoms were just tiny, nothing. They would go away soon and she'd get that rosy bloom she expected to see on all pregnant women.

So the two of them sat down and began to pore over the

documents Falcone had despatched to await her arrival. The Bramante case, Emily soon realized, raised many intriguing questions, some of which, as Arturo Messina readily acknowledged, had never been addressed at the time. This was common in all complex investigations, and one reason why cold-case analysis existed. A fresh eye didn't just see new opportunities. It saw old ones that had been unexploited or simply left unobserved. And sometimes they were the most promising of all.

– 26 –

Beatrice Bramante got up and went to the small sink next to the single hob. She took down a bottle of what looked like cheap brandy from the cabinet above and poured herself a large glass. Then she came back, sat down in front of them, and took a long, slow drink.

'It took me a year to find the courage to ask him,' she said eventually. 'Giorgio is not the kind of man you can interrogate. I imagine you know that already.'

Falcone found his sudden, interior burst of anger receding, found himself hating the fact he was going to have to push this woman to get what he wanted. That self-awareness was something new to him too.

'And he said?'

The words didn't come easily. Beatrice Bramante was crying now, in spite of herself, in spite of the obvious shame she felt as they watched her try, and fail, to choke back the tears.

'He told me . . . there was a time in everyone's life when they had to start growing up. That was all he had to say on the matter. Then he told me he wanted a divorce. Quick. Unchallenged. That was my reward for asking. There was nothing more to say. Nor is there now. This is enough for me, Falcone. Please go.'

Taccone was trying to read the old grubby carpet. Rosa Prabakaran was tidying her notepad into her bag, anxious to get out of there.

Falcone reached over, took the pad out of her bag and put it back in her hands, then stabbed the pen that was still in her fingers onto the page.

'What did that mean, do you think?' he persisted. 'That it was time for Alessio to start "growing up" somehow?'

'He was a child! A beautiful, awkward, spoilt, bloody-minded, mischievous little boy. And . . .'

She threw back her head, as if that could stop the tears.

'And Giorgio loved him more than anything. More than me. More than himself. I don't know what he meant. All I know . . .'

There was a pause as she wiped her face with the sleeve of the grubby blue cardigan.

'. . . is that it wasn't just my son who died that day. I didn't know the man in that cell. I didn't know him when I went to his apartment round the corner. He just looks like Giorgio Bramante. There's some-one else inside the skin. Not the man I loved . . . love. You pick the words. You make them up. You tell the whole stinking world if you want. After all' – the lined, bitter face was glowering at him from across the narrow room again – 'that's what you do, isn't it?'

'When someone's been beaten to death while I sit outside listen-ing, twiddling my thumbs?' Falcone asked. 'Of course. I also try to catch criminals before they can do more harm than they have already. I hope to lessen the hurt that people wish to do to one another, even if they have little desire to do that themselves. It's a foolish idea, perhaps.'

He struggled to his feet and made his way painfully across the room. Then he bent down and took Beatrice Bramante's hands. She stiffened at his touch. His fingers fell on the old blue cardigan, gripped tightly around her palms.

'May I?' he asked.

Gently, he pulled back the cheap fabric of the garment. He knew what he'd see there, why a woman like Beatrice Bramante would hide herself inside those long, baggy sleeves.

The marks on her wrists emerged. Some were fresh, dark red weals, not deep, not the kind of wound inflicted by someone looking to end their own life. She was harming herself, regularly, he guessed. And perhaps . . .

He thought about something that had been nagging at his imagination since the moment he first heard it.

'The T-shirt you gave to the church. The blood on it was yours, wasn't it?'

She snatched her hands from him and dragged the blue sleeves over them again.

'What a clever man you are, Falcone! If only you'd been this perceptive fourteen years ago.'

'I wish that had been the case too,' he replied and returned to the sofa. 'The blood was yours. To begin with anyway. Did you go back to the church again after that?'

'Never. Why?'

'I have my reasons. Why that church in the first place?'

'Where else would I take it? Besides, Giorgio had worked with Gabrielli. He was a part-time warden there. I didn't know anyone else. I read about that little museum of theirs in the paper a week or two before. I . . .'

She sniffed and wiped her nose with the sleeve over her right hand.

'I wasn't myself at the time.'

'When did you tell Giorgio?'

She shook her head.

'I can't remember. In prison. Not long before he asked for the divorce. He thought I was crazy. Perhaps he was right.'

There was another question. It had to be asked.

'Were you harming yourself before Alessio disappeared? Or did it begin only then?'

'This is none of your business. *None* of your business.'

'No,' Falcone agreed, and felt he had his answer. 'You're right. All the same, I think it would be advisable if I asked someone to come round to talk to you from time to time. The social people . . .'

The woman's face contorted in a fit of abrupt fury.

'Keep out of my life, you bastard!' she screeched, stabbing a finger at him from across the room, not minding that her sleeves fell back as she did this, revealing the criss-cross pattern of marks on both her wrists, rising almost to the elbow. 'I will not allow you in here again.'

'As you see fit, Signora,' he replied simply.

It was dark outside. Thick black clouds were rolling in from the Mediterranean, obscuring an almost full moon. Soon there would be rain. Perhaps a roll of thunder.

Falcone waited until they were in the car before giving his orders. 'How much experience do you have of surveillance, Prabakaran?'

She looked bemused.

'I've done the course, sir. Nothing . . . practical.'

'Was the course good?'

'I think so.'

'I hope so. Tomorrow, and until I say otherwise, you will begin surveillance of Signora Bramante. I want to know where she goes. When. Who she sees. Everything.'

'But . . .' She fell silent.

'But what? It's important you tell me if an order is unclear. I abhor being misunderstood.'

'Beatrice Bramante has met me twice now. However hard I try, she's bound to see me. She'll know she's under surveillance.'

The car wound past the market, which was now closed. Falcone peered at the shuttered stalls, the empty boxes and the piles of discarded vegetables littering the pavement outside. As he watched, a burst of squally wind picked up some of the boxes, whirling the rubbish in a spiral, depositing the trash everywhere. A flash of thick greasy rain dashed against the windscreen. The weather was breaking.

'I would be very disappointed if she didn't see you. If the woman has been assisting her husband in this, she's a party to murder already. For her own sake, I do not wish her to become involved any further.'

'But . . .'

'Officer,' he said a little impatiently. 'I owe Giorgio Bramante nothing. He is, as far as any of us understands, the one proven murderer in this whole sorry saga. Beatrice Bramante is different. It may well be that we have to arrest her all the same before long. Nevertheless, we owe her the benefit of the doubt and what charity I can provide. You will follow her. You will ensure you are seen. And at the end of the day you will report back to me. Do I make myself clear?'

Rosa nodded and said nothing. Falcone scarcely noticed. His memories of what happened fourteen years ago were getting clearer all the time. Now he could look back with some perspective, he was beginning to feel distinctly uneasy about several important aspects of the affair.

'We also owe her the truth of what happened to her son,' he added. 'I want Giorgio Bramante. And I want that too.'

– 27 –

After just an hour of work, reading through Falcone's documents, and throwing questions at Arturo, whose replies proved he had a clear and capacious memory, it was apparent that Falcone's papers only covered a part of the story. When Bramante was arrested over Ludo Torchia's death, a grim case of child abduction had turned, instead, into a circus. The police and rescue services were out in force, poring over the Aventino and through the labyrinth of tunnels and caves of Bramante's excavation, looking for the missing Alessio. Hundreds of everyday Romans had abandoned their jobs to join in the hunt. Swiftly, the investigation became swamped by controversy as the implications of Bramante's arrest sank in, and it became apparent that the authorities had little idea how to find the lost boy. Emily recognized the symptoms of a full-scale media onslaught: the blind rage of populous, irrational fury; the angry impotence of a police force driven by legal and public necessities, not what it necessarily believed was correct in the circumstances. Then it all petered out in the unsatisfactory way that was all too familiar in cases involving missing children. Alessio Bramante was never found. His father held out his hands and went willingly to jail. Five teenagers walked free then disappeared, because every lawyer who looked at the case declared, very publicly, that it was impossible to bring anyone to court after the prime suspect had been beaten to death in police custody. The rules of procedure and evidence had been torn to shreds when Giorgio Bramante resorted to his fists to try to bludgeon some information out of the miserable Ludo Torchia. There was no going back.

It was, she thought, a particularly Roman mess, and if they were to stand the slightest chance of peering into this fading mist it was vital, after such an interval, for more insight than lay inside Falcone's hastily assembled documentation.

She pushed the papers to one side and looked at Arturo. A good police officer still lurked there. He went away and made a phone call. It took all of three minutes. When he returned he led her to a small and elegant study at the front of the property then parked himself at a very new notebook computer on the mahogany desk there and began typing. The emblem of the Polizia di Stato flashed up on the screen, followed by an authentication login. Arturo glanced at a slip of paper with what looked like a username and password scribbled in ballpoint, hammered in a few quick characters and they were in.

'Are we hacking into the central police network now?' Emily asked, pulling up a chair.

'No! I'm just . . . deputizing for a friend.' He licked his lips and looked worried for a moment. 'I try to stay up to date, you know. Up to a point. There's a generation of police out there who are more at risk from repetitive strain injury than getting a punch in the face. This is not progress. You have to mix the tools at your disposal.'

'I'd go along with that.'

'Good. You won't tell my son about this little escapade, though, will you? He can be a stuck-up prick at times. The poor soul was born at the age of fifty and he'll stay that way till he dies. Are we one on that?'

'He's your son,' she said. 'Now . . .'

It was all there. All the original reports. All the interviews. Photos. Maps. Even an independent archaeological assessment of Bramante's secret find. He printed out what she asked for. He searched every last digital nook and cranny of the Rome Questura's system, trying to see if there was something they'd missed. Arturo Messina had hung on to his job for as long as he could during the investigation. He only got suspended when the hunt for Alessio was 'scaled down', a euphemism for giving up, he said, with an abrupt and unexpected bitterness. Messina was refreshing his memory with what he was picking out of the system, not finding anything new. When there seemed to be no fresh information to uncover he finally logged off, then they shuffled the stack of papers together and headed for the living room.

Raffaela was there with Arturo's friend. He was an equally lively-looking pensioner type, tall and slim, tanned, with a pleasant, aristocratic face.

'Did Pietro lead you astray?' Arturo asked. 'I'm widowed. He's divorced. Draw your own conclusions.'

She laughed.

'I saw the Duomo. Such wonderful paintings.'

'Paintings!' Pietro declared. 'Luca Signorelli. My favourite's *The Elect and the Reprobates*.' He nodded towards them. 'That's me and him. You just have to work out which is which.'

'Tonight,' Arturo said, 'you're the cook. Pheasant for four, please.'

Raffaela was beaming, keen to help. She disappeared with Pietro into the kitchen, a different woman, Emily thought. The relationship with Leo Falcone was odd, a little forced, a little subservient. She'd moved in after he was shot, cared for him during the long difficult months of convalescence. There was something that puzzled Emily about the bond between them. It was almost as if Raffaela had decided to look after Leo out of a sense of guilt, of responsibility for the tragedy involving her family in Venice which had also almost cost him his life. Free of her old home in Murano, of Rome, and, it seemed, of Leo, she seemed more relaxed, more independent.

Arturo was at the table with the papers again.

'There's very little here I haven't seen before,' he muttered. 'This case was beyond me then and it's beyond me now. Perhaps I should just go and peel potatoes with Pietro in the kitchen and let you women have some time together.'

They heard the pop of a bottle from the back of the house then the sound of laughter. Pietro marched back in, followed by Raffaela. He was bearing a bottle of *prosecco*, she had glasses and plates of supermarket *crostini*. They looked like a couple about to throw a dinner party, which was, Emily realized, quite close to the mark. She and Nic had never, it now occurred to her, been round to Falcone's apartment in the evening. Leo and Raffaela weren't that kind.

'Not for me,' Emily said, turning away the glass with her hand. 'I want a clear head.'

'And I work best with a fuzzy one,' Arturo declared. 'So serve, then back to the chopping board. Some of us have work to do.'

'More fool you,' Raffaela murmured on her way out.

Arturo Messina's face fell for a moment as they left.

'Perhaps she's right,' he said with a sigh, after gulping at the brimming glass, an act she envied deeply. 'What on earth can I do?'

'What you said. Go and peel the potatoes.'

He didn't move.

She reached for the phone.

'I, on the other hand, need to talk to the man who sent us all this in the first place.'

'Not on your own,' he insisted, dashing to plug in the conference phone. 'Leo and I haven't spoken for fourteen years. It'll be a pleasure to listen to his miserable voice again, just to hear the shock.'

She hardly heard him. She found herself staring once more at the photos of Alessio Bramante, printed out with the files. He was an unusual-looking boy. Beautiful, a little effeminate with his long hair and round, open eyes. It was easy to see how the papers would love a story featuring a kid like this: pretty, smart, middle class, with a father who'd killed someone on his behalf. She knew from her time in the FBI that photogenic victims always got the best coverage.

'Do you know what puzzles me most?'

'No,' he admitted. 'Where do you begin? What did they do to the kid? Was he still alive when Giorgio was trying to beat the truth out of that evil little bastard Torchia? And why? Why were those students there? Why Giorgio and his son? There's so much . . .'

She agreed. There was. But the Bramante case had changed in nature once the father was charged with murder. It ceased to be a simple mystery about supposed child abduction. Instead it turned into a public debate about how far a parent should be allowed to go to protect his child. It became as much the story of Giorgio Bramante as his son. More, in a way, because Giorgio was there on every front page, his picture on every news programme. He was an emblem for every last parent who'd ever looked down a dark street and wondered where a son or daughter had got to.

'What puzzles me is simple,' she said. 'You had teams and teams of men. You had mechanical diggers. It says here you virtually destroyed Bramante's archaeological site looking for his son. And still you never found him.'

Arturo Messina licked his lips and, for a moment, looked his age.

'He's dead, Emily,' he said miserably. 'Somewhere inside that hill. Somewhere we didn't find or the cavers didn't dare go.'

She knew she ought to believe that too. But the doubts must have been obvious on her face.

'What else,' Arturo Messina asked, 'could possibly have happened?'

- 28 -

It felt like the old times. Ahead of them, past the long window of Falcone's office, now vacated by the temporary inspector despatched elsewhere that afternoon by Bruno Messina, a team of fifteen men and women were working the phones and computers, sifting records, chasing leads, trying to find an answer to a simple question: where would a university academic turned murderer go to ground in his native city? Something else was familiar too. They weren't finding any easy answers. The scooter Bramante had used to flee the scene in Monti had been found abandoned in a backstreet near Termini station. Trying to locate Bramante on the basis of information like that wasn't going to be easy. From where he'd dumped the bike he could catch the subway, the tramlines, the buses, the trains . . .

Or, Costa thought, he could do what any Roman probably would in the circumstances. Walk. It wasn't that large a city really. From Termini, Bramante – a fit and active man, by all accounts – could be in any one of a number of suburbs on foot within the hour. And there? Costa felt he knew the answer instinctively. Giorgio Bramante was no fool. He'd know, surely, that it was always simplest to be anonymous in a crowd. With time, the police could work the areas where the vagrant populations lived, shiftless, nameless people among whom any fugitive could easily disappear. Bramante may even have known such men in jail. He could be renewing an old friendship, or calling in favours from the past. For a man willing to sleep rough, able to hide in the thousands of underground caves in backstreets and small parks throughout the city, Rome was an easy place to hide. Falcone had his officers running through the usual techniques. But the customary tools – video surveillance cameras most of all – were useless. The scope was too wide, the data too large to absorb. Bramante was a man playing by rules of his own making. That effectively made him invisible.

The TV was running stock photos. The morning papers would repeat the exercise, all with pleas for help and a phone number set up to handle sightings. Costa had no good, clear recollection of Bramante's appearance from their meeting that morning. He'd been too focused on Leo Falcone, too worried that the inspector was in grave danger, to think ahead that much.

Still, the figure he remembered – dressed in black, hat pulled down low, scarf around his mouth, scarcely anything visible of his face – provided enough for him to realize that the photos they had of Giorgio Bramante were hopelessly out of date. Fourteen years ago he'd been good-looking, clean-shaven and sported long, dark hair. Most of the photos taken before his arrest made him look like what he was: an intelligent, probably slightly arrogant university professor. From what little Costa had seen that morning he now understood, very clearly, that Bramante didn't fit that image any more. Nothing could be taken for granted. They were locked inside a sequence of events Giorgio Bramante could have been planning for years. Unlike them, he was prepared, working on the basis of prior knowledge. It was possible, they all knew, that Bramante had managed to track down the elusive Dino Abati under whatever name he now bore. Abati would be thirty-three now. His parents hadn't heard from him in years. But eighteen months before he had been recorded re-entering the country from Thailand. Since then there was no record of him departing through any international airport. Given the freedom of movement within Europe available to anyone with an Italian ID card, that could still put him anywhere from Great Britain to the Czech Republic. Costa wasn't alone in wishing the man was anywhere else on the planet but Rome.

There was a commotion on the far side of the office. Both he and Falcone turned their attention away from the pile of reports on the inspector's desk and looked out into the pool of busy officers at their desks. Gianni Peroni and Teresa Lupo were marching through the aisles throwing out bags of *panini* and cans of soft drinks like a couple of Santas turning up at a child's party.

Leo Falcone laughed. It was an open, honest sound Costa hadn't heard in a while. That of a man who was back in his element.

'I don't know why he's feeding them,' Falcone complained cheerfully. 'At least they can go home. You'd think we were under siege. Being forced to stay here. It's ridiculous.'

'Not for you . . .'

The grey eyebrows rose.

'He could have killed you this morning.'

'He could have killed me this morning,' Falcone agreed. 'So why didn't he?'

'I don't know. Perhaps he thinks this is some kind of a ritual too. Everything has to be done in the right way. None of the men he did kill went easily. A water jet through the chest . . .'

'He hated them more than he hates me,' Falcone said firmly. 'Don't ask me how I know that. I just do. In fact . . .'

He shook his head, disappointed with his own abilities at that moment.

'God. I wish I could think straight. Be honest. How am I doing, Nic? Think before you answer. I may be a touch suspicious here but Bruno Messina could have more than one motive for giving me this job. Yes, you could say it's my responsibility. But if I screw up the way his father screwed up, it won't take much to put my head on the block either, will it?'

Costa hadn't thought of that. Office politics escaped him mostly.

'I think we're doing everything we can. You have the manpower. We've followed practice. If someone's seen Bramante . . .'

'No one really knows what Bramante looks like any more. Except whoever it is that's helping him. We have to go through the motions but I'm not holding out much hope. So how?'

It was the old truism, one that most police officers tried to forget, because it tended to demean all the routine that went with a normal investigation.

'Statistically I'd say . . . out in the street. When his mind's on something else. His work. Or . . .'

He had to add this.

'. . . on the way back.'

Falcone nodded vigorously. His large bald head had lost its customary tan over the winter. He would turn fifty before the year was out and he was starting to look his age.

'Quite right. But here's another statistic for you. Although you'd rarely understand this from reading a newspaper today, a child is many times more likely to be at risk from his immediate family or friends than from a stranger. It's not someone around the corner they need fear, usually. Or some internet stalker. It's those who are close to them.'

Costa nodded. Of course he knew. The assumption, from the outset, was that the Bramantes were a perfect middle-class family, a photogenic one which, in the eyes of some, meant they felt the tragedy more than most.

'There's never been a suggestion that Bramante or his wife abused the child. Has there?'

'No,' Falcone agreed with a shrug. 'The middle classes don't do that kind of thing, do they? At least, not so others get to know.'

'If you think there's something I should be doing.'

'It's done.'

He motioned to some folders on his desk, blue ones, a colour the Questura didn't use.

'I called in the social service reports before you got here. Nothing, of course. We should still have looked more closely than we did. We allowed ourselves to be distracted by the media. The course of action we took was formed by public opinion, not what we should have been pursuing as police officers. Instead of justice we sought vengeance, which is an ugly thing that respects no one, guilty or innocent. The curious part of all this is that I rather had the impression Giorgio Bramante didn't mind. He already knew what he was going to do, even before we put him in court.'

He peered out at the room full of officers, a few laughing with Peroni and Teresa, most head down over their computers.

'And here we are almost fifteen years on, hoping that this time round we can pull some answers out of a machine. Progress . . . What do you think, Nic? How do we break this one?'

Costa had formed firm opinions on that subject already.

'Bramante isn't an ordinary killer. He probably doesn't expect to escape us in the end. Perhaps he thinks he'll become the hero again. The wronged father who came back for justice on the louts who got away in the first place.'

Falcone nodded.

'And the police officer he holds responsible too. Don't forget me.'

'Perhaps,' Costa replied.

'Perhaps?' Falcone asked.

'You said it yourself. I don't think this is about you. Or Toni LaMarca. Or Dino Abati, or whatever he calls himself now. Not really. It's about Giorgio Bramante and what happened to his son. If we could only understand that . . .'

Leo Falcone laughed again and relaxed in his big black chair, putting his hands behind his head.

'You've come on under my tutelage, you know. Where's that innocent young man I nearly fired a couple of years ago?'

'I've no idea,' Costa replied immediately. 'He probably went the same way as that cynical old bastard of an inspector who had this office before you turned up. Sir.'

'A little less of that, Agente. I've got five more years in this job. No more. Perhaps a lot less. I'd like to think that, when I go, you are on the way to filling my shoes.'

Nic Costa found his cheeks going red. Promotion was the last thing on his mind. It was also the last thing an officer like Leo Falcone, who'd had more than a few troubled years of late, was in much of a position to offer.

'I see that Commissario Messina has reminded you the *sovrintendente* exams come up in the summer. You should be studying now. That way you could be getting a pay rise in time for the wedding. A good idea.'

'Sir . . .'

He was grateful that Peroni and Teresa bustled in at that moment. The big man had the remains of what looked like a gigantic cheese and tomato sandwich in one hand and a bagful of canned drinks in the other.

'Rations for the duration,' he declared. 'Teresa and I have checked out the accommodation. The Gulag suite is ours. You two can take the Abu Ghraib wing. We have installed fresh soap and towels because the ones that were in there were quite . . .'

When he stopped, lost for words, Teresa filled the gap.

'Let's put it this way, gentlemen. I wouldn't have touched them. Not even with gloves on.'

'Ugh.' Peroni shivered. 'Quite why we can't just go home beats me . . .'

'Gianni!' she yelled. 'There's a man out there who swished someone's heart out with a high-pressure hose last night. He has our photographs.'

'We joined up for this nonsense to be popular?' Peroni asked.

Falcone harrumphed.

'If Commissario Messina says we're confined to barracks outside of normal working hours then that's how it's going to be. I don't want anyone going walkabout.'

Peroni heaved his big shoulders in a non-committal shrug.

'I'm serious about that, Gianni,' Falcone said severely. 'He took those pictures for a reason.'

'I know, I know. So what news?'

Falcone and Costa were silent.

'Oh,' Teresa said with a sigh. 'This isn't going to be a protracted stay, is it? I mean, I still don't understand why I couldn't go to Orvieto with the other "ladies".'

Falcone raised a long index finger, a man remembering something he should never have forgotten. Teresa responded straight away.

'Orvieto,' she said with a quick and somewhat condescending smile. 'He wants to call the girlfriend, Gianni. Isn't that sweet? I don't remember Leo being so sweet before. In fact, I don't remember him being sweet at all. Nic and Emily getting engaged – and expecting a baby too. Leo being sweet. The fact that there's some lunatic out there with our pictures and a penchant for swishing hearts out. The world's a lovely place now, don't you think?'

Costa didn't like the way Falcone had caught his eye. The expression there wasn't sweet. It was distinctly guilty.

'Actually,' the inspector said quietly, 'it's Emily I need to talk to really. A little advice.'

- 29 -

Four hours later, at just after midnight, the office was empty except for a lone cleaner working away with duster and broom at the far end of the long line of desks, faceless in the shadows. Costa sat by the window, taking breaks from hunting idly through yet more files on the computer to stare out at the bright, handsome moon, high over the rooftops of the *centro storico*, shining down on empty streets and the dead eyelids of closed shops and bars. It was a good time for a man who couldn't sleep to try to think. In February the city didn't stay up late. Come June there'd be people still walking the alleyways outside, happy after dinner, munching on ice creams from the places that stayed open into the small hours, part of the restless summer life of the metropolis. Come summer, too, there'd be a wedding, and a child. Just the thought of those two events dashed Giorgio Bramante from his mind entirely.

What mattered in the end was family, that undefined and indefinable bond that required no explanation, because, to those it embraced, it was as natural as taking a breath, as easy as going to sleep next to the person you loved. As simple as the sense of duty you felt to any child who grew out of that loving relationship.

That, he knew, was what had changed between him and Emily over the previous year. Without Leo Falcone's influence, and the way the crafty old inspector had opened his eyes, he would never have been able to commit to their relationship in the way it deserved. Leo had taught him to relax, to live with his emotions, to take a break from trying to solve the problems of the world for a while. And then get back into the fray. It was a gift he'd never forget.

Costa looked at his watch, breathed hard, felt guilty for a moment, then picked up the phone. She answered, sounding very, very sleepy. He wondered what the villa was like, and the bedroom.

They'd all spent an hour and a half on the conference call that evening, sharing ideas, Falcone and Arturo Messina talking together as if nothing had happened all those years before, Teresa trying to make the most of the scant and largely obvious forensic she'd assembled from Toni LaMarca's corpse, which would receive a full autopsy in the morning. Costa and Peroni had kept quiet mostly, thinking, listening, exchanging that glance they both knew well, a kind of invisible shrug that said: maybe it gets better tomorrow.

'If you're too tired,' he insisted quickly, 'just say so and I'll ring off. I never got the chance to ask how you were on the conference call. It didn't seem right.'

She sighed. There was the impatient rustling of sheets.

'It's nearly one o'clock!'

'I know. I'm wide awake. There's a bright moon. I can't stop thinking about you. What more is a man supposed to offer?'

There was the distant sound of her laughter. He wished he could reach out and touch her, even for a moment.

'Flowers would be in order when you have the time. And champagne when I'm up to drinking it.'

'How do you feel?'

'Fine. Up and down, to be honest. Don't sound so worried. The doctor said it would be like this. It's not unusual, Nic. Men always seem to think their first child is the only one there's ever been in the entire history of the planet. Women know better.'

'Don't shatter my illusions. Please.'

She laughed. He could almost imagine himself lying next to her on the bed, such were the tight, unspoken ties between them now.

'Something's bothering you,' she said. 'Tell me.'

He'd worked just one cold case in his entire career. It was a murder too, though less complex. A man of almost seventy beaten to death in his home in a quiet suburban street out in the suburb of EUR. They'd gone back to the investigation eight years later and discovered that, by then, the neighbours were ready to admit what they'd kept secret before. The victim's son had been involved in low-level drug-running. He'd gone missing two years after his father died and was never seen again. It took three months but eventually they were able to charge a gang enforcer with the old man's murder and that of the son. All over a measly €3,000 owed for cocaine. Time did change the perspective with which one approached a crime. But it hadn't done them any favours in the Bramante case. All Emily had uncovered were questions. Good ones, without any easy answers.

'You said you didn't understand why no one ever found a body,' he answered. 'Is it that unusual?'

He thought he heard a yawn getting stifled at the other end of the line.

'Maybe. Maybe not. It just makes me uncomfortable. They brought in all that heavy equipment. Some thermal imaging gear too. All the reports say those caves go deep. That they get too narrow and dangerous to be explored . . . I still feel uneasy that there wasn't a body. But if he's not there, where?'

Costa glanced at the screen of the computer.

'Anywhere,' he said. 'If he's still alive.'

- 30 -

The labyrinth enveloped them, held them captive in the stone belly of the hill. Ludo Torchia led the way, tugging Alessio's slender arm. The rest followed, getting more and more confused and scared with each lurching step.

After a few minutes Guerino had stumbled badly, cutting his hands, letting the cockerel loose into the gloom again where it flew, screeching, taunting them. Abati was glad of that, though it made Ludo Torchia furious. There were bigger issues to worry about than sacrificing some bird. They were without bearings, deep underground. And the one man who might save them, Giorgio Bramante, would surely be as angry as Ludo Torchia if he discovered what had happened.

Dino Abati knew what the man would be shouting, too, when he came. It was obvious.

Alessio. Alessio. Where are you?

And that, in itself, seemed strange. By Alessio's own account, it was now perhaps thirty minutes since his father had left him alone in the main vestibule at the entrance to the caves. What was Giorgio doing all this time? And why did it need to involve Alessio?

These weren't questions he had time to consider. He didn't feel good. His head was pumping where Torchia got him with the rock. There were lights, coloured lights, chafing at the edge of his vision. The seven of them were now fleeing into a deep, Stygian chasm, trying

147

to illuminate it with their lanterns, hoping that somewhere, in this unknown skein of corridors, there lay some other way out to the world above, one that would help them all – perhaps Alessio too – escape Giorgio Bramante's inevitable wrath.

They turned another blind corner, ran, half fell forwards, tumbling down a steep incline. A sudden rock face loomed up to greet them. Abati took a good look around him and felt his spirits begin to fall. Near the Mithraeum they'd been in relatively well-managed territory, tunnels and small chambers carefully hewn out of the tufa with some forethought. Here they were back in the original workings, so deep inside the hill he didn't want to think about it. The rough walls, the rocks strewn on the floor, the cramped, winding tunnels barely high enough for a man to stand upright . . . everything spoke of a crude, ancient mining operation, not the fabric of a subterranean temple for some cult that liked a little privacy. They were, surely, at the very periphery of the incisions that men had made into the heart of the Aventino. What lay around them was as uncertain, as unknown now as it must have been to the slaves who laboured here two millennia before, wondering whether the next working would hold or collapse on them in a sudden, deadly torrent of stone. Or if a natural fault – there was water hereabouts, and that meant the hill itself was far from solid, even before the miners arrived with their pickaxes and shovels – lay in deadly wait around the corner.

The boy stumbled. A falsetto cry – young, uncomprehending – rang through the narrow corridors surrounding them, fading, disappearing, rising, Abati hoped, to break into the open light of day and tell someone out there to look beyond that old, rusted gate by the Orange Garden and try to find what was happening within.

'You're not hurt,' Torchia spat at the child, dragging him to his feet, scrabbling for the lantern.

Alessio Bramante hung his head and swore, using the kind of word Abati hadn't heard from most of his age. Giorgio was an unusual father, he guessed.

Torchia's eyes widened.

'It's a game, a game, a *game*, you miserable, spoilt little bastard!'

The boy stood still and was silent, just stared at them all with his wide, round intelligent eyes, the kind of stare that said: I know you, I'll remember you, there'll be a price to pay.

'Ludo,' Abati said quietly, as calmly as he could. 'This is not a good idea. We don't know where we are. We don't know how safe these caves might be. I understand places like this better than you and I don't feel safe down here, not without the proper equipment.'

The rest of them stole hopeful glances at Abati. Waiting. Not that he could do much. The flashing lights, the pumping in his head, were getting worse.

There was an exit to the left. They'd come past it in their rush. Another black hole to dive down. Another vain hope of avoiding discovery.

'No,' Torchia said simply.

'Giorgio is going to find out we're here! Please!' Vignola objected. His fat face was wreathed in sweat. He didn't look well at all.

They were quiet, until Abati said firmly, 'Let's just go back now. If we meet Giorgio, at least we're bringing him the kid. Let's not make this any worse than it is.'

Torchia was on him again, hands at his throat, face in his, scary in the way that lunatics are scary, because they don't care what happens to them, or to anyone at all. Abati remembered the feel of the rock on his head again. It could have killed him. Just the memory of it made him giddy.

'I got you ungrateful shits in here,' Torchia hissed. 'I'll get you out. That's who I am.'

'Who?' Abati asked, pulling away from him, realizing with some relief that he didn't much care what happened to Ludo Torchia, or any of them, himself included, any more. It was all too far gone for that. 'Pater? Are you so screwed up in your own head that you believe all that nonsense? That all you need to do is get seven people down here, kill some stupid bird, and everything gets made right somehow?'

'You agreed!'

'I agreed to make sure you idiots didn't come to any harm,' Abati said quietly, turning to go. 'Now I want to see daylight again.'

Vignola's hand touched his sleeve.

'Dino,' he pleaded under his breath. 'Don't leave us here.'

'*Don't leave us here, don't leave us here . . .*'

Torchia was out of control, almost on the two of them, spittle flying from his mouth as he mocked Vignola's words.

'Of course he's not leaving, are you, Dino? A soldier never leaves his battalion. You don't let your comrades down.'

Abati shook his head.

'You're crazy,' he murmured. 'This is real, Ludo. Not some playground adventure. We're in trouble enough as it is.'

'Wrong. Even if Giorgio's guessed someone's here anyway,' Torchia insisted, 'how could he know it's us? Answer me that.'

The flaw in his argument was so obvious. Dino Abati knew straight away he wasn't going to mention it, because that could only make things so much worse.

Then Vignola piped up and Dino Abati wished he'd had the time to grab him by the scruff of his neck and force him to keep his overactive mouth shut.

'Even if he doesn't know, the kid's going to tell him, Ludo. Don't you think?'

- 31 -

Costa had taken a good look at what else was going on in Rome the week Alessio Bramante went missing. This was not an ordinary time.

'It all happened when NATO was in one more terrible mess in Serbia, remember? That was one reason why the authorities told Bramante he couldn't go public. There were enough contemporary ethnic massacres to deal with without bringing in the TV cameras to see some grisly Christian episode from the past.'

'I still don't get it. Would people really get that touchy about something that happened almost 2,000 years ago?'

'What we like to call "the former Yugoslavia" is one hour by plane from Italy. There were boatloads of refugees crossing the Adriatic, turning up on our beaches. This was local for us, not distant pictures from a distant land. You really don't see it?'

She conceded that point.

'But,' Costa continued, 'there was a peace camp on the Circus Maximus at the time. Three, four thousand people from all over Europe. All kinds of people. Hippies. The far left. Just ordinary people too. And quite a few refugees who'd got nowhere else to go.'

'So what are you saying? He was abducted by one of them?'

That was going too far.

'I'm just raising possibilities. Imagine Alessio escaped the caves. Some of them exit not far from where the camp was. Imagine he ran in among the tents there, distraught, frightened for some reason. He didn't want to go home. He didn't know what he wanted.'

This was a possibility. He felt certain of it.

'They'd have called the police, Nic. It's what you do with lost kids. And what could have scared him so much he wouldn't want his own parents?'

'I don't know. But you can't assume the people there would have gone to us in those circumstances. Some would. Some of them wouldn't speak to the police about anything. We're the fascists, remember? Maybe they didn't have access to the news either. They wouldn't know a child was missing, being hunted by hundreds of people.'

The silence down the line told him she wasn't convinced.

'If I'm right, Alessio Bramante could be anywhere now, living under an entirely different name,' he went on.

'He'd be twenty-one or so,' she objected. 'You're telling me he wouldn't have remembered who he was? He would have stayed hidden all these years, with his father in jail?'

'His father would have stayed in jail whether Alessio turned out to be alive or not. Besides, that's your instinct talking, not fact. If you look at actual abductions it's not uncommon for kids taken at that age to become absorbed by the unnatural family they enter. Children try to adapt to the situation around them. Look at your own country. Children who were abducted by Native Americans in the nineteenth century became Native Americans. They weren't looking to go back into white society. They often rebelled if someone tried to force it on them. They didn't think the situation they found themselves in was primitive. It was how the world was supposed to be. If Alessio was somewhere else altogether. Out of Rome. Out of Italy perhaps . . .'

The pause on the line told him she still didn't think much of this at all.

'You always look for the bright side, don't you?' she said gently.

'You were the one who said it was odd there wasn't a body.'

'It is. And I'd love to believe Alessio Bramante's alive and well out there somewhere. I just don't think it's possible. Sorry.'

'Fine. Your turn for a stab in the dark,' he said.

There was a quick intake of breath on the line. He was happy with that. She always rose to a challenge.

'How about this? Giorgio Bramante made the discovery of a lifetime in that excavation of his. Yet, because of the awkward politics at the time, no one would give him the money to make the most of it. No one would even let him tell the world what was down there, which, for the arrogant bastard I suspect he is, must have been even worse.'

'Go on.'

'What if he tried to lose Alessio in those caves deliberately. So that he could run out into the street and shout the houses down. The rescue service would turn up. The media too. His big secret would be out in the open and there'd be nothing anyone could do about it.'

It was an extraordinary idea, one none of them had even come near when they'd been throwing the case around that evening.

'You really think a father would sacrifice his son just for professional pride?'

'No! And this isn't professional either. From what I've read about Giorgio it was personal. That work was his life. But Alessio would be safe. In the end.'

'I'm not sure . . .'

'Nic. I know you're big on family, and so am I. Which is just as well in the circumstances. But there are some tough truths you have to face up to as well. We've all seen what gives in the media. When things like this happen, the focus of all that public sympathy turns on the parents as much as it does on the kids. That's the way it works. The parents are the ones on TV. If they're lucky enough to find the kids no one asks any hard questions. How the hell did they get there in the first place? We're just glad it ended cleanly, keep our doubts to ourselves and hope someone goes round and quietly tells those people never to get themselves in a mess like that again.'

He couldn't argue with that.

'Think it through,' she went on. 'Follow the logic. Chase down the flaws. Please.'

'There aren't any. It's still more far-fetched than mine.'

'Really?' He was starting to recognize that tone in her voice. It demanded attention. 'There were six stupid students down there, trying to raise the Devil or something. Like it or not, something very far-fetched did go on. You know that. So does Leo. He wouldn't be asking me to cold case these files if he wasn't desperate, would he?'

No, Costa knew, Falcone wouldn't. The old Leo would never have placed a single sheet of paper outside the Questura. But the old Leo was gone.

'And Giorgio Bramante beat one of them to death,' Costa murmured idly. 'What the hell was that about?'

'It was about his son,' she said. 'Wouldn't you feel the same way?'

'I'd feel the same way. That doesn't mean I'd do what he did.'

He heard a long pause on the line, then she asked, 'How do you know, Nic? How would anyone know the way they'd respond in a situation like that? Can you be so sure?'

He struggled for an answer.

'I think so,' he said. 'I hope so. Look, it's late. Let me pass all this on to Leo in the morning and see where we get. If you need access to any files . . .'

'Um,' she said cautiously. 'I think we're fine on that, thanks.'

She hesitated.

'Is Leo all right?' she asked, a little nervously. 'He's still convalescent. He could have said no.'

'Leo's looking better than I've seen him in months,' he answered honestly. 'He needed to get back to work.'

'Tell him to call Raffaela from time to time. She hasn't been out much since Venice.'

'I'm sure with you around she'll get over the shyness.'

Emily laughed again, and the sound brought out in him the same physical pang he'd experienced ever since they'd met. There was a note of concern in her voice, all the same.

'Raffaela's over it now. She and Arturo are still downstairs with his best friend working their way through the household grappa cellar. If Leo cares . . .'

Costa thought of Falcone's hungry, intense look as he eased his injured body back behind that familiar desk. It was a big if . . .

'I'll tell him. But . . . Bear with me.'

The light was flashing on the handset: an internal call. He put Emily on hold and hit the answer button.

It was the duty officer at the front desk. Costa listened then cut the line and went back to her.

'I have to go,' he said quickly.

'Is everything all right?' she asked. 'You sound worried.'

'Front desk say that someone claiming to be Dino Abati has turned up looking like a street bum, asking to talk to Leo. No one else would do.'

'That sounds like good news.'

'Maybe . . .'

He looked around the office. The cleaner was gone. The place was empty. This was an operational floor, staffed only during daytime and outright emergencies. As far as he knew no one else was there apart from him and the three individuals asleep in the rudimentary quarters along the corridor.

'That was half an hour ago,' he continued. 'The desk's heard nothing since they sent him up here with some rookie *agente* looking for something to do.'

'Nic?'

The light in the corridor outside failed, followed by those in the office, throwing most of the floor ahead of him into the dark. Only the bright silver rays of the moon, visible through scudding rain clouds, remained, and they travelled no more than a third of the way across the room. He turned to face what should have been the doorway, blinked, trying to adapt to the sudden gloom. It could just be coincidence. Not that he believed in them much.

'Call the switchboard back,' he said quietly. 'Tell them we may have an intruder. Old wing. Third floor.'

She killed the phone without saying a word.

He could just see the extensions printed in the list by the phone. Costa called the first one. A sleepy Teresa answered before Peroni.

'Don't ask questions,' he ordered. 'Just lock the door and keep it that way until someone arrives. Yell at Leo through the wall and tell him to do the same.'

Then, to make sure, he dialled the room he'd been sharing with Falcone.

In the few brief seconds he allowed himself, no one answered.

He swore quietly. At least he'd seen fit to check out a handgun from the armoury that afternoon. It sat in its regulation holster on the desk in front of him. Costa hated wearing the thing. He picked it up, checked the safety was on then, grasping it low in his right hand, got up and walked towards the pool of inky black spreading out ahead of him.

He could picture the corridor in his head, with its glaring white paint and bare bulbs. The emergency quarters were just ten metres or so on from the doorway.

Costa tried to hurry. Desks bumped into him, from all the wrong places. He blinked again, trying to force his eyes to adapt, opened them and thought he could just make out the shape of the area ahead.

A car moved past outside. Its headlight shot through the office, briefly illuminating the area like a flash of lightning. Then it was gone, leaving its visual imprint in his head. Ahead of him Nic Costa saw the single outstretched silhouette of a figure in a familiar pose, one he'd learned to loathe over the years: arm outstretched, weapon ready, moving purposefully, with intent. When the car headlight moved on, he could see the pencil-thin beam of a caver's helmet torch running in a distinct yellow line from the figure's head, cutting through the gloom, aiming towards the rooms where Falcone, Peroni and Teresa Lupo had been sleeping.

'Wonderful,' he muttered to himself, then took a first, tentative step towards the invisible corridor ahead.

- 32 -

'This is enough,' Abati began to say, then took one step forward and found himself falling, head spinning, arms grasping in desperation at little Sandro Vignola's shoulders just to stay upright. He needed a doctor. He couldn't take on anyone like this, particularly not Ludo Torchia who had now, to Abati's dismay, grabbed the child round the throat, and was clutching him, like a shield, like a weapon.

He had his knife out, tight to Alessio's scalp. Dino Abati looked into the boy's eyes and wondered whether he could really understand what Dino was trying to say to him, just with a desperate expression, surely only half visible in the dark.

This isn't my doing, Alessio. Forgive me. I'll try and make it right.

'I don't wanna go to jail, Ludo,' Toni LaMarca pleaded. 'Getting kicked out of college I can handle. But that . . .'

'No one's going to jail. You won't tell a soul, will you, kid?'

Alessio Bramante stayed there, tight in his grip, not saying a word.

'He won't say a word,' Torchia said defiantly.

'So,' Abati murmured, squeezing his eyes open and shut rapidly to try to force some clarity back into his head, 'tell us all, Ludo. Where now?'

A new sound came to them. It was the tentative clucking of the cockerel, fear covered by some small bravado, filtering out from the tiny, narrow tunnel they'd already passed on the left.

No one saw where it went to after it escaped. No one but Ludo seemed to mind.

'There,' Torchia replied, lifting his arm from Alessio Bramante's throat to point at the black chasm behind them. Abati could detect a breath of foul, miasmic air emerging from its mouth. It stank of damp and decay. The very existence of a current of air, however meagre, filled him with the faintest trace of hope. It meant the channel went somewhere, in the end.

'Which goes where, exactly?' Abati asked.

Torchia's foot came out and stabbed him painfully in the shin. The movement released Alessio. The child could have run then. He didn't move.

The kick was directed, as Abati knew without looking, towards the tunnel, so badly hacked out of the damp rock it looked half finished. He staggered a little closer and could taste the dank, stagnant vapour in the air. Somewhere there was a stream, a fissure in the hill, perhaps, one that led into some unknown natural waterway running beneath the people and the cars on the Lungotevere, back into the real world, straight down to the Tiber. He'd stamped, waist-deep, freezing cold, through subterranean torrents like this before. He'd do it again, with a child in his arms if necessary.

'You tell me, Dino.'

'Ludo . . .'

'*You tell me!*'

His voice was so loud it felt as if Ludo Torchia had entered his head, and would stay there, trying to spread his infection wherever he could.

Then another noise. It was the bird again. The black cockerel strutted confidently into view from the hidden crevice ahead, small head bobbing, walking with a mechanical gait, as if it were trying to force from its tiny mind the idea that there might be something worse ahead, worse even than the crazy Ludo Torchia, who now watched it, hungrily.

'Mine,' Torchia barked, grabbing at the bird's flapping wings and the flailing claws.

When he had hold of the creature, when it became obvious what would happen, Dino Abati took the boy by the shoulders and tried to turn him away. He didn't want to watch himself. Only Toni LaMarca's eyes glittered in Ludo Torchia's direction at that moment.

'I thought you needed an altar,' Abati said quietly.

Torchia made an animal grunt then flung a string of foul epithets in his face.

I thought, Abati wanted to add, but didn't dare, a bungled sacrifice, rushed, out of place, out of time, was worse than no sacrifice at all.

There was the sound of wild, frightened cawing, one high-pitched screech, then nothing. An odour – fresh, harsh and familiar – reached them. Blood smelled much the same, whatever the source.

The boy held on to him now, trembling, shaking hard, tight and nervous as a taut wire. Abati gripped him, trying to keep his small, fragile body hidden. Torchia recognized symptoms like these. They stoked his craziness.

Torchia took the black, feathered corpse and walked round each of them, wiping its blood on their hands, and on Abati, his face.

He got to Alessio. Dino Abati watched, not knowing whether his head was really working then. What he thought he saw made no sense. Of his own volition the boy thrust out his fists, worked them deep into the shiny feathers, washing his hands with quick, eager movements.

'Brothers,' Torchia said, watching him. 'See? He understands. Why don't you?'

But he's a child, Dino Abati thought. An innocent who believes this is a game.

'Where do we go now?' Vignola asked.

'Where this dead thing came from.'

Dino Abati looked at the crude, gaping hole of the doorway.

'Sure,' he said.

Discreetly, he reached down and gripped the child's left hand, now sticky with blood, then ducked beneath the sharp stony overhanging teeth, bent the beam of the lantern forwards, and stepped carefully along the ground it revealed, hearing the shuffle of feet behind him, trying to force his hurting head to think.

− 33 −

Costa found the corridor, found the light switch, dashed it up and down, knowing it would be no good. Giorgio Bramante had worked some trick with the central fuse box, blacking out the entire floor somehow. If Costa were to believe the front desk, he'd been in the building little more than thirty minutes, accompanied only by an inexperienced cadet. Not long. It was as if he knew the place already.

Then he remembered what Falcone had said. Bramante was an intelligent, capable man, one used to being underground in the dark, at home in a foreign world where most would be lost, happy inventing a strategy as he went along. One who stored what he saw and held it for use later.

There were interview rooms on this floor. It was just a two-minute walk from where Falcone, Peroni and Teresa had been sleeping, down through the Questura's old narrow corridors to the cell in the basement where Ludo Torchia had been beaten to a pulp. Bramante could be working from memory, with a set plan in mind, one that had been developed and honed over the years he'd spent in jail.

He played his hand in the least expected places, always. And when it came to Leo Falcone he could simply pretend to be someone else, someone who was threatened, not a threat. Someone who could talk their way inside the Questura after midnight, when everyone was a little sleepy, and too tired to ask good questions, because all of Rome, if not Italy, had watched TV, read the newspapers, knew full well that Leo Falcone was searching for a man of that name.

Then Bramante could wait for the moment he found himself alone with a rookie cop, one he could pull into a corner, beat the truth out of, quickly, before anyone else in the slumbering Questura woke up to what was happening.

That truth being: Leo Falcone was still in the building, fast asleep somewhere upstairs, thinking that here, of all places, he was safe from everything.

The idea had a bleak simplicity that made Costa feel stupid for not having expected it. On form, Leo would surely have been ready for that eventuality. But Falcone was struggling to rediscover what he used to be, and that made him vulnerable.

Sorting through the possibilities as he slowly, carefully made his way through the unfamiliar darkness of the Questura, Costa was aware how obvious the situation now was.

He stepped out into the centre of the corridor – as much as he could guess its location – and began to make his silent way behind the figure he'd seen slipping past the doorway, bound for the rooms that lay somewhere ahead in the dark. The gun lay loose in his fingers. Teresa and Peroni would be safe, but a part of his head was already beginning to calculate what Leo Falcone's unanswered line signified.

A sound came to him through the pitch-black space ahead; someone walking, slowly, with more noise than Costa could have hoped for. Then the movement shifted direction, position, too, flitting through the blackness with an infuriating uncertainty, not left, not right, somewhere he couldn't quite locate before there was silence again.

Costa was trying to analyse what had happened when something made him jump inside his own skin.

A man was breathing, heavily, the awkward, arrhythmic wheezings of an individual in stress, no more than a metre or two from where he stood.

Giorgio Bramante was only human, he reminded himself. A killer. A father who'd lost his own son. Criminal and victim in the same skin.

'Give it up, Giorgio,' he said in a loud, clear voice, trying to pinpoint the source of the sound, wondering if he was close enough to reach out and touch him, incapacitate the man with a sudden burst of violence that ought to stay him until help arrived. 'Don't move. Don't even think you've got somewhere to go.'

That uncanny sense of confusion returned through the gloom, and with it the realization that this unreadable world was not a place where anything possessed solidity or certainty. Finally, he caught the tail end of some low, throaty laughter, and the sense that Bramante had changed position, with an astonishing speed, in absolute silence, the moment he had realized how close they were.

'You're up late for one so young, Mr Costa. Are you feeling tired? I'm not. I like this time of night.'

Hearing his own name sent a chill up Nic Costa's spine.

There was a commotion from somewhere beyond where Bramante had to be. The rooms. It was Peroni bellowing in a loud, threatening voice. Costa waited for the fury to subside then shouted, loud enough for everyone to hear, 'Stay inside, Gianni. I've got a gun. This is covered. There's back-up on the way.'

Somewhere.

There were angry noises still from the distant door, Peroni and Teresa's voices in conflict. He could imagine that argument: common sense clashing with instinct. He didn't need that distraction right now.

'That's a pretty girlfriend you have. Nice house, too, out there on the Appian Way. Does a police salary really pay for that?'

'No.' The more Bramante talked, the easier it was to find his position, to keep him stalled. 'It was my father's. Just inherited wealth.'

Bramante didn't answer straight away. When the voice came back again it was different in tone. Less amused. Less human, somehow.

'I wanted Alessio to have that house of ours on the Aventino,' Bramante said without a trace of emotion. 'By that time I'd probably have paid it off.'

'I'm sorry. What happened was a tragedy.' There were men outside on the staircase. He could hear the babble of their confused voices, and the low, mutual tremor of indecision. 'We'll try to find out what happened. I promise you.'

'What use is that, in God's name?'

The vehemence and the volume took him by surprise. Costa took two long steps towards the wall on his left. It was stupid to stay still.

'I thought it's what you'd want.'

He was somewhere different again.

'I wanted that girlfriend of yours,' the voice said, floating casually out of the dark, almost relaxed again. 'She'd have been good for bargaining.' Another dry, soulless laugh. 'And the rest.'

Costa didn't rise to the bait. He wondered what exactly Bramante hoped to achieve by taunting him like this. Some sudden anger, and the exposure that would follow?

'Is that what prison does to you?'

That brittle sound of amusement again. This time more distant.

'Oh yes. It brings out the man inside.'

Bramante was moving down to where the corridor opened up to a larger area outside the emergency quarters, a place used for small briefings and meetings during training sessions. The bunk rooms were on one side, high blacked-out windows on the other. He followed, trying to picture this part of the Questura more accurately in his head. The station was so familiar he thought he knew every last corner. But memory meant nothing without some visual prompts. He'd never expected to have to feel his way around like a blind man, struggling to build a picture out of senses that had nothing to do with vision – hearing, touch, smell. Talents Bramante must have perfected from all that time spent underground.

There were a few desks here. A collection of foldaway chairs that were arranged and rearranged to suit the occasion. Four, five doors, perhaps six, two to the accommodation rooms, the rest for smaller meeting places.

Try as he might, he couldn't remember which door was which, or how the seats and tables had been left that evening. Bramante could have walked through in the light, checking out everything before returning to the stairwell, where, Costa assumed, the fuse boxes were situated, and pitching the entire floor into darkness.

Then, from behind, he heard a sudden burst of noise: men's voices, angry shouts, the sound of metal on metal. Back-up wasn't going to be as easy as he thought. Costa could picture the fire door more clearly than anything else on the floor. It stood, a huge green hunk of iron, atop the staircase, rarely used except in drills, the result of some demand from the fire department. Once someone closed it and threw down the huge clasp, the entire floor was sealed. Bramante had found the time do that somehow, and now the back-up men were busy hammering away against solid steel, screaming at each other to come up with a solution. The building that housed the Questura was, in parts, 300 years old. They'd never got around to installing a lift in this section. It never seemed necessary.

'How long do you think I have, Agente Costa?' the voice asked him, amused, coming from somewhere he couldn't begin to pin down. 'All I want is a little time with my old friend, Leo.'

'There was a tense, hard catch in his voice when he said Falcone's name.

'You hear that?' the man shouted. 'A minute or two of your time? That's all I need. It didn't use to be so precious. I don't remember you hiding away in the dark back then.'

He was moving. Costa thought he was beginning to get a handle on where Bramante might be. Then the men at the doorway broke through with something like mallets, hammering down the old iron, screaming at each other to fight their way inside, their cries echoing down the long, long corridor.

Costa heard a door open ahead of him and a familiar sound: Leo Falcone's pained shuffle, the unsteady gait of a man struggling to be himself again.

There was the sound of a lighter. A small flicker of flame fluttered in the shade on the far side of the room. It just succeeded in illuminating Falcone's aquiline face and the upper part of his body: the bald head, the large, crooked nose, the jut of his silver goatee, and a white shirt, open to the neck.

Costa gripped the gun more tightly, felt how the icy sweat made it slip in his palm, and edged towards the man by the puny flame, knowing that Bramante must be doing the same.

'Fourteen years ago,' the old inspector said nonchalantly, 'I was busy putting you in jail for murder, Giorgio. It seems unfortunate I have to repeat that exercise now.'

Falcone held the flame aloft.

'If you have something you wish to say to me . . .' he began, in a firm, untroubled voice.

The back-up men were almost in but they were still a long way behind. Costa began to move, feeling the gun in his grip, wondering what use it might be, and how dangerous, with so many unseen figures about to fill the shadows around them.

Then Falcone cried out. The flame disappeared. One muffled moan, perhaps more, broke through the darkness which enveloped everything again, throwing Costa off his balance, making him wonder which way was forward, which back.

The iron door fell onto the Questura's old tiles with a crash that roared through the building, shaking the floor. A team of officers, angry, frustrated, were now fumbling in the direction of the small anteroom where Leo Falcone had been engulfed by the night, and something else.

'He's got Leo,' Costa yelled at them. 'Don't shoot . . .'

The words just froze in his throat. Another light had come on now. The pencil-torch beam was lit again, attached to the black helmeted head of a figure who was struggling manically against the far wall, wrestling with Leo Falcone, arms around his white shirt, doing something Costa could only imagine.

He remembered the slaughterhouse, the knives, and the sight of Toni LaMarca, his heart ripped apart while he hung alive from a meat hook, staring at the face of the man who was murdering him.

The weapon hung clammy in his fingers. He could hear men coming down the corridor now, men who'd no idea what they were facing, no clue about how it might be tackled.

Nic Costa recalled the layout of this hidden chamber very carefully, then pointed the weapon sideways, out away from the oncoming team, out towards the dusty glass of the blacked-out windows.

He pulled the trigger, hard. The resulting sound was so loud it seemed to take on a hard, physical dimension, reverberating around him as if multiple firearms had spent their ammunition in multiple dimensions, shaking his head until he couldn't think straight, couldn't sort out what was happening around him in a sea of bodies, heading scrum-like for the white shirt on the floor, dimly visible in the torch beam which was now at the same level as Leo Falcone's body.

There was something on the white fabric. A stain, dark and fluid.

Costa threw the gun to one side, fought his way through the bodies, got to the front until he saw Falcone.

A torch came on from behind him: broad and yellow, all-revealing.

The sight wasn't what he expected. Leo Falcone was glaring at them all, eyes as bright as the blood-stained shirt that stuck to his chest. The figure of a man still clung to him, unmoving, clad in black, with a woollen helmet of the same colour tight around his head.

'Are you . . .' Costa began to ask.

Falcone struggled and got his arms free of the body that covered him.

'Yes!' he spat back. 'Now get him off me.'

Costa took hold of the man's body.

'You'll need a knife,' Falcone said, inexplicably.

'What?'

The rest of them crowded in. Someone brought more torches. He could hear Teresa Lupo yelling to be allowed through. They needed a doctor. They all knew that.

Then, finally, someone found the fuses, flipped whatever switches Giorgio Bramante had worked to send this entire section of the Questura into the darkness he thought of as his own.

The lights came on in a sudden, cruel flood. He blinked beneath them, trying to make sense of what he now saw.

In Leo Falcone's arms was the same man he'd seen in the beam of the torch. The caver's helmet was shattered along one side, revealing a wet and shiny scalp, damp with blood. Something else, bone, maybe, some kind of matter, was visible beneath.

A heavy rope bound Leo Falcone and the figure in black tightly at the waist. It was tied with a serious knot and held with the kind of metal clamp that Costa remembered from his climbing days. One called a krab.

'I didn't shoot him,' Costa said quietly, almost to himself, as he watched Peroni kneel down and start to work on the rope with a penknife, Falcone struggling impatiently all the time. 'I didn't shoot him. I pointed the gun over . . .'

He paused and looked around him. Now it was lit, the room looked nothing like the place he'd pictured in his head. In truth, Costa had no idea where he'd pointed the weapon. It was stupid to have discharged it in the dark. Had it not been for the sight of Falcone, struggling with a man who'd butchered another human being not long before, he'd never have considered it.

Peroni finally worked his way through the rope then helped Falcone struggle to his feet. He wasn't even glancing in Costa's direction. He was looking at Teresa Lupo who was down by the stricken man, feeling for a pulse, starting to work the helmet off his damaged head.

'I didn't shoot him, for God's sake,' Costa said loudly, aware of the chill around him, in the team of men, more than a dozen now, who'd arrived to witness the spectacle.

'What does it matter?' one of them grunted. 'How many people did he kill anyway?'

The officer went quiet. Falcone was glowering at him, livid, looking his old self, for all the grey, sallow pain in his face.

'None,' Falcone said with a scowl. 'Absolutely' – he bent down, reached in front of Teresa Lupo and dragged the remains of the helmet off the dead man's head – 'none.'

The face was older than Nic Costa remembered from the records. But he still had a full head of bright ginger hair, now matted with blood. All the same, Dino Abati's features seemed more lined and worn than was right for a man of his age, even in death.

Costa thought again of the cleaner at the back of the incident room, someone who'd been in the Questura all evening, unquestioned, unseen.

'I didn't kill him,' Costa said again quietly, inwardly relieved.

Falcone peered down at the body which lay on the floor, bent in an awkward, prenatal crouch.

'No, you didn't. Giorgio Bramante shot the poor bastard, while you people were running around like idiots. Now he's . . . where? I don't suppose there's someone with half a brain on the door.'

It was Prinzivalli, the gruff old uniform *sovrintendente* from Milan, who finally found the courage to speak.

'We thought you were in trouble, sir,' he answered quietly, without a hint of irony. 'I'm sure I speak for everyone when I say we're delighted to see we were mistaken.'

Part 2

THE MIDNIGHT GOD

– 1 –

Arturo Messina stood on the brow of the hill at the edge of the Orange Garden, gazing out over the river, lost in thought. Next to him, Leo Falcone waited, trying to be the dutiful *sovrintendente*, struggling to find the right words with which to tell the older man, a well-established commissario, one who carried respect throughout the force, that he might be wrong. Deeply, seriously wrong, in a way that could threaten the entire investigation.

'Sir?' Falcone said quietly in a gap between the loud, throaty roars of the machinery below, two small mechanical diggers warming up their engines, awaiting orders, much like him. It was now late afternoon. Five hours had passed since the boy had first been reported missing by his father. Four hours before Messina had put out the call for the students after listening to Giorgio Bramante's story. Bramante was their professor. He knew them well and had noticed them fleeing the exit of the underground warren of tunnels when he surfaced to see if his son had somehow escaped the caves without him. In spite of hearing his calls, they had fled down the hill in the direction of the peace camp on the Circus Maximus, trying to lose themselves among 3,000 or more people living there in tents, protesting daily about the continuing horrors across the water in what had once been Yugoslavia.

Now every officer Messina could muster was on the case: half hunting for the students, the remainder working with the hundreds of civilians who kept turning up to offer their help in the search for the missing seven-year-old. There were TV crews and packs of journalists kept back from the excavation site by the yellow tape cordoning off the small park overlooking the Tiber. A growing crowd of mute bystanders, some of whom looked ready to turn ugly, was joining them. The story about the students had already got out somehow. Blame was already beginning to be apportioned, with a swiftness and certainty that gave Falcone a cold feeling in the stomach. There was a touch of the mob to some of the people lurking around the Aventino just then. Had any of those students happened to emerge in their midst, Falcone knew that he would have to act quickly to protect them from the public. Rationality and a sense of justice could fly out of the window in cases like these, depriving a good officer of the cold, detached viewpoint that was necessary in all investigations.

While the father joined – almost led – the hunt for the child, his wife was in a police van inside the cordon, saying nothing, staring at the outside world with haunted eyes that seemed to contain little in the way of hope.

And all they had to go on was the fact that, when Alessio went missing, the boy had been deep beneath the dark red earth of this quiet, residential hill, not far from a bunch of students who were probably up to no good. Students his father had heard, and gone to track down, telling his son to stay safe where he was, only to return some considerable time later – how long? No one had actually asked – to find the boy gone, and without having located the intruders either.

In public, Bramante reacted exactly how an individual was expected to in such situations, which gave Falcone pause for thought. Something about the man concerned him. He seemed too perfect, distraught to a measured degree, just enough to allow him to benefit from the sympathy of others, but never, not for one moment, sufficient to allow him to lose control.

There was also the question of the wound. Bramante had a bright red weal on his right temple, the result, he said, of a fall while stumbling through the caves, looking for his son. Injuries always interested Leo Falcone, and in normal circumstances he would have taken the opportunity to explore this one further. That, Arturo Messina expressly forbade. For him, the answer lay with the students. Falcone could not believe they would remain free for long. None had police records, though one, Toni LaMarca, came from a family known for its crime connections. They were, it seemed to him, average, ordinary young men who had gone down into the caves beneath the Aventino for reasons the police failed to understand. Messina seemed obsessed with finding out what they were. The same issue interested Falcone too, though not as much as what he regarded as more pertinent questions. What was Giorgio Bramante doing there with his son in the first place? And why did he have a livid red cut on his forehead, one that could just as easily have come from a struggle as a simple accident?

'Say it,' the older man ordered with a barely disguised impatience. 'Are you worried this will interfere with the homework for the inspector's exams or something? I always knew you were an ambitious little bastard but you could let it drop for now.'

' "Little" seems somewhat unfair, sir,' Falcone, who was somewhat taller than the portly Messina, protested dryly.

'Well? What's on your mind? This is nothing personal, you know. I think you're an excellent police officer. I just wish there was a spot more humanity at times. Cases like this . . . you walk around with that hangdog look of yours as if they don't even touch you. Shame you screwed up that marriage. Kids do wonders for putting a man in his place.'

'We're making many assumptions. I wonder if that's wise.'

'I'm stupid now, am I?'

'I didn't say that all, sir. I'm simply concerned that we don't focus on the obvious alone.'

'The reason the obvious *is* the obvious,' Messina replied testily, 'is because it's what normally gets us results. That may not be fashionable in the inspector's examination today but there it is.'

'Sir,' Falcone replied quietly. 'We don't know where the boy might be. We don't how or why any of this occurred.'

'Students!' Messina bellowed. 'Students! Like all those damned anarchists in their tents, fouling up the middle of Rome, doing whatever else they like, not that I imagine it much concerns you.'

There had been two arrests at the peace camp. They'd had more trouble at religious events. Next to a Roma versus Lazio derby it was nothing.

'I fail to see any relevance with the peace camp . . .' Falcone started to say.

'Peace camp. Peace camp? What did we find down in those damned caves again? Remind me.'

A dead bird, throat cut, and a few spent joints. It wasn't pleasant. It wasn't a hanging offence either.

'I'm not saying they weren't doing something wrong down there. I just think it's a big leap from some juvenile piece of black magic and a little dope to child abduction. Or worse.'

Messina wagged his finger in Falcone's face.

'And there – *there!* – is exactly where you're wrong. Remember what I'm saying when they make you inspector.'

'Sir,' he said, temper rising, 'this is not about me.'

'It begins with "a little dope" and the idea you can pitch a tent in the heart of Rome and tell the rest of the world to go screw itself. It ends' – he waved his big hand at the crowds behind the yellow tape – 'out there. With a bunch of people looking to us to clean up a mess we should have prevented in the first place. Good officers know you have to nip this kind of behaviour in the bud. Whatever it takes. You can't read a bunch of textbooks while the world's going to rack and ruin.'

That was a point of view with which Falcone had a finite amount of sympathy, not that he intended to expand on the point just then.

'I am merely trying to suggest that there are avenues we haven't yet explored. Giorgio Bramante—'

'Oh, for God's sake! Not that again. The man agreed to take his son to school, only to find the teachers are having one of those stupid paperwork love-ins the likes of you doubtless think pass as genuine labour. So he took him to work instead. Parents do that, Leo. I did it and, God forgive me, the boy's in the force now too.'

'I understand that . . .'

'No. You don't. You can't.'

'He didn't take him to work. He took him underground, into an excavation few people knew about, one that he believed was entirely empty.'

'My boy would have loved that when he was seven.'

'So why did he leave him there?'

Messina sighed.

'If there's a burglar in your house do you invite your son along to watch you deal with him? Well?'

'We should interview Giorgio Bramante properly. In the Questura. We should go through what happened minute by minute. He has that injury. Also . . .'

Falcone paused, knowing in his own mind that he was on the verge of being led by his imagination, not good reasoning. Nevertheless, this seemed important, and he was determined Arturo Messina should know. Watching Bramante join the search parties for Alessio on the Aventino that afternoon, Falcone felt sure, at times, that the man appeared to be looking for someone other than a minor. It was as simple as a question of posture. Children were smaller. However illogical, at close to medium quarters, one tended to adjust one's gaze accordingly. Giorgio Bramante, it seemed to him, did not. His eye level was horizontal, always, as if seeking an adult, or someone on the horizon, neither of which made sense for a seven-year-old boy.

Messina's dark eyes opened wide with astonishment as Falcone elaborated. He beckoned with his right arm towards the crowd.

'You expect me to pull him in for questioning because there's something you don't like about the angle of his head? Are you serious? What do you think they'd make of that? Them, and the media?'

'I don't care,' Falcone insisted. 'Do you? There's the question of the wound, his behaviour, and the holes in his story. Those, to my mind, are sufficient.'

'This is ridiculous. Take it from me, Leo. I'm a father too. The way he's behaving is exactly the way any of us would in the circumstances. He couldn't be more cooperative, for God's sake. How the hell would we have found our way around those caves without him? When we have those students, when we know what's happened to the kid . . . then you can sit down and go through your stupid procedures. Now tell me how we can get to that boy.'

'The injury . . .'

'You've been in those caves! It's a death trap down there. Are you honestly surprised a man should stumble in them? Do you think all the world is as perfect as you?'

Falcone had no good answer.

'I agree,' he replied, 'that it is dangerous down there. That affects our efforts to find the boy too. We've gone as far as we dare. It's treacherous. There are tunnels the military don't feel happy entering. We've heard no noises. We've brought in some equipment they use during earthquakes to locate people who are trapped. Nothing. We should pursue all possible options.'

Messina scowled.

'He could be unconscious, Leo. I know that's inconvenient but it's a fact.'

'They tell me he would still show up through thermal imaging if he was unconscious. Given the short time that's elapsed, he'd show up even if he was dead. If he's anywhere we could hope to reach, that is.'

'Oh no,' Messina said quietly, miserably, half to himself, eyes on the ground, detached from everything at that moment, even the case ahead of them.

Falcone felt briefly embarrassed. There was something in Messina's expression he didn't – couldn't – share. A man who had no experience of fatherhood could imagine the loss of a child, sympathize with it, feel anger, become determined to put the wrong right. But there was an expression in Messina's face that Falcone could only guess at. A sentiment that seemed to say: this is a part of me that's damaged – perhaps irrevocably – too.

'Don't let him be dead, Leo,' Messina moaned, and for the first time seemed, in Leo Falcone's eyes, a man beginning to show his age.

- 2 -

'Like father, like son,' Falcone murmured as the three of them shuffled into Bruno Messina's office. They were in the elevated quarters of the sixth floor. From Messina's corner room there should have been a good view of the cobbled piazza below. All they saw now was a smear of brown stone. The rain was coming down in vertical stripes. The forecast was for a period of unsettled weather lasting days: sudden storms and heavy downpours broken by outbreaks of brief bright sun. Spring was approaching, a time of extremes.

Messina sat in a leather chair behind his large, well-polished desk, trying to look like a man in control. It was an act he needed. Costa and Teresa Lupo had taken an early turn of the Questura, checking out the temperature after the disaster the night before. The place was teeming with officers. Local, pulled in from leave. Strangers, too, since Messina had demanded an external inquiry into the security lapses that allowed the attack on Falcone, wisely choosing to endure the pain of outside scrutiny before it was forced upon him. No one yet seemed much minded to blame Leo Falcone or those close to him. How could they? But the low, idle chatter had begun. Scapegoats would be sought.

The commissario had suspended the civilian security officer who had failed to spot that the ID used by Bramante to pose as a cleaner actually belonged to a woman, one whose handbag had been stolen while shopping in San Giovanni a week before and was now on vacation in Capri, a fact that would have been obvious from the personal diary that had disappeared along with the rest of her belongings. The rookie *agente* ambushed by Bramante when he took Dino Abati was now at home recovering from a bad beating, and scared witless, Costa suspected, about what would happen when the inquiry came round to him. Messina was acting with a swift, ruthless ferocity because he understood that his own position, as a commissario only a few months into the job, was damaged. That had led him to put some distance between himself and Falcone as head of the investigation, hoping perhaps to shift the blame onto his subordinate should the sky begin to fall.

The effect was not as Messina had planned. The word that was on everyone's lips that morning was 'sloppy'. The media were enjoying a field day about a murder that happened in the heart of the *centro storico*'s principal Questura. Politicians, never slow to seize an opportunity to deflect criticism from their own lapses, were starting to get in on the act. What had occurred, the wisdom inside and out of the force was beginning to say, took place because the juniors, Messina, in particular, were now in charge. They had lax standards when it came to matters of general routine. They put paperwork and procedural issues ahead of the mundane considerations of old-style policing. No one, it was whispered, had ever accused Falcone of such lapses of attention. Nor would they now throw that accusation in the direction of the fast-recovering individual who was marching around his old haunt like a man who'd rediscovered the fire in his belly.

Messina looked as if he couldn't wait to stamp that fire into ashes. The commissario watched the three of them, Falcone, Costa and Peroni, take their seats, then stated, quite flatly, 'I've brought in someone else to run this case, Falcone. Don't argue. We can't have a man heading an inquiry into his own attempted murder. The same goes for you two. There's a young inspector I want to try out. Bavetti. You'll give him every assistance . . .'

'You're making a mistake,' Falcone said without emotion.

'I'm not sure I want to hear that from you.'

'You will, nevertheless,' the inspector went on. 'I kept quiet for too long when a Messina was screwing up once before. I'm not doing it twice.'

'Dammit, Falcone! I won't be spoken to like that. You listen to me.'

'No!' the inspector yelled. 'You listen. I'm the one Giorgio Bramante came looking for last night, aren't I? These two and their women got their photos taken by that man. Doesn't that give us some rights?'

Messina folded his arms and scowled.

'No.'

'Then listen out of your own self-interest. If your old man had heard me out fourteen years ago he'd never have left the force in disgrace. Do you want to go the same way?'

Messina closed his eyes, furious. Falcone had hit the spot.

Without waiting, Falcone launched into retelling the information he'd managed to assemble overnight, speaking rapidly, fluently, without the slightest sign that he was affected by the previous year's injuries or Giorgio Bramante's more recent attentions. If anyone doubted whether the shooting in Venice had diminished the man's mental faculties, Costa thought, they were unlikely to harbour those misconceptions for long in the face of the precise, logical way Falcone painted, in a few short minutes, a picture of recent events and how he had reacted to them.

Two officers had spent the night checking with contacts in the social agencies and the hostels dealing with itinerants. It was clear Dino Abati was far from a stranger. He had made a polite street bum, one who never asked for much more than simple charity. Those who dealt with him regarded him as educated, honest, and more than a little lost. He stood out too, with that ginger head of hair and his knowledge of the city. Given the facts – Abati was in Italy, outside the normal system of ID checks, social security records and tax payments – the street was an obvious place to look for him. Bramante just happened to be several steps ahead of them.

*

Abati had been due to spend the previous night in a hostel run by an order of monks near Termini. At eleven in the evening, after his free meal and an evening spent watching TV, a member of staff had found an anonymous letter addressed to him, left in the hostel entrance, at the front desk, by an unseen visitor. Abati read the letter then, without saying a word, walked out of the building.

They had recovered the document from a rubbish bin in the communal living room, next to the TV set. It said, simply: *Dino. I was talking to Leo Falcone earlier today. You remember him? He thought it was time the two of you met up. I tend to agree. The sooner the better. Or should we discuss this face to face? Giorgio.*

'Wonderful,' Messina groaned. 'This man is three steps ahead of us all the way. What is he? Psychic or something?'

'Tell him,' Falcone said icily.

Costa kept it short. He'd made this call himself, to Dino Abati's mother, after the local force had broken the bad news, just after eight that morning. Three months before, she'd received a letter, supposedly from the missing Sandro Vignola, asking urgently for Abati's where-abouts. It had contained personal details which made her believe the message was genuine. They were, when Costa checked, the kind of information Bramante, as his professor, would have known: birth dates, home addresses, student haunts in Rome.

'So,' Messina acknowledged with little grace, 'you have got something.'

'More than that,' Costa went on. 'We're checking with the other families too. The Belluccis say they got a similar letter, just as convinc-ing, several months before Raul died. It's a reasonable bet we'll find out the same method was used with the others. That was how Bramante tracked them down.'

The commissario's face fell.

'And we never found out?' he asked, incredulous.

'You said it yourself,' Falcone replied. 'They were distant cases, handled by different forces. No one made the link. Why should they? There's more. Early this morning we sent men round to each of the obvious hostels you'd expect a well-mannered itinerant to use.'

Costa smiled. It was a typical Falcone shot in the dark. Nine out of ten times they never paid off. Then . . .

'Four others close to the Questura, ones that knew Abati, had received an identical letter last night,' Costa said. 'It was delivered some time in the early evening. The one in the Campo has CCTV of the person responsible. He was wearing a cleaner's uniform, with the name of the same private company we use for housekeeping. Their office reported a break-in the previous night. Clothing and money were taken. Bramante planned to drive Abati towards the Questura. Where else would he go? And if he didn't turn up, Bramante had Leo . . . Inspector Falcone. It's called covering your options.'

Messina swore under his breath.

'Good work, Agente,' he muttered.

'I just go where I'm told, sir.'

That was true too. What had occurred possessed Giorgio Bramante's style, something Leo Falcone had recognized from the outset. Everything was planned, down to the last detail, with alternatives should the original scheme go awry.

Even so, Costa felt uneasy. Bramante could have killed both Abati and Leo at that last moment, finished his list for good. And there would have been a good few reading their newspapers the next day who would have felt some sympathy with him.

Instead, Bramante let Leo live, and that seemed to engage – almost infuriate – the inspector more than ever. Costa had seen this steely glint in his eye before, just not for a while. It was obsessive, and not simply because of the personal dimension. The case had become the entire focus of Falcone's world. Nothing now mattered until every last unresolved detail – and that included the fate of Alessio Bramante – was brought to a satisfactory conclusion.

'Look, Leo.' Messina sounded a little conciliatory. 'Put yourself in my position. You're involved in this case. All three of you.'

'We were involved yesterday,' Falcone pointed out. 'It didn't seem to worry you then.'

Messina looked dejected. He wasn't entirely his own man, Costa thought. There would be pressure from above. A young commissario's career could hang on how he handled difficult cases like this.

'Yesterday I thought this was going to be simple. Either you brought in Bramante quickly and covered yourself in a little glory. Or you fouled up and – let's be honest with one another – that would be an end to it. You could retire. Like my father.'

Falcone was unmoved.

'I still don't see what's changed.'

'What's changed? I'll tell you! This bloodthirsty animal isn't running from us. He's got the damn nerve to bring his murderous habits right to our own doorstep. That's an entirely different game. I can't make . . .' He glanced away from them for a moment. 'I can't base my decisions on personal issues. I just want this whole mess cleaned up. Now. For good. With no more bodies. Unless it's Giorgio Bramante's. He's caused us enough grief for one lifetime.'

Peroni leaned forward and tapped the desk hard with his fat index finger.

'You think we want otherwise?'

'No,' Messina admitted, shrinking back into his leather chair. No one liked the look of Peroni when he was getting mad. 'I just don't intend to take any more risks. How would the three of you feel about a little holiday? I'll pick up the bill. Just watch the drinks. Sicily maybe. Take your women along. The pathologist too. Two weeks. A month. I don't mind.'

They looked at one another. It was Peroni who spoke first.

'What kind of men do you think we are?'

'Meaning?' the commissario replied warily.

Peroni answered straight away.

'What kind of serving police officer walks away from a case like this? All to sit in some out-of-season hotel swilling down wine at the taxpayers' expense just because you don't like having us around?'

'It's not that—' Messina began to say.

'What kind of senior officer would even contemplate offering such a thing?' Peroni added, interrupting him.

Messina picked up a pen and waved it in the big man's direction.

'The kind of officer who doesn't like going to funerals. Is that so bad? Understand this. I don't know if I can keep you alive. Any of you. If I can't guarantee your safety in the Questura, where the hell am I supposed to put you? In jail? How would you run an investigation from there, Leo? Answer me that.'

Falcone thought about it for a very short moment.

'I keep this case for two more days. I give you my word I won't put myself in the way of danger. Costa and Peroni here, it's up to them. I think they can look after one another.'

'Correct, sir,' Costa said.

'If there's no concrete progress,' Falcone continued, 'if I don't seem to be on the point of closing Bramante down after forty-eight hours, you give the whole show to Bavetti. That's the deal.'

Messina laughed. It didn't seem to be a sound he made often.

'A deal? A deal? Who the hell do you think you are to come in here and offer me deals? You're a cripple living on past gratitude. Don't stretch my patience.'

'Those are my conditions.'

Messina made that strange dry noise again.

'Conditions. And if I say go to hell?'

'Then I quit,' Falcone replied. 'Then I do something I've never even contemplated before. I walk straight out there and tell those jackals from the newspapers why.'

'Quit,' Peroni repeated. 'I love that word.'

Then he reached into his jacket pocket, pulled out his wallet, withdrew his police ID card and placed it on the desk.

Costa watched, did the same, then added the handgun he'd used to no good purpose the previous night.

Peroni looked at the weapon, then glanced at him.

'You never really liked guns, did you, Nic?'

'There are a lot of things in this job you get to dislike,' Costa said, not shifting his attention from the senior officer on the other side of the desk for one moment. 'It's all a question of learning to live with them.'

Messina glared at them from across the polished desk.

'I'll remember this, you bastards,' he muttered, furious. 'Forty-eight hours, Falcone. After that it's not Giorgio Bramante you have to worry about. It's me.'

– 3 –

They had breakfast in the conservatory: coffee and pastries, and a view out to the Duomo. The weather had changed. Rain clouds had thrown a grey-winged embrace around the hilltop town of Orvieto. There would be no walks today, as the two men had planned. Instead she'd rest, and think about the case a little. Not too much, though. She still felt tired, a little wrong, and it wasn't just being disturbed by Nic's call and the frenzy that followed. She hadn't gone to bed until three, which was how long it had taken to discover he was safe. Even then she hadn't slept well. She couldn't stop thinking of the missing Alessio Bramante, wondering whether Nic's customary, selfless optimism could possibly be correct. Instinct told her the opposite. Instinct was sometimes to be avoided.

Pietro had stayed the night. He looked a little the worse for wear. So did Raffaela, if Emily was honest with herself. She'd retired to a corner with a coffee and a newspaper after a brief conversation between the two of them, an exchange of short pleasantries, a question about Emily's health, a mutual sharing of observations about the predictable nature of men. In spite of the commotion in the Questura, Falcone had never phoned. Nor had he returned Raffaela's call when, in desperation, she attempted to reach him around two. Emily tried to tell her he'd be busy. It hadn't cut much ice. It hadn't deserved to.

Then, after Arturo and Pietro had carefully tidied away the cups and plates, Emily retreated to the study, fired up the computer, spent thirty minutes reading the American papers online: the *Washington Post*, the *New York Times*. Familiar pillars she could lean on from time to time, established icons that never changed, were always there when you needed them. It wasn't the news she sought. It was their presence. Emily Deacon had spent more of her life in Italy than her native America. All the same, she knew she wasn't fully a part of the country she was coming to regard as her home. She lacked the true Roman's frank, open, immediate attitude to existence. She didn't want to face the good and the bad head on, day in, day out. Sometimes it was best to circumvent the subject, to pretend it didn't exist. To lie a little, in the hope that some time soon, tomorrow perhaps, next week, or maybe even never, one could hope to stare the day down without blinking.

And so she read idly, of a world of politics that was now foreign to her, of football games and movie stars, bestsellers she'd never heard of and corporate scandals that mattered not a jot in Italy. After a while Arturo Messina came in with coffee, which she refused. He then sat down in the large, comfy leather chair at the end of the desk, took a sip of his own, and said, very politely, 'You're using too much of my electricity, Emily. Unless you tell me that's something other than Alessio Bramante you're hunting on my computer I will, I swear, turn the damn thing off.'

'I was reading about the New York Mets,' she said, and it was only half a lie. She'd been about to follow up on Nic's comments about what happened to abducted children, and how they were absorbed by the alien culture in which they found themselves. 'But I'm done.'

She leaned back, shut her eyes, and took a deep breath. It would be a long day, with very little to fill it.

'I talked to your Nic last night,' he revealed. 'He's a little concerned about your health. I didn't realize . . .'

Arturo nodded in the direction of Emily's stomach.

'Congratulations. In my day we had this antiquated habit of getting married first then bringing the babies along a little later. But I am, of course, part-dinosaur so what do I know?

'It's the biggest adventure a couple can take together,' Arturo went on. 'Whatever it costs. However painful it is at times, and it will be, I can promise you that. Still, you have to remind yourself. Children give you more than you can possibly imagine. They bring you back down to earth, and make you realize that's the right place to be. When you watch them growing, day by day, you understand we're all just small and mortal and we'd best make the most of what we have. You realize we're all just here for a little time, and now you have something to whom you can pass on a little of yourself before you go. So you lose a few shreds of your arrogance if you're lucky. You're not the same person any more.'

'People tell me that.'

'But you don't understand. None of us ever do. Not till it happens. And then . . .'

A shadow of concern crossed his face.

'Then you can't see the world in any other way,' he continued. 'This is, I suspect, a failing in a police officer. Emily, I don't want to talk about the case if it upsets you. This is a very serious affair. I've asked the local police to put an armed car on the gate here. I don't want you to feel insecure for any reason. Or unhappy. Just read a book. I'll fetch something from town if you like. I can probably get you a real American paper.'

She stared at the distant black and white cathedral, shining under the drenching rain.

'He wouldn't come here, Arturo. This is about Rome. He's playing out his final act. He wouldn't want it anywhere else.'

He laughed.

'I can see why Leo sent you those papers. I wish I'd had someone like you around all those years ago.'

It had to be said.

'You had Leo.'

'I know,' he replied, with some obvious regret. 'And I was very hard on him. Cruel. I don't think that's too strong a word. He brought that out in me. Few people do. But Leo was so damned resolute. As if none of it really touched him. It was just another case. He can be so . . . infuriating. With that cold, detached manner of his.'

'That's not the real Leo. He's a considerate man at heart. He feels the need to suppress that sometimes. I don't know why.'

Arturo raised one bushy eyebrow.

'I'll take your word on that. All the same, I owe him an apology. I keep thinking of what happened then. The stupid, bull-headed way I handled everything. I should have listened to him more. But . . .' He didn't finish the sentence.

'But what?'

'I told you! I was a father too. Leo wasn't. We were two human beings looking at the same facts from different parts of the universe. All I could think of was Alessio Bramante, somewhere inside that blasted hill. Hurt, perhaps. Unconscious. Capable of being rescued, and that is what any father would hope to do in those circumstances. It's a bug, something genetic that just leaps out from under your skin. Save the child. Always save the child, and ask questions later. Every-thing else was a side issue. Leo has this insufferable ability to detach himself from the emotional side of a case. I resented that.'

He dashed back the last of his coffee.

'I envied it, to be honest,' he added. 'He was right. I was wrong. I knew that back then but I was too stubborn to admit it. We should have been asking a lot more while we were trying to find Alessio. But Giorgio Bramante was a good, well-connected, middle-class university professor. And they were a bunch of grubby, dope-smoking students. It all seemed so obvious. I was a fool.'

She reached over and touched his hand. Something seemed to stir inside her at that moment. A warm feeling below the pit of her stomach. It was impossible to tell whether the sensation was good or bad, pleasure or pain.

'We don't know what happened, Arturo. Still. Perhaps those students did kill Alessio. Accidentally, maybe. The caves were danger-ous. Perhaps the child simply escaped them and fell down some hole. And they were too frightened to admit their part in it all. Or . . .'

Nic's idea wouldn't leave her, and it wasn't just because its very substance was so typical of his character, such a telling reminder of why she loved him.

'Perhaps he's still alive.'

He glanced at her, then his eyes meandered to the window, not before she noticed some sadness in them. She hadn't seen that before.

'He's not alive, Emily. Don't fool yourself. That's no way to approach anything.'

'We don't know,' she insisted. 'We're in the dark about so many things. Why the boy was there. Why Bramante left him in the first place. The truth is we don't understand much of anything about that man.'

'That's true,' Arturo admitted miserably.

'Even now,' she went on. 'Where the hell is he? He must have access to equipment. To money. To the news. But I can't believe he's holed up in some apartment somewhere. It would be too dangerous, and Giorgio Bramante isn't a man who'll take unnecessary risks. Not when he thinks he's got unfinished business.'

He brightened immediately.

'Come, come. It's obvious where Giorgio is, don't you think?'

'It is?'

'Of course! He spent most of his life in the Rome the rest of us never see. Underground. Have you never been there?'

'Only once. I went to Nero's Golden House. It made me feel claustrophobic.'

'Hah! Let an old policeman tell you something. The Domus Aurea is just one tiny fraction of what's left. There's an entire underground city down there, almost as big as it was in Caesar's day. There are houses and temples, entire streets. Some of them have been excavated. Some of them were just never fully filled with earth for some reason. I talked to a couple of the cavers Leo called in. They hero-worshipped Giorgio. The man had been to places the rest of them could only dream about. Half of them unmapped. That's where he is, Emily. Not that it does us any good now, does it? If we wanted to find Giorgio today, the best person to ask would be . . . Giorgio! Wonderful.'

She thought about this, and the stirring in her stomach ceased.

'I imagine you never put much store in forensic, did you?'

'Not unless I was really desperate,' he admitted. 'That's all they think of these days, isn't it? Sitting around waiting for some civilian in a white coat to stare at a test tube then point at a suspect line-up and say, "That one". Use it if you have to. But crimes are committed by people. If you want answers, ask a human being. Not a computer.'

'I have a pathologist friend you should meet. She half agrees with you.'

'She does?'

He looked puzzled.

'I said "half". Now, may I make a call?'

Arturo Messina passed over the handset, then, out of idle curiosity, plugged in the conference phone too.

He listened to the brief, lucid and highly pointed conversation that followed then observed, 'I would like to meet this Doctor Lupo some time. You should rest now. The men here must think about lunch.'

- 4 -

The prevailing wind had changed direction overnight. Now it was a strong, blustery westerly, drawing moisture and a bone-chilling cold from the grey, flat waters of the Mediterranean before rolling over the airport and the flatlands of the estuarial Tiber to form a heavy black blanket of cloud, killing the light, casting the city in a monotone shade of grey.

They were standing in the Piazza dei Cavalieri di Malta, shivering against the cold, wondering where to begin. Get nosy, Falcone said. It was, for him, an exceptionally vague command.

Peroni was crouching down, peering through the keyhole.

'I can't see a thing,' he complained. 'Are you sure about this? It's not just one of your tricks?'

'What tricks?' Costa complained, pushing him out of the way to look for himself.

The avenue of cypresses was there as he remembered, and the gravel path, now shiny with the morning rain. His own father had showed him this small secret when Costa was no more than a boy. That day the sun had been shining. He could still recall St Peter's standing proud and grand across the river, set perfectly at the centre of the frame made by the trees and the path under a blue sky the colour of a thrush's egg. But today all he saw after the dark green lines of foliage was a grey, shapeless mass of cloud, deep swirls of cumulus channelling down onto the city, obscuring everything it consumed.

From the corner behind them, which led off in the direction of the Circus Maximus, came a sound that reminded them why they were there. The school was enjoying playtime. The noise of happy young voices rose above the high wall keeping it from the public, a vibrant clamour of life protected from the harshness of the world by Piranesi's tall, white defences, like the ramparts of some small, fairy-tale castle.

'I'm sure,' Costa said and took his head away from the door. The two Carabinieri who were always stationed here, for some bizarre reason deputed to guard the mansion of the Knights of Malta, were looking at them, interested.

'Childhood memories are rarely reliable, Nic,' Peroni declared with a sage nod. 'I spent years convinced I had an aunt Alicia. Right up to the age of . . . oh, twelve or so. The poor woman was completely fictitious. Which was a shame because she was a sight nicer than most of my family.'

He hesitated, looking a little embarrassed.

One of the blue uniforms came over and gave them an evil look.

'What do you want?' the younger of the two Carabinieri asked. He was about Costa's age, taller, good-looking but with a pinched, arrogant face that had an unpleasant turn to it.

'A little comradely help wouldn't go amiss,' Peroni replied, pulling out his ID card and the most recent photo they had of Giorgio Bramante. 'Please tell me this charming individual is fast asleep on a bench round the corner somewhere. We can deal with him after that. No problem.'

– 5 –

Leo Falcone knew it had to be said. Out of necessity. And to bring Arturo Messina back down to earth.

'He could be somewhere else altogether,' Falcone insisted. 'Perhaps they argued. The child ran away . . .'

Messina's scowl returned.

'They didn't argue. The father would have mentioned it. I do wish you'd concentrate on what's important here, Leo. The missing boy.'

'I am,' Falcone replied sharply. 'There's very little left for us to do other than the obvious. The Army have sent in two more specialists to see how far they can get. Those caves are unmapped. From what I've been told some probably run as far down as ground level, then to springs or waterways. The channels could be just large enough for a child, but too small for anyone else.'

Messina nodded at the two small excavators that had been brought there on his personal orders.

'From what I've seen of the map we can lift the lid off the whole thing in thirty minutes. Like taking the roof off an ants' nest. We could see right inside.'

Falcone had been hoping it wouldn't come to this.

'It's not that simple. This is a protected historical site. It was before anyone knew the full truth about what Bramante found here. Now they understand that, the city authorities would have to give permission. Bramante himself would be involved.'

Messina glowered at him.

'There's a child's life at stake here! And you're talking about paperwork again?'

'I'm merely reminding you of the facts.'

'Really. Go get me Giorgio Bramante. Now!'

It took fifteen minutes, during which Falcone received a phone call he'd been half expecting. Bramante was with a team of uniformed officers and civilians combing the grass verge of the rough field that fell down from the Orange Garden towards the winding road that led to the Tiber. He came without a question, without protest. He had a dark, bleak look on his face by this stage. It didn't stop him staring at the photographers when they found him, or pausing briefly to talk to the reporters to make another plea for assistance from the public. The mark on his forehead was a little less livid. Soon, it would look like a simple bruise.

Falcone waited until this short interview was over, saying nothing in response to their questions, wishing more than ever that he could get Bramante alone in a room to himself for a little while. Then they walked to join Arturo Messina who still stood above the entrance to the excavations, staring down at the culvert with its old iron gates, now unlocked. This was a small indentation in the Aventino, almost like a bomb crater, a pocket of flat land on the hill which was reached by a little path that wound down from the park. The miniature excavators had made their way along it. Their operators now sat on the machines which rumbled in the warm late afternoon air, like iron beasts of burden resting before the exertions they knew were to come.

'There's news?' Bramante asked the moment they arrived.

'No—' Messina began to say, then Falcone interrupted him.

'We have Ludo Torchia, sir. He was picked up in a bar the students use in Testaccio. Somewhat drunk. He's at the Questura now.'

An unexpected grin broke Messina's gloomy features.

'See, Giorgio! I told you. We make progress.'

The man wasn't paying much attention. He was staring down at the excavators.

'What are you doing?' Bramante asked warily.

'Nothing,' Messina answered. 'Without your permission.'

Bramante shook his head.

'This is . . .' The digger drivers were looking up at them in anticipation. 'A historic site. You can't just destroy it . . . Not again.'

Messina put a hand on his shoulder.

'We can't go any further down there without those machines. If the boy's still inside we could lift off the roof and see a hell of a lot more than we can now.'

'It's irreplaceable.' He shook his head again, then added, sourly, 'I suppose it's too much to expect the likes of you to appreciate.'

Arturo Messina blinked, somewhat taken aback by this vacillation.

'You're exhausted. It's understandable. You don't have to be here,' Messina continued. 'Go home to your wife. You've done everything you can. This is our job now. I'll send someone to be with you. Falcone. Or someone less miserable.'

Bramante glanced at them and licked his lips.

'You've got Ludo,' he said quietly. 'I know him. If I speak to him, perhaps he'll see sense. He wouldn't want this damaged either. Just give me some time.'

Falcone was shuffling from side to side, frantically coughing into his fist. Interviews in the Questura were for police officers, lawyers and suspects. Not the desperate parents of missing children.

'Let me think about this,' Messina replied. 'Falcone. Take Giorgio back to the Questura with you. I'll be along very shortly. I want to see what happens here. And *I* begin the questioning. No one else. Well?'

Falcone didn't move.

'An interview conducted in the presence of a potential witness, as Professore Bramante undoubtedly is, would be . . . rather unorthodox. It could cause problems with the lawyers. Immense problems.'

Messina smiled then put his hand on Falcone's arm and squeezed. Hard.

'Fuck the lawyers, Leo,' he said cheerfully. 'Now off with you.'

Falcone caught the expression in his superior's eye. Messina wanted the two of them out of there. He wasn't waiting for anyone.

'Sir,' Falcone replied, and led Giorgio Bramante to a squad car, closed the door on him, and ordered the driver to take the man to the Questura to await his arrival.

After which, he lit a cigarette, took two rapid draws from it, then threw the thing beneath one of the parched orange trees.

The relationship was damaged already, Falcone thought. There was no more harm to be done.

He walked back and joined Messina who stared at him, furious.

'You're disobeying my orders. How do you think that will look on the report sheet when it comes to the promotions board?'

'There's something wrong here,' Falcone replied. 'You know it. I know it. We have to—'

'No!' Messina barked. 'That boy's missing. Once those machines go in, I could turn him up at any moment. Until we get to the bottom of that, I don't give a shit what you think, or what Giorgio Bramante gets up to. Understood?'

- 6 -

The older Carabinieri officer laughed. It wasn't an entirely unpleasant sound.

'You think we don't know who Giorgio Bramante is?' he asked. 'We work the Aventino. We're not strangers here.'

'So you've seen him?' Costa asked.

The two of them exchanged sly glances. It wasn't supposed to happen like this. They were rival forces, one civilian, one military. Not exactly at loggerheads, but rarely bosom friends either.

'Listen,' Peroni went on in his best, charming voice, one that was at odds with his thug-like build and appearance, 'we can either play the game and pretend we don't exist. Or we can have an easy, amicable chat and then go our own ways. I won't tell if you won't. Where's the harm in that?'

'He came here two or three weeks ago,' the older one said, and got a filthy look from his colleague for his pains. 'He put some flowers down in the park over there. Where the kid went missing, I guess.'

'No one ever said he was a bad father,' Peroni agreed.

That got the young one going.

'He was the best kind of father you could get, wasn't he? Some scum go and kill his kid like that. What the hell do you expect? If you've got kids . . .'

'You've got kids?' Costa asked.

'No,' the young one answered with a surly expression.

'Then—' Costa was beginning to say until a painful dig in the ribs from Peroni stopped him.

'I've got kids,' the big man went on. 'If anyone touched them . . .'

'Quite,' the young one nodded.

'He never came back?' Costa asked.

The two of them glanced at each other again.

'The wife did,' the older one replied. 'We didn't know who she was until one of the mothers from the school pointed her out. No one gets to keep any secrets around here. It's that kind of place.'

'What did she do?' Peroni asked.

He grimaced. He seemed a decent man.

'She put down some flowers too. Then she sat in that park for hours. It got so late I wondered if I shouldn't have gone and talked to her. It was freezing, for God's sake. But she went in the end.'

The officer hesitated, wondering whether to say what was in his head.

'You think he might be around here?' he asked finally. 'After what went on in the Questura last night? What a mess. I don't envy you cleaning up after that.'

Peroni patted him on the arm and said, very sincerely, 'Thanks.'

'Lax,' the young one said. 'Downright lax. That's what it was.'

The older one rolled his eyes, looked at his colleague, then said, with a sad air of resignation, 'You know, I wish you'd keep your mouth shut a little more often. It just leaks out crap day after day.'

'I said . . .' He was getting red in the face.

'I don't care what you said. These men asked for our help. If we can give it to them we do.'

Not a word.

'One thing,' the friendly one continued, nodding at his colleague. '*He* spoke to Bramante. Didn't you, now? He walked right up to him, as if the man was a football star or something. Did you get an autograph, huh, Fabiano? Have you washed your hand since he shook it or what?'

Fabiano's face got a touch redder.

'I told him what I thought. That he ought never to have gone to jail for what he did.'

197

'You mean for killing someone?' his colleague demanded. 'Doesn't look like it was that much out of character either, does it?'

'I'm just saying . . .'

'I don't want to hear what you have to say. Here' – he took a note out of his pocket and threw it at the officer – 'go down the road and buy me a coffee. The usual. One for yourself if you want it. And two for our friends here.'

'We don't have time,' Costa said. 'But thanks anyway.'

They watched the younger Carabinieri shuffle off across the road, tail between his legs.

'You know what worries me?' the man said, shaking his head. 'If it all happened again, same situation, same people, an idiot like Fabiano there would make exactly the same mistakes. He'd still think he could fix it all with his fists.'

He peered into their faces.

'Let me tell you two something. He was no hero. I don't judge people on how they look. I'm not that stupid. But there was something about him. He let that moron of mine suck up to him as if he was God or something. It was . . . bad.'

Peroni nodded.

'Understood.'

'No. Listen. I'm not so good with words. Meeting him felt very creepy. Same with his wife too. I've seen what happens when you lose a kid. It's not easy. But all those years on, looking as if it happened yesterday . . .'

Costa hadn't given Beatrice Bramante much thought. Rosa Prabakaran was keeping an eye on her. If she was involved, she'd surely keep away from her ex-husband from now on.

'Do you think the two of them met? The wife and the husband?' he asked.

'I didn't see it. They came here on different days. Who's to know?'

He seemed as if he needed that coffee. And something else too. As if he wanted to say what was on his mind before his colleague returned.

'I'll tell you one thing, though. It wasn't just the once. He came back one more time. Five days, a week or so ago. Went in that place over there.'

He pointed along the square, to a small dark door with a sign by it, unreadable from this angle.

'There being . . .?' Peroni prompted him.

'Where he used to work,' the officer said, as if it were obvious. 'Where all those archaeologists are doing whatever they do. He went in there and didn't we just know about it. They were shouting and yelling. We could hear them from here. I was about to go and ask whether someone needed a little help. But then he came out again, face like thunder, then just walked off down the road as if nothing had happened.'

Costa stared at the sign on the wall: the archaeology department of La Sapienza had a small office here, hidden behind a wall, just like the mansion of the Knights of Malta. Giorgio Bramante had turned down his old job. But he'd returned to where he used to work in any case, and he wasn't a man who did anything without a reason.

'Are they still investigating the site?' he asked. 'The place where Alessio went missing?'

The Carabinieri officer shook his head.

'Not if they've any sense. It's all cordoned off down there. Whatever happened to it back then left the whole area a death trap. Every time it rains badly we have a mud fall. Kids mess around in it from time to time. If we find them they go home with boxed ears. And I mean boxed. I don't want them coming back.'

Peroni looked at Costa, stared at his shoes and sighed.

'What's wrong?' the officer asked.

'I just cleaned them this morning,' he moaned.

– 7 –

It was almost seven before Arturo Messina felt able to leave the Aventino. A lazy orange sun hung over the Tiber. Its mellowing evening rays turned the river below into a bright still snake of golden water, patterned on both sides by two slow-moving lines of traffic. The squad car, with its blue flashing light and siren, worked its way through them laboriously. He didn't have the heart to yell at the driver to make better progress.

He cast a final glance back towards the hill. There were crowds gathered on the Lungotevere below, and on the brow too. No one moved much. Even the jackals of the press were beginning to look bored. Messina had been a police officer all his life, worked uniform, plain clothes, everything, before joining the management ladder. He understood that feeling of stasis, of wading through mud, that gripped an investigation when the first buzz of adrenalin and opportunity was lost. There were now only a few hours of light left. The machines had struggled against the patch of ground hanging precipitately beneath the Orange Garden. What initially seemed a simple task had turned into a nightmarish attempt to shift a small mountain of earth and soft stone that kept collapsing in on itself. The amateurish surveyor supplied by the company that brought in the excavators appeared hopelessly out of his depth. Not one of the archaeologists from Bramante's team was willing to help; they were too infuriated by what was happening. With Giorgio Bramante departed to the Questura there was no one in the vicinity who could give them an expert opinion on how best to proceed.

So they blundered on, Messina naively believing the job would become simpler as they progressed. Like scooping out the top of an ants' nest and peering inside, he'd told Leo Falcone. He was fooling himself. The truth was much more messy. The nest was long dead. The interior was a labyrinth of tunnels and crevices, dangerous, friable, liable to collapse. One of the excavator drivers had been making noises about quitting because it was too risky to continue. The Army sappers had withdrawn and sat watching the proceedings from the grassy mound by the park, smoking, an expression on their faces that said: amateurs. The machines had already reduced to rubble what, to Messina's untrained eye, looked like some extensive underground temple, shattering visible artefacts, ploughing the remains, and what seemed to be a plentiful scattering of broken bones, back into the red earth. There would, he knew, be a price to pay.

None of which mattered. Only one thing did. Of little Alessio Bramante there wasn't a sign. Not a shred of clothing, a footprint in the dirt, a distant cry, a faint breath or heartbeat picked up by the sensitive machines Falcone had brought to bear on the job.

Messina stared out at the traffic and said to himself: a boy cannot disappear magically of his own accord. Their only hope now was to prise some truth from Ludo Torchia. And soon. Whatever it took.

He sat upfront in the car as usual. He didn't like to think of himself as a superior. He was their leader. The man who showed them the way forward. That was what troops – and police officers were troops of a kind, even if they weren't Carabinieri – needed.

The driver was one of the uniformed men he used regularly. Taccone, an uninspired but essentially decent drone in his mid-thirties, someone who was struggling to master the *sovrintendente* exams. Not a bright, ambitious, questioning individual like Falcone. A commissario needed his foot soldiers, Messina thought, just as much as a good officer.

'What would you do if someone took your kid like that?' Messina asked, not much expecting an answer.

Taccone turned and stared at him. There was something Messina had never seen in his eyes before.

'Just what anyone would do,' Taccone said quietly. 'I'd take the scumbag into a small, quiet room. I'd make sure there was no one around I couldn't trust. Then . . .'

He was a big man. He'd probably done it before, Messina guessed.

'Those days are past, my friend. We live in regulated times. Procedure is what matters. The fine print of the law. Working by the book.'

The traffic was getting worse and worse. The flashing blue light and the siren were doing them no favours. Cars, buses and trucks blocked both sides of the Lungotevere as it wound past the small piazza of the Bocca della Verità. The peace camp occupied almost the entire area of the Circus Maximus beyond, a ragtag army of tents and bodies sprawled beneath the evening sun, covering every inch of the bare and scratchy green grass that had once been an Imperial racetrack.

Taccone swore, ran the police Lancia up onto the broad pedestrian pavement, floored the pedal and drove a good 400 metres, scattering walkers, not minding whom he pissed off. Then he found a break by the next lights, forced his way into the moving traffic flow, began bullying everything else off the road.

They were outside the Questura in a matter of minutes. A mob of reporters, photographers and TV crews milled around the entrance. They knew a suspect was inside the building, Messina guessed. Even if some creep inside the force hadn't told them for a few illicit lire, Giorgio Bramante surely had when he arrived. He was that kind of man. He rose to the media, whatever advice he received to the contrary. Bramante felt wronged, and a man who was wronged would always be moved more by a sense of injustice than common prudence.

Taccone braked hard to a halt, scattering the scrambling hacks.

He turned and stared balefully at Messina.

'Those days are only past, sir,' he said slowly, 'if we allow it.'

– 8 –

When Emily called she suggested it might be a good idea to tie up soil samples and any other ground artefacts. She didn't say: I'm fine, don't worry, and by the way, it's very nice holed up out here in some swanky mansion in Orvieto while you play cut and stitch with the latest corpse on the production line.

Americans, Teresa Lupo said quietly to herself. Everyone needed a work ethic. The trouble was they craved one even when they weren't working.

Fifteen minutes later the thing crawled out of dead Toni LaMarca's throat. She screamed when she saw it. This was a first in the morgue. So was the worm. She'd seen many strange items on the shining silver table that was the focal point of her working life. None had yet scared her, not seriously. But watching – close up, since she was taking a good look at the dead man's face at the time – a pale flabby beast with prominent eyes and a triangular head, its whole slimy body the length of a little finger, slowly wriggle its way out of a dead man's throat then settle on his lips was enough to make her shriek, something Silvio Di Capua found extraordinarily amusing.

Thirty minutes later Silvio had called in the friend of a friend who turned out to be Cristiano, the evolutionary biologist from La Sapienza. Cristiano was one of the tallest human beings Teresa Lupo had ever seen, a good head higher than both she and Silvio, as thin as a rake, utterly bald, with a cadaverous face and bulbous eyes. He could have been anywhere between nineteen and thirty-seven, but he didn't look the type to be interested in girls.

The worm turned him on.

He spent thirty minutes peering at it from every angle through a magnifying glass then asked, anxiously, 'Can I keep it?'

'The worm is in police custody, Cristiano,' Teresa explained patiently. 'We can't let a creature like that go walkabout simply because you've taken a fancy to him.'

'It's not a him. It's a him and a her. Planarians are simultaneous hermaphrodites. This little fellow . . .'

She closed her eyes and sighed, unable to believe anyone could talk so affectionately about the disgusting piece of white slime now meandering around the small specimen dish Silvio had found for it.

'. . . pre-dates the ice age. They have the sexual appetite of a seventies rock star. Five times a day man if he can lay hold of a partner, and he doesn't much care about the condition either. Also, if you chop him in half he can grow a new head or tail. Or even several.'

'So "he" is a he,' she observed slyly.

'I was being conversational for a lay audience,' Cristiano insisted.

'You're too kind. Does he have a name?'

'Two. We used to call him *Dugesia polychroa*. Then they decided some dead academic called Schmidt, who did a lot of work on the subject, needed something to be remembered by. So it got changed to *Schmidtea polychroa*.'

'Cristiano,' she said, taking his skinny arm. 'Let me be candid with you. Things are just a touch busy around here at the moment. For example, this "little fellow" worked its way out of the open mouth of a gentleman who got his heart hosed out in a slaughterhouse, and that doesn't happen too often. Also, last night someone broke into the Questura, probably looking to kill a good friend of mine, then shot dead a potentially important witness in this very case. I hope to work my way round to him a little later. My colleague Silvio was of the opinion that this creature might provide some significant information for us. It would delight me immensely if you could give me some small clue as to whether he's correct.'

She paused for effect, then demanded, 'What is it?'

'A flatworm.'

'Just any old flatworm?'

Silvio got in on the act.

'There's no such thing as "any old flatworm", Teresa. If you'd spent a moment reading a few papers on evolutionary biology you'd know that. These things . . .'

'Shut up!' She squeezed Cristiano's arm. 'Just tell me, before you go, how it got there. Could it have been inside him when he was alive?'

'Are you serious?' he asked, big eyes bulging. 'Who'd let that crawl down their throat?'

'I meant as a parasite or something. Like a fluke.'

'Planarians aren't parasites!'

He looked as if she'd insulted a relative.

'What are they then?'

'Scavengers, mainly. They feed on dead meat.'

'So it could have crawled down his mouth when he was dead? Or unconscious?'

He shook his bald head in violent disagreement.

'Not while he was unconscious. These things didn't live that long by being stupid. They stay away from anything that's breathing unless it's smaller. They're pretty good at devouring young earthworms if they can catch them but that's as far as it goes.'

She thought about this.

'Habitat,' she said. 'They live in the earth. They come out when they're hungry. This man was found in a crypt alongside a hundred or so skeletons from the Middle Ages or whenever. A natural place for them, I guess.'

'No.'

She wished he wouldn't treat her like an idiot, just because she hadn't spent a joyous afternoon inside the pages of *Lifestyles of Rich and Famous Worms* lately.

'Why not?'

'Where's the food? Where's the water? They need water. Without it . . .'

That ruled out one way Toni LaMarca could have got a slimy white flatworm down his throat.

'How about a slaughterhouse?' she suggested. 'They're full of meat. Water, too. They could just come out of the drains at night for a munch on the leftovers.'

Silvio sniffed.

'That was a very clean slaughterhouse,' he said. 'I took a good look at those drains. They were putting all the right chemicals down them. I doubt anything could live if it got that much disinfectant poured on its head every night. I know I couldn't.'

She looked at Cristiano, hoping.

'If the drains are disinfected properly,' he said, 'you wouldn't get planarians. Even they have limits.'

And so have I, she thought.

The previous evening, whiling away the hours in the Questura intelligence office, she'd stolen a good look at the papers on LaMarca's disappearance. It had taken a while to track down the boyfriend who'd been kidnapped by Giorgio Bramante as bait. A while, too, to persuade him to talk. When he did he told them something interesting. Toni LaMarca had been taken two nights before his body turned up at Santa Maria dell'Assunta, not the one night they'd first thought. It was clear from the autopsy that he'd died soon after he was taken, too, in the slaughterhouse, she supposed. The church had been visited by the woman caretaker the day before she found the body. She'd seen nothing unusual. That meant Bramante had stored LaMarca's corpse somewhere – out of some unforeseen necessity – before moving it to the final location. Then, some thirty-six hours or so after the killing, he'd left the clue in Sacro Cuore to what he had done.

There was dirt under LaMarca's toenails, traces of earth on his body that forensic were looking at. But the kind of information she'd get from those sources only meant something with corroboration. Dirt wasn't unique like DNA. If they had a suspect location, they could look for a match. But without a starting point everything they had was like the stupid white worm. Information that lacked context, data floating on the wind with nothing concrete to make it useful. It could take weeks to track down, if ever.

'So where?' she wondered.

Cristiano shrugged.

'Like I told you. Near water. Near a drain maybe or a culvert. Underground, overground. You choose.'

'Thanks a bunch,' she grunted. 'You can take your pet home. Provided' – she prodded the worm nerd in the chest – 'you promise to name him Silvio.'

He hesitated and risked a glance at his friend.

'You mean you don't want me to work on him? Run a few tests? They're fatal, naturally, but I don't think the animal liberation people will start squealing. I mean, it's not like he's an endangered species.'

Her mind was already running elsewhere. She wanted him out of there.

'Worm autopsies are not my field, Cristiano. Talk to Silvio about it. In his time.'

'But . . .'

'But nothing.'

'Tell her,' Silvio ordered.

'Tell me what?'

'It's the sex thing again,' Cristiano said. 'You didn't hear me out.'

She looked at her watch.

'Thirty seconds.'

'It's a question of allopatry or sympatry, whether they're sexual or parthenogens . . .'

'I will, I swear, hit someone soon. Get to the point.'

'OK. Some populations of planarians overlap and mate with each other. Some stay apart and reproduce parthenogenetically. They develop female cells without the need for fertilization. Some . . . kind of do a little of both.'

'I *will* . . .'

'In Rome we have sexual types and parthenogens, and they're allopatric. Which means they live in geographically diverse communities and are basically slightly different versions of the same organism. It's a big deal. We have underground waterways that have been untouched, sometimes unconnected, for 2,000 years. What that means is that over the centuries we've come to have hundreds of communities of planarians and no two are exactly the same. There's a team that's been logging them for over a decade at La Sapienza along with a couple of other universities too. I'm amazed you never heard of it.'

'I never kept up on worms,' she muttered. 'One more personal failing. So what you're saying is that if you dissect his love tackle under a microscope you can tell me where he came from? Which waterway?'

'Better than that. If he's in the database I can tell you whereabouts. Whether it's the head of the Cloaca Maxima or the outlet. They're that distinct.'

She picked up the specimen dish and peered at the creature wriggling inside it.

'I'd like to say this is going to hurt me more than it hurts you,' she murmured. 'But it won't. Silvio – that's you, not the worm – kindly find this gentleman a white coat, a microscope, a desk and anything else he needs. We have human beings who require our attention.'

– 9 –

Judith Turnhouse didn't have the words 'academic bitch' stencilled in gold on a sign in her desk. As far as Peroni was concerned she didn't need them. Costa watched the body language as they entered the woman's office in the outpost of La Sapienza's archaeology department on the Aventino and felt his heart sink. It was hate at first sight. Turnhouse looked mid-thirties, tall, excruciatingly thin, with an angular face framed by lifeless brown hair. She sat stiff and serious behind a desk where everything – computer, files, papers, keyboard – had been tidied into a neat, symmetrical pattern.

Before Costa could even finish his introduction she took one look at their cards and said, 'Make it quick. I'm busy.'

Peroni breathed a deep sigh and picked up a small stone statue on her desk.

'What's the hurry?' he said. 'Does this stuff go off or something?'

The woman removed the object from his hands and placed it back where it belonged.

'This is our year-end. I've a budget to approve and an annual report to write. You can't do research without a proper administrative structure to back it up. We tried that once before. It was a disaster.'

Costa glanced at his partner and, uninvited, the two men took a couple of seats opposite the desk. Judith Turnhouse just watched, her sharp, pale grey eyes noting every moment.

'Giorgio Bramante's disaster?' Costa asked

209

'I might have guessed. In case you hadn't noticed, Giorgio doesn't work here any more. They gave me his chair a few years ago. It's a big job. Especially if you do it properly.'

Peroni looked puzzled.

'I thought Giorgio was a star. That's what everyone tells us.'

'Giorgio was an excellent archaeologist. He was my professor. I learned a lot from him. But he couldn't handle admin. He couldn't handle people, either. It was all about the research, and nothing about people.'

'Even a painter needs someone to pay for his paint,' Costa suggested.

She nodded, thawing a little.

'If you want to put it like that. Giorgio thought everything revolved around the pursuit of some holy grail called academic truth. The result? We found one of the greatest undiscovered archaeological treasures in Rome. Now it looks like a building site. It's tragic.'

More tragic for Judith Turnhouse, it seemed to Costa, than the loss of a young boy.

'You were in on the secret?' Peroni asked.

'Of course. You can't work a site of that size on your own. Giorgio took five of his best post-grad students into his confidence and told us what was going on. We laboured down there for a year. Another three months and we could have been in a position to tell people what we had.'

'Which was?' Costa answered.

'The largest and most important Mithraeum anyone's ever found in Rome. Probably the best source of information we were ever going to have on the Mithraic cult.'

'And it's all gone.'

'No,' she snapped. 'It's all in little pieces. In fifty years' time, perhaps, when everyone's forgotten about Giorgio's mess, maybe they'll come up with the budget to try to put it all back together. Maybe. Not that it will matter to me by then. Just because what I work with is timeless doesn't mean I think I'm that way myself.'

Peroni took out a pad.

'The other students. We'd like their names.'

She thought about arguing for a moment, then reeled off what he wanted. One now worked in Oxford, two in the States, and the last was a professor in Palermo. She hadn't seen any of them in years.

'Is that it?' she asked.

'We're trying to find out where Giorgio might be now,' Costa replied. 'We're trying to understand what happened back then. Whether that can help us today.'

'I don't—'

'We're trying, Professor Turnhouse,' Peroni interjected, 'to understand what happened to Alessio too. Doesn't that make you curious in the slightest?'

She hesitated, gave Peroni a dark look, then said, 'If you really want my help, you can cut out that kind of bullshit. I didn't have anything to do with Alessio getting lost. I have no idea what happened to him. You're the police, aren't you? Isn't that your job?'

Costa slid a hand across to Peroni's arm and stopped the big man reacting.

'Agreed,' he said. 'Which is why we're here. What was Giorgio like back then?'

She said something short and monosyllabic under her breath then stared deliberately at her watch.

'Also,' Costa added, 'what's he like now? Changed, or what?'

She stopped looking at her wrist and gazed straight into his face. Judith Turnhouse wasn't a woman who felt scared of anything, he thought. She was a senior academic, an important cog in an important wheel, at least inside her own head. She wasn't much interested in anything else.

'Now?'

'He came here. A week ago maybe. He had an argument with someone. So loud even the Carabinieri outside heard it. Then he stormed off. My guess is he had that argument with you.'

She toyed with the pen on the desk.

'Really?'

'You know,' Costa continued, 'on that basis alone I could go to a magistrate. Giorgio is a convicted killer who's picked up his old bad habits. He's a threat to the community. I could ask for papers that would let me go through everything here. Your computers. Your files. Every last site you're working on inside that hill . . .'

'We're working on nothing,' she grumbled. 'Everything is elsewhere these days.'

Peroni smiled and folded his very large arms over his chest.

'We could sit here looking at you for so long that year-end report will be about next year. If you're lucky.'

Her pale, anxious face was taut with some inner, constrained fury.

'Or,' Costa suggested, 'we could just have a friendly chat, a look around that site and be out of here by twelve. It's up to you.'

Judith Turnhouse picked up the phone then said, in an accent still marked by her native American, 'Chiara? Cancel all my appointments.'

She glared at them.

'Persuasive pair, aren't you?'

'Rumour has it,' Peroni concurred.

'You.' She pointed at Costa. 'The polite one. Start taking notes. I'll tell you everything I know about dear, sweet Giorgio, past and present.'

She went to a floor-length cupboard by the window and removed a bright orange all-covering suit, stepping into it in an easy, familiar fashion.

'After that,' Judith Turnhouse added, 'I'll show you what was once a miracle.'

– 10 –

By seven o'clock they still had only the one student, the one suspect: Ludo Torchia. The others would, Falcone suspected, be found soon. They weren't the kind to stay invisible for long. They dabbled in drugs, and, Ludo Torchia most of all, took a close, almost unhealthy, interest in Giorgio Bramante's theories about Mithraism. But nothing Falcone had seen made him suspect they were capable of cooking up the conspiracy the media were looking for.

Torchia had been placed in the last interview room in the basement, a former cell with no window to the outside, just an air vent and bright lighting, a metal table and four chairs. It was the place they reserved for more difficult customers, and ones they wanted to frighten a little. There were four other rooms adjoining it, running to the old metal staircase that led up to the ground-floor offices. No one else was in for questioning that night. Falcone was leaving them open for the remaining students when they were found. The Bramante case was the Questura's sole focus, and would remain so until either a resolution emerged, or it became apparent that the moment was lost, and the investigation would gradually subside into the low-key, quiet operation that would acknowledge what Falcone now believed to be true: Alessio Bramante was already dead.

Under instructions to await Arturo Messina's arrival, he had spoken with the student only to establish the bare essentials: his name, his address. Everything else – all the routine checks and procedures – were to wait. Messina was, it seemed, playing this game by ear. It seemed a dangerous and unnecessary response to the hysteria now being played out in the street and on the TV.

Falcone also decided that Giorgio Bramante, to the man's obvious fury, would wait elsewhere until Messina's arrival. He half hoped he could make his superior see sense. Then, at ten minutes to eight, the commissario returned to the Questura. Falcone took one look at his face and realized it wasn't even worth the effort. The man looked as angry as Bramante himself, though lost too, something which Falcone did not see in the father.

'The others?' Messina demanded.

'Still looking,' Falcone replied. 'We'll find them.'

'Doesn't matter,' the commissario grumbled. 'One will do. Where's Giorgio?'

Reluctantly, aware that there was no sense in arguing, he went to fetch the man himself.

Giorgio Bramante didn't say a word when he saw Messina. That, in itself, Falcone found interesting.

Messina clapped him on the shoulder and peered into his eyes.

'We will find your boy,' he said firmly. 'Give us twenty minutes with this creature to ourselves. If we have nothing after that . . . it's your turn.'

– 11 –

It was hard to believe there had ever been anything here of value. Beyond the Orange Garden, on the steep slope that led down the sharp riverside incline of the Aventino, adjoining the Clivo di Rocca Savella, was what now looked like a rubbish dump. The ground was uneven, part grass, part dun earth. Spent plastic bottles were strewn around in patches of debris beneath low, meagre scrub. Costa spotted two used syringes before they'd even scrambled down the muddy narrow path that led from the park above, then wound, by a snaking, perilous route, on to the throng of the riverside road below.

They stumbled through the mud until they found a small platform of even earth. The rain had stopped, probably only for a little while. Judith Turnhouse had dragged up the hood of her caving suit. She looked around, screwed up her face, then pulled the hood down again.

'This is it?' Peroni asked.

'This was it,' she replied.

Costa kicked over a couple of sods of grass. There was stone beneath, the ribbed surface of what looked like some kind of column.

'They brought in the bulldozers,' she added. 'They tore down everything. When we found it, all this area was still beneath the earth. There was an original entrance fifteen, twenty metres away, by the park up there.'

'You mean it was made that way?' Peroni asked. 'Underground? Why?'

215

She shrugged.

'We don't know. A place like this could have helped us understand. Mithraism was some kind of male cult, most popular among the military. It involved strict codes of behaviour, a series of rituals and hierarchies, with just the one leader who had absolute power. Apart from a few, cursory contemporary descriptions that survive, we're speculating about the rest.'

Peroni scowled at the area around them. There were, Costa could see, what looked like the remnants of blocked-up tunnelways and even a few small holes. Large enough for a child, perhaps, nothing more.

'So,' Peroni went on, 'this was like all that black magic stuff you still read about in the countryside from time to time?'

'No!' she replied quickly. 'It was a faith. A real one. Followed very carefully, in secret, by thousands and thousands of people. Christianity was underground for most of three centuries before it became the dominant religion. The day that happened, the day Constantine won his victory at the Milvian Bridge, is when everything here was destroyed the first time round. Somewhere in there' – she pointed to what looked like a former entrance, now blocked with rubble and wire mesh to keep out intruders – 'we uncovered the remains of more than a hundred men who'd been gathered together and slaughtered. By Constantine's army. It couldn't have been anyone else. The evidence is still there somewhere. It was one reason Giorgio felt so nervous about letting people understand the full extent of what we found here. There were . . . resonances.'

Peroni glanced at Costa. The two of them had discussed this idea already.

'If Alessio got lost, it would all have been made public anyway, wouldn't it?' Costa asked. 'Could that have been why he brought the boy here?'

She treated the question as if it were irrelevant.

'Search me. You had fourteen years to ask that of Giorgio.'

'Then why did he come back to see you?' he persisted.

She actually laughed.

'It was ridiculous. He wanted to get back all his old files. His reports. His maps. Everything he'd worked on.'

'And?' Peroni asked.

'I threw him out! He worked for the university. Everything he produced during his employment is legally ours. I wasn't giving it all away.'

'I imagine he didn't like that,' Costa said.

'That's one habit he's not lost in jail,' she replied. 'Giorgio always did have a temper. He was screaming at me as if I was still some timid little student of his. That I don't take. Not from anyone.'

The woman hesitated. There was more.

'I ran off some copies of the maps he wanted. That was as far as I was willing to go. I was going to phone and tell you people about it when I read what was happening.'

She went quiet.

Peroni nodded.

'When?' he asked.

'This afternoon.'

'After the year-end budget?'

'Don't patronize me.' Judith Turnhouse spoke with a slow, hard fury.

Costa was poking around at the hill edge of the clearing. There was a multitude of potential openings and tunnels in the hundred metres or so of ground that stretched from the fence by the narrow Roman alley, and ended in the sheer face of the hill on the other side.

'Where could a child have gone in a place like this?' he asked, almost to himself. 'Why didn't they find him?'

'I don't know!' she declared, exasperated.

'You went down there,' Peroni pointed out.

'Yes! And that's exactly why I don't know. The conditions here were the worst I've ever encountered. Giorgio took such risks I sometimes wondered if we'd get out of the place alive. Some of the underground tunnels were so fragile you could bring down a landslide just by putting your hand against the wall. It's a nightmare down there. There are manmade tunnels, natural fissures, drainage . . . Some parts link up with at least two branches of the Cloaca Maxima in ways we don't even understand. Also, there are ways down to springs that emerge in the riverbed too. If a child got lost in there he could find a hundred different holes to fall down, and every one of them would claim him. Or . . .'

She stared at them.

'Someone could have thrown him down one.'

'You knew those students,' Costa stated. 'Would they have done that?'

'Ludo Torchia was a twisted bastard. He could have done anything. But I still believe . . .'

She thought of something. Judith Turnhouse walked over and picked up one of the empty water bottles, one with a very visible bright-red label.

'If you want to understand what we're standing on here – a honeycomb no one, not even Giorgio, got round to mapping – watch this.'

The woman took the top off the bottle, scooped some earth into the neck as ballast, and walked over to one of the few open fissures in the rock behind.

'This is a trick we learned when we were working here. My bet is it happens even more quickly now than it did back then. More rain. More erosion. Watch . . .'

She beckoned them to come close, held the plastic bottle over the hole and let go. They heard the thing bouncing off rock, softer, softer. Then a distant splash into water. Then nothing, except the continuing soft ripple of a distant current, moving somewhere beneath them, constant.

'We thought this was a natural culvert, never part of the temple at all. There's some kind of channel that descends, meets something else in the hill, then runs to the river. See there?'

She pointed towards the city, at an area of foaming water on the near side of the bridge before Tiber Island.

'By the weir there's a peripheral outlet of the Cloaca Maxima, on the bend. You can just about make it out. The head itself is Claudian. There's a modern arch around it they made when they built the road and the flood defences.'

Costa caught the gap in the line of the flood wall, almost directly by the churning waters of the weir.

'Got it,' he said.

'As you'll see in a moment, somehow – and for the life of me I fail to see how this is possible – that little channel here works its way through several hundred metres of horizontal rock and ends up there. What we're standing on is porous, fault-ridden stone, full of holes and hidden passages we can't even begin to chart. If a child went down a place like that . . .'

She sighed and looked at her watch.

'So how is your eyesight? Mine's not so great these days. I'm afraid this is the only party trick I have.'

'Very good,' Costa replied, watching the bobbing debris like a hawk.

They waited five minutes. No red bottle appeared.

'When did you last try this?' Peroni asked. 'Before Alessio disappeared or after?'

'I don't remember. After, I think.'

'So it's years?' he went on. 'The drain probably got blocked.'

She shook her head.

'No. That's just not possible. We know when there's a drainage problem around here. We've got sites that flood straight away. We have to do something about it. There's been nothing like that for a long time. On a day like this' – she pointed at the foam on the weir. Small white horses, lively, wild – 'without a blockage it should be running more freely than usual. The channel's still open here. You heard it yourself. I don't know . . .'

For the first time since they met her Judith Turnhouse looked uncertain of herself, vulnerable, capable of thinking that there might, perhaps, be something in her world that hadn't been discovered, labelled, and filed safely away for the future.

'This may sound stupid but I don't think this is quite right,' she said, so quietly it seemed she didn't like to hear the sound of her own self-doubt.

Costa glanced down. There was a narrow, slippery path that led to the alley of the Clivo di Rocco Savella. Then a short walk across the busy Lungotevere to some steps that ran close to the weir.

The waters looked cold and grey and angry.

'I may need your suit,' Costa observed, and heard nothing, no complaint, no objection, in return.

- 12 -

He was twenty-one but didn't look fully formed to Falcone's eyes. Ludo Torchia had the shifty, stupid grin of a teenager, one who'd done something bad, and was now challenging them to find out exactly what.

Messina sat opposite. Falcone took a chair in the corner and pulled out a notepad.

'We don't need that,' Messina said immediately.

Falcone put the pad away and closed his eyes for a moment. From what he'd observed of Torchia already, confrontation was exactly what this strange young man wanted.

'Do us all a favour, son,' Messina began. 'You know Professor Bramante. You know his boy. Tell us where Alessio is. Don't make things worse.'

Torchia sniggered and stared back at them. He had the smell of cheap, stale wine about him.

He began to pick at his fingernails.

'I don't talk to scum like you. Why should I?'

Messina blinked furiously then managed to calm himself.

'This is a police matter,' he said through clenched teeth. 'When I ask you a question I want an answer.'

Torchia leaned over the table, looked the commissario in the eye and laughed.

'I didn't hear a question, moron.'

'*Where's the boy?*' Messina yelled.

'Dunno,' he said, then went back to picking at his fingernails.

'Tell us why you were in that place,' Falcone intervened, and ignored the caustic glance he got from Messina.

'I am Giorgio Bramante's student,' he replied, as if talking to a child. 'I have the right to visit any academic site he's working on.'

Falcone struggled to interpret Torchia's attitude. It was resentful, aggressive, unhelpful. But the student was at ease too, and that seemed odd.

'You mean Bramante invited you there?' he asked.

'No!'

An angry flush finally rose in Torchia's cheeks.

'I had to find it for myself. You ask him why that was. We were supposed to be a family. Students. Faculty. All together. The only secrets were supposed to be the ones we shared.'

'This isn't about the site. It's about the boy!' Messina barked back at him, leaning over the table, spittle flying from his mouth.

Torchia didn't even flinch. Falcone had seen this type before. Even if Torchia did get a beating, he probably wouldn't mind that much. It just validated what he thought to begin with: that he was in the company of the enemy.

'I was there to see what was mine by rights,' he said slowly. 'Something Giorgio should have shown us a long time ago.'

Falcone pulled his chair nearer the table and looked Torchia in the eye.

'A child is missing, Ludo,' he said. 'Somewhere in a place that's treacherous. You were seen leaving it. You ran away . . .'

'Nobody likes the police,' he said quickly. 'Why should I help you?'

'Because it can help Alessio?'

'I don't know anything.'

'You ran away,' Falcone repeated. 'All of you. There was a reason for that. We need to know what that reason was. If something bad has happened to Alessio you can see, surely, that you will get the blame. Unless you tell us . . .'

'I didn't see the boy.'

He was lying. As if this was all a game. Ludo Torchia was toying with them, it seemed to Falcone, simply because he felt like it.

'Who else was there?' Messina asked. 'Give me the names.'

'I don't betray my comrades,' he said, then went back to staring at his fingernails.

Messina looked at the end of his tether. Torchia appeared immovable. What emotion he possessed was contained, suppressed, tightly inside his own skinny frame.

None of the standard process had happened either, all thanks to Messina's direct instructions: put Torchia in a room and let him stew. The formalities, the words that were supposed to be read . . . all the prerequisites of interviewing a suspect. A good lawyer could have a field day with the holes they'd already left open. Messina had allowed himself to become obsessed with the boy, not any possible conviction that might follow. This was, in Falcone's eyes, foolish, and dangerous. The Questura had lost two high-profile cases of late, cases where guilty parties had walked free simply through breaches of procedure. It could so easily occur again.

One practical job had never taken place either. A physical search.

'Turn out your pockets,' Falcone said.

A glimmer of fear flashed in his eyes. Ludo Torchia had remembered something.

'Turn out your pockets, Ludo,' Falcone repeated. 'I want to see everything. Put it slowly in front of you, item by item. Don't leave out anything.'

He swore. Then he reached into his trousers and withdrew a few tissues, some notes, and some coins. A set of keys. A lighter and some cigarettes.

The backs of his hands were covered in scratches. Fingermarks, Falcone thought, and reflected, miserably, that, had proper procedures been followed, this would already have been noted, already be the subject of forensic investigation.

'You're hurt,' he observed.

Torchia looked at his hands and shrugged.

'The girlfriend got a little fresh last night. You know what they're like.'

'I didn't think you had a girlfriend.'

He laughed.

'The jacket too,' Falcone ordered.

'Nothing in there.'

Messina was round the table and on him, big fists grabbing at the cheap cloth. Torchia squawked, a little scared, but defiant still.

'I said—' the student screeched, trying to fight off Messina's strong arms.

The commissario pulled something from his right-hand jacket pocket and placed it on the table. Falcone stared at the object. It was a pair of cheap toy spectacles, the kind you saw at funfairs. The lenses were semi-opaque, divided into glittering sections.

'Alessio had a pair like that when he went missing,' Falcone said quietly. 'His father told us. They were a birthday present. He turned seven yesterday.'

No one spoke for a moment. Then Torchia reached forward, picked up the spectacles, put them on, pushing them back on to the bridge of his nose when they fell forward.

'Found them somewhere. That's all. Christ. I can see a million of you ugly fuckers now. What kind of a crappy toy is that to give a kid for his birthday?'

He was taking them off when Messina threw the first punch. It caught Torchia on the back of the neck, sent his face flying down hard into the metal table. Blood spattered from his nose.

Messina had got in five or six more blows by the time Falcone reached them. Ludo Torchia was on the floor, cowering, arms around his face. Falcone couldn't help but notice he was laughing.

'Sir,' Falcone said quietly, to no avail. '*Sir.*'

Messina dashed in a last kick then allowed himself to be pushed back towards the cold, damp brick wall of the cell.

'This is pointless,' Falcone insisted. 'If the boy's alive, he won't tell. If he's dead and you beat it out of him, we won't be able to take him to court. This . . .' He said the words slowly. '. . . won't . . . work.'

Torchia was still laughing. He wiped the blood away from his mouth. He looked as if a couple of teeth had got shattered by Messina's feet.

'Kick away, you fat old bastard,' Torchia hissed. 'I wouldn't tell you shits a thing. Ever.'

Messina backed off. There was a wild look in his eyes Falcone didn't recognize. He was lost for a way forward. And there was only one, Falcone knew that. Patient, persistent police work. Slow, relentless questioning. None of which felt good in the light of one certainty which was, he felt, now spreading inside the Questura and out: Alessio Bramante was already dead somewhere. It was just a question of recovering the body.

'Give him to the father,' Messina ordered.

Torchia's eyes sparked with a mix of fear and interest.

'What?'

'Talk to me or talk to Giorgio Bramante!' Messina bellowed.

Torchia wiped the blood from his face and mumbled, 'I've got nothing to say to any of you. I want a lawyer. You can't go beating people up like this. *I want a lawyer. Now.*'

Messina got up and threw open the cell door. Bramante already stood there, waiting, still as a statue, powerful arms folded over his chest.

'Ludo,' he said simply.

'No,' Falcone declared immediately. 'This is not possible. This is the Questura . . .'

'We're getting nowhere,' Messina snapped, taking Falcone by the arm.

Falcone couldn't believe his ears.

'Sir, if anyone should hear of this.'

'I don't care!' the commissario yelled. 'Not about this stinking moron. I just want that boy.'

'I could observe,' he suggested.

Messina pushed him outside, ignoring his protests.

'You've an hour, Giorgio. Undisturbed. You hear me, Falcone?'

Bramante stepped round them without a word, walked into the cell, and slammed the iron door behind him.

The corridor outside had lost a fluorescent tube some nights before. It left the place in semi-darkness. Falcone moved into the light as much as he could. He wanted Messina to see his face.

'I disassociate myself from this decision completely,' he said quietly. 'If I'm asked what happened, I'll tell them.'

'You do that, Leo,' Messina replied. 'I hope it helps you sleep at night. But if you set foot in that room before the hour's up I'll have your scrawny backside across the coals first. You'll never make inspector. I promise. You'll never show your smug face in this Questura again.'

Then he walked off. Giorgio Bramante and Ludo Torchia were alone together in the small cell, in the dark bowels of the Questura, the last room in a basement corridor, far from sight.

Falcone went into the empty interview room next door, took out one of the small metal chairs, set it by the side of the cell, and waited.

It took scarcely a few minutes for the first sounds to eke their way under the metal door. Not long after, the screaming began.

- 13 -

The racket of the traffic almost disappeared once they'd descended the steps to the Tiber. Costa had rarely been on the broad riverside pathway during the day. At night, this was a place for the homeless and the crooked, the city's lost and forlorn, men and a few women all looking to stay hidden. He hardly recognized the place now. The water margin was green and luxuriant, with a straggle of cow parsley, wild fig and laurel bushes falling down towards the grey sweep of the river. Two lean, black cormorants skimmed the surface, gleaming dark darts, as they sped towards Tiber Island.

Then something rat-shaped but much larger ran from a small, leaking spring by the land edge, crossed their path no more than three metres ahead, racing to safety in the undergrowth to their left.

Peroni almost leaped out of his skin.

'What the hell was that?'

'Coypu,' Judith said. 'They were brought in for their fur, then went native. They give the rats something to fight.'

'You must come here a lot,' the big man said, looking uncomfortable at the thought that giant, foreign rodents were thriving in the centre of his adopted city.

'We work underground,' she said caustically. 'I thought you understood that.'

The outlet was so large the pathway had been extended in front to form a bridge over the surging race that was roaring out of the ancient stone mouth. The original exit was probably some three metres high, almost a perfect semicircle, three layers of old stones now set in grey mud and water. It stood inside a huge modern enclosure that must have run almost to the road above and seemed to incorporate other, more modern drain outlets, funnelling them into the same rough, thrashing gush of grubby water as it fed into the river, just above the weir.

Straggly trees fought feebly through the mud on either side of the channel. Shredded plastic rubbish and paper hung from their bare branches like lost Tibetan prayers, waving feebly in the renewing drizzle. The same kind of litter lay trapped in the broken and ragged wire storm guard that had once protected the lower half of the structure, and was now broken in multiple places.

Something lurked in the darkness at the back of this hidden cavern, dug deep into the underside of the road above. Costa squinted into the gloom, took out his pocket torch, and tried to see what it was.

'I really think I need that suit,' he was saying, when there was a splash beneath them. Judith Turnhouse was in the grubby water, furious, screeching at the makeshift building just visible in the man-made cavern ahead.

She stormed over to the old drain and clambered up onto the modern structure above it.

Peroni stared mournfully after her.

'It's OK, Nic,' he muttered. 'I'll do it. Your clothes are so much nicer than mine.'

'You're too kind,' Costa said, and leaped in anyway. He got there just a second or two behind the woman, while Peroni was still thrashing through the brown mud.

It was a home of kinds. Some old timber and scaffolding thrown together to make a shelter held together by industrial polythene and scraps of tarpaulin. There was a low, battered picnic table inside and a little folding stool. Plus the remains of some food. Recent. A few scraps of bread and meat that, to Costa's eye, had probably been gnawed at by a rodent after some human had discarded them.

The woman was going a little crazy. This was, he supposed, her territory in a way. The stone entrance almost looked as if it belonged in a museum, the city crest now barely visible.

'How dare they?' she screeched. 'How dare they?'

'They're homeless,' Costa replied, and suddenly remembered, with a sharp twinge of guilt, how long it had been since he followed his father's dictum: one gift a day to the poor, without fail.

But the poor didn't normally leave scraps of food lying around for the rats to finish.

He walked into the shelter. It didn't smell any worse than the drain outside. There was no effluent around here, only dank, stagnant water and the kind of refuse that stayed around forever, modern plastic and metal.

Costa kicked over the stool and ran a foot through the rubbish that lay on the floor. Some newspapers, and a few sheets from an office printer. He picked them up. The crest of the archaeological department stood on the top. Beneath was a computerized map of what appeared to be a drain system somewhere in the vicinity of the Villa Borghese, across the city.

Peroni caught up with him, a little out of breath. He stared at the paper, then the woman. She was poking her way into one of the side drains. It didn't look modern at all now Costa saw it close up.

'Signora Turnhouse!' Peroni yelled. 'Do not go in there. Please.'

She didn't take any notice.

'Damn,' Peroni muttered. 'He could still be around, Nic.'

'Agreed,' Costa said, and scrambled across the slimy stone towards her, shouting to the woman to be still.

It worked this time. She stopped. He reached her, got in front, hoped she understood there was a reason a gun now sat in his hand.

'This isn't how I remember the place,' she said, sounding a little scared. 'I can't put my finger on it. This isn't as old as the rest. Fifteenth, sixteenth century maybe. We used to use it for study work. A group of us went in here with Giorgio the first year we were here. It was different somehow. That's impossible.'

Costa worked his way in front of her. The entrance to the drain was under two metres high at this point. A meagre stream of thick, muddy water gripped his ankles in a bone-chilling embrace. He pointed the torch into the gloom and saw nothing. Not a man. Not a thing, until a large black animal shape scuttered through the grimy water into the darkness. The woman followed him then, after a couple more steps, anxiously grabbed his jacket.

'There!'

Peroni yelled that he was calling in back-up. Smart move, Costa guessed. If there was anyone around it was a good idea to let them know they would soon have more to deal with than a couple of puzzled cops and one increasingly jumpy archaeologist.

'What do you see?' he asked, then, before she could answer, found his eyes adapting, realizing what was wrong.

Something was obstructing the route ahead. It almost looked like the larva of some gigantic insect, bulging out from the rock wall of the culvert. Except it was red brick, not the dried husk of an insect's egg. Modern red brick, weakened by something pushing from behind. The pressure of water, perhaps, since what they seemed to be looking at was, he now came to realize, the artificial cap of something that could only be a side drain running into this main channel, one that had, at some time within the last few years, been blocked, and subject to the growing pressure of whatever sporadic force of liquid had built up behind.

The pointing between the bricks was rough and cracked and failing. A steady stream of dank rain water now ran through the base, filtering through the rough cement before falling into the broader flow that swirled in an icy embrace around their feet.

Costa took three steps forward and shone his beam on the foot of the protruding brickwork. It looked weak, on the verge of collapse. He stuck out his toe and pushed at the lowermost part. Soft cement crumbled as he watched. A single brick fell, then another, then the entire underside of the small, circular wall in front of him collapsed completely and fell into the grubby stream.

A mountain of rubbish that must have been building for years followed: cans and dead wood, paper and an unidentifiable thick brown sludge.

Then a bottle with a bright red label, one that was familiar. Followed by another object, something Costa dreaded to see. And a smell, organic, vile, fetid, that was at once both alien and familiar.

The woman began shrieking. The loud, manic sound of her voice

echoed around the artificial cave in which they stood, becoming
magnified by the brickwork enclosing them, drowning out the steady
rush of the water at their feet.

Behind the gobbets of refuse vomited into the sewer something
else dangled down over the brickwork, what lay behind it still hidden,
thankfully, in the shadows.

It was the hand and upper arm of a human being. The fingers were
now stiff, off-white digits of bone. Tatters of pale dun flesh ran through
taut, open tendons to the wrist, somewhat shredded in areas by what
looked like geometric teeth marks.

It was a very small hand, Costa thought. Not that of a man.

- 14 -

Rosa Prabakaran had spent most of her life feeling prominent, feeling as if the eyes of those around her were always watching, asking: why? There was no reason a woman of Indian extraction couldn't join the state police. No reason she couldn't do anything she liked. The colour of her skin was not her problem. It was theirs. All the same, she didn't like feeling as if she was something to be stared at. Falcone's admonition – which amounted to, 'I want her to see you' – grated. It was unprofessional. It was unwanted.

So, for the first time in her brief career, she disobeyed orders. After catching up on the news of the overnight attack at home, trying to absorb it, she took out some things she hadn't worn in a long time. Bright, young clothes, from a time before the police, when she had felt free of responsibilities. A short, pencil-thin skirt, a shiny leather jacket, red shoes. She put on make-up, raked out her business ponytail and let her long brown locks hang around her shoulders.

It was a touch sluttish, she thought, regarding herself in the mirror. But Beatrice Bramante would surely never recognize her now. She looked like one of the naturalized Indian girls, the kind who hung around the bars and clubs and shops near the Piazza di Spagna, picking up Italian boyfriends, living the modern life, all quick pleasures, and nothing to worry about afterwards. Her father would be out selling umbrellas like crazy in the rain, at twice the normal price, because that was how the street traders worked. She was glad. He'd have worried more about her looks than the fact that she was walking out of the door to try to break some lead in a murder investigation, and in doing so prove some kind of point to people like Inspector Leo Falcone.

There was a handgun in the small patent leather handbag that hung around her right shoulder on a gold chain. He might have worried about that too.

Just before ten she took the Number 3 tram to Via Marmorata. Then she walked down to the street where Beatrice Bramante lived and parked herself in the café opposite, playing with a *cornetto* that was still hot from the oven.

After almost two hours and three coffees, she watched Beatrice leave her apartment block through the big iron gates at the front, nodding to the caretaker in his little cabin on her way out.

Rosa followed the woman to the market where she bought some vegetables, bread and a little cheese. She recalled Beatrice during the awkward interview with Falcone, trying to hide the scars on her wrists, grabbing for the booze bottle when he pushed too hard. She didn't look like a woman who coped well with today, let alone tomorrow.

Finally, Beatrice went to one of the butchers' stalls. Rosa remembered something else from the previous day, something dark. It was the woman from Santa Maria dell'Assunta almost fainting in this very place, nauseated by what she'd seen, and by the visible reminder of it on the stalls. Hunks of bright red meat, white fat, little puddles of blood gathering on the marble slabs beneath. The harsh, organic smell of raw flesh.

Rosa looked at the sign above the stall where Beatrice had stopped. It was a horse butcher's. *The* horse butcher's. She'd asked before. There was only one in the market. This was the place where Giorgio Bramante had worked, half the time killing the animals at the slaughterhouse out in Anagnina, the rest bringing the meat here.

Beatrice Bramante was talking in an animated fashion to a man behind the counter. A man in his early thirties wearing a blood-stained coat and the white pork-pie hat butchers seemed to favour.

Then the man stood closer to Beatrice, staring at her with admiring eyes, slipping some parcel of meat illicitly into her hands. He followed this with a brief, sudden kiss, one that took the woman by surprise, so that she glanced around nervously, wondering if anyone had seen.

Rosa had ducked behind a towering pile of fruit boxes the moment she saw Beatrice turning in her direction. There, her nostrils full of the ripe, acid smell of winter lemons from Sicily, she felt her lungs tighten, her fingers grip the little patent bag, with the handgun inside. She'd left the police radio at home deliberately. This was a statement. I'm on my own. But she had her phone, and if she called Leo Falcone, told him she was standing just a few metres away from someone who might be Giorgio Bramante himself, none of that would matter.

She moved out from behind the lemon boxes again. They were still talking, still close. She took a good look at him. The man was quite striking in a damaged way. Not muscular, but not a college professor either, even one who'd spent the last fourteen years in jail. She'd seen the photos of Giorgio Bramante. They'd warned her he would be different. But not this different. And why would he return to the old job like this? It seemed inconceivable.

She remembered Teresa Lupo's advice: *Either look or don't look. Just don't half look.*

The reason she assumed this was Giorgio Bramante was simple: the man and the woman treated each other with a casual, intimate familiarity.

As she digested this thought the butcher reached forward and lightly brushed Beatrice Bramante's cheek once more. Then she walked off, out from under the market's iron roof, covering her head against the rain, striding back towards her apartment, eyes on the pavement.

Beatrice is not alone, Rosa Prabakaran said to herself. She has a lover. One who worked with Giorgio. And surely must have known him.

This was valuable, she thought. In a different light, Leo Falcone would be grateful for it. Yet she was immediately aware that he would see instantly she had come to possess the intelligence through what he would view as illicit means, in direct contradiction to the orders he'd issued.

Of itself it was useless, of such limited value that its revelation could only serve to reveal her duplicity.

'I need more,' she whispered.

When the market closed she followed him back to where, she assumed, he lived. It was in a block near the old slaughterhouse, a massive complex now being turned over to the arts, not far from the Monte dei Cocci, the small hill of Imperial-era pottery shards that was Testaccio's one tourist attraction. At night half the city came here for the restaurants and the clubs. In the day it was deserted. Only a handful of visitors were heading for the arts exhibition. She stared at the gates of the old slaughterhouse. They'd left the huge original headstone over the building: a winged man wrestling a complaining bull to the earth by the ring through its nose. And beneath both of them a sea of carved bones, animal and human, all grimy stone after years of exposure to the weather.

Lost for what to do next, she hid from the rain in a tiny café opposite. After a while her mobile phone rang. She cursed the intrusion as an unfamiliar, unexpected voice came on the line.

– 15 –

It was hot that night in the basement of the Questura. Falcone was left alone outside the cell, a punishment for defying Messina so much over the progress of the investigation. His penance was to listen to a young man being beaten to the brink of death, a point from which there would be no return.

He had sat there for so long, racking his brains for some possible solution, some excuse which would allow him to contravene Messina's direct orders and enter that dreadful room. There was only one, and he'd known it from the outset. What was happening was wrong. Nothing could justify it, not the mysterious disappearance of a young boy, nor the likelihood that Ludo Torchia was involved. Wrong was wrong, and any police officer who tried to run away from that simple fact would surely, one day, pay the price.

When he could take no more – Bramante was left alone in the cell with Torchia for fifty minutes, Falcone was to discover later, though it seemed much longer – he threw open the door, began to say something, and found the words failed in his mouth. This was a sight he knew would never fully fade from his memory.

Giorgio Bramante stood over his victim, still furious, still wanting to go on, hate and a lust for some kind of vengeance burning like bright beacons in his eyes.

'I'm not done yet,' this learned, respected college professor yelled. 'Didn't you hear your orders, man? I'm not done yet.'

'There,' Falcone said, 'you are wrong.'

Then he picked up the phone to the front desk, ordered the duty medic to come immediately, and called for an ambulance. After which he dialled the central complaints bureau, described, in brief, the situation as he saw it: an act of outright brutality warranting a criminal investigation had happened in the heart of the Questura. When he heard the hesitation on the line he left them in no doubt that, should they decide to play deaf, he would take the matter higher and higher until someone, somewhere would listen. There was no going back.

He put down the handset. Giorgio Bramante was glaring at him with such hatred that, for a moment, Falcone feared for his own safety.

- 16 -

Even for Giorgio Bramante, used to hardship, the weather was bitter. After he'd fled the Questura, surprised at how easily he'd avoided capture, he trudged for two hours along deserted roads which still followed the route of the old Imperial highways, finally passing the Porta San Sebastiano around 3 a.m., and walking until he found what was once the Via Latina. There he planned to spend the rest of the night, and much of the coming day, dry, if not warm, in the depths of a set of closed caverns, not far from the Ad Decimum catacombs, ten Roman miles from the city, close to what would once have been a military encampment.

This was the most remote of his several potential hiding places. There were ones much closer to the *centro storico*, caverns and remains of underground streets that had never been mapped over the centuries, known only to a handful of scholars. He could live hidden away like this for months undetected, with space, with the food he bought surreptitiously during the day, coming out only when necessary.

Circumstances forced him to wait, to be patient. There was only a little work to be done now, but this was the most important of all. So he sat, in the cold, bleak cavern, thinking about the day, and what knowledge he had come to possess of this place over the years.

The present site had been discovered by a local farmer trying to break up the soil for vines. The family had kept the find secret for a decade, hoping there was some hidden treasure in its subterranean web of tunnels. All they uncovered were tombs and bones, niches hacked into the stone, row upon row, tunnel upon tunnel. And, on the final, lowest level, the temple, which they scarcely looked at once they realized there was nothing glittering among its stones.

In late Imperial times this had been a modest agrarian community, probably no more than a few farms and a small army barracks for men guarding the gatehouses and tax-collection points of the Appian Way. The temple had none of the grandeur of the great altar hidden deep within the Aventino. Mithras and the bull were crudely carved. The scorpion squeezing at the beast's groin was scarcely recognizable. The place was a token of the old religion, one that the archaeologists, once they learned of it, decided to overlook in favour of the more obvious Christian remnants that had followed its creation: the insignia of the Cross, the legends carved into the walls that hinted someone, perhaps a saint, had rested here briefly after martyrdom.

On the first Sunday of each month a local archaeological society led a small gaggle of visitors down through the simple, modern, concrete entry-cabin on the surface, taking thrill-seeking tourists beneath the earth to see the skeletons and what remained of the ancient funereal decorations. No one spoke of Mithras. The religion that had once been Christianity's principal rival – though Bramante doubted any of the men who had worshipped here would have seen it that way – was a myth to amuse children. A fairy story, a fable to file alongside Aesop.

That worked to his advantage. The site, situated half a kilometre along a narrow, now unused farm track, in a field abandoned by a farmer who found more profit in subsidies for growing nothing than planting young grapes, was remote and little visited outside that one, fixed event. The archaeologists wouldn't be back for another two weeks. He had privacy and security. And, thanks to the caring city authorities, electricity too, since a single cable feeding electric lights ran through virtually the entire network of caverns, stopping short only of the Mithraeum, which no one wanted to see.

The previous day had exhausted him. Unwittingly, he'd slept for eight straight dreamless hours before waking. Now he sat on the first level, by a series of niches, under the dim illumination of the bulbs and the grey light of day slipping down a slender ventilation shaft that led from here to the surface. In this sector all but one of the graves were empty. In the last alcove lay a female skeleton, carefully posed for the visitors, a real human being, someone who had walked and breathed in the fields above some 1,700 or more years before, her remains now arranged for the curious, like a waxworks dummy from a travelling circus.

Bramante still understood the archaeological mind. His former colleagues were historians, not grave robbers, and would move only what was absolutely necessary. The bones remained, in all probability, where they had been found, which meant that he knew the girl's name too, since it was carved over the tomb with the odd added inscription – 'nosce te ipsum', 'know yourself' – a sign, surely, that there was more here than the obvious. Above the alcove, the handiwork so poor one had to work to interpret its meaning, was a simple tableau, no more than two hands high: a young female figure in a shift, standing, leaning on one leg, holding a cat in her arms, stroking its head, in a pose that was so timeless, so natural, it made any parent's heart ache. At her feet stood a cockerel and a goat. Bramante had accompanied a couple of tours here. He'd listened to the guides talk fondly of the carving, citing it as an illustration of the idyllic pastoral life lived in the vicinity. He'd kept his own opinions to himself. People saw what they wanted to see. For him, as a rational investigator, one who tried to sift small nuggets of truth from the dust of history, it was important to deal with the facts. The cockerel and the goat were common emblems in certain kinds of Roman statuary, notably pieces of a ritual and votive nature. They were there as sacrifices, not emblems of the kind of bucolic Heaven Virgil tried to portray in his poetry. The truth was probably more mundane and more complex. While the girl clearly lived, and died, in a Christian community, it was one that, like many, kept alive the old gods, furtively, with covert references, in much the same way that the followers of Jesus had done before they came to power. The bird and the goat were there because the girl, in the mind of her mourners, was about to kill them, to dedicate a sacrament to Mercury who would decide whether her transition to the next world would be swift and painless.

Bramante reached for the bag of food and drink he'd bought in the supermarket at San Giovanni two days before. The self-heating instant coffee tasted disgusting but at least it was warm. He ripped open a pre-packaged cake, took a bite, idly examining the label. Alessio had loved these. The boy always had a sweet tooth. It was a bad habit, one his parents had found hard to discourage.

Then he looked again at the inscription above the tomb and the small, familiar assembly of brown and white bones, the fragile simulacrum of a once-living human being.

'*Salute*, Valeria,' Bramante said quietly, toasting her with the disgusting coffee. He thought to himself: I hope Mercury listened when you called. I hope you haven't spent the last 1,700 years waiting for him to wave you on.

The young police officer lived not far from here, with his girlfriend. She was an attractive woman. Bramante would have taken her had a hostage been necessary. It wasn't personal.

He thought of the blonde American and the way men amused themselves in jail. All the effort, alone and with others, all the concentration on the corporeal elements of the act, as if the cerebral didn't matter for a moment. He was aware that, at that moment, he could so easily have done exactly what many did in prison: a minute or so of grunting effort, then a kind of relief. But there was a young girl in the room, albeit a dead one. And Giorgio Bramante needed – prized – real contact.

He needed so much. He . . .

His breath began to come in short, pained gasps. His eyes started to sting.

It took just a thought to bring on an attack now. This had the makings of one as bad as any in recent days. The buzzing came back, drove a sharp, agonizing stake between his temples. His hands began to tremble. His whole body began to shake so hard he spilled some of the foul, scalding coffee on his hands as he struggled to put the drink on the floor.

The stupid cake got flung into a corner by the spasmodic jerk of his arm, down into the dark where the rats could find it. Bramante didn't care any more. He just threw back his head, teeth clenched tight, let the rage take him.

Madness, maybe. That's what the woman doctor in the hospital had hinted at. Guilt perhaps, she said once, and that was the time he killed all future appointments.

Psychiatrists didn't really believe in psychopomps, invisible beings that could try to achieve their ends through ordinary humans, hoping, perhaps, in his case, to find some possible fate for Alessio, wherever he might be, longing to be home, at peace, joined with the grey world that lived alongside the present one, flitting in and out of its consciousness at will.

He wasn't sure he believed in them himself. At moments like this it didn't really matter.

Eyes closed tightly, teeth grinding, sweat running down his brow, Giorgio Bramante saw the picture forming in his head and tried to fight it, knowing the effort was futile.

After an effort to resist – a second? a minute? an hour? – he opened his inner eye and found himself back in the place that never really left him any more: Piranesi's square on the Aventino. He was on his knees, neck upright, head straining, eyes ready to burst from the pressure behind them as he sought in desperation to see something through the keyhole in the door of the mansion of the Cavalieri di Malta.

It was Alessio's voice in his ear, filling his head. Older now, and full of some emotion his father had never noticed in life. Determination. Hatred. A cold, mocking detachment.

'Can you see it?' this young-old imaginary creature asked.

He didn't answer. There was no point in talking to a ghost.

'Well?' the voice asked in a louder, harder, crueller tone. 'Or are you just thinking about yourself again, Giorgio? Who's next on the list? The skeleton in the corner?'

He'd no idea how long the fit lasted. When it was over, when his muscles relaxed and his jaw unclenched, aching, teeth sharp and edgy from the prolonged effort of crushing them together so hard it felt something might break, Bramante was dismayed to find he'd pissed himself. He got up, grateful only that he wasn't in his caving suit, climbed out of the jeans and pants he was wearing, scooped some icy water from the bucket he'd brought with him, towelled himself down, then put on the last pair of clean underwear and jeans he had.

He threw the dirty ones into the corner, as far away from Valeria's alcove as he could manage. Then he sat down, recovered the coffee and the cake, ate and drank and thought.

'No,' he said, staring at the bones of a long-dead girl called Valeria. 'I didn't see it.'

After finishing the food and drink, he took out the little digital camera he'd stolen from a Chinese tourist dawdling outside the Pantheon three weeks before and began to flick through the pictures.

The blonde American girl was very pretty. Given the opportunity and the reason, he would have liked the chance to take her. He flicked through five frames, watching her walk from the entrance of the Palazzo Ruspoli, out into the Via Corso, fighting his own desire to linger because he was getting hard, in spite of himself, in spite of the watchful dead judgemental presence of the bones in the corner. Then he passed over Falcone and his woman, then the other two.

The weather was made for work like this. He could go anywhere, do anything, take pictures where and when he liked, and none of them knew.

He returned to the last few frames on the camera, the shots he'd noted very soon after they were taken, from the café across the road near Santa Maria dell'Assunta. He'd drunk a cappuccino and eaten a sandwich, watching Falcone and his men bicker and fumble their way inside the old abandoned church.

It was easy to read Leo Falcone, Bramante thought. His smiles were so rare they had to mean something. At that moment, captured in the distance, across the road, behind the yellow police tape, Falcone was looking at someone with – not affection, Bramante thought – but a kind of respect. The sort he seemed to reserve for the young these days, judging by the way he kept close to the short, bright *agente* with the beautiful girlfriend.

He stared at the picture, once again felt certain of its use to him, but remained surprised, almost shocked, all the same. The police had changed in almost a decade and a half. That made things so much easier. Before he put on the office cleaner's uniform the night before he'd walked into a café and sat in front of a computer for half an hour, preparing his options. It hadn't been difficult to track down the name of the only recent female Indian recruit to the Rome police. They liked to make a story of ethnic recruitment these days. The woman had been in most of the city papers three months earlier, with a photo. And her name.

Rosa Prabakaran.

There were only three Prabakarans in the book. He'd hit lucky first time. It was the girl's father. Bramante posed as a senior officer from the Questura, concerned that he'd been unable to get through to Rosa on her private mobile number, worried that he hadn't heard from her, and that perhaps they had the wrong details.

Giorgio Bramante knew, by now, how to work on the emotions of a parent. Fear unlocked any door.

He rubbed his hands together to give his fingers life, then took out the number her father had given him. Then he looked up to make sure he was beneath the air vent, checking the signal on his phone. One bar. Enough to get through, though probably with a lot of distortion, which was not, of itself, a bad thing.

She picked it up on the third ring. Her uncertain voice crackled and hissed through the ether.

'Agente,' Bramante said with an easy authority. 'This is Commissario Messina. Where are you exactly? And what are you doing?'

– 17 –

It took Falcone a good five minutes to negotiate the stone steps down to the river. Teresa Lupo and her team were there already. On the far bank a group of photographers and TV cameras were setting up positions. The morgue team was busily erecting grey canvas barriers around the mouth to the drain. Everything seemed to be in place.

Costa and Peroni were sitting under a temporary awning by the waterside, escaping the constant drizzle. They were with a woman Falcone recognized. It took a moment to place the name: Judith Turnhouse, who had been cursorily interviewed during the inquiry fourteen years before.

He beckoned to the men to join them, remaining out in the rain which, with its constant cold, seemed to keep him alert.

'Well done,' he said. 'You've achieved more than fifty officers plodding along in Bruno Messina's footsteps.' He paused. 'Are you sure?'

'It looked like a child to me,' Costa said, nodding towards the grey canvas by the drain. 'Teresa and her people are in there now.'

'Is this possible?' Falcone asked. 'It's a long way from the Orange Garden.'

'Definitely,' Peroni replied. 'She' – he nodded towards Judith Turnhouse who sat motionless under the awning, eyes pink from tears – 'showed us.'

Costa shuffled, uncomfortable with something.

'We shouldn't jump to conclusions,' he said. 'The boy could have been looking for a way out. It's not a pretty thought. If he was in there. Alive.'

'We had search parties!' Falcone objected.

Peroni nodded at the drain, built into the underside of the road, reachable only by wading through mud and filthy water.

'Would they have looked in there? Why? Who would have guessed he could have got that far?'

Falcone scowled.

'None of the archaeologists gave us an ounce of cooperation. If they had, perhaps we would have found this place. When we know for sure, let's get the media in. I want a full statement broadcast as soon as possible. Perhaps if Bramante hears it, if he understands we've tried to give him some answers . . .'

The two men looked at him, puzzled.

'It might be enough to persuade him to come in,' Falcone suggested, aware of the cool reception he was already getting. 'He can't hate me that much. Lord knows he's had two chances to kill me already and not taken them. If it's the boy, what else can he want? Bramante can't stay hidden for ever.'

Costa didn't say anything. But there was an expression in his eyes Falcone recognized. A look of doubt. The kind of look, Falcone suspected, he himself had once used on Arturo Messina.

'I want to go in there,' he said.

The two men glanced at each other.

'It's difficult,' Costa explained. 'Even for us. You need to wade through mud. There's very little room. Teresa has hardly any space to work in.'

'I am,' he said, voice rising, 'the chief investigative officer in this case. I will see what I want. I . . .'

Costa didn't budge. Friendship and work didn't mix, Falcone reflected, and that was because they were right. He wasn't up to this kind of physical effort. He gave up and hobbled to sit on the wall, out in the gentle rain, watching the slow-moving mass of the Tiber.

Costa and Peroni came and joined him, one on each side.

'You don't want me to carry you, Leo,' Peroni said. They were out of earshot of the rest of the team. He didn't mind the familiarity any more. 'I will if you want. But . . .'

'No.' Falcone touched Peroni lightly on the arm. 'I don't want you to carry me. I'm sorry. It's this damned . . .'

He stared at his feeble legs.

'It's feeling I'm not pulling my weight.'

He stopped. Two figures had appeared from behind the grey screen masking the mouth of the drain: Teresa Lupo and her assistant, Silvio Di Capua. He was holding a small notebook computer in his arms, tapping with one hand, staring at the screen. The pair were conversing rapidly.

'I believe we have news,' Falcone said softly, and felt a strange emotion in his heart: dread accompanied by relief.

She said one last thing to Di Capua, who returned behind the canvas afterwards. Then she walked over to Judith Turnhouse, spoke to her briefly, and finally joined them, sitting down next to Peroni, looking a little wary.

'I wish I still smoked,' she announced. 'Don't the rest of you have that feeling from time to time? You excluded, Nic, since we all know you've never had a real vice in your entire life.'

'News, Doctor,' Falcone insisted.

'News?' She tried to smile. 'We have a positive ID. Absolutely certain.'

'I knew it!' Falcone said, excited.

'Hear me out,' Teresa interrupted. 'We have an ID. Unfortunately . . .' She stopped and screwed up her large, pale face. 'Do I really mean that? How can I even think that way?'

'Teresa!' Peroni cried in exasperation.

'Unfortunately – or fortunately, whichever way you wish to look at it – it isn't Alessio Bramante.'

– 18 –

She was young, a rookie, it said in the paper. That didn't mean she was stupid. There had to be rules about the use of private calls.

'I'm where Inspector Falcone sent me, sir,' she replied hesitantly. 'Testaccio. To watch the mother.'

'With whom?'

'On my own. Inspector Falcone said . . .'

'I wasn't told that.' He let a little impatience drift into his voice. 'I don't understand why you're not with the rest of the team. Do you think Inspector Falcone has some kind of . . . bias against you?'

'No, sir.'

But it took her a second to say it.

'So what do you have to report?'

'She went shopping in the market.'

'And?'

'She met a man. At the horse butcher's, where Giorgio worked.'

'You've told Falcone this?'

'Not yet . . .' She sounded less than convincing. 'I was about to report in when you called.'

'Leave that to me. Tell me about this man. Young or old?'

'Perhaps thirty-five. I believe he was a fellow prisoner of Bramante's. I don't know if this means anything . . .'

'Tell me.'

'It looked as if he and Signora Bramante had a relationship. He kissed her.'

Giorgio Bramante breathed deeply and stared at the still skeleton in the corner.

'Did she look pleased by this?'

'She looked . . . guilty. I think she hoped no one would see.'

He wanted to scream again. He wanted to shout so loud these old walls would shake.

'Did she go home with him?'

'No. She left on her own. He went back to his apartment when the market closed.'

'Men take advantage sometimes. You know this, surely?'

'Sir, I think . . .'

'Men take advantage in all kinds of ways. I feel Falcone has taken advantage of you. Would you agree?'

Silence again, but a brief one.

'I don't feel it would be appropriate for me to comment.'

'You're very loyal. I like that. Has she seen you?'

'No . . . No one's seen me.'

He thought about this.

'Listen to me, Agente. This case is more complicated than it appears. Between ourselves, more complicated than Leo Falcone can begin to appreciate. Do you understand what I'm saying?'

'I'm not sure . . .' she began.

'I need to discuss this with you, in confidence. What you've been asked to do. How you feel about it.'

'Sir . . .'

'Where are you now?'

'In a café near the old slaughterhouse in Testaccio. The horse butcher lives close by. I followed him home.'

'Good. Stay where you are. I'll send someone to replace you in an hour. Until then, if Falcone calls and orders you to do otherwise, listen, then ignore him.'

'I . . .'

Human beings were motivated by what mattered to them.

'You do want to progress in the force, don't you, Prabakaran?'

'Yes, sir.'

'Then do as I say.'

He picked up the photos in his left hand and took a second look at her. She was an interesting young woman. Different. For some reason she clearly sought to hide the truth of her appearance while working.

'My man won't know you, Agente. Describe to me what you're wearing.'

He listened carefully, relishing the meek embarrassment in her soft-toned voice as she explained the nature of her disguise, and the reasoning behind it.

'Wait for him,' he ordered, then cut the call and glanced at the bones in the alcove. He felt happy again, renewed, excited.

'They come from all four quarters of the known earth, Valeria,' he said quietly. 'They come not knowing what they might find.'

– 19 –

The rain ceased. A little late-afternoon sunlight broke briefly over the Tiber. This gave Falcone the excuse he needed. Planks were placed on the mud, and with great care they lowered him down to the water level, and accompanied him behind the screen, slowly making their way to the mouth of the old drain. When he reached the end of the temporary wooden structure he clambered onto the platform to reach the newer, larger arch in the ground beneath the busy road above. He was so exhausted by that stage he needed a break. Teresa Lupo took the opportunity immediately.

'You' – she prodded Peroni in the chest – 'are certainly not going any further. We've enough to deal with in there already without having someone throw up all over the place. In fact, I would strongly advise all three of you to take one short peek down that big black hole, breathe in the stench, then grab a few of those little collapsible picnic seats we brought along for the occasion and listen to me.'

'I am the officer in charge,' Falcone protested. 'I need to see for myself.'

She folded her arms and stood directly in his way.

'It's slippery and dark and treacherous in there. I don't even want to think of what might happen if you fell over, Leo.'

'I am the officer in charge,' Falcone repeated, outraged.

'True,' she replied, then pulled up one of the metal chairs, opened it with a quick, hard flick of the wrist and sat down.

'So you can find your own way in and I won't talk to you. Not a word. Or you can stay out here and I will. What's it to be?'

Peroni was the first to take a chair for himself. The others followed, with Falcone still grumbling.

'I thought it was a child,' Costa said. 'It looked like a child.'

She sighed, called Silvio Di Capua over with the notebook computer, found something, and turned the screen round to face them. It was a collection of photographs of a teenager with his family. He was a good head shorter than his father, who was a rotund, smiling, ordinary-seeming man, and the two older figures Costa took to be brothers. The picture was taken on a beach somewhere: five people at an ice-cream stand, happy on holiday, faces trapped in time, looking as if nothing would ever come along to disturb their contentment.

She hit the keyboard. The next image was of dental records: upper and lower teeth, and a name in the right-hand corner.

'We had all this on file from missing persons,' she explained. 'It was just a question of pulling it out. Sandro Vignola was a very short kid. No, a very short person. He was twenty-two when he went missing. It's an understandable mistake, Nic. You wanted to find Alessio Bramante.'

'We all want to find him,' Falcone interjected.

'Yes,' she agreed. 'We all do. Unfortunately I can't help you there. But if you'd like to hear about the body I do have . . .'

They said nothing. She smiled.

'Good. Let's make this quick.'

She shielded her eyes against the sudden harsh sun and stared at the sky.

'For one thing, I don't think this weather's going to last. The heavens are going to open some time soon and when that happens everyone here is going to be swimming in mud. For that very reason I've told Silvio that some time in the next twenty minutes we will be putting this poor soul into a body bag and taking what's left of him out of here. I seriously suggest you three, and any other of your colleagues who are of a gentle disposition, do not witness this event.'

The three of them sat hunched on their little chairs, saying nothing.

'Good,' she declared, clapping her hands. 'Now listen carefully, please . . .'

- 20 -

Rosa Prabakaran didn't know the man. He wore a dark, somewhat shabby winter jacket, pulled tight against the rain that was now dashing down in vertical stripes from a black, churning sky that had rolled over the last of the afternoon sun. His hood, sodden and glossy from the downpour, was close into his head. There was just a snatch of face and two bright, glistening eyes. Intelligent eyes. Interested.

Then he pulled an umbrella out from under his jacket. It was bright pink, the kind of cheap junk her father sold during weather like this.

'Agente,' he said cheerfully. 'You should be prepared for all eventualities.'

His eyes ran her up and down, the same look she'd got from men everywhere in Testaccio that day, though perhaps with a touch of amused irony. Rosa Prabakaran cursed herself for dressing like this. It made her anonymous to Beatrice Bramante. To everyone else it was a sign screaming: *look at me*.

'Thanks,' she said, and took the umbrella, wishing, as she did, that she could see more of his face. Commissario Bruno Messina hadn't made himself clear on the phone. She didn't know why she was being dragged off surveillance like this. To start some kind of disciplinary action against Falcone? That idea concerned her. She didn't like the man, but she didn't feel vindictive towards him either. In truth, she'd taken a more high-profile role in the case at the beginning than she could ever have expected. It was scarcely a surprise that Falcone reduced her position to that which her experience actually justified.

The tiny café was deserted. The woman at the till was starting to stare at them.

'Aren't you going to have a coffee? What's the rush?' She had to ask too. 'What's your name?'

'Pascale!' he replied immediately. 'Didn't Messina tell you? Jesus, things are in a mess . . . I don't know where all this is going. Do you?'

'No. The coffee.'

He pulled the hood around his head more tightly and peered at the rain which was now a grey sheet obscuring the frontage of the old slaughterhouse. The figures on the portico roof were unclear. The man and the bull were one in their struggle for life.

'I don't want coffee,' he said. 'You don't have the time for it.'

'Pascale,' she repeated.

Rosa Prabakaran tried to remember whether she'd ever heard the name before.

'I've been away for a while. Sick. Ask Peroni for a reference next time you see him. Or Costa. You know his American girlfriend?' The look came again. 'My, is he a fortunate man.'

'I'll ask them,' she said, and unhooked the cheap clasp on the umbrella, began thinking about the long walk to Via Marmorata where she could get a bus or a tram.

'Where's the woman now?'

'At home, as far as I know. She doesn't go out much.'

'And the man? This butcher you saw?'

Her eyes went to the plain public housing block across the street.

'He went in there. I haven't seen him come out.'

The figure followed the direction of her gaze.

'Did you watch all the time?'

'Yes,' she lied, badly. Watching suspects was fine. Watching the door of some cheap little apartment block, noting people who didn't interest you come and go, was deadly boring. When the sun came out briefly she'd disobeyed Messina, walked and found a bench by a small grassy slope on the Monte dei Cocci, sat there, thinking of nothing, for a long time, feeling useless, unwanted. She came back to the café on the hour, when Messina said his man would turn up. Even then she'd just been daydreaming. Reading the papers. Wondering what she'd have been doing had she taken up the offer of a junior lawyer's post in the criminal practice near the courts in Clodio. Not looking like a hooker, waiting to be relieved of duty in order to betray a man she scarcely knew, that was for sure.

She didn't know where the butcher was, and a part of her didn't care.

'You really think they're lovers?' he asked.

'Messina mentioned that?'

'I'm taking over from you, aren't I?'

Rosa Prabakaran thought about what she'd seen. It couldn't have lasted more than thirty seconds. Could you really read an entire relationship from a single, snatched glimpse into the lives of two complete strangers?

'They didn't want anyone to see them. He kissed her. She didn't . . .' The right word was important. '. . . she didn't seem to object. That's all I know.'

She caught a glimpse of his mouth then. It had a downturned expression, severe, serious, judgemental.

'This happens all the time,' he said. 'A man goes to jail. His best friend comes round to sample the goods. That's the trouble with the modern world. People have no sense of duty or propriety. A little messing around outside the nest here and there . . . no one minds. So long as that's all it is. So long as it doesn't mess with the family or get in the way of what's important. A man needs a sense of priority. The trouble is, these days they just don't care. They live their lives through the end of their dicks and nothing else. This lacks . . . balance.'

She didn't like him. She wanted to go and meet Bruno Messina, give him what he wanted, then surprise her father with a bottle of good *prosecco* to celebrate all those rip-off umbrellas he'd sold this freezing, wet, baffling spring day.

'He's all yours,' she said, and headed for the door. His hand stopped her.

'Let me give you a lift to the station or somewhere,' he said. 'You're going to get drenched, and frankly you're not dressed for it.

I've got a civilian vehicle. No one's going to know. Besides . . .' He glanced again at the block across the street where the butcher lived. 'I don't think he's going anywhere now, is he?'

They walked round the corner, a long walk, 300 metres or more, with him holding the umbrella over her head, letting the rain run down his black hood. He was parked on a little road that ran away from the old slaughterhouse, down what looked like a country lane, narrow, empty, desolate. A line of shattered pot shards from the grassy banks of the Monte dei Cocci had spilled onto the street, dislodged by the rain. They stepped over them and walked towards a white commercial van, parked on its own by a couple of large overflowing dustbins from the restaurants and night clubs up the street.

He stopped at the rear.

'You never asked to see my ID,' he said, and there was a hard, censorious tone in his voice. 'You know, if I was to tell someone that, the commissario, say, it wouldn't go down well for you.'

'I'm sorry.'

She felt exhausted. He'd moved the umbrella now so it didn't cover her properly. The rain fell on her legs, which were cold, and felt exposed. She was shivering.

'It's important you see it,' he said. 'I keep things inside.'

She wasn't thinking straight, but something still told her this was wrong.

He placed a fist firmly in her back and edged her towards the doors. There were no windows at the rear. Something was painted on the sides that she couldn't quite make out. Lettering and a symbol, all in blood red.

He got out some keys, worked the handle and opened the doors. Then he nudged her forward to look. She blinked. There was a man inside, trussed like a turkey for Christmas, some kind of rag around his mouth, hands bound behind his back, ankles tied tightly together so that he lay on the floor able only to roll helplessly around, saying nothing, going nowhere. The interior of the van was spotless, antiseptically clean, and now his own pointless floundering meant he was careering around it, bumping into white industrial boxes full of meat.

The trussed man on the floor had frightened, familiar eyes. It was the butcher from the market. She knew that the moment she saw him, and was amazed that her first emotion was fury: anger directed at herself for being so stupid.

'What do you give a condemned man?' asked the voice behind her, which was different now. More cultured. More distanced from the interested, human emotion he must have summoned up from somewhere to get her here. 'Anything he wants, I guess. Otherwise he just takes it.'

Her hands were shaking now as she fought to get the bag off her shoulder, struggling to find the gun she'd secreted inside. The strap caught. Then his powerful fist wrapped itself around the cord, snapped it, flung the bag and the precious gun into the gutter.

She thought about fighting, tried to remember the self-defence lessons she'd learned so carefully in the training school out on the Via Tiburtina, day after day, arms and hands hurting, bruises rising on her shins. But this wasn't a classroom. He was strong, so much more powerful than she could ever be. His hands moved everywhere, grasping, hurting, forcing. Hands that seemed to enjoy what they were doing: pushing her down onto the white metal floor of the van, next to the trussed butcher, winding a rag around her mouth, one that tasted of something raw and chemical, tying her hands, her ankles, securing her in a few swift easy moments as surely as a man preparing a beast for the knife.

She stared up at him. He saw. The hood came down. It wasn't the face from the photographs. Not quite. Giorgio Bramante, in the flesh, had only a passing resemblance to the man she thought she would see. He was greyer, more sallow-faced, with the complexion of someone dying from the inside out, of some cruel disease, like a cancer gnawing away relentlessly. Except for the eyes, which blazed at her.

The eyes were happy. Hungry. Amused.

- 21 -

Costa listened. He thought he was getting blasé about this kind of detail. He was wrong. What had happened to Sandro Vignola, if Teresa was right – and it was difficult to see how she could be mistaken – was as vicious and heartless as anything Bramante had done to his other victims. Perhaps more so, and that made Costa ask himself: *was this different somehow?*

There was much work to be done on the remains, which had suffered badly from animal attack and substantial decomposition in the airless, damp enclosure of the drain. This would take days to complete back in the morgue, and require outside assistance, possibly from a private lab or that of the Carabinieri. But two facts were clear to her already. Vignola had been gagged – the cloth which had been tied round his mouth to prevent him calling for help was still in place. And he'd been hobbled, hand and foot, so that he could scarcely crawl.

'Hobbled with what?' Falcone asked.

Teresa shouted to one of the morgue monkeys. He came out with a strong nylon tie, with a buckle on one end. It stank.

'I'm only guessing here,' she said, 'but I'd put money on the fact that's the same kind of hobble they use in a slaughterhouse. Remember, Bramante was working in one while he was in jail. He could have lifted a couple of these things when he came out for the weekend. Also . . .' She looked at Peroni as if to say sorry. '. . . just to make sure, he broke both of the victim's ankles. Performed after the hobble went on, so perhaps he was worried his original idea wouldn't stick.'

'This idea being?' Peroni asked.

'He crippled Sandro Vignola and put him in the drain. Then he capped the end of it with bricks. It wouldn't take long. Not if he knew what he was doing. I asked the American woman earlier . . .'

She nodded at Judith Turnhouse, still sitting under the awning, now talking quietly, calmly, to a policewoman.

'One of Bramante's many specialities as an archaeologist was the early use of brick and concrete. Apparently they knew an awful lot about that, even 2,000 years ago. They could run up the right mortar for a situation where there was damp. They knew about what kind of material to choose so that it didn't fall down after a couple of years. That's what he did here. He hobbled Sandro Vignola. He made sure he couldn't utter a sound. Then he walled him up in there and left him to die.'

Peroni said something indistinguishable.

'I imagine,' she added, 'that we'll find the cause of death was starvation. Not that it helps very much. I couldn't see any obvious wounds apart from the broken ankles. Here's another thing I learned from the American too . . .'

She looked pleased with herself for a moment. 'Walling people up and leaving them to die was one way some Roman cults treated those they believed had betrayed them.'

Falcone didn't look remotely interested. This surprised Costa.

'You mean Bramante's taunting them with their own rituals or something?' he asked.

She flicked a thumb at Di Capua.

'I don't know what I mean. All I know is this. Geek boy over there did a little research on the web before this lot came in. Everything to do with Mithras happens in sevens. There were six kids and Giorgio. There were seven different levels of stature in the temple, ranked beginner to god. Does it mean anything? I don't know. But here's a fact he found. Every level has a sacrament. Which, before you jump to conclusions, could just mean a gift. An offering. Or it could be a sac-rifice too. An animal. They killed a lot of animals back then, and not necessarily for food either. Or it could be some kind of ordeal. One of which was being left alone in some dark, deserted cave, wondering whether anyone was ever going to come back and let you out.'

They took this in, still wondering.

'Seven stages, seven sacraments,' Teresa added. 'By my reckoning, he's still one short.'

'I'm not much interested in ancient history, Doctor,' Falcone said severely.

'Giorgio is,' Costa reminded him. 'It was his life. Just as much as being a father. Perhaps the two weren't separated at all. Didn't he say you were number seven?'

Falcone stared at him. Once Costa would have felt a little awed by the older man's presence. Once he would have been too scared to utter a comment like that. But Falcone had changed. So had he. And now the inspector was regarding him with a curious expression, one that bore no animosity and possessed, instead, something not far from approval.

'A complex case doesn't necessarily demand complex solutions,' Falcone declared. 'So this killing happened, what . . .'

'Eleven years ago.' She shrugged. 'I'm amazed we've got as much to work on as we have, what with the rats and the water.'

Falcone scowled, a familiar gesture.

'And there's absolutely nothing here that's going to be of any use to us today? No forensic? Nothing? We know this was Bramante's work. He's hardly likely to deny it when we find him.'

The three men stared at each other miserably.

Teresa Lupo clicked her fingers at Silvio Di Capua.

'If you people are going to ask me a question,' she said, 'it would be polite to wait for an answer before you dive into your own personal pits of gloom. Show them, Silvio.'

Di Capua bent down. There was a transparent plastic case in his hand. Inside it wriggled a large white, corpulent worm, of a kind Costa had never seen in his life, and would feel happy never to encounter again.

'Planarian,' Di Capua said firmly, as if it meant something, and pointed towards the drain.

Teresa rapped her fat fingers on the box and beamed at the thing when it moved.

'It's a worm,' Peroni observed.

'No,' she corrected him. 'Silvio is right. It's a planarian. Our friend in Ca' d'Ossi had one too. It didn't come from there. It didn't come from the slaughterhouse. It came from some underground place where Giorgio stored him before moving him in with all those other dead people.'

'It's a worm,' Falcone said.

The Lupo forefinger waved at them, like the wagging, warning digit of a school teacher about to deliver up a secret.

'A very special worm,' she said. 'I've decided to call this one . . . Bruno. What do you think?'

- 22 -

The ambulance fought through the busy streets of the city, rocking violently across the cobble stones of the *centro storico*, battling the traffic to find the hospital at San Giovanni. The police doctor, Foglia, sat next to his patient, ignoring the two medics, who seemed to be working on Ludo Torchia out of duty rather than conviction.

Falcone took the chair opposite, held on tight for the ride, and didn't shrink from the man's severe gaze.

'This was not my doing, Patrizio,' he said in the end. 'Save your anger for someone else.'

'You mean these things simply happen in our own Questura and no one notices? What the hell is going on, Leo?'

'There's a child missing,' Falcone replied, and found himself depressed to discover how much he sounded like Arturo Messina. 'In cases like this people become different. Giorgio Bramante is a highly respected university professor. Who was to know?'

'So we allow parents to carry out their own interviews now, do we? If you can call it that.'

Falcone shrugged.

'If they're parents like Bramante. Reputable, middle-class citizens who could, I imagine, make a phone call to the right person if they wanted. This was not my decision. I opposed it as vigorously as I was able. But I am a mere *sovrintendente* around here. I was overruled. I regret that deeply. I disobeyed Messina in the end and stopped this when I was able.'

Torchia wasn't moving. Falcone didn't know a lot about medicine. Nor did he want to know much. All he saw were all the usual totems he associated with a life about to fail: oxygen and syringes, masks and mechanisms, crude toys fighting a useless battle against the inevitable.

'You could have stopped it in the first place,' Foglia said with a scowl.

'Probably not. Messina would simply have dismissed me and put someone in there who would have done nothing anyway.'

'You could have told them upstairs!'

He tried to smile.

'Messina *was* upstairs. Please. We've been friends for so many years. Don't imagine these things didn't run through my head.'

Foglia seemed to have given up on the injured man, judging by the way he allowed the medics to do everything. This surprised Falcone. He was a good doctor. A good man.

'Is there nothing you can do?'

He grunted at that.

'As one of my illustrious forebears once said, "I cannot cure death".'

They had been close for many years. When Falcone was still married, they'd made up the occasional foursome with Foglia's wife, an administrator at the opera house.

'Perhaps Messina and his kind have a point,' Falcone replied idly, thinking aloud as much for his own benefit as anyone else's. They were in the wide straight line of the Via Labicana now, a medieval pope's highway to the great church of San Giovanni in Laterano at the summit of the hill ahead. The hospital wasn't much further. This part of Ludo Torchia's journey was coming to an end.

'What?' Foglia replied, his voice becoming high-pitched with disbelief. 'Beating a man to death has a point?'

'Not for me but, as I am constantly reminded, I'm no parent. You, Patrizio, are.'

They were lovely kids, two girls, twins, fast approaching the age at which they'd go to college. Foglia and his wife would, he knew, be heartbroken when they left home.

'Imagine this was Elena or Anna,' he went on. 'Imagine you knew that she's still alive somewhere, but she won't be for much longer. She's underground. Trapped, perhaps on purpose. Frightened. Unable to do anything to help herself. And this . . . individual can tell you where she is. Possibly.'

There was a new chill in the ambulance. Falcone ignored it.

'Put yourself in that situation, Patrizio,' he went on. 'You don't want vengeance. You don't care about anything but the child. If this man speaks, she may live. If he remains silent, she will surely die.'

Foglia wriggled on his chair.

'What would you do in the circumstances?' Falcone demanded. 'Rattle off a suitable section of the Hippocratic oath then walk out of the room and start phoning around for quotes for the funeral? Not that you can be certain there will be one, naturally, because the odds are we'll never find a body; that you will never know what happened to your own flesh and blood. You will go to your grave with that big, black hole burning inside you till the end—'

'Enough!' Foglia yelled. '*Enough!*'

The ambulance lurched to a complete halt. A trumpet voluntary of car horns rose in harmonic unison and filled the air with their angry cries, like some crazed ironic fanfare for the dying man on the stretcher.

The older medic, a man in his forties, who was watching the oxygen machine like a hawk, took hold of the tube running to Torchia's mask, waited for the row outside to lessen a little, then said, 'I'd beat it out of him. Without a second thought. If I thought it would help right now I'd squeeze this oxygen supply until the bastard came clean. What else can you do?'

'And if he's innocent?' Falcone asked.

'If he's innocent,' the medic answered straight away, 'he'd say so, wouldn't he?'

Not always, Falcone thought. Sometimes, in the middle of an investigation, logic and rational behaviour went missing. In sensational cases it was by no means uncommon for some troubled individual to walk into the Questura and confess to a crime he had never committed. Some strange, inner guilt drove people to the most curious and damaging of acts on occasion. Perhaps Torchia was culpable of something dark and heinous he didn't want to share with a couple of police officers. There was no guarantee that it had to do with the disappearance of Alessio Bramante.

'We can do what we're paid to do,' Falcone replied. 'We can try to find out what has happened, to sort some facts from the mist. That sounds a little feeble, I know, but sometimes it's all we have. Besides, someone tried to beat the truth out of him and look at the outcome. He didn't say a single helpful word as far as I can gather. We still don't know where the boy is. Which means . . .'

What? He still wasn't sure.

'Perhaps he is genuinely innocent. That he was in the wrong place at the wrong time, though I doubt that. Or he wanted Bramante to do what he did for some reason. It gave him some satisfaction.'

Foglia shook his head.

'What possible motive could he have for that?' he asked.

Falcone felt a little ashamed. It had been wrong of him to personalize the case in the way he had, to put that cruel picture inside Foglia's head. It had disturbed his old friend, who was now red-faced, exasperated and, unusually for him, confused.

'Listen to yourself, Leo.'

'I don't know. I honestly don't, Patrizio. And I wish I did.' He hesitated. 'Is there any chance he'll live?'

Both of them, the doctor and the older medic, shook their heads in tandem.

'Will he regain consciousness?' Falcone asked. 'I was clinging to some faint hope he might tell a stranger something he wouldn't disclose to Giorgio Bramante. If there was a personal reason behind this that we don't understand, perhaps I'd have a chance.'

'He's not coming back,' the medic muttered, then gingerly opened the door and peered outside. The driver was there, lighting a cigarette. He stared back at them, guilty at first, then smiled, the quick, cheeky Roman smile everyone used when they were caught out. Falcone listened to the man's brief explanation and quickly understood what was happening. There was an accident in the road ahead. They were stuck in solid traffic going forwards and back. It would be some time – perhaps more than fifteen minutes – before they got to the hospital.

The medic swore, closed the door and tugged his colleague's arm. The other one was a thin, unremarkable young man with a head of long blond hair. He was still watching the dials and the screens, a little nervous, as if he hadn't seen many deaths before.

'Don't waste your time,' the older man said. 'I'd put money on him being gone by the time we get there. Is that right?'

Patrizio Foglia must have seen many men and women die. All the same, there was something in his eyes at that moment which Leo Falcone didn't recognize.

The doctor stared at the monitors attached to Ludo Torchia, whose breathing seemed shallow and faint.

'I believe so.'

'You should have stayed in the Questura,' Foglia said with some faint note of reproof barely hidden inside his voice. 'You have some of the other students, don't you?'

'We have,' Falcone agreed. Probably all of them by now. As he'd expected, they weren't good at hiding.

'Then they can tell you,' the doctor suggested.

Falcone shook his head and looked at the still figure.

'Not after this. They're surrounded by lawyers. They don't need to say a thing. Why should they? We've allowed one of them to be beaten almost to death in our own interview room. They can stay silent for as long as they like. We can't even use it against them.'

'I need a cigarette,' the older medic complained. 'We're not going to be moving for a while.'

'As a doctor,' Foglia murmured, 'I shouldn't say this. But go and have one. Both of you.'

The younger medic looked baffled.

'I don't smoke.'

His companion caught something in Foglia's expression.

'I'll teach you,' he said, and led him out of the ambulance.

Falcone sat there, silent, lost for words.

Foglia took another look at the monitors.

'He's dying, Leo. There's nothing anyone can do.'

'So you said.'

'You really think he might have talked to you?'

'I don't know, Patrizio. This case makes me realize I know very little indeed.'

Foglia stood up and walked over to the equipment cabinet on the wall of the ambulance, reached in and took out a syringe, then, after checking carefully, an ampoule of some drug.

'If I'm lucky, I may be able to bring him back to consciousness for a minute or so. It would be appreciated if the pathologist made no mention of this in his autopsy. I quite like my job and it's a sight better than prison.'

He primed the syringe, checking the level very carefully.

'Well?' Foglia asked. 'We don't have all night. Neither does that boy.'

Falcone felt embarrassed.

'What else will it do to him?'

'He'll probably die of heart failure within fifteen minutes or so.'

'No!'

'He's dead anyway, Leo!'

'I said no, Patrizio. I've already arrested one man for murder tonight. Don't make it two.'

He laughed, without conviction.

'I'm a doctor. We all make mistakes.'

Falcone couldn't believe this was happening.

'Don't do it. Please. For your own sake.'

'What about the boy?'

Falcone tried to argue, but the words weren't there.

'Exactly,' Foglia went on. 'Either way I'm not going to get to sleep tonight.'

He found a patch of clear skin between the bruises on Torchia's bare right arm, plumped up the vein with the same professional care he would have used on a patient in the Questura surgery, then slipped the hypodermic deep into the flesh.

It took less than a minute. Almost to the rhythm of the horns outside, the student's chest jerked. Suddenly, his eyes opened, blinking at the bright light above the surgical stretcher.

Falcone moved over to crouch by the stretcher.

'Ludo,' he murmured, and found his throat was dry, his voice sounded distant and foreign. 'We need to find the boy.'

Torchia's swollen, blackened lips moved, shiny with blood and spittle. He said nothing. All his energy was, at that moment, spent focusing on the light above him.

He sobbed, choked back a liquid, guttural cough and managed to turn his head, just five degrees or so, in their direction.

Falcone caught a glimpse of his eyes. He looked like a child himself at that moment: alone, scared, confused, in pain.

Then something came back, an unreadable certainty in his face, and Leo Falcone felt, against his own wishes, that he'd been wrong all along. Torchia did know something about the boy, and even now the memory amused him.

'Say something,' Falcone pleaded, and thought they were the feeblest words he'd ever uttered in his life.

- 23 -

Unaware that a fat white planarian, recently dissected in the morgue below, had come to bear his name, Bruno Messina sat in the large leather chair in his office looking like a man at the end of his tether.

'So there's nothing?' he asked, half furious, half pleased he was able to launch this accusation in their direction.

Costa had to nudge his boss for an answer. He'd been staring out of the window, into the night, lost in thought, as if remembering something. Fragments from the Bramante case of old kept re-entering the conversation they'd had on the way to the Questura, like flotsam released from the depths of some murky sea, surfacing in Falcone's troubled mind. There had been a moment when Costa wondered whether it would be wiser for him to retire from the case altogether, to make way for a younger, more physically sound man such as Bavetti, the inspector Messina had tried to introduce that very morning. Then, just before the car parked in the secure piazza behind the station, Falcone had taken a call from the intelligence team chasing Bramante's movements in the city and, in the space of one minute, conducted the kind of intense, rapid-fire interrogation of a junior officer no other man in the Questura could begin to match. The old Leo Falcone was there when needed. He was just distracted, for reasons Costa couldn't quite comprehend.

*

The team had stayed at the murder scene by the river for two hours in all. When they returned to the Questura Falcone had summoned a meeting of all the senior officers in the case, along with Teresa Lupo and Silvio Di Capua. That had taken more than ninety minutes. It was now just past eight o'clock, a time when shifts changed, when stalled investigations risked falling into a mood of stasis, indolence and, eventually, despair.

'Furthermore,' Messina added, 'you disobeyed my express orders. You left the Questura.'

'I thought I was only a prisoner at night,' Falcone replied, without the slightest hint of guile. 'I apologize if there was some misunderstanding.'

'I never . . .'

Messina gave up in exasperation.

'What are we supposed to do, Leo? One more day and all we have is one more body.'

'That's not quite fair, sir,' Costa interjected. 'We know that Bramante has been trying to find his old maps of underground sites.'

'That narrows it down,' Messina said dryly.

'We know from Bru—' Peroni corrected himself. 'We know from the worm we found down by the river that he didn't keep the last victim there.'

'I say again: that narrows it down.'

'But it does,' Costa objected. 'The worm Teresa got out of Toni LaMarca isn't in any of the databases. That means we know where Bramante *didn't* hide him before he took the body round to Ca' d'Ossi.'

'Tell me something you do know!'

'Of course,' Falcone replied, taking control of the conversation, and allowing Costa a glance that said: mine now. 'There are something like 150 registered subterranean archaeological sites for which La Sapienza have no planarian records. The university archaeological department has a further forty-three that are not officially registered but were visited by Bramante in the course of his work. That means he could have used any one of them, or somewhere else entirely.'

'This could take years!'

Falcone laughed.

'No. A couple of days at most, I think. We could start now, but in the dark . . . he'd be gone the moment he heard something. Wherever he is, he knows it well and we don't. When we send in men we need to have a team outside on the exits. Besides, we have other work to do.'

Bruno Messina sighed.

'Nearly 200 sites . . .'

'That's the total,' Costa interrupted. 'It's coming down all the time. We can rule out some because they're not close to running water, so it's highly unlikely there would be a planarian population. Also, we ought to assume he's in reasonable proximity to the Aventino. This is the area he knows best. He took LaMarca's body to Ca' d'Ossi using a stolen car. We found it near the Circus Maximus this afternoon. It has LaMarca's blood in the trunk. Bramante was running a considerable risk there. An intelligent man would wish to minimize that. He wouldn't be far away. Tomorrow, from seven on, we start looking in a radius out from Ca' d'Ossi.'

Messina almost exploded.

'This is ridiculous. How many searches can you perform a day? Ten? Fifteen? You could have men out there now.'

'I've already told you,' Falcone shook his head. 'It would be counterproductive in the dark. Besides, Bramante has no one left on his list but me. I'd like this finished as soon as possible too. But, being realistic, there is no rush. If I don't have him when my time runs out, I hand everything over to Bavetti. He can have the credit. I don't care. And' – he paused to make this point, which seemed to him an important one – 'we should not fall into the trap of acting first and thinking afterwards. That's happened too much in relation to Giorgio Bramante already. It's almost as if he expects it of us.'

'If that's a criticism of my father, Falcone . . .'

'No, no, no.'

The inspector looked dissatisfied, with himself more than anyone. When Costa compared him with Peroni, it was hard to believe these two men were around the same age. Gianni had found something over the past eighteen months. A new life, the odd blossoming of love in autumn with Teresa, had revived him, put colour into his battered, farmer's features, a spring into his step. Falcone had been brutally wounded in service, a shock from which he had yet to recover fully, both physically and mentally.

A stray thought entered Costa's head at that moment: what if he never quite made it back? How would Falcone, a man whose self-knowledge had a candid, heartless intensity, be able to face that fact?

'This is not about your father,' the inspector insisted. 'Or me. Or any of us here. It's about Giorgio Bramante and his son. His son more than anything. It's the same now as it was fourteen years ago. If we could find out what happened to the boy, all of this would be over. Had it been Alessio in that hellhole down by the river today, Bramante would have been walking into this Questura tonight to give himself up. I'm convinced of that.'

'Closure,' Messina said, and nodded sagely, in agreement. 'You could be right.'

'Please don't use that kind of trite cliché around me,' Falcone said immediately, sending a red flush to Messina's choleric face. 'I may not be a parent but I surely understand one thing. When you have lost a child there is no closure. It's a myth, a convenient media fantasy which the rest of us adopt in order to allow ourselves to sleep at night. You'll be asking me to "move on" next . . .'

'I may well,' Messina snapped. 'Bavetti's chasing your heels, Leo.'

'Good. I like competition. If we find the boy, discover what happened to him, Giorgio Bramante will give himself up because he's lost what's currently driving him. His anger would seem to be directed solely at me by this stage, though I still fail to understand why. Uncovering the fate of that child will take the sting out of that rage, supplant it with what should have been there in the first place, and for some reason never was: the natural response of a father. Grief. Mourning. The kind of grim and bitter acceptance we've all seen for ourselves before.'

Messina snorted.

'I didn't realize psychology was your subject.'

'Neither did I until recently,' Falcone replied. 'I wish I'd made this discovery earlier. But there you are. So' – he leaned back in his chair, stretched his long legs and closed his eyes – 'this morning you said we had another forty-eight hours.'

'This morning you held a gun to my head,' Messina replied, offended.

'I'm sorry, Commissario. Genuinely. We haven't had a good start to this relationship, have we? I imagine, in the circumstances, it's inevitable. You blame me for what happened fourteen years ago. So does Giorgio Bramante, come to that.'

'I want no more surprises,' Messina emphasized, bristling at the thought. 'No more trips outside the Questura. No more wild goose chases.'

Falcone threw his arms open wide in protest.

'I said! It was a misunderstanding.'

Bruno Messina drew in a deep, agonized breath.

'Very well,' he conceded. 'You go nowhere. None of you. Not till it's daylight. If you have nothing come Thursday this is Bavetti's case. You three can get out of my sight for a while. Everything runs so smoothly without you around. Why is that?'

Falcone struggled to his feet, holding on to the desk for a moment, then let go, standing unaided. Costa restrained the urge to help him. A point was being made. His bald, avian head, upright, bright-eyed, fixed each of them in turn. He looked tired. But then they probably all did. A part of the old Falcone was still there. A good part.

'Perhaps you're just not looking hard enough,' the inspector suggested.

Messina shot him a furious glance.

'Don't push your luck,' he said with menace. 'It's not that great at the moment, is it?'

'A day,' the inspector emphasized. 'That's all I ask. I will bring you Giorgio Bramante. That' – he clicked his fingers at Costa and Peroni, then pointed at the door – 'is a promise.'

The three of them stood outside, by the corridor window a little way along from Messina's office, glad to be out of his presence.

'How, exactly?' Peroni asked.

They didn't get an answer. Falcone was stomping down the corridor with an awkward gait, not looking back for a moment.

- 24 -

They'd turned off the Via Galvani quickly, parked somewhere; maybe, she guessed, in one of the deserted dead-end alleys on the far side of the Monte dei Cocci. There was no escape. Bramante had walked round to the back of the van, punched the butcher hard in the face once when he tried to resist, then tied the two of them tightly together with thick, tough climbing rope. Then he'd disappeared, for hours. She'd watched the daylight die in the front windows of the van as night fell, trying to find some way of communicating with the sweating, terrified man to whom she was tethered. It was impossible. Finally, she'd persuaded him to help her kick the walls of the van for long periods on end, and still no one came. Not until Bramante returned, threw open the doors, face furious from the noise, fists flailing at the butcher again.

After that Bramante got in the front and drove for no more than ten minutes, uphill – the Aventino, it could be nowhere else – then down a winding road, meeting no traffic, travelling so quickly they rolled around in the back, bumping into each other, tethered by the climbing rope, close enough for her to see the all-consuming fright in her fellow captive's eyes. The vehicle came to an abrupt halt. The doors flew open. Briefly – all she saw were the distant lights of a tram, the Number 3, it couldn't be any other – they were outside, before being dragged down a stony path, falling, tumbling on the hard stones and cold damp grass, winding up in some dank passageway that had an old, rank smell of age and distant sewers.

She'd been on a history trip when she was in school: the catacombs somewhere out on the Appian Way. They smelled like this, a strong, pervasive reek, organic and earthy, that had probably hung around for centuries.

Rosa Prabakaran hated being in the catacombs, not that she let this show. It felt as if she were trapped in the grave.

Finally, pushed on by Bramante's feet and fists, they found themselves in some subterranean chamber. Not large. Not complete, either, because part of it was open to the night air, letting in some soft, slow drizzle that curled down from a dark velvet sky in which stars were faintly visible.

There were chambers off this principal vestibule, guarded with iron gates, modern ones, designed to keep out intruders.

Bramante unlocked the cell to the right, opened the door, and took out a large clasp knife.

The butcher whimpered and stared in horror at the weapon. Bramante cut through the thick climbing rope with one strong swipe, then propelled the man inside with a vicious kick in the back. He fell on the floor in a pained heap. The door closed behind him with a clatter.

She closed her eyes, found herself wondering what this meant, then immediately fought to stifle the thoughts that rose in her head.

Bramante pushed her through into the adjoining chamber, closed the door behind him, locked it. He had a set of keys, she noticed. Several, on a chain, the kind a caretaker would use. Or an archaeologist, going back to his old haunts.

He propelled her forward again until they were standing close to the end of the room, then found a large electric lantern on the ground and turned on the light. A broad yellow beam illuminated what appeared to be a cavernous chamber, with brick walls clinging to the rock and earth around them. One corner was open to a luminous night sky. Some dim illumination from an artificial bulb surely joined the light from the stars and an unseen moon there. A man or woman at ground level just might have seen them from the right position, a thought that gave her no comfort, since Bramante must have realized this too.

They had to be somewhere central yet sufficiently deserted for him to avoid detection. Rosa racked her brain to imagine such a place in the heart of Rome. There were, when she came to think of it, scores, possibly hundreds. Abandoned excavations, old archaeological finds that never had the pulling power to bring in sufficient tourists to keep them open. The city was a honeycomb of ancient sites, some on the surface, many more below the dark, dank earth. Giorgio Bramante doubtless knew them all.

He came and stood close behind, one large, strong hand curling round to lay his palm flat on her stomach. His face crept close to hers, his breath, hot and anxious, panted in her ear.

Then the blade rose in his other hand, flashed past her eyes to press hard against her cheek. It was cold and damp, and she could detect the sharp edge of the metal on her skin. The tip found the corner of her gag, lifted it, cut through fabric. The material fell away and she found herself choking, too scared to say anything, aware he still had the rope in his hand, aware, too, that Bramante was a smart man, a man who would never have returned to her the power of speech if it could have been of any possible use.

'Do you know what this place is, Rosa?' he whispered.

'Don't call me that,' she said, once the choking ended, struggling to adopt a quiet, firm tone to her voice, one that didn't expose the fear she felt.

'A woman with self-respect,' he murmured. 'That's important. So. Again. Do you know what this place is, Agente Prabakaran?'

'Some . . .'

She shrank in on herself, cold in the flimsy, stupid clothes she'd chosen.

He was hard. She could feel the anxious pressure as he held her close.

'. . . temple.'

'Ten out of ten,' he said, and, thankfully, released his grip, just a little.

Giorgio Bramante pulled a pocket torch out of his jacket and played the light on the object in front of them, filling out the yellow light of the lantern. It was an altar, perhaps five metres long and two high, with a stone surface that was still flat and level.

Like a table. Or a hard rock bed. Something was carved on it. He noticed it caught her attention. Bramante pushed her forward.

'Can you see it?' he asked, and there was some unfathomable bitter note, tinged with sadness, in the words.

Carved into the face of the altar was the long, muscular shape of a creature being wrestled to the ground by a burly figure who wore a winged helmet and held a short, stabbing sword tight in his right hand. The animal's face was contorted: bulging eyes, flared nostrils, a living thing struggling for life. Bells rang in her head. It was like the statues on the old Testaccio slaughterhouse, a man overpowering a colossal bull, intent on slaughter. Only there was more to the image here. A dog was licking the blood that ran from the beast's throat. A scorpion was pulling hungrily on its taut penis. This was a freak scene from a vivid nightmare.

'It's insane,' she murmured, and closed her eyes because he was roaring again, like a beast himself, pulling her into him, dragging her head close into his body until his mouth was in her hair, his torso locked tight against the curves of her back.

He glanced at the altar and the figures there.

'A man is either Mithras or the bull,' Giorgio Bramante said quietly. 'The giver or the gift. After which he is nothing.'

She caught a glimpse of his face and regretted it immediately. His eyes weren't quite human. They were dead. Or absent of humanity. She wasn't sure which.

He leaned ever closer into her, pressing so hard now it hurt, and whispered eagerly, 'I spent so long in prison. No women. No pleasure. No comfort . . .'

She closed her eyes and tried to remember what they told every woman in the force about a situation like this. Only one word remained clear in her head.

Survive.

– 25 –

Whatever drug Foglia had given Ludo Torchia seemed to be racing through the young student's blood system, like some deadly spike of adrenalin. He lay there taut, rigid, eyes wide open, acutely alert, taking in their faces, taking in the din of the traffic outside: horns and angry human voices, an ordinary evening in the Via Labicana, such mundane noises to accompany the end of a human life.

Falcone was astonished to find those sounds were still there, fourteen years after the event, alive in his head, so real he could hear them. And Ludo Torchia's face too: shock mixed with something not short of amusement. The face of a guilty man, Falcone had realized that on the instant. A guilty man, too, who was in no mood to be helpful in his dying moments.

'Say something.'

Falcone mouthed the same words now, alone in his office, trying to marshal his thoughts in the way he used to with such fluent ease. It was all getting harder and it wasn't just his injuries. He was starting to feel old. Even before the gunshot wound in Venice he'd passed some invisible point in his life, a moment of profound change, when all his past skills simply solidified inside him and stayed there, clinging on, hoping to defy the years. If they found Bramante the following day, Messina still had him in his sights. There would, he now knew, be no new talents, no fresh challenges. The time was approaching when he would have to pass on the reins to a new generation. Nic Costa one day, or so he hoped. Barring some kind of a miracle, only the sidelines waited for Leo Falcone: administration or some other corner of bureaucracy before the inevitable retirement. This part of his life was coming to a close, and he had no idea what could possibly replace it.

Or how he could even begin to approach that task without putting the present case into some kind of compartment he could label 'resolved'. He'd snapped at Messina over the grim word 'closure', unfairly perhaps, because a part of Falcone did want this issue finished, for good. Not just with Bramante back in jail, but with the fate of the boy uncovered too. He believed, with every instinct thirty years of police work had given him, that the two were inseparable.

His mind wandered back to the ambulance again. Everything in those last moments was so hazy. It had been hard to catch Torchia's final, murmured words.

Reluctantly, because he knew the pain it would cause, he took out his personal address book and found Foglia's number. The doctor had retired from the Questura six months after the Bramante case. Both men knew why, though they had never discussed the matter. Falcone knew Foglia would never be able to live with the consequences of what he'd done, perhaps all the more because they were never brought to the light of day. Teresa Lupo's predecessor in the morgue had quietly overlooked whatever substances he found in Torchia's blood – an act of deliberate negligence which Falcone knew he could never expect from her. So the best Questura doctor Falcone had ever worked with took early retirement and, when his children left home for university, departed his native Rome for good to live on Sant'Antioco, a small, little-visited island on the west coast of Sardinia, a place that seemed, to Falcone, to say: *don't visit.*

All the same, he did go, some five or six years before, spending a few quiet days watching the sea from the couple's large, modern villa above a modest holiday resort, passing pleasantries, never talking about work.

It was enough.

Falcone dialled the number, waited, then heard Foglia's familiar voice. He sounded a little older. A little more settled than Falcone remembered. After the excuses and brief exchanges of news, the retired doctor took a deep breath and announced, 'I know why you're calling, Leo. You don't need to beat about the bush.'

The Bramante case had made big headlines fourteen years ago. It was back up there now, louder than ever.

'If I had any alternative, Patrizio.'

'My God, you must be desperate if you need the likes of me.'

'I just . . .'

Foglia was spot on. He was desperate.

'What do you want?' the voice on the line demanded. 'If it's a free holiday we'd love to see you. Please come. May or June when the fresh tuna are in. I'll teach you how to fish. How to relax.'

'I'll take you up on that,' Falcone promised.

'No, you won't. Does it make you feel good? To know you were right about Giorgio Bramante? That he was some kind of animal all along?'

'Not at all,' he replied honestly. 'I wish to God I'd been wrong. That he'd just come out of jail, gone to a quiet academic job somewhere then put the past behind him.'

'But he couldn't, could he? Not without knowing.'

'No.'

Falcone could recall precisely Torchia's dying words in the back of that ambulance, amid the cacophony of horns and angry human voices outside. They hadn't made sense at the time. They didn't now.

'You must have seen many people die, Patrizio. Does it matter what they say?'

'Rarely. I had one miserable, tight-fisted old bastard tell his wife to turn off the lights afterwards. That was one to remember.'

'And Ludo Torchia?'

There was a pause on the line.

'*Meglio una bella bugia che una brutta verità.*'

The words were just as Falcone remembered, spat out by the dying Torchia one by one, punctuated by some kind of ironic, choking laughter.

Better a beautiful lie than an ugly truth.

'Funny old saying at the best of times,' Foglia declared. 'They seem to me the dying words of an actor, someone who is playing a game in his head, even to the end. Do you have any idea what he meant?'

'The beautiful lie was surely Giorgio Bramante. The idea that he was some kind of loving father figure, the man we took him to be.'

'And the ugly truth?'

'There you have me.'

There was an awkward pause on the line. Falcone had no idea what it signified.

'You will visit us again one day, Leo, won't you? It's lovely here in the spring. We would both enjoy your company.'

'Of course. You heard nothing more? There was a moment . . .'

When Torchia had closed his eyes again, as the drug seemed to wear off, Falcone, furious, desperate, had thrown open the doors of the ambulance and screamed at the two medics there to find some way, any way through the mass of cars and buses and lorries blocking the Via Labicana. It was a slender hope, but perhaps there had been some few words that had eluded him.

'He said nothing more. I'm sorry.'

'No. I'm the one who should apologize. I should never have dragged this back into the light of day for you. It's unfair.'

The silence again. A thought pricked at Leo Falcone's mind. Patrizio Foglia did have some secret weighing on his chest, surely.

'There's something I never knew, isn't there?' he asked.

Foglia sighed.

'Oh God. Why does it have to keep coming back? Why doesn't the man simply mourn his own child and find himself a life somehow? Or put a gun to his own head for a change?'

'Tell me what you know. Please.'

He could never, not in a million years, have predicted what he heard next.

'I took a close interest in the autopsy,' Foglia said softly. 'I had good reason, as you must appreciate.'

'And?'

'There was clear evidence Torchia had anal sex that day. Brutal. There was blood and bruising. It had . . . culminated too. Possibly rape. Possibly sadomasochistic. I am not an expert in these matters.'

Falcone's mind went blank. Without thinking he said, 'Those boys were down those caves for some kind of ritual. There were drugs. I imagine we shouldn't be surprised.'

He heard Foglia's long, pained intake of breath over the phone.

'It wasn't in the caves, Leo. The evidence was plain and fresh and incontrovertible. This happened shortly before he died. In the Questura. In the cell where you and Messina and Giorgio Bramante questioned him.'

Falcone's vision became blurred. He caught his breath.

'And you told no one?' he asked, incredulous.

'I asked the pathologist to leave it out of his report. He was . . . accommodating. The Questura was in enough trouble already. Did you really want another scandal on your hands? Whether it was Bramante, Messina . . . or you . . . either way, it would have rebounded on us. Besides, what use could it possibly have been? Torchia was dead. Bramante was in custody. You had your man.'

'*The boy!*' Falcone responded, aware he was yelling down the phone, unable to stop himself. 'What about the boy? Had I known that . . .'

These were the early days of DNA. They could have identified Bramante as the sexual assailant too, surely, and that would have changed the entire complexion of the case.

'Then what?' Foglia demanded crossly. 'Do tell me, Leo. I would love to know.'

'Then perhaps . . .'

There could be no instant answer. What mattered was that he had been robbed of some knowledge that was, surely, useful, if only he could begin to comprehend its significance.

'I'm sorry,' the voice on the line said. 'I wanted an end to it. We all did. I wish . . .'

'Good night,' Falcone snapped, then slammed down the phone.

He sat alone, placed his head in his hands, didn't mind at that moment what a passer-by seeing him like this in his office would think.

Was this the ugly truth? That Giorgio Bramante was not simply just a careless father, but a man gripped by some dark, secret side to his character too? If it was, his wife, with her self-inflicted wounds and her compulsive need to paint their lost child, over and over again, must surely have known.

He swore as another realization struck him. The young Indian detective had been deputed to followed Beatrice Bramante all day long. He'd never even looked for her report.

Falcone keyed the name 'Prabakaran' into the computer.

It came up with nothing since the previous evening.

'Novices . . .'

She would be home by now. He let a low curse slip from his lips, then looked up her mobile number, picked up the phone, and dialled it, steeling himself for the conversation that would follow, one in which he would remind a junior officer that no one on his team ever went off duty without filing a report.

The phone rang three times. A man's voice answered.

'I would like to speak to Agente Prabakaran,' he said impatiently, adding, 'This is Inspector Falcone.'

There was a pause.

'Leo,' said a cold, amused voice at the other end. 'What kept you?'

- 26 -

Peroni was trying to nail down possible underground locations for Bramante in the company of the worm geek, two archaeology students the intelligence team had dug up and a roomful of maps. So Costa found a quiet corner in the office and called Orvieto. Her voice sounded distant, lacking the warm, confident timbre he'd come to expect. Emily was just a few hours away by car but it felt as though she might be on the other side of the world. The others were having dinner; she was alone in her room, resting. It wasn't like her.

'What's wrong?' he asked.

'Nothing. I just didn't want company. Also, it pains me to watch others enjoying good wine when I can't join in.'

'How do you feel?'

There was a pause. This was so new for both of them. The doctors had said she should expect to feel tired, perhaps depressed from time to time. Yet she had no one to share this with now. Raffaela knew nothing about motherhood. Arturo Messina, who had been an extraordinary source of support for her in his own absence, did what he could, but he was still a stranger.

'Perhaps I'll go and see someone tomorrow,' she conceded eventually. 'It's only a little thing.'

'You can do that tonight,' he said immediately. 'Why wait?'

'Because I know what they'll say. They'll sigh and think: here's another first-time mother teetering on the edge of panic. All because

283

it's new to her. Nothing more. Children come into the world all the time.'

'They won't mind. That's why they're there.'

'No,' she said firmly. 'They're there to treat sick people. I'll see a doctor in the morning, just to reassure us both. I've no reason to think there's anything wrong really. I simply feel a little out of sorts. That's all.'

He didn't push it. He knew her well enough by now not to argue.

'When will I see you?' she asked.

'Messina's given us one more day. After that, if Bramante is still out there, Falcone hands over to Bavetti. We'll be gone from the Questura, all three of us. We don't meet Messina's approval. He doesn't sound much like his father.'

'No,' she replied, and he could hear a note of sadness in her voice. 'There's some distance between those two and I don't really understand why. Fathers and sons. I thought it was supposed to be some special kind of bond women were meant to envy. They don't seem to have a relationship at all.'

Costa thought of his own family, the constant, abrasive difficulties he'd experienced with his father, almost till the end when he was in a wheelchair, stricken too, and their mutual frailty brought about some painful, redemptive reconciliation that still pricked like an awkward needle when the memories came back. So much time wasted on stupid arguments, from both sides. Marco Costa never made life easy for anyone, himself and his own flesh and blood least of all.

'Just one more myth,' he murmured.

She waited for a moment, then said, 'No, it's not. I never knew your father. I really wish I had. Even so, I see someone else in your eyes from time to time and I know it has to be him. You two had a link going between you that never existed for me with my own dad. Or my mom either. And it's not just you. I've noticed this before. It's men. I think . . .'

Another, longer pause, one that told him she wasn't sure she ought to say this.

'You think what?'

'In a way, once you become fathers, you feel guilty if you feel you're just living in the moment. When a man has a son he develops some sense of duty that tells him the day will come when he'll pass on the torch. One generation to the next. And that's what's driving you all crazy about this case. Not the missing kid, or rather not just the missing kid. You see a world where that all got taken away. Some kind of sacred bond that's been broken. Even Leo . . .'

'Leo doesn't have children!'

'Neither do you. But you both had fathers. Have you heard him mention his? Ever?'

'No.'

Costa's gaze wandered to the glass-fronted office across the room where Falcone was still working, pale-faced. It was gone eleven. He looked as if he could go on for hours.

'If you want to discuss the case,' she went on, 'it doesn't bother me, really. Feel free.'

'I don't have anything left to tell you. We think we can start to narrow down where he's hiding tomorrow. It's just a standard operation: search the possibilities, eliminate what we can until we find something. As far as Alessio's concerned . . .'

The shadow of the lost boy hovered behind everything like a ghost. Without telling anyone Costa had, during his break earlier that evening, driven over to the little church of Sacro Cuore in Prati, talked to the church warden there, a good man who was a little scared and puzzled by what had happened. He had spoken with the plain-clothes officer on surveillance outside on Falcone's orders, satisfied himself that the likelihood was that Bramante had never been near the place that day. Then he'd returned to the church, gone into the little room, with the strange, unworldly name, Il Piccolo Museo del Purgatorio, looked at the items on the wall, the blood-stained T-shirt in particular, and tried to imagine what all this meant to Giorgio Bramante.

Plain screws fastened the glass to the case on the wall. They would be simple to remove. What eluded him was the rationale: it was a public act with a private meaning.

Bramante blamed Ludo Torchia and the other students for Alessio's fate. That much was clear. But an intelligent man couldn't fool himself either. He was the father. He carried the responsibility for his young son. He had brought him to that place. He bore his share of the blame too, blame that had somehow translated itself, in his wife's head, into an act of self-mutilation: cutting her own flesh to stain a garment belonging to her missing son, and placing it on the wall of this dusty place that smelled of emptiness and cold, damp stone. Was this act – Bramante placing a mark of his victims on the missing child's shirt – some way in which he hoped to make amends?

'Perhaps you're right, Nic. I tried to disregard what you said because it seemed so you.'

'Right about what?'

The memory of Santo Cuore bothered him for some reason that was out of reach.

'That he didn't die in that hill. Someone, surely, would have found something.'

But that idea, which he'd come to dismiss himself, now raised so many unanswerable questions.

'Someone would have known. He would have come forward, Emily. Surely.'

'There was the peace camp at the Circus Maximus. You found out about that.'

'True . . . but that was fourteen years ago. I've no idea how we could start work on that today.'

'Quite . . .' He heard a deep breath on the line. 'Have you talked to Teresa about this?'

'No,' he replied, baffled. 'Why should I?'

'Women have conversations with each other that men avoid. All you see is the present. Teresa has an interesting past too.'

'Meaning?'

'She was a student firebrand back when she was young. Are you surprised?'

Not for a moment, he thought. And it had never occurred to him. Emily was right: all he saw was the woman he'd come to know and admire over the last few years. He'd no idea of the journey that had brought her there.

'I can imagine that. You think she'd know about this demonstration?'

'Look at the newspaper cuttings yourself. If you were young, radical and living in Rome back then it's difficult to see how she could have avoided it. She would have been around the same age as the one who died. Torchia, wasn't it?'

'She would,' he agreed, though the very idea seemed alien and improbable.

'Here's another thing that struck me. It's absolutely clear these students were doing something weird down there. You found the cockerel. They'd sacrificed that, right?'

'There was a dead bird. They'd been messing around. I'm just guessing. None of them gave a statement because of what happened to Torchia.'

'They weren't there for class, that's for sure. So let's say it was some kind of ritual.'

'Let's say.'

'Where do you think they got the idea?' she asked. 'Everything they knew about Mithraism they learned from Giorgio Bramante.'

This conversation was beginning to depress him. He could hear some tension, some excitement in her voice, the same emotion he witnessed when they'd worked together officially, just once, on the same case.

'What idea?'

'Anyone can look this up, Nic. No one understands much about Mithraism but what we do know suggests it was an organized, highly ritualistic cult that demanded a gift from its followers if they wanted to progress through the ranks.'

'Seven orders, seven sacraments,' he said, recalling what Teresa had told them.

'Precisely. And it's not unreasonable to think that the higher you progressed, the more you had to offer in return. It's not that different to the kind of hierarchical structure you get in the Masons or some modern cults. Or the FBI, for that matter.'

'No.' He wasn't even going to countenance this. 'We've been here before and I still won't accept it. I can't believe any father would put a child through pain or worse just because of some ancient ritual. A stupid student – Torchia, maybe. Not a man like Bramante.'

'I told you!' Her voice rose, in volume and pitch. It worried him. 'Maybe it went wrong. He probably never thought for a moment that Alessio would be harmed. He just wanted to initiate the boy into the mysteries or something. Or take part in his own sacrament. I don't know. Who's to say Torchia wasn't part of that game, unwittingly, maybe? Who's to say that's why Giorgio Bramante beat him to death? Out of revenge. And to make sure none of us ever really got to know what happened down there?'

He was silent. It was a good point, even if he felt, in his bones, it needed to be challenged.

'Perhaps the reason you never found Alessio,' she continued, 'is because he just didn't want to face his father after whatever happened. He couldn't bear the sight of him for one more minute.'

'So a seven-year-old child walks out into Rome and just disappears?'

'It's happened before. You know that as well as I do. He could be alive. He could have fallen victim to some genuine maniac out there, somewhere else, say in that peace camp. Nic . . .' That pained intake of breath again, as she steeled herself to say something he didn't want to hear. 'At some stage of your life you're just going to have face up to the fact that there are some mad, bad people out there and it doesn't actually matter why they're like that. What matters is stopping them harming the rest of us.'

Others said that kind of thing to Falcone all the time. He could imagine the very same words coming from Bruno Messina.

'We all want it stopped, Emily,' he said, trying not to sound censorious. 'Understanding them makes it easier.'

'Not always. When it's all this close, understanding makes you start to put yourself in his shoes. Trying to think like a father who's lost a son, and I don't think it's that simple, do you?'

'No,' he admitted. Something about the entire case continued to elude them all, he thought, and it wasn't straightforward, simply a question of motive or action or opportunity. It was in the grey area that existed between people who knew each other, loved each other, once upon a time. 'We shouldn't be talking like this. Get some rest. Just give me a day or two and then we'll get back to normal.'

He heard a note of dry amusement on the line.

'If I wanted "normal", I wouldn't be about to get married to a police officer. I just don't want you hurt. And I want to go home.'

Home.

It was astonishing how such a short, simple word could carry so much warmth and hope and trepidation inside it. Home was the place everyone was seeking in the end. Even the lost souls who'd supposedly touched all those exhibits that wound up on the walls of the little museum in Prati. Perhaps that was what Giorgio Bramante ultimately wanted too: to help the child that lived in his head find some kind of peace through the elimination of those he held responsible for his fate. All of whom were dead now, except for a single police officer whose only crime had been to intervene in a vicious beating deep in the heart of his own Questura, to do his duty.

Something didn't add up.

Costa looked at his watch and, without quite thinking, or knowing why, asked one last question.

'Why would a woman, a mother and wife, someone with an apparently idyllic family life, cut herself? Deliberately, regularly? Because it wasn't idyllic, obviously. But why beyond that? And why still today?'

He waited and when she spoke she was quieter again. Perhaps a little shocked.

'She did that?' Emily asked.

'The blood on the T-shirt in that church. The first blood, when she took it there. It's hers. She admitted it to Leo. He said there were fresh scars on her wrists when he saw her, too.'

'Oh . . .'

Emily was considering his question, in that measured, rational way which was one of the last parts of her personality that hadn't turned Italian.

'Self-harm is complicated, Nic. It's usual a form of self-loathing. The woman places no value on her own existence for some reason. Perhaps she is clinically depressive, or expressing guilt. Perhaps there are other reasons. A husband who's having an affair . . . I don't know. Aren't there psychologists on the force who can tell you this?'

'Of course,' he confessed. 'It's so much easier talking it through with you. I understand what you say, for one thing.'

'I will,' she said severely, 'start charging for these services soon.'

Something caught Costa's attention. It was Leo Falcone crossing the half-empty office in his direction, with that serious, engaged expression on his face, the one that meant something was happening.

'You're out of our league,' he said to her quickly. 'We could never afford you. Now promise me you'll see a doctor tomorrow. Then on Thursday I'll be around. Whether it's here, Orvieto, or the moon, I don't care. I will be there.'

'It's a promise,' she said.

Falcone watched as he put down the phone. He looked as if something was wrong.

'Sir?'

'I want you to find Peroni. I want you to look up everything you can find on Giorgio Bramante that's been back-filed. Anything and everything, however apparently trivial.'

Costa was puzzled.

'Isn't that all in the reports from the original case?'

'No!' Falcone replied, exasperated. 'Bramante was already in custody, ready to plead guilty. It was regarded as wasted effort.'

Costa caught his eye. Falcone looked worried.

'I see . . . I'll do it straight away.'

'Tomorrow morning, first thing, talk to the mother again. Find out exactly what her relations with him were. Don't pull any punches. Perhaps I was a little restrained.'

'Agente Prabakaran—'

'Never mind Agente Prabakaran!' Falcone snapped. 'Just do it, Nic!'

Costa already had the following day mapped out. It would consist of ticking off potential lairs for Bramante until they found him. Or some evidence that they were on his trail.

He was silent. There was something in Falcone's tone, a tense, distanced note that reminded him of the old Leo, the one no one ever liked. There was no colour in the old inspector's cheeks, no blood in Leo Falcone's face at all.

Then something happened that Costa had never witnessed before. Falcone leaned forward, just a little, and patted him gently on the back, a gesture that was familiar, almost paternal.

'I'm sorry,' he said apologetically. 'It's been a long day. I find it hard sometimes. The truth is' – Falcone's eyes focused on something across the office, perhaps nothing at all – 'I've always found it hard, if I'm being honest with you. I simply made a point of never showing it.'

He seemed embarrassed by this sudden show of emotion.

'I've put you down for that *sovrintendente* exam,' he went on. 'I want you to take it. This summer. Before you get married. You'll walk through, you know. It's time you started making progress around here.'

Costa nodded, lost for words, unable to protest.

'And Gianni,' Falcone asked. 'Where is he?'

'With the maps and the worm people.'

'Tell him I'm grateful for all the work he's put in these last couple of days. It wasn't needed. Not from either of you, really.'

'Leo . . .?'

'This is work, Agente,' Falcone interrupted him. 'Don't ever forget that. It's friendship too. I understand that, of course. But this profession comes first. Always. The work. The duty. They never go away.'

'Is there something wrong?'

He smiled and then that bony hand came out and patted him on the back again. This time it didn't require any conscious forethought.

'I'm tired, that's all. Giorgio Bramante is a master of timing, but I imagine you've noticed. Now . . .'

He cast his beady eyes around the room, a look designed to stiffen the spine of anyone thinking of slacking.

'I shall have a quick word with the troops, then I'm done for tonight. We can talk in the morning.'

'Goodnight,' Costa murmured, then went back to the job.

– 27 –

Beautiful lies. Ugly truths.

In Ludo Torchia's dying words lay a universe of possibilities, a million ways to uncover what made Giorgio Bramante the man he became, and exhume the fate of his son from the red Aventino earth beneath which, if logic meant anything, his remains still surely lay.

But these, Falcone reflected as he reached the staircase, were matters of conjecture. What stared him in the face now was plain fact. Rosa Prabakaran was in Bramante's hands. He'd heard her screams down the phone when he asked for proof. That sound had sent a chill, of fear and fury and shame, down Falcone's spine. Afterwards, he was aware he'd noticed something else too: a tone in Bramante's voice that was never there even fourteen years before. Prison had coarsened this man, made something that was bad to begin with worse. Before, there had been some humanity in the man. His concern for his child had, Falcone was convinced, always been real. Now that was gone, had been torn from him, gone for good.

When Bramante said he would kill the young policewoman if Falcone didn't take her place, he was simply stating a fact. When he spelled out the conditions – the place, the time, one in the morning, an hour away, the absolute absence of any other officers on pain of Prabakaran's death – Bramante's voice had the firm, unshakable assurance of a university professor handing out an assignment. None of this was to be the subject of argument. Falcone did as he was told, or the woman died. It was as simple as that, and what Falcone found a little disconcerting was how easily he was able to agree to the man's demands.

There was no alternative. No time to put together a team. No need to risk Costa and Peroni, two men he felt he'd leaned on too much of late in any case, yet again.

This time was his and his alone.

He glanced back at the office to make sure no one was looking. Then, gingerly, ignoring the pain from his limbs, he walked slowly down the stairs to the ground floor and headed directly to the front counter.

Prinzivalli, the *sovrintendente* from Milan, a man he'd worked alongside for three decades, stood there alone, sifting papers. Falcone's spirits fell. He didn't have the heart or the talent to push this man around. They had known each other far too long for that.

'Can I help, sir?' the *sovrintendente* asked, raising a puzzled, grey eyebrow. He played rugby in his spare time and had once managed the same team in which a young, very different Nic Costa had played. Prinzivalli was as solid and trustworthy a police officer as Falcone had ever worked with.

'You're under orders not to let me out, aren't you?'

The *sovrintendente* nodded.

At that moment the bells of the old church around the corner intervened: twelve chimes. Falcone listened to the sonorous chorus of metallic sound, a collision of dissonant notes that had, he now realized, followed his life in the Questura for more than thirty years, from raw cadet to old, tired inspector. It was now midnight in the *centro storico*, a time he had always loved, an hour when the modernity of Rome all but vanished and the streets seemed made for people, not machines. When, in his younger, more fanciful years, he could almost imagine the old gods seeming to rise from their distant graves, making the city alive with their presence, a magical place, where everything was possible.

Prinzivalli coughed, interrupting his reverie.

'Commissario Messina made it very clear that he does not want you to leave the premises. You wouldn't want to argue with him, would you?'

'He's not his father, is he?'

293

'No.' The man in the uniform gave this some thought. 'But he is commissario.'

Falcone cast an eye at the surveillance camera. It had a blind spot. If you stood between the counter and the back desk, no one saw you. It was common knowledge, useful sometimes.

He beckoned Prinzivalli there.

'Have I ever asked you to disobey orders before, Michele?'

'Yes,' the man replied dryly.

'Then we have precedent. The situation is this. I will explain it once, then you shall open the door for me. Understood?'

He said nothing.

'Bramante has taken that young *agente*, Rosa Prabakaran. Unless I meet him' – he glanced at his watch with a small theatrical flourish – 'alone and in an hour, he will kill her.'

'Good God, Leo!'

'Please. I have very little time. We know the kind of man Bramante is. We know he will do as he says. I cannot for the life of me put together a team to accompany me in the time available, not one that I can trust to stay unnoticed. I have to do this on my own . . .'

'He wants to murder you, man!'

Falcone nodded.

'So he says. But this is irrelevant. If I go, Prabakaran may live. If I don't she will most certainly die. The girl is young, a little naive and my officer. My responsibility.'

Prinzivalli stayed silent.

'What I would like you to do is this. Wait until one. If no one's noticed I'm gone by then, notice for them. Raise hell. Do whatever you see fit.'

'Where are you meeting him?'

Falcone eyed him.

'I'm not saying.'

'Leo . . .?'

'I told you. This happens on his terms or she's dead. Now, will you open that door or not?'

'You are a bad-tempered, stubborn old bastard. There are people who can help.'

'Yes,' he said emphatically. 'You.'

The *sovrintendente* looked at Falcone in his office suit, then snatched an overcoat, his own, no doubt, from the stand by the door and threw it at him.

'It's bitter out there,' he added and stabbed at the button on the counter. The security gate flipped open.

'Thank you,' Falcone said and, without looking back, walked outside.

The night was cold, the kind of bone-numbing cold Rome could deliver at times, one that seemed at odds with the burning, airless heat of summer, just a few months away. He shuffled on the gigantic overcoat, hobbled down the street towards the cab stand and waited, thinking.

There was always time for beautiful lies and ugly truths.

Falcone didn't want to wake her. Besides, he knew she listened to the messages on her mobile phone religiously, never wishing to miss any human contact. Raffaela Arcangelo had experienced so little in her life. They were, in that sense, very alike.

So he called the number, waited until the robotic voice asked for his message, and then spoke, aware that he would say things – true or false; he wasn't sure which – that he could never have broached in person.

'Raffaela,' he began, self-conscious, even in the dark, deserted Roman street, waiting by the cab rank, on a cold winter night, a little ashamed that, freed from the very real human rapport he enjoyed with her, it was so easy to say what he wanted. 'There is something I must tell you. I apologize you must hear it like this. Unfortunately, I have no choice.'

There was a light sweeping the cobblestones. A cab, coming from the Piazza Venezia perhaps.

'This cannot go on. The game we're both playing, neither wishing to say what we really feel. I'm grateful for what you have done for me, but that is all. I don't love you, and I don't wish either of our lives to be damaged by some sad pretence that I do. This isn't your fault. If I were capable of loving, then, perhaps, it would be you. I have no idea.'

The car approached. It was looking for trade. Falcone waved.

'I am unsure precisely why you chose me. Perhaps out of pity. Or guilt. Or curiosity. It's unimportant. What you should understand is that a man reaches a point in his life at which he realizes he is looking at the remainder, the diminishing part of his existence. What lies ahead . . .'

It was a shiny, old black Mercedes. Still talking, Falcone climbed in and waved to the driver to wait for a moment.

'What remains does not – cannot – include you. I'm sorry. I wish—'

Something interrupted him. The harsh, inhuman beep of a machine echoed in his ear. Then a message. The phone would listen no more. These sentiments, like everything else, were finite. Falcone wondered, for a moment, what he'd left unsaid. Nothing. Everything. There was a door to be closed, and no point in wondering what lay behind it once the deed was done.

The cab driver turned round to stare at him. A man about his own age, he guessed, with a tired, lined face and a drooping moustache.

'Are we going somewhere?' he asked.

'The Aventino. The Piazza dei Cavalieri di Malta.'

The man laughed.

'You won't see anything through that keyhole at this time of night, friend. Are you sure?'

'Just drive,' Falcone said sourly, then looked at the phone again before thrusting it deep into the pockets of Prinzivalli's thick and capacious overcoat.

Part 3

THE SEVENTH SACRAMENT

- 1 -

They had been marching, lost, through the labyrinth for what seemed to Alessio Bramante to be the best part of twenty minutes, not once seeing a hint of daylight, not for a moment hearing anything but the echo of their own voices and a distant trickle of water. How long would his father wait before coming back to reclaim him? When was this game meant to end?

He tried to remember what had happened in Livia's house on the Palatino, when his father had abandoned him inexplicably. There, Giorgio had been gone for longer than this, so long that Alessio had amused himself by closing his eyes and imagining he could hear the voice of the long-dead empress, her hard Latin phrases demanding instant obedience, the way that powerful grown-ups liked.

A test was not meant to be easy, otherwise it was no test at all. But this ritual involved obedience too, and there Alessio Bramante was lost, uncertain how to act. Perhaps soon there would come a roar from behind them: Giorgio Bramante, like the Minotaur bellowing for its prey in the caves in Crete, stalking them, slowly, methodically, through the subterranean veins of the Aventino.

He had no idea, and nor did they. Holding the hand of the tall figure in the red suit, with the wild, curly hair that almost matched, Alessio Bramante moved ever deeper into the warren beneath the Aventino, aware that they were all equally trapped, equally tied to one another, in hierarchies of dependence and control, beneath the power and judgement of his father.

Dino – he had revealed his name in a quiet moment, as they stumbled through the dark – hoped to play the part of saviour. The one who rescued the initiate who would become Corax. Some minutes after the argument, he had dragged Alessio ahead then led the boy into a Stygian corner.

'Alessio,' he had said, very earnestly. 'I won't let him harm you. Don't worry. Stay close to me. Do what I say, please. Ludo's just . . . a little crazy.'

The boy almost laughed. Dino didn't understand.

'He's frightened of my father,' he replied, and knew this to be true. 'What can he do to me?'

'We're all a little frightened of your father,' Dino answered ruefully. 'Aren't you?'

'I'm not frightened of anything. Not you. Not' – he nodded back towards the footsteps of the others, fast catching up – 'him.'

'Well, good for you,' Dino said, and tousled his long hair, an act that made Alessio shrink away from his grip, disgusted by the expectation of weakness.

Alessio really wasn't scared. There was no need to be, not even as they travelled further and further into the network of tunnels that ran ahead of them in all directions, driven, it seemed, by Ludo's terror at the unseen wraith that lay between them and escape. This was an adventure, a physical human set of moves on a gigantic, three-dimensional chess board, manoeuvres with an end in mind. One that only he seemed to recognize fully.

Death was a part of the ritual too. Every old book, every story his father had recounted to him, said that, unmistakably. This, not simple, greedy curiosity, was why Alessio had watched every instant of the bird's end at the knife of Ludo Torchia, determined to be a witness, a participant, curious, too, to see what the grey ghost looked like when it emerged from the shadows.

He wanted to talk to each of them about it, to pose questions, gauge their varying reactions: crazy Ludo, the short, studious one called Sandro, big, stupid Andrea and quiet, frightened Raul, who never spoke. Even Toni LaMarca, who had a crooked, evil set to his eyes, one that gave Alessio pause for thought. And Dino, too, who regarded himself as Alessio's friend. He wanted to ask them what the creature would have felt. How long it would have remained conscious. Whether they felt different afterwards (as he did, surreptitiously reaching down, when no one was looking, to dip the fingers of his left hand deeper into the pool of damp, sticky blood on the ground, determined to have more than the rest).

There was no opportunity for talk, except with Dino, who was – Alessio understood without thinking – unlike the rest of them, a virtuous person, someone whose imagination was limited by his innate goodness. Dino didn't want to be here, deep in this game. He didn't believe in gods and rituals and the power they might exercise over ordinary men.

The others fell through the doorway into a new, narrower, low cavern where Dino and he had come to a halt. They looked breathless, tired, all five of them. And scared.

It was Toni, perhaps the only one among them Alessio thought it was wise to fear, who spoke first.

'Where are we going?' he asked. 'Is this really a way out?'

'Shut up,' Ludo said, half-heartedly.

The lanterns were losing their power. The illumination had taken on that dying, yellow hue Alessio knew from the times at home when he'd creep beneath the sheets, play with the toy lantern he owned, seeing how long it could stay alive in the dark.

'We can't keep stumbling around like this,' Dino said. 'We've been going down. I don't know this hill very well. I don't have any way of judging in which direction we've been headed.'

He aimed the faint beam of his little pocket torch into the thick, velvet blackness ahead. It revealed nothing but rock and a continuing line of empty tunnel.

'We'll hit a dead end here,' he said. 'Or worse. And if these torches are gone by then . . .'

Ludo didn't say anything. Alessio watched his face. It was interesting. Engaged. It didn't recognize the boundaries that constrained the way someone like Dino would think.

'If we're caught down here without light,' Dino went on, 'we're in real trouble. This isn't about getting thrown out of university. This place is dangerous.'

'That's why you feel alive,' Ludo replied, and Alessio realized he approved of that answer.

Ludo's eyes hunted round each of them, looking for a target. Finally, they fell on Alessio.

'What do you think,' he asked, 'little boy?'

Alessio said nothing. Somewhere inside himself he felt some small beast rise on red wings.

'Spoilt little brat,' Ludo went on, bending down, in a way that spoke condescension in every crook and bend of his lanky, lean body. 'What does some rich little kid, whose daddy thinks he knows everything, have to say for himself, huh?'

Alessio flew at him then, nails scratching, fingers flailing, let out some furious, pent-up rage that had been waiting so long to surface.

He made a discovery at that point too. When he felt this way, when the world was nothing but some bleeding scarlet wall of flesh and pain at which he could claw with his strong, lithe fingers, nothing felt wrong, nothing existed that could be labelled 'good' or 'bad', 'right' or 'wrong'. In the wild and screaming place to which his anger took him lay some kind of clear, hard comfort he'd never quite found before.

It elated him. Ludo was right. It made him feel alive.

His fingers tore at the hands of his foe. His nails scratched and found purchase on skin. Ludo was yelling, words of fear and pain and frenzy.

'Shit!' Ludo screeched. 'Shit! Shit! Shit! Get the little bastard off me. Get . . .'

Alessio stopped then smiled at him. The marks of his own fingers ran in parallel scrawled lines down the backs of Ludo's hands.

It didn't prevent him getting the knife out. Alessio stared at the blade. It was still stained with the blood of the cockerel, the bird that had choked out its life, drop by drop, somewhere in these caves, not far away, he guessed. In a place his own father might well have passed by now, if he'd started looking.

'Ludo . . .' Dino murmured.

Alessio glanced at him. Dino was weak. It was part of his character. He wouldn't stand in Ludo's way. Nor would any of them. They were, he saw, lesser creatures, on a lower part of the hierarchy.

He raised his small hand, still painful from clawing at Torchia the moment before, a calm, unhurried gesture, one that said: *quiet.*

He watched the knife rise in front of him.

'This would be so easy . . .' Ludo began to mutter.

The rest of them stood around like scared idiots. Alessio wondered what his father would have said in a situation like this. And whether this was all part of the test.

Alessio Bramante looked into Ludo Torchia's eyes, recognized something there, and waited until Ludo saw this too.

Then, and only then, he smiled and said, 'I know the way.'

- 2 -

They'd searched all night, more than a hundred officers in all. Every last part of the Aventino. Every car park. Every blind alley. They'd made a cursory run past all the sites that appeared on Falcone's lists, not that there was much to see in the dark, much to do beyond a check for recent tyre marks.

Now they were engaged in a muddled, directionless conference of team leaders in the large, crowded room next to Falcone's empty office, Costa and Peroni tagging along because it was unclear to whom, exactly, they were answering at that moment. Precious little was apparent at all, even after nine hours of solid, sometimes frantic, labour.

The one firm lead Messina and his new inspector Bavetti had to show was something Costa thought Falcone would have picked up in minutes. Early the previous afternoon Calvi, the horse butcher, had reported one of his three vans stolen. The vehicle possessed a cargo compartment that was, for obvious reasons, impossible to see into from outside, and highly secure. It was still unaccounted for, though every police car, marked and unmarked in the city, now had its number. Gone too was Enzo Uccello, Bramante's cellmate and fellow worker at the horse abattoir, who had failed to return to work at 4 p.m. as expected. Maybe they'd been right to think that Uccello was helping Bramante on the outside. Bavetti certainly considered that a strong possibility. It occurred to Costa that, if true, this told only part of the story. Enzo Uccello had been sent to jail three years after Bramante. He was inside, without parole, when the earlier killings took place, of no practical use whatsoever. What help he had to offer Bramante was surely limited to the last few months.

Details like these didn't seem to bother Bavetti, a man who was a little younger than Bruno Messina, tall, nondescript, and apt to speak little, and then only in short, clipped sentences upon which he seemed unwilling to expand. Both men appeared uncertain of themselves, racked with caution, because they feared the consequences of failure. There was a severe lack of experience in the Questura at that moment, and it would make the search for Leo Falcone and Rosa Prabakaran doubly difficult.

Not that Costa expected to be engaged in it for much longer. Messina's patience was wearing thin. He'd barely spoken to them all night. And now, in front of several other senior officers, he had virtually accused them of being party to Leo's disappearance.

Costa had laughed, had been unable to do anything else. The charge was ludicrous. Why would they aid Leo in doing such a thing? And why would they wait for Prinzivalli to raise the alarm? It was ridiculous and he told Messina so to his face.

Peroni took it more personally. He still stood, big, scarred face close into Messina's florid features, continuing to demand an apology and a retraction, something the rest of the men in the room would have loved to hear from this green commissario's lips, which was one good reason why it would never happen.

The big man tried for the third time.

'I want that withdrawn. Sir.'

Messina was still trying to bluster his way out of it. Peroni was drawing nods from the older men in the room, which did little to help their cause. There would be a reckoning when this was done, Costa knew, and he found himself caring little about which way the blame would fall. Leo was missing, along with Rosa Prabakaran, who had, he assumed, been taken as the price of Falcone's surrender, in the same way Bramante had done with his earlier victims. Now they had no idea what had become of either of them. The game, once again, was entirely in Bramante's hands. Messina and Bavetti lacked both the foresight and talent to second-guess the man. Perhaps Leo Falcone did too, though things had seemed a little more equal when he was around.

'Do you want us on this case or not?' Costa asked, when Messina avoided Peroni's demands again.

The commissario leaped to the bait, just as Costa had expected.

'No,' he spat back, as much out of instinct as anything. 'Get the hell out of here. Both of you. When this is over and done with, then I'll make some decisions about your future.'

'We know Leo!' Peroni bellowed. 'You can't kick us out just because it makes your life easier.'

Messina looked at his watch.

'Your shift's over. Both of you. Don't come back till I call.'

Costa took Peroni's elbow and squeezed. For the life of him he didn't understand what Messina would have left to talk about once they were gone. He and Bavetti looked lost for what to do next.

'Worms,' Costa said simply.

Bavetti screwed up his pinched face. The man hadn't even taken a good look at Falcone's papers before taking over the case. He'd just sent officers out into the Rome night, looking everywhere, flinging manpower at shadows.

'What?'

'Remember what Leo was chasing before all this began. He had a lead. Today, we were going to narrow down all those possible places Bramante could have been staying before. There's a whole map of them downstairs. Inspector Falcone planned to visit them. One by one . . .'

Just then a nearby phone began to ring. Costa walked over to pick it up, dragging Peroni in his wake.

The conference went on behind them, a ragged, monotonous drone of confused voices. But at least Bavetti seemed to be talking about investigating Falcone's list of possible sites.

Costa said, wearily, '*Pronto.*'

It was a uniform man calling from a car in the field. He was struggling to maintain his composure. Costa listened and felt a cold stab of dread run down his spine. He asked the important questions and made some notes of the answers. Peroni watched him in silence, knowing, in that shared, unspoken way they both recognized now, that this was important.

After a minute, he put down the phone and interrupted Messina's rambling attempt to sum up the case so far.

'I'm talking,' Messina snapped, not listening for a moment.

'I noticed,' Costa replied without thinking. 'I think we've found Agente Prabakaran.'

He paused. The man struggled for words.

'She's in Testaccio,' Costa continued, as Peroni walked over to their desks and picked up the car keys and their phones. 'The horse butcher opened his shop late because Uccello never turned up for work. In the cold store . . .'

He shrugged.

'Is the woman alive?' Messina asked.

'Just about,' Costa replied. 'There's a man's body too. She was tied to him. It doesn't sound . . . pretty.'

The local officer he'd spoken to had become almost hysterical when Costa pushed him on the finer points.

'More,' Bavetti demanded, suddenly finding his voice. 'Details.'

'Details?' Costa asked, amazed. Bavetti looked as confused, as lost for a course of action, as Messina.

'What? Where exactly? How . . .?'

Peroni came back. Costa looked at him and nodded.

'I believe, Commissario,' the big man replied, dangling the car keys, 'you said we're off duty.'

Messina's florid face became a livid red.

'Don't play games with me, Peroni! Damn you!'

Costa turned round and slapped the notebook firmly into the commissario's fleshy hands, with a sudden, vehement force.

'Someone's found a dead man and a half-dead woman who appears to have been raped. Beyond that . . .'

He didn't say another word. Peroni was heading for the door, with the speed of a man half his age.

- 3 -

'I know the way,' Alessio repeated, making sure he didn't stutter.

Ludo stopped for a moment. The knife glittered, stationary.

'Little boys shouldn't tell lies,' he said menacingly.

'Little boys don't.'

He pulled the end of the string from the spent loop on his belt, the short section, which had broken when he first tried to attach it. The main ball had run for several minutes, tugging on his trousers. None of them had noticed back then, in the temple room, as he'd paused for a moment, untied this second loop, and allowed the string to fall on the floor, floating against his legs, still tickling like some dead, falling insect.

He held the piece of string in front of him, staring into those crazy, scared eyes, thinking of chess and how he'd played with his father, hour after hour, in the bright sunny garden room in a house no more than a few minutes' walk from here, out in the light of day. This, too, depended upon the endgame.

Alessio had fought to memorize each turn they took since that moment: left and right, up and down. He could, he felt sure, retrace their steps, find a way back to the fallen string and the corridor to the surface, one of seven, one that Giorgio Bramante had surely not taken when he disappeared.

He could lead them out of the caves, unseen. Or . . .

Games always involved a victory. Winners and losers. Perhaps he had a gift, a sacrament, to make too: six stupid students, trespassing where they weren't wanted.

'A piece of string,' Torchia said, taunting him. 'Is that supposed to make a difference?'

'Listen to him,' Dino Abati cautioned. 'We don't have many options left, Ludo. Sooner or later we stumble into a hole. Or into Giorgio. Which would you prefer?'

'Ludo . . .' Toni LaMarca whined.

'I know the way out,' Alessio said again, and wanted to laugh. 'I can take you past my father. He won't even see you. He won't even know you were here. I won't tell.' He smiled, and held up his left hand, still sticky with the cockerel's blood. 'I promise.'

Torchia stared at his fingers, thinking.

The knife slipped down below the line of the boy's vision.

'If we do this,' Torchia threatened, 'you don't say a word. Not to him. Not to anyone. We don't talk about you. You don't talk about us. That's the arrangement. Understood, little rich boy?'

'I'm not rich,' Alessio objected.

'Understood?'

He looked at the knife, reached forward with his hand and pushed it gently out of his face.

'I won't tell a soul,' Alessio said. 'I swear.'

– 4 –

For once the traffic was light. They made it to Testaccio in little more than seven minutes. Four blue marked cars stood outside the market, lights flashing. Peroni knew the most senior uniform man on duty. He nodded them through into a corner of the building that was now deserted except for police. Word had gone round. The stalls were closing for the day.

Rosa Prabakaran sat in a huddle next to a bread stall, one female officer either side, a blanket over her hunched frame, clutching a mug of coffee steaming in the cold morning air.

Peroni walked over and, without thinking, placed a hand on her shoulder.

She shrieked. He shrank back, muttering curses about his own stupidity, taking the stream of abuse from the women as he did so.

Costa had been in these situations before. At some point Rosa Prabakaran would disclose what had happened, quietly, at her own pace, to some trained officers, all of them female, who knew how to listen. He didn't need to do more than look at her to understand what, in part at least, she had been through.

'Agente,' Costa said quietly. 'Commissario Messina will be here shortly. I suggest, very strongly, you insist on being taken back to the Questura, and talk in your own good time.'

The blanket had slipped. He'd caught sight of something unexpected: a flimsy, provocative slip of a dress underneath. Torn and muddy. She'd seen he'd noticed. After that her eyes didn't move from the floor.

Costa walked around the back of the horse butcher's stall, the shelves white and empty, and waited for the pale-faced uniformed man at the door of the cold store to get out of the way.

Then he went inside, aware immediately of the stench of meat and blood.

Peroni followed him. The two of them looked at the shape on a hook in the corner.

'That's not Leo,' Costa said eventually.

'Thank God for that.'

'Too short. My guess is Enzo Uccello.'

Peroni, a squeamish man at the best of times, made himself stare at the cadaver.

'You've a better imagination than me, Nic,' Peroni admitted. 'I don't envy you that.'

He walked outside. Costa joined him almost immediately. Messina and Bavetti were there now, all bluff and bluster, officious voices in a sea of uniforms. Teresa Lupo and her team had arrived too. The pathologist was seated next to Rosa Prabakaran, talking quietly to her.

Peroni strode over to the young *agente*, kept well back this time, bent down on one knee, on the far side from Teresa.

'Rosa,' he said quietly. 'I know this is a terrible time to ask. But Leo. Did you see him? Do you know what happened?'

She closed her eyes. When she opened them again they were glazed with tears, so shiny she couldn't be seeing a thing, except, Costa thought, some unwanted mental images of what had happened.

'No,' she said quietly.

Peroni glanced at Teresa, pleading.

'Leo's a good man,' the pathologist said quietly, persistently. 'I know you didn't get on well, Rosa, but we really need to find him.'

Something, some memory, made her convulse, hand to mouth. Teresa Lupo hugged her shoulders, tight, in a way no man could, perhaps for a long time.

'I don't know.' She choked with fury on her own ignorance. 'He just did what he did, then took us here. I didn't even know about Inspector Falcone until these men came. What was he doing?'

'He gave himself up to free you,' Teresa said quietly. 'That's what we think, anyway.'

Her head went down again.

'You should go back to the Questura now with these officers,' Peroni said, nodding at the uniform women. 'You take it easy. Tell them what you want. Just . . .'

Rosa Prabakaran's agonized, tear-stained face rose to look at them.

'I didn't ask him to do that,' she cried. 'I didn't *know.*'

'Hey, hey, hey!' Peroni said quickly. 'Leo would have done that for any of us. That's . . .' He cast an ugly glance in the direction of Messina and Bavetti, who'd just walked out of the cold store, and now stood, white-faced and shocked, talking in low tones to each other. 'That's what comes naturally to some people.'

She dragged an arm across her face, like a child, angry, ashamed.

Then the two senior officers marched over briskly, trying to look unmoved.

'I want,' the commissario announced to everyone in earshot, 'everything focused on finding this bastard Bramante from now on. We assume Falcone is alive. When Bramante has killed before he has usually made his handiwork very obvious. Until that is the case – and I pray it won't be – we assume Falcone is a prisoner, not a victim. I want officers armed at all times. I want helicopter surveillance. And the hostage rescue unit. I want them too. The firearms people.'

Costa blinked.

'Firearms?'

'Exactly,' Messina concurred.

There were two specialist state police hostage teams in the city, one focusing on negotiation, the second specifically trained to deal with urgent, high-priority incidents involving captives. Messina was making it clear he wanted the latter. The team existed more out of pride than necessity. The Carabinieri and the secret services handled most security events. But what they had, the state police wanted too.

'If Leo's a hostage,' Peroni observed, 'the last thing we want is a bunch of people pointing guns at the man who's holding him.'

'You're experts on hostage-taking now, are you?' the commissario barked. 'Is there anything you two don't have an opinion on?'

'We're just trying to pass on what we think Inspector Falcone would say in the circumstances,' Costa added.

'Leo Falcone walked out of the Questura against my direct orders! He's just made things ten times worse.'

Messina glanced down at Rosa Prabakaran. It was an unfortunate gesture. He looked as if he really didn't want to see her at all.

'What happened here, Prabakaran?' he demanded. 'I need to know. Now.'

Teresa Lupo stood up and prodded a stubby finger into his dark, serge coat.

'No, Commissario. Not now. There are protocols and procedures for situations like this. They *will* be followed.'

Messina's big hand flapped close in her face. 'You're the pathologist here,' he bawled at her. 'You do your job, I'll do mine. I want to know.'

'Know what?' Teresa demanded, standing her ground.

Costa broke in.

'Agente Prabakaran has nothing to tell us about Inspector Falcone. She wasn't even aware he'd been taken until someone told her this morning.'

'I am the commanding officer. I demand a full report—'

'Oh please,' Teresa interrupted. 'Don't you have eyes, man? Can't you see what happened?'

'Remember your place,' Messina hissed, and stuck out a beefy arm to push her out of the way.

Costa watched what happened next with amazement, if not surprise.

Teresa Lupo's arm rose in what seemed to him a passable imitation of a boxer's rapidly drawn right hook, caught Messina on the chin, then sent the large commissario spinning back into the arms of Bavetti, who just managed to break his fall as the man hit the stone market floor.

A barely hidden ripple of amusement ran around the officers, uniform and plain clothes, watching the scene. No one, except Bavetti, moved a muscle to help the prone man. Teresa turned to Costa and Peroni: 'Do you really think Leo could still be alive?'

'Bramante was in no rush to kill him before,' Costa insisted, adding, with a glance at Messina, half dazed on the ground. 'We could be in luck. If we had something to offer him . . .'

'Such as?' she asked.

'Finding out what happened to his son,' Costa suggested.

'This is ridiculous,' Messina snapped savagely, scrambling to his feet, not yet ready to look Teresa Lupo in the face. 'If we didn't get to the bottom of that fourteen years ago what chance is there now?'

She shook her head in disappointment.

'For you, Commissario, I suspect the answer is none indeed. Silvio?'

Di Capua, who was just loving this, made a military salute. She threw her briefcase across to him with one easy movement.

'You know the routine. Check for anything at the scene that can narrow down that list of potential sites Leo left us. Once the gentlemen here have ceased walking around with their chins dragging on the floor, they will, I trust, realize their time will be better spent trying to find the living instead of gawping at the dead.'

'Done,' Silvio replied. 'And you?'

She stroked her forehead with the back of her large hand then emitted a long theatrical sigh.

'If anyone asks, I have a terrible headache. Ladies?'

The two female police officers were helping Rosa Prabakaran to her feet. Teresa Lupo took one big stride towards them, sending Bruno Messina scampering back as she approached.

'I think,' she said, 'it's time to leave this place to the weaker sex.'

'You two,' she added, pointing to Peroni and Costa, 'excepted.'

- 5 -

The hospital seemed to be run by nuns, silent, unsmiling figures who drifted around busily, taking patients and equipment and pale Manila record folders around the maze of endless corridors that ran in every direction. It was in a beautiful Renaissance building not far from the Duomo, a massive, ornate, four-square leviathan that, from the outside, looked more like a palace than a place for the sick, or those just thinking of joining them. Arturo had insisted on accompanying her. They sat together on hard metal chairs in a small waiting room with peeling paint and rusty windows that gave out onto a grey, damp courtyard, its cobblestones shining with the constant rain. There were four other women in front of her in the queue, waiting patiently with telltale bulges in their tummies, only partly covered by the magazines they read intently.

Emily Deacon, who was still slim, still, in her own mind, only half attached to the being growing inside her, glanced at them and felt an unwanted sense of shock. This is me too, she thought. This is how I will look a few months down the road.

Arturo, ever the observant one, noted, 'It all goes, you know. The weight. Usually, anyway. I know women think men are just beasts who're interested in nothing but their looks. It's not like that. I always found it hard to take my eyes off my wife when she was pregnant, and I don't mean that in the way you think. She was radiant. It's the only way I know of putting it.'

'It doesn't feel particularly radiant when you're throwing up at seven in the morning. Men get spared the hard parts.'

For a moment he looked hurt. She'd told him about the conversation she'd had with Nic. Arturo had made his own inquiries after that. The way the case was going in Rome depressed him too.

'Not really,' Arturo commented. 'They just hit us later, in more subtle ways. I don't want you worrying about Falcone by the way. I know that's a stupid thing to say, and that you will anyway. When we get back I don't want you hanging off that computer all day. Or the phone. I'll unplug both if you're going to be obstinate.

'Since this is a time for speaking out of turn,' he went on, 'I should say that I did not find Raffaela's reaction to be quite what I was expecting. Were things . . . well with her and Leo before? I'm prying here, of course, so feel entitled to tell me to get lost.'

They hadn't been getting on, not really, she thought. Leo and Raffaela had come back from Venice dependent upon each other in ways that were, to some extent, inexplicable. He needed someone to nurse him through his physical frailty. That much was understandable. But Raffaela's urge to fill this role – one which was not quite, Emily believed, the same as a craving for love and affection, both of which had been denied her for years – continued to puzzle her.

'I don't know, Arturo. I was never very good at relationships until Nic came along.'

'You only need one. The right one, which can be hard, I know. But you're there already. Stupid old men see things they were blind to when they were stupid young men. I can see that. I look forward to meeting this Nic of yours.'

'I'm sure you'll like him.'

'I'm sure too. And yet he gets along with Leo! Don't tell me the man's changed. I know that's impossible. He walks out into the night to try to save this poor young *agente* for whom he feels responsible – not that he is. What else does he do? Phone his lover to tell her it's all over. And how?'

Raffaela had revealed all this over breakfast, her face grim with fury and spent tears. Then she had insisted on taking a car back to Rome to return to their apartment and await developments.

'By leaving her a message!' Arturo declared, making a broad, incredulous gesture with his hands. 'Is this Falcone's interpretation of kindness? That, before you go out to meet some murdering bastard who hopes to kill you, a man must call home and leave a few words on an answering machine, telling a woman who loves you it's all over?'

She'd thought about this already. Quite a lot.

'I think he meant it as kindness. Leo's a little uncomfortable when it comes to personal matters.'

'True. But you see my point? This is precisely what I had to deal with fourteen years ago. Stubborn as a mule, utterly insensitive to the feelings of others and – this is the worst, the very worst – quite uncaring about his own skin too. Being selfless is not necessarily a virtue. Sometimes it's just downright infuriating, a way of saying to other people, "You can care about me, because I'll be damned if I care about myself."'

She smiled. He had Leo to a T. She liked Arturo Messina immensely.

'And the worst thing is,' she replied, 'you do care. I do. I think you do too. Even after all these years.'

'Of course! Who wants to see a good man go out into the night to face Lord knows what? Even if we have had our arguments. He was right, though. He understood Giorgio Bramante a lot better than I did. If only I'd listened . . .'

'Nothing, in all probability, would have been any different. Leo was no closer to finding that boy than you, was he?'

'*Meglio una bella bugia che una brutta verità.*'

'Excuse me?' she asked.

'Ludo Torchia's final words. Years ago I bullied them out of the doctor who was with him. I was a good bully. Believe me. Leo knew already, of course, not that he was any the wiser.'

The four women ahead had gone now. Surely her time would come soon.

'I was a police officer,' he went on. 'I was used to the idea that there were ugly truths out there. But something about that case fooled me. I found myself looking for beautiful lies. That a father's love was always perfect, always innocent, especially when it came from a seemingly good, middle-class intelligent man like that.'

'We don't know it wasn't.'

'Perhaps. But there was something wrong with Giorgio Bramante and in my haste I refused to acknowledge it. Why? Because I didn't want to. Because I couldn't bear the idea, I couldn't stomach the notion that he might somehow have been at fault too.'

He shuffled the raincoat on his lap, a little nervously.

'Leo never played those games. He had never had to learn that they were part of growing up, for a father, and for a son. That both needed some beautiful lies between them, because without those fabrications there was only the dark and the gloom to fill their lives when things got bad. I pitied Leo for that back then. I still do now. We need our self-deception from time to time.'

The surgery door opened. A nurse waved towards them.

'I hope to God they can find Leo before more harm's done,' Arturo added quickly. 'And this will be our final word on this subject until your Nic is here.'

She walked in, conscious that sitting in that rigid chair had somehow made the aches worse. The doctor was a woman: slim, mid-fifties, dressed in a dark sweater and black trousers. She looked harassed, too busy to deal with stupid, time-wasting questions.

After a brief discussion of her history the doctor asked, in a peremptory fashion, 'What do you feel is wrong?'

'There was a tiny amount of bleeding. Three days ago. And then again this morning.'

'These things happen,' she said with a shrug. 'Didn't your physician in Rome tell you that?'

'He did.'

'So. A man. Did you feel comfortable with him?'

'Not entirely,' she admitted.

The doctor smiled.

'Of course not. This is your first time. You should have a woman to talk to. It makes everything so much simpler. Signora, there must be a reason why you came. Please.'

'I have a little cramp in my side.'

Her expression changed.

'Persistent?'

'For the last few days it's been there most of the time.'

'How many weeks are you?'

'Seven. Eight, perhaps.'

'Where is the pain exactly?'

Emily indicated with her hand. 'Here. I had my appendix out when I was a teenager. It's almost the same place. Perhaps . . .'

'You have only one appendix.'

She asked some more questions, the personal ones Emily was now beginning to field almost without thinking. It was easier with a woman.

Then the doctor grimaced.

'What about your shoulder? Is it stiff? Strained perhaps?'

'Yes,' she said, unnerved by the connection the woman had made. It had never occurred to her to place the two sensations together. 'I thought perhaps I'd wrenched it.'

'Have you ever suffered from a pelvic inflammatory disease?'

This was all too close.

'I had chlamydia when I was twenty. It was nothing. They cured it, they said. Antibiotics.'

She scribbled some notes.

'Did your doctor in Rome ask any of these questions?'

'No.'

The woman nodded, got up and reached into the medical cabinet by her desk, taking out a syringe.

'We will need a blood test, naturally. And an ultrasound. A special one, I think. We have the equipment here. Your husband?'

'My partner's working.'

'What is work? He should come. This is important.'

It was only an hour since they'd spoken. Nic seemed so engrossed in the search for Leo Falcone. It was impossible to divert him from that.

'I have a friend with me. Outside.'

The woman came over. She smelled very strongly of old-fashioned soap. The needle went into her arm. Emily was, as always, amazed how dark blood appeared in real life.

'What's wrong?'

'In a little while I hope we will know. Your friend can bring some things for you?'

She blinked.

'I'll be staying?'

The woman sighed and looked at the papers on her desk.

'Emily, bringing children into this world is a game of chance. In some ways, the odds are better now, because we know more. In others, they're worse, because of our habits, and little demons like chlamydia. Sometimes events have consequences, long after we've forgotten them.'

The doctor paused, wondering, it seemed to Emily, whether to go on.

'Listen to me,' she said. 'You're an intelligent woman. I don't imagine this thought hasn't run through your head. One in a hundred pregnancies in our wonderful civilized world is ectopic. They are more common in women who have suffered pelvic inflammatory diseases. The symptoms are . . . your symptoms. Do you want the truth?'

No, she thought. A beautiful lie. The woman was on the phone, speaking rapidly, with authority.

'I want the truth,' she said when the call ended.

'We will see what the ultrasound reveals. If there is a baby in your uterus, then fine. You will stay here, I shall look after you, and it is entirely possible there is nothing to worry about at all, though you will not leave until I am satisfied of that. If the uterus is empty then this pregnancy is ectopic. Your baby is in the wrong place, somewhere it cannot survive. In that eventuality, what I shall be endeavouring to do is ensure that you will be able to conceive again. Parenthood is often a question of persistence, and I say that as a mother myself.'

She felt cold and feeble.

'My name is Anna. Please use it.'

The doctor stuck out a slender, tanned hand. Emily took it, and found her fingers in a warm, powerful grip.

'Anna,' she said.

'Are you sure you don't want to call your friend in Rome?'

There was a nun at the door already. She held a grey hospital gown and a pale Manila folder. Behind her stood Arturo Messina, leaning to see into the room. He looked curious, apprehensive and, for once, lost.

But all she could think of was Nic, trying to cope with an investigation that was falling apart, worried to death about the disappearance of Leo Falcone, a man who, she'd long recognized, had become a kind of substitute father for him.

'I'm sure,' she said.

- 6 -

They sat in a large, empty café around the corner from the Testaccio market, stirring three excellent coffees. Teresa had waved for another one already, and was rapidly munching her way through a second honey and hazelnut pastry the size of her fist.

'So now that's out of the way,' Peroni asked, 'what career were you thinking of next? Chief negotiating officer with a reconciliation service or something? You know the kind of thing. Two people who hate each other's guts walk into the room and you state that, unless they promise to leave loving one another to pieces, you'll punch their lights out.'

'Messina, Messina,' she moaned, pausing for a big bite of the pastry. 'I told you. The man's doomed already. I don't believe in kicking people when they're on the ground but there's nothing wrong in giving them a little nudge, is there? This woman mingles for Italy, boys. I mingled greatly this morning, with people you wouldn't even dare talk to. Messina has three days, four maybe, no more. Once this mess is over, however it works out, he'll be despatched to Ostia to take notes for the committee designing the next generation of parking tickets. They overestimate his abilities in my opinion, but for now I'll let that pass.'

In the space of ten minutes they'd accomplished much. Being free of the ties of the Questura, answerable to no one, made it easy to act quickly. On the way out of the market Teresa had summarized the growing dissatisfaction with Messina upstairs in the Questura. Then, after briefly agreeing on their options, they'd made three calls to pet journalists they knew: radio, TV and a newspaper. It was important the news got out soon. There was one point on which they and Bruno Messina were at one. As long as there was no body they would assume Leo Falcone was alive. Prabakaran and Uccello had been in his hands for more than twelve hours. He was not a man to be hurried.

'You really think this fantasy about a new lead on the son will keep Bramante from hurting Leo?' she asked.

The story, which was pure fabrication, would be on the radio and TV headlines within the hour, and in the early-afternoon editions of the papers.

Costa shrugged.

'For a while maybe. It can't do any harm. Bramante's got to be curious, hasn't he? Leo thought the man would give it all up if only he knew. Besides, he must realize that if he murders a police inspector we're not going to focus much time on chasing what happened to Alessio.'

'Leo's not himself,' Peroni pointed out.

'I'm not so sure about that,' Costa said.

'Nic,' Teresa said, shocked. 'He walked out in the middle of the night to get that poor girl freed. Who's to know this bastard wouldn't have killed them both?'

It was Peroni who spoke.

'No. Bramante wouldn't do that. He's bad, but bad within his own rules. Which are, I suspect, pretty much set in stone.'

'He kidnapped poor Rosa!' she objected. 'And the rest! That's what kind of man he is.'

Costa recalled Falcone's words as he left the previous night. Check out Bramante before the nightmare began. He'd played around with the records database for a few minutes before Prinzivalli raised the alarm.

'He is that kind of man,' Costa agreed. 'Or at least, he could be. Leo asked me to run some checks to see if we had anything on him before Alessio disappeared.'

'Well?' Peroni asked.

Costa grimaced.

'It's a touch inconsequential. There'd been two complaints of sexual harassment from students a couple of years before.'

'Anyone we know?' Teresa demanded.

'No. They didn't want to push it either. Someone had spoken to the university and got the usual tale. Students made up that kind of story all the time. It was impossible to prove either way.'

'Doesn't tell us much, Nic,' Peroni pointed out, disappointed. 'They probably do get that all the time.'

'How often?' Costa replied. 'The officer who went to the university had discovered there'd been other complaints about sexual intimidation too. They dealt with them internally. They said they couldn't release the details. For legal reasons. The two female students who complained to us wouldn't push the case. Bad for their degrees. So that was where it ended.'

Costa stirred the dregs of his coffee and fought off the urge to buy another. Even if Bramante was a sexual predator, it was difficult to see how that knowledge would help them in their present predicament: finding out what happened to the son. Though it might explain his wife's habits with knives.

'How long will it take them to work through Leo's list of sites?' Teresa asked.

'A day, two maybe,' Peroni said. 'That is going to be a long and tiresome job.'

'I wouldn't want to be banged up in some subterranean hellhole with Leo for two days,' she muttered. 'He'd drive me crazy, and I've grown to like him. I can push Silvio to narrow it down. Maybe Rosa will come up with something. But we don't have much time, gentlemen.'

Yet . . . Costa still struggled with some hidden aspect of the case.

'What if Leo's not what he really wants,' he suggested. 'He's just the route to getting it.'

'You mean Alessio?' Teresa asked, wrinkling her big nose in the way he'd come to recognize, an expression of intense disbelief.

'Perhaps. I don't know what I mean. I just feel that, if all he wanted was Leo dead, it would have happened by now. Yesterday or the day before. And also' – of this he was sure – 'I think Leo feels the same way too. He's been curious about something. What's really driving Bramante. He has been all along, and didn't want to let us know.'

'Too much talk,' Peroni interjected. 'We're free of Messina. We can do any damn thing we like. So what's it to be? Back into the hill?'

'Alessio's not in the hill,' Costa replied. 'I don't think he was ever there, not when they were looking. We would have found him.'

'Then where?' Teresa wanted to know.

'What if Alessio was too scared to return home for some reason?' They looked at him, dubious.

'Bear with me for a moment,' he said, and outlined his thinking.

Most of the roads from the summit of the Aventino would not have been appealing to Alessio Bramante. The Clivo di Rocca Savella was surely too steep and too enclosed to attract a scared child fleeing his own father. The streets that led to the Via Marmorata in Testaccio would pass too close to his own home for comfort.

There was only one obvious direction: to the Circus Maximus, and the huge crowd that was gathered there at the time, a sea of people in which a frightened young boy could surely lose himself.

'He'd end up in the peace camp. There was nowhere else for him to go.' Costa glanced at Teresa. 'Emily told me you were involved in events like that when you were young. She thought you might have been there.'

Teresa Lupo blushed under Peroni's astonished gaze. This was, Costa realized immediately, a part of her past the two of them had never shared.

'I had a rebel streak back then,' she confessed. 'I still do. I just disguise it well.'

'Really?' Peroni wondered with a sigh of resignation. 'You were there when all this happened?'

She winced.

'No. Sorry. I was asked. But at the time I was in Lido di Jesolo sharing a very small tent with some hairy medical student from Liguria who thought – wrongly, I hasten to add – that he was God's gift to women.'

Peroni cleared his throat and ordered another coffee.

'Even Lenin had holidays, Gianni,' she continued defensively.

'Not with hairy medical students in a tent,' Peroni grumbled.

'Oh, for God's sake,' she snapped. 'I apologize. I had a life before we met. Sorry. We all existed before. Remember? What the hell were you two doing fourteen years ago? It's OK, Nic. I can answer that in your case. You were at school. And you?'

Peroni watched his *macchiato* getting made on the silver machine.

'We'd just had our second child. I was like Leo, a *sovrintendente* waiting to take the inspector's exams. I got three weeks' paternity leave, more than I was owed but some people upstairs were in my debt. The weather was beautiful, from May right through to September. I remember it so clearly. I thought . . .' He grimaced. 'I thought life had never been so good and it would all just roll on like that forever.'

Costa recalled that year too. It was then that his father first started making mysterious appointments with physicians, the beginning of a slow, unremarkable personal tragedy that would take more than a decade to unfold.

'It was a beautiful summer,' she agreed. 'Unless you happened to be living on the other side of the Adriatic. I stayed in that stupid little tent for two weeks, with some jerk I didn't even like. You know why? I couldn't face it any more. Thinking about all the horrors that were going on then. It wasn't that long since the Berlin Wall fell, and we'd all sat around for a couple of years waiting for the global paradise of happiness and plenty to reveal itself. What did we get? Wars and massacres. A little more madness with every passing day. Just a little local conflict in the Balkans, some small reminder that the world wasn't the safe, comfortable place we all dreamed it would be. We went from there to here in the blink of an eye, and for the life of me I don't remember much of what happened in between.'

She shook her head.

'I went because I was running away. Sorry.'

'No problem. It was a wild hope.'

'Damn right. There must have been thousands of people there!'

Costa had checked that too.

'The authorities said two thousand. The protestors said ten.'

'The authorities lie. They always do.'

She downed the last of her pastry.

'Mind you, ten's a bit much. You really thought I'd remember some child wandering around looking lost? You haven't been to many demonstrations, have you? They're full of lost kids, of all ages. It's just real life only magnified. Chaos from start to end.'

'I suppose . . .' he said, thinking.

Peroni stared at his new coffee. 'So what the hell do we do now?'

Falcone would have achieved more than this. He wouldn't just have imagined where Alessio might have wandered. He would have looked ahead, trying to work out how this fact might be extracted from the hazy lost world of fourteen years before.

'The newspapers would have taken photos,' Costa said, almost without thinking. 'We could try the libraries.'

'Nic,' Peroni groaned. 'How long would that take? And how willing do you think they would be to help two off-duty cops and a nosy pathologist?'

'We just gave three of them great stories!' Teresa objected.

'For our own reasons,' Peroni went on. 'They're not stupid. They don't think we're doing this out of charity.'

'Vultures,' she spat out, so loudly the waiter gave them a worried glance.

'Vultures perform a useful social function,' Peroni reminded her, but by then Teresa was bouncing up and down on her seat with unbounded excitement, scattering pastry crumbs everywhere as she did so.

'You two really have led sheltered existences. There's more to the media than a bunch of political cronies in flash suits. What about the radical press? They were surely there.'

Peroni gave her his most condescending look.

'You mean long-haired people like that individual you shared a tent with? Teresa. Listen to me, dear heart. The radical press hate us even more than the others.'

'Not,' she said, slyly, 'when you're in the company of a comrade.'

- 7 -

The paper was in a small first-floor office above a pet shop in the Vicolo delle Grotte, a half-minute walk from the Campo dei Fiori, in a part of Rome rapidly being taken over by expatriates and tourists. On the steep internal staircase Costa, who'd lived nearby a few years back and found it hard to afford the rent even then, muttered something about this being an expensive home for a weekly publication dedicated to liberating the downtrodden masses.

'You misunderstand the patrician breed of Italian socialist,' Teresa declared, taking the steps two at a time, looking keen to reacquaint herself with this lost piece of her past. 'This is about raising the proletariat up to their standards, not bringing them down to the hoi polloi.'

At the head of the stairs was a tall, gaunt, elderly man with a long, aristocratic face and a head of thinning, wayward grey hair. In his bony hands he held a tray bearing four full wine glasses. It was not yet eleven in the morning.

'If they were Carabinieri I wouldn't let them on the premises, you know,' he announced in a high-pitched, fluting voice of distinctly upper-class origin. 'I still have my principles. I am Lorenzo Lotto. Yes, I know what you're thinking. Is it the one you read about in the papers all the time? Rich son of that family of wicked oppressors who pollute the Veneto with their factories? It is indeed. They should find something better to write about. A man does not choose his own parents.'

He thrust the tray at them.

'I was thinking of the painter,' Costa said.

Lotto's beady eyes looked him up and down.

'How extraordinary, Teresa,' the man declared. 'Trust you to find the one police officer in Rome with half a brain. That Lorenzo died destitute, scribbling numbers on hospital beds for a living, though he was a better man, and a better artist, than Titian. I am a mere revolutionary, a small yet significant cog in the proletarian machine. Drink, boy. Tame that intellect or you'll be counting paper clips in the Questura for the rest of your life.'

'It's a little early for us, Lorenzo,' Teresa pointed out.

'Tush, tush. This is from the wicked family's private estate. You can't even buy it in the shops. Besides, one should always take alcohol when meeting a former lover. It dulls the senses, and God knows we both need that.'

Teresa blushed.

'This day just gets better and better,' Peroni groaned and walked in ahead of them.

They'd phoned first in order to check what material the paper possessed from the nineties. Teresa had sounded hopeful. *La Crociata Populare* was not, in spite of its name, popular, though it remained a crusade on the part of its wealthy owner. But it was meticulous about its forty-year history and, unlike most of the small left-wing weeklies, it didn't fill its pages exclusively with columns and columns of dense, unreadable text. Several well-known photographers had begun their careers working for Lorenzo Lotto's pittance salary, the bare union minimum. Even Pasolini had submitted material from time to time during the paper's brief heyday in the early seventies.

As Lotto led them through what passed for an editorial floor – a shabby room with four desks, three of them unoccupied – Costa's hopes began to fall. He'd read *La Crociata* himself from time to time. The photos were good. And numerous. It would surely take an entire library to catalogue all the negatives, contacts and prints from over the years.

Lotto led them to the corner where the one visible member of staff, a small, timid-seeming young woman, sat in front of a gigantic computer screen, working on what looked like the next issue. A headline screaming about government corruption yelled out from it in bright red, heavy type.

'Katrina,' he said quietly. 'It's time for you to go clothes shopping.'

Her eyes flashed at him, baffled, a little in awe.

'Here.'

Lotto reached into his pocket and pulled out a wad of notes. She took them, smiled and scampered for the door.

'The redistribution of wealth,' Lotto said quietly. 'I pay them what the unions demand. But they're my children really. The only ones I have.'

'Pictures, Lorenzo,' Teresa reminded him.

'I know.'

He punched some keys on the computer then beckoned them to join him. At Lotto's bidding Costa sat down in Katrina's chair and looked at the screen. There was something marked 'Library' there. He clicked on it and saw an entry form.

'Now what?' he asked.

'The state will be brought down by its ignorance of modern technology,' Lotto remarked. 'I could drag in a thirteen-year-old child off the street and he'd know more about this than you.'

Keywords, Costa thought. Clues. You typed them in. The stupid computer tried to guess what you meant.

'Every photo that has ever passed through our hands is stored somewhere in there,' Lotto boasted. 'Not just the ones we printed. *Everything*. Forty-three years' worth. It cost me a fortune. Without it I doubt even I could keep this place afloat.'

'You're a picture agency now?' Teresa asked.

'As well as . . . And why not? Engels was a clerk in Manchester when he was keeping Marx and his family from starving in London. Industry and investment, Teresa. Unfashionable these days I know . . .'

Costa typed in: *peace camp*.

What seemed like a million tiny photos appeared on the screen.

'Typical lazy liberal thinking,' Lotto declared. 'Dialectical materialism, boy. Ideas will only come from precise material conditions. Not obscure generalities.'

'You sound like my father,' Costa snapped.

'Ah,' Lotto replied, warmly, for the first time. 'I thought you were that one.'

He leaned over and whispered in his ear.

'Do you know a year?'

'Of course.'

'How about a date.'

'Exactly.'

'Good. Why not try that?'

Costa typed in the exact day.

The screen filled again, with just as many photos.

Lotto leaned over and looked at the screen.

'We had five different photographers supplying material to us then. Everyone wants their picture in the paper, don't they?'

'How many?' Costa asked.

'Look at the screen! Eight hundred and twenty-eight. Thirteen rolls of thirty-six shot film, including the blanks and the failures, naturally. It costs more to take them out than leave them in. You should think yourself lucky. We're all digital now. Never mind the quality, feel the width. It would be ten times that if you were looking today.'

Costa hit on the thumbnail of the first image. It leaped to fill the screen. They could have been looking at anything. A rock concert. A demonstration. A weekend camp. Just hundreds and hundreds of people, quiet, apparently happy under the sun.

'What about time?' Costa asked.

'Sorry. Film never recorded that.'

'What about,' Teresa asked, 'telling it, "Find me a young boy in a peculiar T-shirt"?'

'It's a machine,' Lotto said severely. 'Are you going to drink my *prosecco* or not?'

'Later,' she said.

He grumbled something inaudible and wandered off. Teresa and Peroni pulled up chairs on either side and started peering at the scores of thumbnails in front of them.

'If we can scan five a minute we're done in under three hours,' Peroni said, and made it sound like good news.

Costa began flicking through the first photographer's rolls. A good third of the shots digitized by Lotto's machines were useless: out of focus, accidental. The rest were mainly mundane. A few were simply beautiful: sharp, observant, wry pictures of people who didn't know the camera was there, candid shots still bright with their original summer hues, frozen in time.

After half an hour, with his right hand starting to tire, Costa hit the button, and turned up yet another roll. The film had changed. The light was different, older, more golden, the kind that fell on Rome as the day was coming to a close.

He clicked through five more frames then stopped. None of them spoke for a moment.

The child stood centre-frame, and for once this was a subject that did look into the camera. He still wore the T-shirt they'd all come to associate with this case, the seven-pointed star of the Scuola Elementare di Santa Cecilia. This was Alessio Bramante, some time during the early evening of that fateful day, when every police officer in Rome, state and Carabinieri, was looking for him.

He was holding the hand of an untidy, overweight woman of middle age, a woman with a blank, rather puzzled expression on her flat, featureless face. She wore the kind of long pink cotton shift Costa expected of these events, and large, open-toed sandals. Next to her was a skeletal, sickly-looking man, perhaps fifty, perhaps older, with a pinched, tanned face and a skimpy grey beard that matched the meagre hanks of hair clinging to his skull.

Neither of them looked remotely familiar from any of the photos of witnesses or related individuals Costa had seen, and tried to commit to memory, in the case.

But that wasn't the worst thing. Peroni put it into words.

'Good grief,' the big man said with a sigh. 'We got it wrong all along, didn't we?'

They stared at the screen, grateful he was the one who had the guts to say it.

'I thought we were looking for a nice kid,' Peroni said, finishing their train of thought.

'It's just one photo,' Teresa reminded him.

It was, too. One photo of a child, no more than seven, turning to stare towards the camera, his features tautened into an expression of pure hatred, of unimaginable, unspoken violence directed straight into the lens.

'He was Giorgio's son,' Peroni pointed out.

'Perhaps he still is,' Costa added quietly.

- 8 -

Back in the Questura, Bruno Messina was beginning to feel a touch more in control. Now he sat at the head of the table in his own conference room, a smaller, more private place than the sprawling quarters Falcone preferred when talking to his staff. Messina believed in delegation, in keeping his immediate officers under full scrutiny after which they – in the current jargon – 'cascaded' down his desires, and pressure, to those below.

Bavetti was there with two men of his choosing, along with Peccia, head of the specialist armed squad and his deputy. Forensic had, to Messina's displeasure, decided they wished to be represented by Silvio Di Capua from the path lab, in place of the absent Teresa Lupo. He would, he thought, deal with her later. There was a mutinous atmosphere in that part of the Questura, and she surely bore much of the blame. Technically, though, they were separate departments, answerable to civilian officers. It would take a little while and some persuasion for him to work a result there.

Di Capua had brought to the meeting a lanky, bald, odd-looking individual from the university who introduced himself as 'Doctor Cristiano'. This odd pair had turned up with a laptop computer, a set of maps of the city and a report produced principally by Peroni the previous evening.

'Let me make it abundantly clear,' Messina said, opening the meeting, 'that my first priority in this investigation is the safe and early release of Inspector Falcone. Nothing is to be spared to that end. No expense, no resource. Is that understood?'

The police officers nodded gravely.

Silvio Di Capua, who had clearly learned at the knee of his mistress, rolled his eyes and declared, 'Well . . . *yes!* Did you drag me away from my work to tell me that?'

'I want our priorities clear,' Messina insisted.

'The living – if indeed Leo still is living – come before the dead. I must try to remember that in future.'

'What do we have, Bavetti?' Messina cut in.

The inspector cleared his throat and adopted a formal tone of voice.

'Prabakaran is being debriefed by two specialist female officers. This is a slow and patient process, as the procedures allow.'

'I don't want it too slow and patient,' Messina interrupted.

'Of course.'

'Has she said anything?'

'She's saying a lot, sir. The officer is being extremely helpful in the circumstances. Prabakaran is a brave and conscientious police woman . . .'

'I hate to interrupt the hagiography here,' Di Capua broke in, 'but does she by any chance have a clue where she was held?'

'We haven't got that far,' Bavetti said, taken aback at being interrogated by forensic.

'Well, what the hell are you asking her about?' Di Capua demanded.

'The woman was raped. She's with two specialist officers who are trained in dealing with cases like this. They're going through what happened very carefully . . .'

'Fine,' the pathologist went on. 'Let me point out two things. First, we know she's been raped and we know who did it. Second, Falcone's missing. Asking this poor woman about her getting raped doesn't help us find him. We need locations. We need facts.'

Bavetti shrugged.

'There are procedures . . .'

'Screw the procedures!'

Di Capua looked at Bruno Messina, pleading.

'How,' he demanded, 'do you think she's going to feel if Leo turns up dead at the end of all this? Particularly if there's something lurking in her head that could have saved him?'

Messina nodded.

'He has a point,' the commissario said. 'Made with forensic's customary grace, I must say, but he has a point.'

'Thank you,' Di Capua went on, nodding at the uniformed Peccia and his colleague. 'Now to the gun people, please? Explain.'

'We are here,' Peccia replied coldly, 'at Commissario Messina's request.'

'What for? Target practice? We don't have a clue where Giorgio Bramante is. Why the hell are you playing cowboys and Indians at a time like this?'

Messina's face reddened.

'If Leo Falcone is alive I want him kept that way. Whatever it takes. When we track him down, I'm not dealing with this animal. If they get a clean shot, he goes.'

Peccia nodded, and looked satisfied with that idea.

'Aren't there "procedures" when it comes to shooting people?' Di Capua asked sarcastically.

'Screw the—' Messina began to say, then checked himself. 'You're here to offer forensic input. Nothing else. Is there something you have to say?'

Di Capua took hold of the papers in front of him and slapped them on the desk.

'Peroni's report—'

'Peroni's report tells us nothing,' Bavetti interjected. 'It's a list of possible underground sites which Bramante may or may not have visited at some stage in the last week. It's a shot in the dark.'

'Most things are,' Di Capua replied. 'Tell them, Cristiano.'

Dr Cristiano tapped the computer keyboard idly and said, 'We know from the planarian samples we have already that the site used to store the body from Ca' d'Ossi was somewhere the university has never looked for genetic material. Last night your officer and I worked to try to narrow down the scope of listed archaeological locations which could fit this description. Numerically it amounts to—'

'Days of work,' Bavetti said. 'Weeks. For what?'

'To chase down one of the few facts you have,' Di Capua said. 'The body from Ca' d'Ossi was stored somewhere known to Bramante, near water, with a planarian population that has not been logged by La Sapienza. So what are you doing instead?'

It was Bavetti who rose to defend the investigation.

'House to house. Throughout Testaccio and the Aventino. Someone must have seen him. All we need is one lead.'

Di Capua almost leaped out of his seat.

'What? All you need's a miracle? Do you think he's waiting for you in some Testaccio tenement? Think about what we know about this man. Everything he does is underground. Living. Killing. Planning too, I'd guess. Those places are his. Out of sight in some subterranean city we don't even know. And you're going door to door, showing people photos? I don't believe it.'

The man from La Sapienza shook his bald head and said, 'Gentlemen. I am no expert in these matters. But this seems a little illogical to me.'

'What the hell is this freak doing here?' Peccia asked, furious.

'Trying to tell you people something,' Di Capua broke in. 'Listen to me and try to understand. You know nothing. We know nothing. But the nothing we know is smaller than the nothing you know, and I think we could make it smaller still. So small that, with a little help and a little luck it just might, at some point, become something.'

Messina did listen.

'What do you want us to do?'

'Prabarakan knows where she was picked up. She must have some idea how long it took to get there in the back of that van. Ask that. It's a start.'

The commissario paused for a moment then turned to Bavetti and muttered, 'Do it.'

'Sir. The idea is to allow the victim to tell her own story . . .'

'Do it!'

Messina used the ensuing five minutes to listen to a more detailed explanation of what Peroni had been working on the previous evening. As he did so he was aware of an uncomfortable realization: he had rejected Peroni's ideas because they were a part of Falcone's investigation, the kind of long-shot, imaginative leap that he regarded as typical of the inspector. He was envious of that facility, and it had coloured his behaviour. This was bad police work. And worse, bad leadership.

Bavetti got a call back. They waited and listened.

He put down the phone and said, 'Bramante drove her somewhere close by to begin with.'

'Close?' Di Capua asked, incredulous. 'Don't give me words like "close"? Minutes? Seconds?'

'A minute. Perhaps two.'

'So they were still in Testaccio? Near the market?' Di Capua asked, and unfolded a city map on the table.

'Yes. After that, much later, in the evening, they drove for no more than eight or ten minutes.'

'Quickly, or was there traffic?' Di Capua demanded.

'Very quickly. Without stopping. Uphill then downhill.'

The young pathologist smiled at that.

'He went from Testaccio on to the Aventino. It's familiar.'

'And then?' Messina asked.

'Let's assume he continued in a northerly direction.'

Di Capua took out a red felt-tip pen and drew a circle on the pristine map. It ran from the foot of the Aventino by the Circus Maximus, stretching past the Colosseum to Cavour directly north, then to the Teatro Marcello in the east, and as far as San Giovanni to the west.

'Not good,' Cristiano grumbled. 'There's as much under the surface there as there is on it.'

'How many on our list?' Di Capua demanded.

The university man hammered at the keyboard.

'Twenty-seven. Sorry.'

Messina shook his head and murmured, 'Impossible.'

'Do you have archaeological data in there too?' Di Capua asked.

Cristiano nodded vigorously.

'Naturally.'

'How many of that twenty-seven have a Mithraeum?'

The bony fingers flew.

'Seven.'

Di Capua cast an eye over the computer screen.

'One of those is San Clemente. I hardly think he's going to be hiding in a busy church next to the Colosseum, not with all those Irish priests crawling around above him. That makes it six.'

He scrawled crosses on the map and pushed it over to Messina.

'Unless you have a better idea,' Di Capua added.

Bavetti bristled, furious.

'We're not even a third of the way through door to door!'

Silvio Di Capua opened his hands in a gesture of desperation.

'This is all I have, Commissario Messina,' he said softly. 'And do you know something? It's all you have too.'

Messina hated Teresa Lupo and her minions. They were intrusive and irresponsible. They never knew when to shut up either. Just one thing got them off the hook. They were right, more often than any forensic squad he'd ever known, more often, even, than the overpaid teams of the Carabinieri who had every last computer and gadget the Italian state could afford.

'We need someone who's familiar with these sites,' Messina pointed out.

Di Capua nodded.

'We've been talking to Bramante's replacement. The American woman. Judith Turnhouse. She knows these digs, probably as well as he does. I can call.'

'*I* can call,' Messina replied. 'Get me your best men, Peccia.' He stared at Bavetti. 'Door to door. What was I thinking? I lead this myself. We start at San Giovanni.'

Silvio Di Capua perked up and came over all cheery.

'Are we invited?' he asked hopefully.

'No,' Messina declared, then pointed to the door.

- 9 -

When they compared Lotto's shot with the stock photo Peroni had lifted from the Questura it was clear Alessio's long hair had been cut roughly, perhaps just minutes before this shot was taken. Someone was attempting to disguise his true identity, with his compliance, or so it seemed. All the same, there wasn't much to work with. Ordinarily, Costa would have called the Questura and passed everything to intelligence. The TV and the papers could be running the photo within hours. If the couple were Italian, someone had to know them. If they weren't, the odds were they could still be traced through European and international links.

There were two problems: time and Bruno Messina. Running to the media with names always proved a lengthy business. Possible leads had to be sifted from hundreds, perhaps thousands, of incoming calls. Bruno Messina wouldn't be interested. Not today, not when he had a policewoman who had been viciously assaulted and an inspector who was taken from under his nose. Messina wanted Giorgio Bramante's hide, and the whereabouts of the man's son seemed, on the surface, to offer nothing to assist that particular quest.

They talked through the options and got nowhere. Then they ran through the frames in the film around Alessio's first appearance. He was in two of them, with the same couple, no one else. These were after the first. He was no longer glowering hatefully at the photography. They'd taken off the giveaway T-shirt and replaced it with a plain red one marked with a hammer and sickle. He still didn't seem happy. To Costa he looked like a kid on the edge, one who'd do anything at that moment – however dangerous, however stupid – just to prove that he could.

Teresa muttered something and went off to fetch Lorenzo Lotto. He returned with the girl, who was now wearing a new bright white cotton shirt and looking very pleased with herself.

'Explain the problem,' Lotto demanded.

Costa pulled up the original photo.

'We need to know who the two people with the child are.'

Lotto eyed him suspiciously.

'Why?'

'The child's been missing ever since,' Teresa replied, on the brink of exasperation. 'We'd like to know what happened to him. This isn't some capitalist conspiracy, Lorenzo.'

He harrumphed.

'You have to expect me to ask. Katrina?'

The girl motioned to Costa and let her fingers fall on the keyboard.

Katrina spoke, finally. She had an accent. It sounded Scandinavian.

'I can find out.'

She did something with the computer, drawing a rectangle on the fabric of the woman's shift, then hit more buttons with flashing fingers, clicked on something that Costa recognized, in the brief instant it was on screen, as the word *similarity*.

Scores of thumbnails filled the screen, most of them in situations they hadn't yet reached, on different film stock, from different photographers. The woman was in all of them. Katrina had tracked her down through the unique colour and pattern of her clothing.

'What next?' Teresa shouted.

'I keep telling you!' Lotto complained. 'It's a machine. Ask the right question and you just might get an answer.'

'Who were they with?' Costa asked.

'I like this man,' Lotto declared. 'I liked your father, too, by the way. Katrina . . .'

She flicked through the photos faster than Costa could count them. After a minute she closed in on a sequence of four. The couple were at a stand of some kind. There were publications for sale, and a large banner behind, with an anti-American slogan and the name of some left-wing group Costa had never heard of.

'Ooh.' Lorenzo Lotto's face creased with an expression of extreme distaste. 'I'd quite forgotten those people ever existed.'

'Who are they?' Costa asked.

'They *were* a bunch of tree-hugging lunatics. Wanted us all to return to the woods and eat leaves. Try telling that to some Fiat worker in Turin who's about to lose his job to a sweatshop in the Philippines.'

'Lorenzo!' Teresa chided.

But he was on the phone already, talking in a low, private whisper none of them could hear. The conversation lasted less than a minute. Then he put down the phone, scribbled something on a pad, and passed the paper to Katrina.

'Email all four photos to this address now, please.'

Peroni shuffled uncomfortably on his big feet.

'Do we get to know with whom you are sharing our evidence?'

Lotto's grey eyebrows rose in disbelief.

He leaned forward and pointed at a large, bearded man seated behind the stand, in front of the banner. In one shot he was talking animatedly to the couple. The light was brighter. This was earlier in the day, before Alessio's arrival.

'The likes of us inhabit a small world these days,' Lotto said simply, bestowing upon Teresa a short glance of reproof. 'Him.'

They were silent. Then the phone rang. Lotto picked it up, walked away from them until his voice was indistinct again, and spoke for a good minute or more, making notes continuously.

The call ended. He came back and allowed himself a brief smile.

'The man's name was Bernardo Giordano. He died two years after these photographs were taken. Cancer. So much for living on leaves. Give me tobacco and alcohol any day.'

'What about the woman? Did she have kids?' Costa demanded.

'They had a nephew who came to live with them in Rome some years back. It seemed he stayed a very long time. Family problems back home supposedly.' Lotto winced. 'They were a strange pair. Even for the Vegetarian Revolutionary Front or whatever they called themselves. They wouldn't have anything modern in their lives, apparently. Not even a phone.'

'The woman's still here?' Teresa asked.

'Yes, but it may not be the same child. Not the one in the picture,' Lotto cautioned. 'There are still several hundred photos you haven't even looked at. I was starting to enjoy your company.'

'I'll go through the photos,' Teresa promised.

He sighed and tore off a strip of the paper from his notepad.

'She still lives at the same address. Flaminio. Her name is Elisabetta, and don't shorten it or she'll kill you. Three minutes by car, the way you people drive. Don't raise your hopes too much. The "nephew" left home a while back. Also, she's somewhat crazy, it seems. A diet of leaves . . .'

Costa took the note gratefully and looked at his watch.

'I wish we could work that quickly,' he grumbled.

'I am delighted,' Lorenzo Lotto replied, 'you can't.'

– 10 –

It looked little these days but the Flaminian Way was one of the oldest and most important roads in Rome, a busy route into the city built two centuries before Christ, running directly from the Capitol through the Apennines to modern Rimini on the Adriatic. Half a kilometre ahead it crossed the Tiber at the Milvian Bridge, a landmark that, Costa now recalled, had something to do with Giorgio Bramante's obsession. It was here that Christianity had become all-powerful in Rome, here, not far from the modern trams and the buses locking horns with frustrated motorists, that much of Western mankind's history was shaped in a fateful battle some eighteen centuries before. The past shaped the present; it always had, it always would, and that knowledge informed his professional outlook as much as his personal one. The line from there to here was omnipresent; part of his job was to try to discern its path in the surrounding darkness.

The rain had ceased by the time they got to the address in Flaminio that Lorenzo Lotto had given them, a narrow back alley behind the main road, close to the point where the trams changed direction, filling the air with their metallic wheezes and groans. It was an old, grimy block. The woman lived in what an estate agent would have called the 'garden apartment'. In truth, it was the basement, a dark, dismal-looking place down a set of greasy steps. Peroni opened the rusted iron gate bearing the name 'Giordano', stared down the algaed steps to the flecked red door which stood behind two rubbish bins and muttered, 'I don't know about you, Nic, but I never much liked cats.'

The stench of feline urine was everywhere, rising like a fetid invisible cloud from behind the stairwell, made worse somehow by the recent downpour.

Elisabetta Giordano didn't just refuse to have dealings with the phone. She didn't answer the doorbell either. Peroni kept his index finger hard on the button at the head of the steps for a good minute and heard nothing. Maybe it didn't work. They couldn't hear anything. Nor was there a neighbour around to offer a clue as to whether the woman might be at home, not until they were halfway down the stairs. At that moment an old man appeared behind them, waving a skinny fist in their direction.

'You two friends of the old witch?' he demanded.

'Not exactly,' Peroni replied. 'Is she around?'

'What am I, social services? Why's it my job to look after these lunatics anyway? What do I pay taxes for?'

Costa was getting impatient. There was nothing to be seen inside. The windows were opaque with dirt and dust. All he could make out behind them were a few grubby curtains; it was impossible to tell whether anyone was at home.

'Have you paid much in tax recently, sir?' he asked nonchalantly and immediately regretted it.

'Paid a fortune in my lifetime, sonny! And what do I get for it? Nothing. I phoned you morons two days ago!'

The men looked at one another.

'Phoned who?' Peroni asked. 'About what?'

'The social! That's who you deadbeats are. I know your look. All cheap clothes and bored faces. You'd think that boy of hers would come back and help from time to time. Not that the young lift a finger for anyone these days.'

Costa took three steps upwards towards the man, who stood his ground, leaning on a hefty stick. He showed him his card.

'We're not social. What did you call about?'

The man looked a little taken aback by the realization he was talking to the police.

'What else? What we've all been complaining about for years. The noise. Crazy bitch. Plays music all night, all day. Yelling to herself and calling it singing. She shouldn't be left on her own like that. We've told them a million times.'

'She sings to herself?' Peroni asked.

'Yes! She sings. Sounds worse than her stupid cats. Would you like to live next to that?'

'No,' Costa said and put away his card.

'Also' – the stick came out and jabbed perilously close to Costa's face – 'it wasn't just the singing. The last time she was yelling and screaming worse than ever. Why do you think I called?'

Costa looked at him.

'Yelling and screaming what?'

He hunted for the words.

'Like she was in trouble or something,' the old man said grudgingly. 'But don't start getting on your high horse with me. We've put up with all manner of shit from that woman over the years. If I called for help every time she went bananas you'd be here three times a day.'

'Have you heard her since?' Costa asked.

He looked guilty all of a sudden.

'No . . .'

'Where do you live?'

The man looked Costa in the face and didn't seem so sure of himself then.

'Number five. First floor. Almost above. Been there twenty-two years.'

'Go home,' Costa said. 'We may want to talk to you later.'

He didn't wait to see if the old man did as he was told. Costa walked down the steps, got in front of Peroni, and stared at the door.

The smell was bad. Peroni sniffed and screwed up his big, placid face.

'I hope I'm wrong,' he said miserably, 'but I don't think that's just cat.'

- 11 -

Lorenzo Lotto was right: the Questura ought to have these toys. They probably did but all the familiar obstacles – procedures, bureaucracy, inter-office feuding – got in the way. Photo records lived with intelligence, a bunch of secretive, surly computer freaks who were capable of doing a great job, but only on their terms, and if they and they alone pushed the buttons. Large organizations choked on their own fat, whether they were police forces or big companies. It was just one of those things. Teresa had known that for years. What she'd never understood was how quickly technique and skill had progressed out in the real world, where machines and working practices were embraced without the need for committees or long consultative procedures. Lorenzo and Katrina could achieve in minutes what would take her days. And that was another good reason not to slink back to the Questura, apologize for slugging the duty commissario – a first, for her, but something that could be overcome – then trying to lend some weight to the hunt for Leo Falcone.

She liked toys. They intrigued her. She wondered about their possibilities.

After Costa and Peroni left, Teresa spent forty minutes with Katrina going through the photos of Bernardo and Elisabetta Giordano, finding a few more frames with Alessio Bramante in them, learning nothing. He didn't look quite as angry in the others. He didn't look totally normal either. Something had happened to the child that day.

It had sent him scuttling down from the Aventino, fleeing something that could, if there were such a thing as logic in this case, only be his father. It was also, it seemed to her, quite out of reach. Kids ran away, of course. They probably had sour, bitter faces like this when they did so. It was possible Alessio had run in the wrong direction. That a couple of sickly left-wing leaf-eaters like the Giordani were child molesters or, worse, simply looking for an opportunity to find their next victim.

But it didn't feel right. She'd got Lorenzo to call a couple of other people and check on them. The same message came back from everywhere. They were solitary, decent, if deeply weird, people, who didn't like the modern world, hated mixing with their fellow human beings outside gatherings of other tree-huggers but would, when called upon, perform acts of extraordinary kindness up to the point that their meagre standing in society allowed.

Bernardo had been a tram driver all his life. His wife worked part-time in a bakery. The word 'ordinary' didn't do them justice. But they'd kept a 'nephew' for years too, a kid who became a teenager then left. Only two facts seemed to be agreed upon about him: he didn't go out much, even when he got older. And Elisabetta, possibly with help from some fellow leaf-eaters, educated him at home.

There had to be more. Teresa had drunk one of Lorenzo's glasses of *prosecco* – which was so good she steeled herself against accepting another – then sent him back fishing again. One question bothered her. The old one: money. Even leaves didn't come for free. When Bernardo was dead, one of Lotto's informants said, Elisabetta had given up her job at the bakery. This didn't ring true. A tram driver's pension wouldn't provide enough money to retire on. Most women in those circumstances, particularly one with a child to raise, would have looked for more work, not abandoned what she had.

Lorenzo came back and shook his head. No one knew where she got her income, and it intrigued plenty too. She never seemed well off. She never seemed short. It was one of life's mysteries.

'Another for the list,' she grumbled, then stared at Katrina who was starting to look bored. There were no more images of Elisabetta's horrible shift to be found. The machine couldn't find anything reliably on the basis of a face. People changed too much when seen from different angles. The mind was used to working in three dimensions. Stupid chunks of silicon weren't.

She looked at the final picture of Alessio. He was mute, a little surly, holding Bernardo's hand – or, more accurately, being held by him, since there was a tight possessiveness to the man's grip that surely said: this one won't run away again.

'The T-shirt he was wearing to begin with,' Teresa murmured. 'The one with a seven-pointed star.'

She glanced at Katrina who pulled up a photo with it on almost immediately.

'Is that too much for a machine?'

'I don't know,' she replied. 'I can try.'

The keyboard clacked. Some invisible digital robot went off on its whirring work.

'Seven is a magic number,' Katrina said, apropos of nothing.

'Only if you believe in such things,' Teresa muttered.

The screen cleared. They had most of the photos they'd seen before. Katrina did something to get rid of them. Just three remained now.

Teresa Lupo stared at them and, to her surprise, found herself wondering exactly where she stood on the subject of magic.

'Be there, be there,' she whispered, stabbing at the speed-dial keys on her phone.

The plain, idiotic beep came back at her: unavailable. She swore. *Men.*

This couldn't wait. She called Silvio Di Capua on his personal mobile.

'Greetings, minion,' she said. 'Now get a piece of paper and write this down.'

'What happened to, "And how are you this fine day?"'

'I'm saving it for later. Take these names to Furillo in intelligence. Just say to him I am now calling in the debt I'm owed and if he so much as tells a soul without my express permission I can guarantee his small yet highly embarrassing medical secret will be on every Questura noticeboard come Monday.'

'Subtle persuasion. I like that. Messina's out there ticking off the sites Peroni had down for Leo, by the way. I am personally responsible.'

'Congratulations. Tell Furillo to look at everything. Debt claims. Criminal. Motoring. Social services. Everything he can lay his prying little paws on. I want to know about records. In particular, I want to know about connections.'

'Done. Names.'

She gave him Bernardo and Elisabetta Giordano, and their address, and crossed her fingers as she spoke. Even leaf-eaters had to step out of line from time to time.

'More?'

She looked at the photos on the screen. They weren't great. This was a guess, perhaps a bad one. All the same . . .

'One,' she said.

- 12 -

The site they first visited in San Giovanni looked more like a bomb crater than an archaeological dig. It stood close to the busy hospital that ran down from the piazza, a mass of buildings, some old, some new, that, in one form or another, had been providing medical aid to the citizens of Rome for something like sixteen centuries. Peccia and his men had changed into their preferred work uniform: black, all-covering overalls, and, for the handful ready for action, hoods. They were carrying slim, modern-looking machine pistols. Messina, a man who had always preferred to stay away from firearms, had no idea what kind they were or why Peccia would prefer them. They just looked deadly. That, he guessed, was enough.

There was, naturally, a procedure. The interior layout of the target was established. A form of entry was agreed. Then a small number of men – Peccia had twelve in all – made the first sortie, watched by back-up officers.

Bruno Messina observed, uneasily, as the squad entered the low, algaed tunnels of the site next to the hospital's main accident and emergency unit. These men had the slow, mechanical gestures of trained automatons, jerking their way through the open corridors and half-hidden chambers of some ancient, underground temple as if they were taking part in some video game. He knew now why Bavetti preferred sending uniformed officers, men and women with visible faces, out into the city to ask questions. It seemed more human, more of a real response than this puppet show.

The woman didn't help either. Messina had called her personally at the office she kept in the Piazza dei Cavalieri di Malta, the same place, they now knew, that Falcone had been driven to early that morning, to await his fate. Everything about this case seemed to hinge around the Aventino. It irked him that Judith Turnhouse was unable to find a suitable location for Bramante to hide on the hill itself – the site beneath the Orange Garden had been quickly ruled out. So, he had arranged for her to be picked up and brought to the Questura, to run through forensic's short-list, nodding in agreement as she saw the list of names there, adding one herself as a possibility.

She was a thin, hard, emotionless woman, Messina thought. There was, too, a condition.

They stood above the abandoned dig, watching two black-clad figures work their way towards what appeared to be a cave running underneath the busy main road. One of the men rolled something like a smoke grenade into the darkness. There was a small explosion and a plume of white cloud. Nothing else. No figures exiting theatrically, arms in the air.

'I told you, Commissario,' the American woman snapped. 'I do this on the understanding that there will be no damage to these locations. None whatsoever.'

'We have a man missing,' Messina replied, almost pleading.

'That's not my problem. These sites are irreplaceable. God knows they get little enough care as it is . . .'

Peccia, who was watching his team with the aloof distance of an army general, leaned over and said, 'They are nothing more than fireworks. A small flash of thunder to daze anyone who's in there.'

'No one's in there!'

'How do you know?' Messina asked.

She shook her head.

'I just do. I spend half my life in these places. You get a feel for them. Whether they're current. Whether someone just gave up on them years ago. This site' – she glanced down into the pit of rubble and spent rubbish blown in from the road – 'it feels dead. You're wasting your time.'

Bavetti pulled out the map and thrust it in front of her. 'Where would you go? If you were Bramante?'

'Straight to the nearest asylum. The man's crazy. Why try to look into his head?'

'This isn't helping us,' Messina said. 'Think about it. Please.'

'I can't think like Giorgio. No one could. If you wanted the site that was most interesting archaeologically then I'd be looking at Cavour. If you wanted space, privacy, you'd go for the one near San Stefano Rotondo. Tick them off. Send in your little action men and see what they find. Just don't ruin anything.'

Three of Peccia's officers, part of the team that had been held back in reserve, rifles at the ready, stood there listening. Black masks, black guns, black clothing. They didn't look like police at all. Messina was beginning to have misgivings all round.

'What's the most obvious place?' one of them asked. 'The first one you'd go to?'

'That's easy,' she replied. 'The site at the eastern end of the Circus Maximus. Where it meets the Viale Aventino. Everyone in this business knows that one.'

The men glanced at each other.

'But it's so public,' she cautioned. 'You're in the centre of Rome. There are big roads on either side. You can see into it from miles around, from the grass, from everywhere.'

'Is it all like that?' Messina asked.

She thought about the question for a moment, trying to remember.

'Actually, no. I haven't been there for years. If you know what you're looking for, in some ways it's one of the most interesting Mithraic sites we have. Now that you people have destroyed what was on the Aventino. There are several extant underground chambers. There's a . . .'

She stopped, realizing their interest.

'What?' Bavetti demanded.

'There's a very good Mithraic altar. Giorgio fought a long battle to keep it there, to stop it going into a museum. He wanted it to stay in place.'

'The map, quick,' Peccia said.

One of the team rifled through the document bag they had and came up with a complex architectural chart. It was large; two of the men in black stretched it out so that everyone could see. Judith Turnhouse's eyes were glued to the complex illustration in front of them.

'I never did much work there,' she confessed. 'It's a lot bigger than I remember. Three levels. All those rooms.'

'The corridors are narrow,' Peccia said. 'Something like that will take us longer to clear. We'd have to be careful. I'd need to send a small team in first.'

Messina screwed up his eyes and stared at the illustration in the corner of the map. It was, he presumed, of the altar: a helmeted man fighting to subdue a struggling bull, forcing a short dagger into the dying animal's neck.

'Prabakaran was taken uphill then, for a short distance, down,' he commented. 'It would fit with him driving through over the Aventino.'

Judith Turnhouse nodded in agreement. Energetically. She'd thought of something else, it occurred to Messina.

'Well?' he asked.

'I just realized,' she said. 'Giorgio's old house. It was above this part of the Circus. When you sat in his garden and looked down towards the Palatino this was what you'd see.'

Peccia shuffled nervously from foot to foot. The rescue team hadn't done work like this in living memory. Messina wondered, for just one second, whether he ought to call in more specialist help. But it was one man. A man who had brought the state police disgrace twice now. It was no one else's job to bring him to justice.

- 13 -

Costa took out his gun, pushed against the door, pushed harder, then gave the old, peeling wood a kick. It didn't budge. This wasn't the movies. In the real world a man couldn't go anywhere he liked with a simple shoulder charge.

'I can try,' Peroni offered.

'Let's do this the easy way.'

Costa walked to the nearest window, broke through the upper panes with the butt of his pistol, found the latch, unlocked the lower half and, with some considerable effort, managed to lift it. Then he clambered through and found himself in a malodorous dark pit.

The stench was so bad he hated having to breathe.

He walked back towards the door and found the light switch. Just three weak, bare bulbs pulsed with a little yellow light when he did so. The apartment was a hovel: mess on the floor, papers and clothes, food, too. He located the latch on the door and unlocked it from the inside. Peroni walked in and glanced around.

'I wish your girlfriend was here,' Costa murmured. 'This smells like her line of work.'

'True,' Peroni replied.

He was scanning the room, not looking at the floor. Costa was aware, as always, of Peroni's squeamish side.

'What are you looking for?' Costa asked.

'Something personal. Anything.' He walked over to the fireplace and examined everything that stood above it: small, cheap ornaments, a tiny vase of plastic flowers. 'What I'd really like is a photo. Do you see any?'

There wasn't one in the room, not visible anyway. And this was procrastination. They'd been in the apartment long enough now to know what lay waiting for them . . .

There was a half-open door ahead, possibly to the single bedroom in the property. Costa took four purposeful strides and threw it wide open. He was greeted by a warm, miasmic smell, a cloud of flies, and, in the corner, several sets of twinkling, feline eyes.

He reached for the light.

Peroni, who had followed behind him, spookily silent for such a large man, swore, turned round and went back to the entrance, back to where the cat pee was predominant.

Costa stayed and took this in.

There was a body there, lying on its back, rigid on the bed. The woman was in a dressing gown, her hands taut around her throat.

One step closer and he'd seen all he needed. The knife was still in her body, plunged deep into the larynx. Her fingers gripped the shaft and the blade. Black gore had caked around the neckline of her grubby nightdress. As he watched, one of the cats ran from across the room, dashed onto her chest, and began to lick in a proprietorial, threatening gesture, staring at him, daring him to intervene.

Costa yelled at the thing then shooed it away with a violent gesture. It ran into the shadows and waited.

He tried to hold his breath as he took a good look around. Then he went back to where Peroni now stood. The odour was still there, identifiable: cat piss and old dried blood.

'Is it what I think?' the big man asked.

'Stabbed in the throat. Probably as she lay in bed. As you noticed, there are no photographs at all. Just this . . .'

He passed Peroni the photo frame he'd found in the room. The glass was broken. Half the picture had been torn away. What remained showed the sickly-looking Bernardo Giordano out of doors, standing, smiling proudly, the way a man would have done if he were being photographed next to someone, a child perhaps, of whom he was inordinately proud.

'What the hell's going on, Nic?' Peroni asked. 'Why would Giorgio Bramante want to kill some crazy old woman out here? Did he know about Alessio?'

Costa shook his head. A knife in the throat? Torn-up photos?

Peroni took two steps up the stairs, found a patch in the lee of the wall that had been left reasonably dry, sat down and stared at his partner.

'If we do nothing but call in about this, Messina will have our hides. I don't care a damn about that. In fact, unlike you, I might welcome it. But we'll either get thrown into a cell to await his pleasure or bullied into going back on duty then waiting on him and Bavetti to read the instruction manual on how to start a murder investigation. If Leo has any time at all it's not that kind of time.'

Peroni hit the target spot on. He always did. Costa wondered whether he'd ever be able to work with another officer when the big man finally gave into temptation and took retirement.

'I agree,' Costa said.

'So what do we do?'

'When we have something we can work with, we go. And make a call on the way out.'

Peroni nodded.

'And when will we have something?'

'As soon as we talk to the old man.'

Peroni smiled. He wasn't slow. He'd picked it up instantly too. He just wanted Costa to make the connection, to take the lead he knew was there already.

'*You'd think that boy of hers would come back and help.*'

'Exactly.'

Finally, something was moving. His head felt light and clear, the way it did when a case began to open up.

They walked back up the stairs, grateful for what might almost pass as fresh air. As he hit the top step, Costa's phone rang.

- 14 -

Giorgio Bramante turned the torch to his watch and frowned. Falcone sat on the broken stone wall in his cell, following his movements in the gloom.

'Are you in a hurry, Giorgio?'

'Perhaps they're happy to let you rot,' Bramante replied without emotion.

'Perhaps,' he agreed.

From what he could work out – Bramante had taken his watch after searching him in the piazza after the taxi had left – Falcone had spent a good half a day or more trapped in this subterranean prison, locked behind an iron door in a chamber of brick, rock and earth that seemed as old as Rome itself. To his faint surprise he had been treated with a distant respect. No violence, not much in the way of threats. It was as if Bramante's mind was, in truth, elsewhere, on other matters, and Falcone's taking was simply a step along the way.

He had been given a blanket and some water, left alone there for hours, though Falcone had a feeling Bramante never strayed far from the site. The man had a mobile phone and a pair of binoculars. Perhaps he simply walked to the distant entrance they'd passed on the way in to see if they were still alone. Perhaps he was waiting . . .

Now that he was back he looked as if he would stay for good, perched on the remains of an old, upright fluted column outside the iron gate, unwrapping a supermarket *panino*.

'I could use something to eat,' Falcone suggested.

Bramante looked at him, grunted, then broke the sandwich in half and passed some through the bars.

'Is this the last meal for a condemned man?' Falcone wondered. 'I'd always pictured something more substantial.'

'You're a curious bastard, aren't you?'

'That is,' Falcone replied, nodding, 'one of my many failings.'

'You were curious all those years ago.'

'About you, mainly. There was so much that puzzled me.'

'Such as?'

Falcone took a bite of the food.

'Why you took Alessio there in the first place.'

Bramante cast him a dark look.

'You don't have children.'

'Enlighten me.'

He looked at his watch again.

'A son must grow. He has to learn to be strong. To compete. You can't hide them from everything. It doesn't work. One day – it comes, always – you're not around. And that's when it happens.'

'What?'

'What people think of as the real world,' Bramante answered wearily.

'So being left alone in a cave. Somewhere he was frightened. That would make Alessio stronger somehow?'

Bramante scowled and shook his head. There was something Falcone, to his dismay, still didn't grasp.

'I never had the courage to think about parenthood,' he confessed. 'When I married, it was one of the first things my wife learned about me. You'd think she would have worked that out before. Being a father seems to require something so selfless. To raise a child knowing that, in the end, you must send it on its way. Cut the strings. Let it go. Perhaps I'm too possessive. The few things I love I like to keep.'

The last sentence surprised him. Falcone wondered if he really meant it. He wondered, too, how Raffaela Arcangelo was feeling. It had been a cruel, hard way to say goodbye. That was the point.

Then he heard something from above, a loud, high-pitched sound. The screech of a police siren.

'But at the age of seven?' Falcone added. 'It was too young, Giorgio. Even a man like me knows that. You were his father. You, of all people . . . I still find this hard to accept.'

Bramante reached into his jacket pocket and withdrew a black handgun. He pointed it straight through the bars, holding the barrel a hand's length away from Falcone's skull.

The inspector took another bite of the sandwich, finishing it.

'I hate processed cheese,' he said. 'Why do people buy this rubbish?'

'What is it with you, Falcone?' Bramante snapped. 'Don't you know how many men I've killed?'

'I've a pretty good idea,' he replied. 'But you didn't kill Alessio, even if a part of you feels you did. Yet that is what instils the most guilt in you. Surely you see the irony?'

Bramante didn't move.

'I had hoped,' Falcone went on, 'to find him. Not just for you. For his mother. For us all. When a child goes missing like that it breaks the natural order somehow. It's as if someone's scrawled graffiti on something beautiful, something you pass every day. You can fool yourself it doesn't really matter. But it does. Until someone removes the stain you never feel quite happy. You never come to terms with what's happened.'

'And you're that person?'

'I'm supposed to be. I failed. Sorry.'

'And he's still dead,' Bramante insisted.

'You don't know that for sure. I certainly don't. We searched everywhere. Ludo Torchia never said he was dead. Not to me. Nor to you either, I think. Did Ludo say anything? You beat him so hard. I would have expected . . .'

'Just lies. Lies and nonsense. My son is dead,' Bramante repeated.

'As someone once pointed out, in the end so are we all.'

He almost laughed. The gun went down.

'A police inspector who quotes ancient English economists. Who'd have thought it?'

'I *am* the curious sort.'

There was another siren now. Perhaps more than one. Closer.

Falcone took a deep breath, knowing he had to ask, uncertain of the consequences.

'When you and Ludo had sex in the cell . . . Was that the first time? The only time?'

Giorgio Bramante blinked, unmoved by the question, thinking carefully of an answer.

'I expected to be asked that fourteen years ago. Not now,' he said eventually.

Falcone shrugged.

'Pathologists are fallible too. This particular one decided to save you the embarrassment. He felt some sympathy towards you, I imagine. Many people did.'

'But not you?' Bramante asked in a cold, unfeeling voice.

'No,' Falcone agreed. 'Not on the information I saw presented to me. Was I wrong? Was that the first time?'

'The second, I believe,' Bramante said. 'Or third. I forget. A lot of students passed through my classes. Opportunities arose, on both sides. They meant nothing. To me anyway.'

'Except,' Falcone pointed out, 'he didn't meet his side of the bargain.'

The man's face darkened.

'He laughed in my face and said he still didn't know. Or care.'

Falcone nodded.

'Which is what he told us.'

'*It doesn't matter!*'

'I—'

Bramante rattled the gun against the iron bars to silence him. Then he unlocked the door and waved the weapon down the chamber. Falcone understood. There was a reason he'd returned when he did. He knew they were approaching. Perhaps there'd been a call, from a person on the outside. Perhaps . . .

Falcone thought of the ritual and the mysteries, the ideas Giorgio Bramante – and Ludo Torchia – had played with all those years ago. Powerful as they were, they remained myths. He was still convinced that what took Alessio Bramante from the world was something both more mundane, and more terrible.

Slowly, with stiff and painful limbs, he shuffled out of the cell then, when he was beyond the bars, placed his hand against the wall to steady himself. Immediately, with a sense of revulsion, he snatched it away. Something was there: a fat white worm, the size of a little finger, was working its way up the damp green stone, almost luminous in the darkness.

Falcone turned to look Bramante directly in the face.

'What if I could still find him?'

Bramante hesitated. Just for a moment. Just enough for Falcone to see that somewhere, buried deep inside the dark tangle of hate and confusion that was Giorgio Bramante, a flicker of hope, of belief, still existed.

'It's too late.'

Bramante was edging him forward, towards something emerging out of the murk.

Falcone's eyes fell on the far end of the chamber, a place partly illuminated by wan, grey daylight falling through what he took to be a gap in the earth above.

Something stood there that had not been visible in the dark when he arrived. It was low and long, the colour of good marble. A ceremonial slab of some kind. An altar, Falcone realized.

'Keep moving,' Bramante, the old Bramante again, hissed, propelling him with the barrel of the gun.

He took a few stumbling steps of his own volition. A smooth white stone slab, dusty, but still impressive, stood at waist height in front of him. On the perfect marble surface – Istrian, he thought – was a near-geometric pattern picked out in dark red.

Leo Falcone had seen sufficient crime scenes to recognize this pattern. These were classic blood spatters, fresh, too, he thought.

'Agente Prabakaran,' he muttered. 'We had an arrangement.'

'She's safe,' Bramante insisted. 'Safe and busy damning my name, no doubt. With good reason. I've no complaints.'

Bramante ran his hand across the stains, sweeping through the dust and blood.

'I had another to deal with. He wasn't someone you'll miss.'

'Seven rituals, seven sacraments,' Falcone murmured quietly, almost as an afterthought. 'Aren't you there already?'

'Not with those who count,' he answered, reaching beneath the altar to withdraw a coil of rope that was stored there, then something else. A long, slender knife, with a waving blade. Something ceremonial, Falcone thought. Something, he realized, looking at the discoloured edge, that had been used of late.

– 15 –

'Nic?'

She simply spoke his name and received, in return, such a torrent of words they silenced her immediately. Emily Deacon recognized this in Costa now. It was the momentum of the case gripping him. In this instance, a case that had far more personal resonance than most.

There was little she could do but listen. And think. Arturo had exercised his influence. She had a private room overlooking a narrow lane leading up to the Duomo, with an attentive nurse who'd already apologized for the fact that there would now be nothing to eat until the following day. He sat outside alone.

And Nic was so wrapped up in what was happening in Rome, so engrossed in the hunt to unravel the fate of the man who'd become a surrogate father over the years. She envied him. That kind of activity had always made her feel alive when she worked in law enforcement. You disappeared inside the case. It was one reason you did the job.

There was news too. Not of Leo, but of a party who might prove the key to finding him. She listened intently and found herself asking, in spite of herself, 'He's alive?'

It seemed so improbable. Disturbing, too, from the brief details Nic outlined.

Alessio Bramante had, for reasons which remained unclear, apparently walked from the Aventino to the peace camp on the Circus

Maximus, met an odd couple from one of the left-wing groups there, and, it seemed, had not simply left with them, but been brought up almost as an adopted child until leaving home some time during his mid-teens, perhaps four or five years ago.

She recalled what Nic had said about abducted children. How they assimilated the environment in which they found themselves. All of this was, she now realized with a brief shock of alarm, quite understandable. Normality, to a child, was the situation he or she faced in everyday life. If Alessio Bramante didn't return to his real home within weeks he would, surely, be lost forever. He was seven when he disappeared. What memories he had of his life with Giorgio and Beatrice Bramante would be entirely coloured by the picture of the world painted by those who replaced them. It was possible, she thought, with a growing dismay, to take a child and, with sufficient will, turn it into an entirely different creature. History was full of dictators who had created their own armies of admirers from the schoolroom.

'You'll never find him, Nic,' she said with conviction. 'If he remembers his real parents at all, he'll hate them. It's probably more like a dream to him than anything. You can't possibly hope to help Leo like this.'

'No?'

He sounded amused, the way he always did when there was more information to come.

'Tell me,' she ordered.

'We got it from one of the neighbours. They hardly met the kid. The couple never mixed. Never after the man died. The neighbour didn't even know Alessio's real name. He thought he was called Filippo. But we know what happened to him. He left home at sixteen. A little while later he came back on a visit.'

'Well?'

'In uniform. He was a police cadet, Emily. Unless he's quit for some reason, Alessio Bramante, or whatever name he uses now, is a working officer in the state police.'

She didn't know what to say.

'We're going back to yell at people in the Questura until they

365

come up with something. We know which year's intake he's got to be in. Even if he's managed to use a different name . . .'

'There'd still have to be addresses, referees,' she suggested, wishing she was with him now, feeling the adrenalin rising as this palpable lead rose to the surface.

'Exactly.'

'Why would someone like that join the police?'

There was a silence at the other end. Then Nic asked, 'It's not that strange a career choice, is it?'

'No. You know I didn't mean that. It's just so . . . odd, somehow. Why would someone with that kind of screwed-up background want to sign up?'

'Perhaps because of it. I don't know.'

'Me neither. You'd best go find him.'

'Of course.' He hesitated. She could feel the embarrassment on the line. 'I'm sorry. I never even asked. What happened at the hospital?'

'Just routine tests,' she said quickly. 'All the usual things I'm starting to get used to. There's nothing to worry about. You track down your missing schoolboy. And Leo. After that . . .'

'I can't wait,' he said quickly.

The door opened. One of the nuns walked in and scowled at the mobile phone. Emily said her goodbyes and put the handset back in her bag.

'Is it time?' she asked.

'*Si*,' she said, nodding. 'I have to do this. A little bee-sting.'

Emily Deacon rolled up the sleeve of her green hospital gown and looked away.

- 16 -

Bruno Messina cast a weary eye at the Viale Aventino. The rain had stopped. A little weak sun was struggling against the falling shade of late afternoon. Behind him the traffic backed up all the way to Piramide. To the east a solid, angry line of cars ran as far as the river. Vehicles traversed the city like blood through arteries. Everything was interlinked. One single blockage in the south could cause chaos in the north. He didn't want to know what was going on elsewhere. Messina had turned off his personal radio, intent on avoiding calls from the Questura. This was too important.

The first team to arrive at the site had discovered a woman's bag flung away close to the entrance. Inside was Rosa Prabakaran's police ID card, a clumsy lapse, perhaps indicative of the man's state of mind. Bramante's options were closing. Messina was determined that here, at the south-eastern end of the long, grass rectangle beneath the gaze of the Palatino, the man's bloody adventures would finally come to an end.

He put Bavetti in charge of dealing with the barriers to keep out traffic, spectators and the media, a job that seemed to fit his talents. For the rest he would lean on Peccia, who seemed energized by the challenge ahead, one for which his men had practised long and hard over the years, with very few real-life opportunities in which to test their mettle.

Messina drove past this place every day he went to work and, like most Romans, had scarcely given it a second thought. It was, he now realized, much more than the simple stretch of open land it appeared to be.

He stood by the empty tramlines, facing the length of what had once been a great stadium, trying to understand the geography of what lay before him. To his right stood the honey-coloured ruins of the former Imperial palaces, now reduced to a network of multi-storeyed arches, rising up the hill, their shattered tops like jagged teeth, yet still high enough, grand enough, to reach the summit. Like many a Roman schoolchild he'd been taken here on a class trip. He could remember the view to the Forum and the Colosseum and Trajan's Markets, across the hideous modern thoroughfare built by Mussolini. It was like gazing down on the city from an eagle's nest. The greener lee of the hill, looking south, always seemed more serene, part of a different, more ancient place, one, Messina ruefully reminded himself, Giorgio Bramante knew better than most.

What had once been the racetrack of the stadium was now grass with a dirt track worn through by the feet of amateur runners. At the far end, from his present position, the view to the Tiber was blocked by a long, low office building. To his left ran the park that led to the Aventino. Ahead, before the shallow dip of the racetrack, was some-thing Messina had scarcely noticed in almost four decades. A small tower – like the remnant of some shrunken medieval palace – stood remote in a meadow of long grass.

Blocked off from the stadium by a tall green wire fence stood the familiar detritus of the archaeologist's trade: white marble stones cast in irregular lines, some still showing evidence of fluting; indeter-minate rows of low brick walls rising from the soil like old bones; rusty metal gates and barriers delineating a pattern that was impen-etrable from the surface, marking out some subterranean warren of chambers and alleyways dug out of the rich, damp soil and the rock below.

And, to his left, on the Aventino side, the low, shallow roof of some more important site, rusting tin sitting over the half-visible entrance to God knows what. As a child Messina had gone into the bowels of the Colosseum, come to understand that the ancient

Romans liked to build underground, finding it a hospitable place to hide practices that were never fit for the light of day. There could be a subterranean enclave the size of the old stadium itself running from the small arched entrance, little more than a cave, that was visible from where he now stood.

Giorgio Bramante doubtless knew. Perhaps he picked this place for that very reason. Perhaps, it occurred to Messina, he had no plans to run any further, not after the final death, the last sacrifice to his lost son.

Messina couldn't shake from his head the image of Prabakaran's bag, left idly by the entrance to the site. It was almost an invitation, and that thought left him feeling deeply uneasy.

The American academic was poring over the set of maps which she had asked to be brought from the university. Messina joined her, eyed the complex maze of corridors and chambers described there, on multiple levels it seemed, and asked, 'Do you understand this site, Professore Turnhouse?'

She looked at the map and pulled a sour face.

'I told you. It's not a project I've ever been involved with directly. Giorgio worked on it when he was a student. It's hardly been visited in years.'

She peered at the paper, squinting hard.

'Also,' she added, 'this map is twenty-five years old. It's not accurate. The site's changed since then. I think there's been some ground collapse that isn't described here. It's tricky.'

'What is this place?' Peccia asked.

She stared at him. There seemed to be a little annoyance in her face.

'I sometimes think this city is wasted on the Romans,' Judith Turnhouse declared. 'This was part of the barracks of the third cohort of the Praetorian Guard. The same military unit that had the temple on the Aventino. They were wiped out when Constantine invaded Rome. Giorgio always had a thing about that.'

Peccia looked puzzled.

'An underground barracks?'

'It wouldn't all have been underground back then,' she replied.

'Only part. The temple. The ritual quarters. The ground level of the city has risen considerably over the years. You really never noticed?'

Messina shook his head.

'There's a temple here as well?'

'They were soldiers. Most soldiers, certainly in the Praetorian Guard, were followers of Mithras. That, ostensibly, was why Constantine slaughtered them. They were the heretics all of a sudden.'

'What does this tell us?' Peccia demanded crossly.

She peered at him, unmoved by the man's aggression.

'If you don't need me here,' Judith Turnhouse said slowly, 'I will quite happily go back to my work. I was rather under the impression you wanted to know where Giorgio might be in this rabbit warren. There are three levels of tunnels. Probably close to a hundred different chambers and anterooms of different dimensions. This map doesn't tell you perhaps 80 per cent of what it's like now. You could spend the next two days wandering around down there. Or I could make an educated guess. It's your call.'

'So you know where this man is?' Peccia asked, with a childish degree of sarcasm.

She shook her head.

'No. Do you?'

'What about there?' Messina asked, determined to seize back the direction of this argument, pointing to the emblem on the map: the picture of the altar, with its powerful figure, subduing the bull. 'This is the temple, isn't it?'

'Read the fine print. I told you, this place has changed.'

They stared at the paper. Sure enough, something had been scribbled underneath.

'I think,' she added, 'that's Giorgio's handwriting, by the way. It says the altar has been moved. The original position' – she pointed towards the Palatino – 'was over there. Where you can see a visible collapse in the ground. Whatever they found, it didn't go into a museum or I'd know. So it's a safe bet it's somewhere else inside this complex for safe-keeping.'

She looked them both in the face.

'And, for what it's worth, yes, I think that would be where Giorgio would go. This is all some kind of ritual for him, isn't it? Sacrificing the people he blames for Alessio. Where else would he be?'

Messina stared at the labyrinth of lines on the map. 'Where the hell do we begin?' he asked of no one in particular.

Judith Turnhouse peered at the map, scrutinizing what looked like an indecipherable maze.

'I can tell you how I'd proceed in there. I can see where a professional archaeologist would want to go. If they moved that altar, it can't be that far away.'

'So where?' Messina asked.

She laughed in his face.

'I'd need to be inside. It's not something you can read from a map. I'd have to see what it's like on the ground.'

'No, no, no, no,' Peccia began to say. 'This man is armed. I will not have a civilian around. It's impossible.'

Messina couldn't avoid the woman's gaze. She wanted to do this for some reason, and he wasn't remotely interested in what it was. All he cared about was Giorgio Bramante. And, he reminded himself, the fate of Falcone.

'Professore,' he said. 'This may be a dangerous offer you're making.'

'Giorgio hates you people,' she insisted. 'He has no reason to harm me. I don't believe, for one moment, that's even a possibility. Perhaps if I'm there, someone he knows, I can talk a little sense into him. I can try anyway. I wouldn't say we're the best of friends but at least he doesn't loathe me. Are you really going to pass up that possibility?'

'Sir . . .' Peccia began to say.

'If the Professore wishes to help,' Messina interrupted, 'it would be foolish to reject her offer.' She muttered some short thanks. 'I must insist,' Messina went on, 'that you follow the strict orders of Peccia's men. This is important.'

'I'm not intent on getting myself killed. You don't need to worry about that.'

'Good.' Messina stabbed a finger at the map. 'I want a team down there within twenty minutes. Look at this map. Listen to Signora Turnhouse. Go where she suggests. Your men in front. Always, Peccia.'

'Sir . . .'

Peccia seemed to expect something else.

'What are your orders?' he asked.

Messina didn't fully understand the question.

'If Falcone's alive, get him out of there.'

'And if Bramante resists?'

'Then do what you will. If there's a body at the end of this, let it be his. No one else's. You hear me?'

Peccia gave him a cold look.

A large black helicopter flew overhead, the roar of its blades so loud it blocked out the hard, desperate timbre Messina could hear in his own voice. He waved to Bavetti and ordered him to call off the surveillance flights. They were, surely, no longer needed. Then he ordered Peccia to begin. The man grunted and walked off to one of the dark blue vans, all of them covered in antennae, from which his unit operated. He returned with four individuals, each dressed in black, each carrying the same short, deadly-looking military machine pistol Messina had seen before, a highly mobile weapon, it seemed, with an open metal stock.

They were all about the same height: young, alert, detached. They didn't appear much like police officers at all. More like soldiers, ready for battle.

'We have no idea what you'll meet down there,' Messina said. 'Inspector Falcone may be alive or dead. If the former, I wish him to stay that way.'

'We negotiate?' one of them asked.

'You see if that's an option, by all means,' Peccia declared.

Messina shook his head.

'This man is not going to negotiate. If he says he is, it's just a ploy. He kidnapped Falcone in order to kill him. Just as he's killed others.'

'People change when they're cornered,' Peccia said.

'Giorgio Bramante does not change. You order him to lay down his weapons and hand himself over. If he doesn't comply, you act accordingly. Do I make myself clear?'

The men nodded. One of them glowered at the woman, an expression of bafflement and aggression on his face.

'Who's the civilian?' he asked.

She held out her hand. He didn't take it.

'My name is Professor Judith Turnhouse,' she said. 'I'm an archae-ologist. I think I can help you find him.'

The four of them glanced at each other. The leader grimaced.

'We can find him ourselves,' he muttered, then retrieved a black hood from his pocket and pulled it over his head.

'That,' Messina said firmly, 'I very much doubt. Professore?'

She took the map and displayed it in front of them. Her thin, nimble fingers began to work their way across its surface, following each line, travelling across the maze, tracing each chamber, each passage, every last dead end.

– 17 –

It took him five minutes to get his bearings. The thread was where he remembered it, left on the floor, just at the point where the one he now knew as Andrea, big, stupid, but strong, had grabbed him in the dark.

They went quiet when he found it. They were all grateful, even Torchia. All games, all rituals, had to come to an end, one way or another.

He couldn't begin to imagine what Giorgio would say if he found out what they'd done. Alessio had seen his father's fury in full flight only occasionally and it had left him chilled and shaking. Once he'd witnessed him beating his mother, an act that was too much, one that made him intervene, small fists flying, miniature mimics of his father's, struggling to separate them. Women were weak and in need of protection. That was something the young Alessio Bramante never questioned. What they required – all three of them – was to become closer, to wind themselves into each others' lives, so tightly nothing could come between them again, ever.

What was needed, it occurred to him, was a sacrament, and fate, or perhaps some destiny the child had found in this labyrinth, had provided one: six stupid students who thought they could get away with trespass, dreamed they could sneak into some secret, holy place, desecrate it with their clumsy rites, then walk out, free, untouched.

Smiling to himself, confident, he went on running the thread through his fingers as they walked slowly up the corridor. There was no light yet. But if he continued for a minute or more it would be there, surely. The sun. Escape. Freedom for the interlopers. They would be like the cowards rescued by Theseus, ungrateful for their release, unworthy of saving.

He caught his breath. This was such a momentous decision, one that would shape the rest of his life. To let Ludo and his fellow students flee out into the bright, burning day, unseen by Giorgio, unscathed. Or to deliver them, unknowing, into his father's hands and final judgement.

Alessio stopped. Dino Abati, who was following closely, as if he was still some kind of protector, bumped into him from behind.

'Can you see it?' Dino asked. 'The entrance?'

'Not yet,' Alessio replied, and, secretly, pulled hard on the string, felt it give some distance ahead, fall down to the ground, like a feather descending against his bare legs on its way to the rocky ground.

One more pull. He let go with his fingers. It was gone.

Seven doors, seven corridors, and a web of interlocking passageways between. Some that led to paradise. Some that led to hell. Life was a set of choices, good and bad, easy and difficult. It was impossible to avoid them.

In the light of Dino's torch he could see a doorway he'd noticed when he'd fled, laughing, from the entrance chamber which must now lie less than thirty metres in front of them.

He thought he could sense his father's presence in this area, could hear – and perhaps this was an illusion – his breathing, heavy and anxious in the dark, multiplied, echoing from the walls.

Perhaps he'd been lost longer than he thought, and Giorgio was getting restive after all this time, with anger to follow soon after.

Either I take the prize or they do, he thought to himself.

'This way,' he said, and veered left, into the square stone doorway.

Alessio Bramante didn't need to look back. They were sheep. Desperate sheep. They would follow, even for a child, one whose courage shook inside him, trembling like a leaf in the strong winds of autumn, clinging to the branch, wondering how long its tenure on life might last.

– 18 –

Emilio Furillo lived by the belief that switching from front-line police duty to running the Questura's information system was a solid, safe career move, one that saved him from dealing with both the fists of drunks on the street and the anger of dissatisfied superiors in the office. Now he stared at the jabbing finger of Teresa Lupo and wondered whether it was time to reassess that position.

'It seems,' he said, in a hurt tone of voice, 'extraordinarily cruel that you should use a personal confidence in order to seize preferential access to the filing system. And through a third party too.'

Three months before he'd quietly approached her about some problems he'd been experiencing in his marital life, anxious to know if a particular drug would offer a remedy. He'd managed to thrust most of this to the back of his mind until Silvio Di Capua, her chief morgue monkey, came in grinning that morning with an unsubtle reminder, accompanied by a demand to leapfrog the data queue.

She glowered at him now.

'What?' the pathologist barked.

'I thought there was such a thing as doctor-patient privilege.'

'I am not your doctor. You are not my patient. What you are is someone who came to me looking for a place to score cheap Viagra.'

'Look,' she went on. 'This is not why I'm here. You have the names. That thing in front of you is the computer. Try getting them up for me, if you'll pardon the expression.'

Di Capua's request went against all established procedure. The system was there for the Questura, not the morgue.

'This is quite untoward . . .' he grumbled.

'Oh, for God's sake, Emilio. Don't you know what's going on out there? Leo Falcone's been snatched by that murderous animal he put away years ago. I'm trying to help.'

'That,' he snapped, 'is the job of the police.'

'The names,' she insisted. 'Just look—'

It got worse. Two other people he didn't want to see walked in. Furillo felt more emboldened with this pair.

'I heard about you,' he told Costa and Peroni. 'After she smacked the commissario this morning you walked out. Result? You are off duty. Everyone here knows that. Good day.'

'This is important . . .' Costa began to say.

'Everything's important!'

'Also,' Teresa Lupo objected, 'I was here first.'

The two pulled up chairs and didn't look ready to leave. Furillo wondered, for a moment, whether he really could call the desk downstairs and insist this trio be ejected from his office.

'We think we can identify him,' Peroni said. 'Does that get us up the line?'

Teresa squirmed on her chair, obviously reluctant to let go of her position, but interested too.

'You have a name for Alessio now?' she asked.

'Not exactly,' Costa volunteered. 'But we know what happened to him.' He paused. 'Alessio joined the police. He became a cadet. That would be four years ago. One of the neighbours saw him in uniform.'

She looked at them, momentarily lost for words.

'The police?' she asked. 'As in you people?'

'As in us,' Peroni agreed.

'Emilio,' Teresa Lupo said. 'Kindly put me on hold. Call up all the cadets from four years ago who had a home address in Flaminio.'

'This is not . . .' he began.

She was staring at him malevolently. 'Of course,' she added, 'if you're too busy, my friends and I could always retire to the canteen for a little chat.'

Furillo muttered furiously under his breath, dashed something into the keyboard, and turned the screen for them to see.

There were sixty-seven cadet recruits with city addresses that year. The only one from Flaminio was female.

'Satisfied?' he asked.

They peered forward and looked at the names and addresses on the screen. The two men deflated visibly. Teresa Lupo nodded and said nothing.

'What about the rest of Italy?' Costa asked.

Furillo worked the machine.

'How much time do you have? There are over 1,800 names there.'

He smiled then. This felt good.

'Any more questions?' Furillo asked.

'Where are those damned searches I asked for on *my* woman?' Teresa Lupo demanded, slapping her plump little fist on the desk. 'Where are the—'

He hit the right keys.

'Here,' he replied. 'I did them earlier. I just wanted to hear you ask nicely. I'm still waiting.'

Then he ran down a summary of what he'd found. There was nothing, Furillo said, to connect Elisabetta and the late Bernardo Giordano with her other woman whatsoever.

Peroni shook his head.

'That's the late Elisabetta, too, by the way,' he said. 'We just passed the case on to what few detectives are still left working upstairs. Who the hell is "her other woman"?'

'However . . .' Furillo continued, only to be ignored completely.

'The woman I found in Lorenzo's pictures after you left,' Teresa Lupo explained, interrupting. 'She was with Alessio in the peace camp before he met the Giordanos. My guess is that she's the one who brought Alessio to them. It looked that way. She was a member of their weird little group of Trotskyite tree-huggers. Lorenzo checked.'

Costa and Peroni glanced at each other.

'*What* woman?' Peroni demanded.

There was that infuriating know-it-all smirk on her face again, and from the look on the men's faces it got to them as much as it did to Emilio Furillo.

'The name I was asked to check,' Furillo interjected, 'was Judith Turnhouse, if that's any help.'

'Thanks,' she spat at him. 'Spoil all my surprises!'

Costa shook his head, baffled.

'You're saying that Judith Turnhouse took Alessio to the peace camp that evening?'

'I'm saying more than that. I looked her up in the phone book. She lives in some tiny studio apartment at the back of Termini. Cruddy place for a university academic, don't you think?'

Costa remembered the clothes she wore the first time they met her. Cheap clothes. Academics of her stature weren't badly paid at all. The money had to be going somewhere.

'Via Tiziano, 117a,' Furillo said, pointing at the screen, and getting ignored all round.

'In one of those photos,' she continued, 'Judith Turnhouse seems to be passing them money. What if she didn't just take the boy there? What if she was his fairy godmother or something all those years? Paying for his keep out of her own salary? Elisabetta must have needed that, surely, after her husband was gone.'

She paused.

'Elisabetta's dead too?' she asked.

'Murdered,' Peroni replied. 'Three nights ago. All the rest of this is . . . speculation.'

'Damn it, Gianni!' Teresa pulled out the prints she'd had made from Lorenzo's machine. 'Look at them. Tell me this isn't her.'

The two of them leaned over and examined the photos.

'It's her,' Peroni agreed instantly. 'But what does that mean? She's out with Messina now, trying to help him track down Bramante and Leo. It doesn't make sense.'

'Signora Turnhouse . . .' Furillo began.

Teresa Lupo waved her heavy arms in the air.

'She was protecting Alessio from his father! What else could it be?'

'From what exactly?' Peroni asked. 'And why? For all these years?'

'Enough! *Enough!*'

Emilio Furillo never shouted. A loud voice always seemed, to him, an admission of defeat. But there were times . . .

They stared at him, aware how rare his sudden ill-temper was.

'Emilio?' the pathologist asked.

'I told you there was no connection between this Signora Turnhouse and the Giordanis. None that I could see.'

They waited.

'That does not mean,' he continued, 'that I found nothing.'

'Out with it,' she ordered.

'Some years ago this woman was stopped for speeding outside Verona. I have the full report on the system . . .'

'Summarize it,' Peroni said.

'She received a spot fine. However, there was a man in the passenger seat. He was forced to show his papers. Normally this wouldn't be a matter of records, of course . . .'

They waited.

'On this occasion,' Furillo continued, 'it was. The man was a prisoner out on weekend leave.'

She blinked at him, open-mouthed, like a freshly landed tuna.

'It was Giorgio Bramante,' Furillo announced. 'To save you some time I checked these dates against the incidents on the list Falcone circulated. This was the weekend the farmer, Andrea Guerino, disappeared. He was later found murdered. Not far from Verona. Make of it what you will.'

It took a little while before any of them spoke.

'Judith Turnhouse was helping Giorgio?' Peroni asked finally, amazed. '*And* keeping his son?'

Costa's mind kept returning to that first meeting with the American academic, and how it had come about. Everything had seemed so easy.

'The reason we spoke to her was because she and Giorgio had a very loud, very public argument, with the Carabinieri within earshot outside,' he pointed out. 'Those officers were always there. The two of them must have known someone would have made the connection. Someone would come, and then she could take us to the body Giorgio had left down by the river. He wants his victims seen. Not hidden away forever.'

Peroni nodded, catching on instantly.

'She told us she would have called if we hadn't arrived,' he pointed out. 'I'm sure that was the truth. So we've just been picking up the crumbs this pair have been dropping for us all along. Where does Alessio come in?'

'Tiziano . . .' Furillo said, without the least sign that Costa heard him.

'And now,' the young detective went on, 'she's leading Messina directly to Bramante.'

'Why?' Peroni demanded.

'Because it's what Bramante wants,' Costa replied immediately. 'She pointed us to the fact he was looking for those underground maps. That's what Messina is using right now. This is . . .'

It was clear in his head. He just lacked the precise words.

'A kind of performance. His last act. Leo is his finale. Giorgio Bramante wants to be found. The man needs an audience.'

He glanced at his partner.

'Giorgio Bramante never killed Elisabetta Giordano. He never even knew she existed. But if Judith Turnhouse had been playing both sides . . . Paying the woman for years. Perhaps even after Alessio left home. She had a reason to keep Elisabetta quiet. The best there was. It could have destroyed everything.'

Costa spoke with authority and a rapid, quick intelligence, Furillo thought. His demeanour reminded the older man of Falcone himself.

'We've got to let Messina know,' the young *agente* added, reaching for a phone. 'Now.'

Furillo raised a finger.

'Hostage situation. The commissario has called a radio silence for everyone except the control room and I would seriously advise you three not to show your faces there at the moment. As I was saying, Tiziano—'

'Alessio would be an *agente* by now,' Teresa Lupo said. 'A fully formed one, newly emerged from the cocoon. Where *is* he?'

'*Tiziano!*' Furillo yelled. 'Are you people listening to me or am I some kind of computer peripheral here?'

Teresa Lupo reached over and patted his right hand.

'Emilio,' she said sweetly. 'You're *never* peripheral. Not to me. We're just a little . . . stumped.'

'God, I wish I had that on camera,' Furillo sighed. 'Judith Turnhouse lives at 117a Tiziano. If you look here' – he pointed at the screen – 'you will see that one of the recruits from four years ago, FILIPPO BATTISTA, gave the same address in his recruitment forms. Perhaps he is a lodger. I don't know. However, he is now attached to . . .'

'. . . the airport,' Peroni read from the screen.

Costa was already dialling the Fiumicino police office. They waited as he dashed off a rapid-fire set of questions then put down the phone.

'Filippo Battista still lives in Tiziano,' Costa said quietly. 'The *sovrintendente* thinks he's shacked up with some stuck-up American girlfriend almost twice his age. A little domineering, or so the gossip goes.'

'Is he on duty?' Peroni asked.

Costa grimaced.

'He was on rest day until Messina asked for volunteers. Somehow he got to hear about this and talked his way onto the team. He's in the armed response unit looking for his own father.'

The three of them took this in for a moment. Then Furillo watched them flee the room.

'You're welcome,' he muttered to himself, grateful, and a little guilty, that this was their problem, not his.

- 19 -

These caves were new to him. No comforting thread to run through his fingers. Just black damp walls that seemed to go on forever, twisting serpent-like through the hillside. Alessio led, the six of them followed, stumbling upwards on the rough-hewn rock floor, eyes fixed on the torch in the child's hand, a circle of yellow light waning as the batteries wound down.

Then a sharp corner, one that took them all by surprise. Someone fell painfully on the hard floor and let loose a low, frightened curse. The electric light flickered, became first the pale colour of dry straw, then the dark, fading ochre of the moon in a polluted Roman night sky.

After that, nothing. The dark engulfed them. Ludo Torchia started swearing, started going crazy again, yelling for something to cut through the shadows ahead.

There was nothing left. No batteries that worked. Just two matches, which Toni LaMarca lit in quick succession, only to see them extinguished by some rapid draught of air, swirling at them from a direction he couldn't discern.

Torchia was getting violent now. Alessio recognized the tone in his voice: fear and fury in equal quantities. They were arguing with each other, the fragile bond of mutual preservation that had kept them together shattering in this all-consuming darkness.

He was scared, too. What confidence the torch had imprinted on his mind was gone. Alessio Bramante couldn't hide from the knowledge that he was lost deep in the stone maw of some ancient hill, with men he didn't like, at least one of whom wished to harm him.

But the worst lay in his imagination. At that moment he could feel the tons and tons of rock and dead red earth weighing down over his head, pressing in on him from all sides, racing down his small, constricted throat to steal the air from his lungs.

The grave was like this, he thought. And this *was* a grave too, for many before him.

When he tried to shout – *Daddy! Daddy!* – he could scarcely hear his own voice. Just the mocking sound of Ludo Torchia somewhere behind him, a malevolent, hateful presence, rising from the rocky intestine of the Aventino, intent on harm.

'Daddy! Daddy!' Ludo yelled. 'Where is he now, little boy? *Where are we . . . ?*

Lost, he wanted to say. Lost and adrift in the lair of the beast, stalked by the Minotaur, which was never a real monster – Alessio Bramante had come to understand this now – but a malformation that lay inside a man, waiting for the catalyst to its birth to emerge.

All hope of victory, of delivering them like a prize, had disappeared. In his small, trembling frame, bravado had given way to terror. He wanted to see his father. He needed to feel that strong hand grip his, to be led out into the light and safety, the way only a father could.

How long had he been abandoned?

He didn't know any more. They could have been in the caves ten minutes or an hour. It was impossible to say. All he knew was that he'd never heard his father's voice. Not once. He'd never heard him call, try to bring this game to a close.

You don't care, Alessio Bramante whispered under his breath. *You never cared. Not about anything except yourself.*

A picture came into his head. Giorgio and his mother arguing, sending him out of the room when the fighting grew too loud. And, after that, crouching by the door, an illicit spy, wondering what came next.

The noises rose in his head. He'd known they would all along. This was what violence sounded like. Now he heard it twice over: in his memory, and in the melee growing behind him, an angry swell of fists and feet, struggling to follow, to find him and exact some kind of brutal, unthinking revenge, because that is what frightened men did when they could think of nothing else; that was the natural solution.

The sounds came from somewhere else too. In the darkness ahead.

A hand clutched his shoulder. He shook in abject fear.

'Alessio . . .'

The voice was taut but not unfriendly. He recognized it. Dino: the weak one.

'There's air coming into this tunnel,' Dino said. 'It's a way out. Just run towards it. *Quickly!*'

He didn't wait. He knew the sounds they were making too well: the animal grunts of brute survival, of human beings in fear for their lives.

Alessio Bramante breathed in the dank draught just discernible in the blackness, tried to imagine the direction from which it came, and ran, ran wildly, not fearing the rocks or the sharp corners in this hidden labyrinth, knowing that there was only a single hope of safety, and that lay outside, in the light, under the bright, forgiving sun, and the familiar streets that could take him home, to his mother, cowering, as she imagined the anger of Giorgio Bramante's return.

Pater.

The word slipped from his hidden memory and entered his head. This was what Giorgio had hoped to be, and failed. A real pater guarded his children. He tested them, watching from the shadows, ready to intervene when needed.

You left me, the child thought, with bitterness, and stumbled ahead, feeling the current of stale air grow stronger, smelling a hint of freshness inside it. Even, as his steps drew ahead of those who followed, something sweet, like orange blossom, the fresh, fragrant scent of life, began to drift from the living world into this bleak, cold tomb.

Then those sounds that had raged in his head became real, formed in front of him.

He stopped. Someone bumped into him. Dino's low, urgent undertone returned.

'*Move!*'

He let Dino's arm propel him forward, stopped again, checking himself. There were two voices ahead, though the noises they made weren't familiar, words he could understand and interpret, but an incomprehensible babble of heat and emotion and some hard, animal savagery he'd never understood.

Pushed again, he lurched forward, seeing light now, the pale, weak illumination of real electricity. It took no more than three steps to enter the chamber. They followed, tumbling into one another, tumbling into him, a sea of discordant, confused voices, falling into silence. Seeing, like him.

Seeing.

No one spoke. No one dared.

Alessio Bramante stared wide-eyed at the sight that lay in front of him, looking like some crazed living painting, two bodies tight against the wall, moving in a strange, inhuman fashion. He held his breath, refusing to allow his lungs to move, wondering whether, if he tried hard enough, he could freeze this scene out of his life altogether, wind back time to the point that morning where he was peering through the keyhole of the mansion of the Knights of Malta, seeing, through the stupid fly-eye glasses, a myriad worlds, none of which contained the comfort of the dome of St Peter's, great and grand on its throne across the Tiber.

It didn't work and he knew why. That was a child's game and from now on he would not be – could not be – a child.

Sometimes, he realized, the Minotaur didn't need to hunt at all. Its victims came willingly, like gifts, like sacraments, delivering themselves into the lair of the beast.

– 20 –

'Talk to me, Nic,' Teresa Lupo ordered. 'Play Leo. I'm struggling here.'

Costa had done his best to race the unmarked red Fiat, siren screaming, a pulsing police light hastily attached to the roof, from the Questura, through the Forum, past the Colosseum, to the site at the Circus Maximus. The traffic was as bad as he'd seen: gridlocked in every direction, angry, solid. For most of the way, Costa had been driving on the broad pavements, sending pedestrians scattering. At the Colosseum he'd abandoned the road completely.

Then the options ran out. There was only road from this stretch on, and it was an intemperate line of stationary metal, pumping foul fumes into the heavy, damp air of coming spring. Costa's head felt ready to burst. There was too much information in there for one man to absorb and a nagging, subterranean sensation of guilt too: Emily had gone to hospital. Costa was aware, soon after the last conversation ended, that it had been entirely one-sided. He'd scarcely asked about her at all. The hunt for Leo Falcone had caught fire. There seemed nothing else in the world at that moment. And this, he understood all along, was an illusion. Whatever happened to Leo – or had happened already – there would be a tomorrow, a future for them to share. He didn't understand how that could have slipped to the back of his consciousness so easily, as if this cruel and stupid amnesia came naturally, a gift of the genes.

It was impossible to address just then. He stared at the sea of vehicles ahead of him and cut the engine.

'They couldn't both know,' Costa said, thinking as he spoke. 'If Giorgio realized his son was still alive none of this would have happened.'

Peroni glowered angrily at the line of traffic. They were still the best part of a kilometre from the broad sweep of green behind the Palatino.

'Agreed,' he said. 'So who's pushing the buttons here? Judith Turnhouse. She helped Giorgio kill those students over the years. Why? And why the boy, for God's sake? What did he ever do?'

Costa had been a police officer long enough to understand that the simplest reasons were always the best ones, the same reasons that had existed for a couple of millennia: love, hate, revenge, or a combination of all three.

It came without thinking.

'He gave her the means,' Costa said, and threw open the driver's door.

There was a motorcycle courier a few metres away, smoking a cigarette, seated on his machine. The man was truly bunking off; his sleek, fast Honda could have cut through the traffic easily if he rode the way most Romans did.

Costa got out and flashed his ID card.

'I'm requisitioning the bike,' he said, then took hold of the lapels of the rider's leather jacket and propelled him off the seat. 'Gianni? Can you ride pillion?'

Teresa was out after them.

'What about me?'

'Sorry,' Costa apologized.

The courier drew himself up to his full height, tapped his chest and said, 'What about *me*?'

Then he took a good look at Peroni and backed off.

'No scratches,' the man said.

Costa turned the key, felt the bike dip as Peroni's bulk hit the seat behind him, tried to remember how to ride one of these things, then crunched his way through the gears, watched by the pained owner.

He eased it gently onto the broad pedestrian dirt path that ran from the Colosseum to the Circus Maximus, the route of the Number 3 tram, a quiet, leafy thoroughfare, a place for pleasant evening promenades before dinner.

There was a photographer ahead. A woman in a white wedding dress was posing next to her new husband, the Colosseum in the background. Costa steered slowly round, making sure not to splash up some mud, then opened the throttle.

The bike hit a steady fifty km/h along the dirt track, beneath the bare trees on this quiet side of the Palatino.

It took just a couple of minutes. There was scarcely a soul along the way, just a few tourists, a handful of curious spectators and, as they approached the open ground in the distance, a growing number of police vehicles, officers and the media, penned into a surly crowd.

Without being asked, Peroni took out his ID card, leaned sideways from the seat, letting everyone see his large, distinct face, one known throughout the city force.

No one stopped them, not until they reached the yellow tape that barred everything from going further. They were at the edge of the Circus Maximus. He could just make out the racetrack shape on the grassy field, a knot of blue police vans in front of it, and a small sea of bodies, some uniform, some plain clothes.

Again, Peroni's presence got them through without a word. Costa came to a halt, let Peroni dismount, struggled to put the heavy bike on its stand, then scanned the crowd of officers, pinned down Messina, in his smart dark suit, and walked up to face him. The man had the static, nervous energy senior officers possessed when they were awaiting the results of an operation they'd ordered.

'Where's Judith Turnhouse?' Costa wanted to know.

Messina glowered at him.

'You're off duty, sonny. Don't tempt my patience. I've enough to throw in your direction later.'

He didn't look as confident as he was trying to sound. Peroni pushed back Peccia, who was hoping to elbow them out of the way, then Costa took a deep breath and began to explain to Messina, as concisely and accurately as he could summarize it, what they now knew.

The blood drained from the commissario's swarthy features as he spoke. Peccia turned quiet and pale too.

'Where is Filippo Battista?' Costa demanded.

Peccia's eyes turned to the entrance to the subterranean workings beyond the sea of uniforms.

'Let me guess,' Peroni interjected. 'He was a volunteer. Nic? Let's finish the talking.'

The two men were ready to go. Peccia started barking orders: more guns, more bodies.

'No!' Costa yelled. 'Don't you understand the first thing about what's going on?'

'Educate me, Agente,' Messina said quietly.

'We're here because Giorgio Bramante – and Judith Turnhouse – summoned us. Maybe for Leo, in Giorgio's case. As for the woman . . . *I don't know.*' He paused. 'But I know this. The more men and weapons you pour into that place, the more chance there is they'll get used. You'll look bad enough with a dead inspector on your hands. Do you want Alessio Bramante dead too?'

Peccia's back-up team looked ready. They had metal-stocked machine pistols and black hoods pulled tight over their heads. Peccia himself had a weapon in his own hands too. He looked at Messina with ill-disguised contempt and said, 'We will take care of this.'

'You've got four men down there already, one of whom is the man's son!' Messina barked. 'And that woman . . .'

'I told you we didn't need the woman. Battista is one of ours. We *will* take care of this—'

'Leo Falcone is my friend,' Costa interrupted with an abrupt vehemence that silenced the pair of them. 'I am not waiting any longer.'

'No,' Messina replied quietly. He closed his eyes, looking like a man who was about to break.

'Listen . . .' he began.

'I don't have time. *We* don't have time,' Costa answered.

'*Listen, damn you!*' Messina yelled.

He had a black, lost look in his eyes. Costa glanced at his watch and thought: maybe a few seconds.

'I'm sorry,' the commissario went on. 'My father wrecked this case fourteen years ago through his instinct. I hoped to rectify that by being detached, whatever that means. I didn't . . .'

He shook his head and stared at the distant golden walls of the broken palaces on the green hill, as if he wished he were anywhere else at that moment.

'How the hell do you and Falcone cope with all this? It's not . . . natural.'

'We cope,' Costa answered instantly. 'Now, if you'll excuse me.'

Peccia joined them as they started to move.

'Stay here,' Messina ordered. 'This is my responsibility. No one else's.'

One of the men in black stopped in his tracks. Then he held out the short, lethal-looking weapon: a gift.

Messina shooed it away with his hand.

'There are three armed men down there I ought to be able to rely on. I think that's enough weapons for one day. Agente?'

Costa was already heading for the entrance. He paused.

'Allow me the privilege, please,' the commissario insisted, and took the lead.

- 21 -

Giorgio Bramante's knife caught a shaft of dying sunlight from a crack in the earth above. Falcone watched it, unmoved, thinking. Bramante had tied his hands behind his back, pushed him around, into the position he wanted. This was not, he thought, the way a man who was about to die would be treated. Bramante's attention lay elsewhere. Falcone's presence in this close, damp underground chamber, next to the altar, was of importance to this event. But he was a prop, not the central actor, much as he'd been in Monti when Bramante seemed to want to snatch him. And in the Questura too, the night before last.

There was a faint sound down the corridor, the route by which he assumed they'd approached. The gap in the rock was narrow, barely wide enough for two men. What little Falcone knew about tactical training told him this was an impossible position to attack. Anyone entering the room would be fatally exposed to Bramante's view the moment they arrived. And given a broad, uninterrupted view of the scene ahead of them, two men at an altar, one apparently about to die.

Then there was a single, distinct sound: the voice of a woman, her Italian still bearing the faint imprint of an American accent. Judith Turnhouse. Falcone recognized her hard monotone from their brief conversation by the banks of the Tiber the day before. He couldn't begin to imagine what reason she had to be there or why a police team that was surely attempting to operate with some secrecy and surprise would allow her to break silence in this way.

He and Bramante stood upright before the altar in anticipation, like figures on a stage. The woman's voice still drifted to them sporadically, approaching. As the police team grew closer, Bramante took hold of Falcone's coat, held him at his side, held the knife to his throat, eyes on the entrance, both bodies exposed to the line of fire.

Falcone didn't struggle. Instead he said, quite calmly, 'You're a poor thespian, Giorgio. I'm pleased to find something at which you don't excel. It makes you more human.'

'Be silent,' Bramante murmured, not taking his gaze from the dark cave mouth ahead. A lone torch danced there, like a distant firefly, one more sign to give away their approach.

Falcone had been unable to shake from his head the words of Teresa Lupo by the Tiber the night before when he'd believed, for a few brief moments, they might have solved the riddle of what happened to Alessio Bramante. And what Giorgio himself had said to him in Monti, when he was almost snatched. When, if Falcone was honest with himself, he could have been taken too, had Bramante pushed his luck.

'The seventh sacrament,' Falcone said, peering into Bramante's face, which now betrayed some trace of fear, and that made him a little more human too. 'It's not me at all, is it? This is about you, Giorgio. It was all along. Is suicide not enough? Is that dead child trapped in your imagination so hungry that he needs his father's blood too, along with all the rest?'

The figure next to him flinched.

'If he is dead,' Falcone pressed, 'he surely doesn't require this spectacle. If he isn't, do you think he'd be happy to know?'

The dark, intelligent eyes flashed at him for a moment.

'You don't understand,' Bramante muttered. 'You've no idea what's in my head.'

'I'd willingly listen,' Falcone said. 'If we'd had this conversation all those years ago . . .'

The man's face went dead.

'Then you'd hate me even more than you do now, Falcone. This is simple. They kill me. Or I kill you. Nothing else. Which would you prefer?'

393

Falcone waited a moment, thinking about his physical state, what worked, what was still struggling back to health. One thing, above all, he'd learned these last three days: he wasn't weak, he was merely, to some unknowable extent, damaged.

A flood of yellow illumination burst into the chamber: four torches searching, probing. Finding.

With all the remaining strength he could muster, Falcone abruptly twisted hard on his best ankle, forced his body round in a fast, powerful spin, tore himself from Bramante's grip, rolled left, kept on rolling, aware that the man's attention was divided now, between the captive he'd lost, and the group ahead of him – black suits, black masks, four men and Judith Turnhouse, whose eyes shone with anticipation, like a fury leading them on.

'No weapons!' Falcone barked, rolling two more turns on the floor, far enough away now that Bramante could not easily reach him. '*No damn weapons! That's an order!*'

The dark figure still stood in front of the altar, confused, struggling for some form of response.

Four black barrels rose in a line, aimed directly at the man with the knife who was frozen in front of them, waiting.

The woman was screeching something Falcone couldn't hear.

'Secure the prisoner,' he ordered. 'Get the knife. One of you only. The rest, cover.'

A single masked figure walked out of the line without being asked. He lowered his machine pistol and took one step forward.

Bramante held the silver blade in front of him, point upwards, looking as if it could go anywhere.

'Put it down, for God's sake,' Falcone barked at Bramante, tugging himself to his feet, leaning against the raw rock wall at the edge of the chamber, feeling the breath come back into his lungs. Feeling well, if he was honest with himself. Already, he was thinking of the Questura. An interview room. He'd be in charge. The deal he'd cut with Messina hadn't yet run out. 'And one of you get over here and cut these ropes.'

Falcone closed his eyes, fought to clear his head, which took more than a moment. He'd always been proud of the way he could claw his way back to some form of competence, some quick, avid intelligence, even in the most pressured of situations. This was a particular skill, one he hadn't lost after all.

'We need that conversation, Giorgio. We will *have* that conversation. I want this finished, once and for all . . .'

He opened his eyes, determined to control this situation. Then he fell silent. The two of them had acted so quickly, so quietly, that, during his brief, self-indulgent reverie, he'd not heard a thing. Three officers in black were now being pushed, weaponless, to one side of Bramante, hands in the air. One of their pistols sat easily in Judith Turnhouse's hands, pointed in their direction. The other two weapons lay on the floor, out of reach. The fourth individual in the team moved his gun slowly from side to side, from Bramante to his colleagues and back.

Judith Turnhouse was staring in Falcone's direction, with a bitter malevolence.

'You think,' she spat at him, 'you can take this from me? After all these years?'

'I apologize,' he replied honestly. 'I simply had no idea.'

He glanced at Bramante, who looked uncharacteristically helpless.

'But then I'm not alone in that,' Falcone added. 'Signora Turnhouse—'

The dark, ugly weapon in her hands swung round and pointed directly at his head. To his surprise, Falcone found that, for the first time since leaving the Questura the previous evening, he was genuinely in fear for his life.

'Say one more thing,' she muttered, 'and I will, I swear, empty this into your head and enjoy every moment.'

She walked forward and, without a word, took the blade from Bramante's hand. There was not a sound, not a gesture of protest.

Bramante shook his head, opened his hands, looked at her, glanced at Falcone, then stared at the woman again.

'What is this?' he asked, baffled, a shred of anger rising on his face. 'We agreed.'

'I've something to show you,' she said, and nodded at the man by her side.

The figure in black crooked the weapon under his left arm, then with his free hand dragged the hood off his head.

He was a handsome young man, Falcone thought. A little young for the job. A little naive, not fully in control. He stood erect in the half-darkness, Bramante's height, his build too. And with his looks, though they seemed paraphrased, more exaggerated somehow, so that the resemblance was obvious only by comparison.

Alessio Bramante let the hood fall to the floor then took up the gun again, angling the firearm – casually, with uncertainty? Falcone couldn't decide – towards the figure in front of the altar.

'See him, Giorgio!' Judith Turnhouse demanded, her voice anxious and excited, her torch shining into the face of the young man in front of him. '*See!*'

Bramante watched as her hands fell on his dark head, caressed his full black hair, fell down his body, reached towards his groin, lips on his young neck, damp, hungry, a gesture to which he submitted, Bramante's eyes never leaving the man in front of him, not for a moment.

'He has your eyes,' she murmured. 'Your lips. Your face.' She smiled, white teeth a glimmer of brightness in the shade. '*Everything.* I raised him to be you and not you. I raised him to be mine and you never even guessed.'

The boy – Falcone could think of him as nothing else – uttered the faintest breath of an objection. She never heard.

'Alessio?' Bramante asked, his voice a croak, his hands outstretched, face creased with shock and bewilderment. '*Alessio?*'

The shape in black recoiled, waving the weapon from side to side.

'Don't call me that! Don't you *dare* call me that!'

A chill entered Leo Falcone's blood. A terrible thought began to dawn in his imagination when he heard that dreadful sound.

The voice was wrong, too high, almost falsetto, marked with unimaginable pain and burden, breaking with some inner fury struggling to escape from inside his chest.

Judith Turnhouse's caress turned to a grip. Rigid and determined, her fingers tore into the head of fine black hair, turned his face to hers.

She took hold of the weapon in the young man's hands, thrust it hard against his chest, and said, '*Remember.*'

- 22 -

A seven-year-old child stands stiffly erect, feet frozen to the cold red earth, icy sweat trickling down his spine, motionless, like a living statue, fixed in a chamber half-lit by torches, a bare room, with no ceremony, no decoration, nothing of age about it at all.

A mundane place, a side room, an afterthought in a hidden maze of wonders. A place to hide, to flee for furtive, shameful reasons.

He can't speak. Creatures tread wildly at the back of his mind, primeval figures that have lurked there since his earliest days of remembering, waiting for the moment to emerge.

These primitive beasts tear his dreams to shreds. Ambitions shrivel to become bitter, dry fragments of a lost world.

Dreams . . .

. . . that he would deliver a gift, a sacrament, to his father.

. . . that inside this precious offering would be something to heal them all, mother, father, son. To fire the rough, malleable, formless clay of their fragile family, set it firm, young to old, old to young, a bond that was natural, would last a lifetime, until the torch got handed on, as it always would, one black day when a life was extinguished, its only remaining flame the memories burning in the head of the one who remained.

All these intimate emotions, all of a child's deepest, most private aspirations, expire at this moment, in this half-lit nothing of a place.

Nor is this small death a solitary affair. Others bear witness and add to the shame.

Behind him, the child Alessio Bramante hears them.

Sheep.

Terrified sheep, giggling in fear and, in Ludo Torchia's knowing voice, some threat, some dark knowledge there too. Like the boy, they understand that what they see now will mark them forever, enter their lives, bringing with it the poison of a memory that can never be smothered.

Nothing, from this moment forward, will be the same, the child thinks, unable to take his eyes off what he sees, unable to believe that it continues, even though his father . . .

Giorgio, Giorgio, Giorgio

. . . knows someone is there, has acknowledged their presence with a single backwards glance over his shoulder, eyes rolling wildly, like a beast's, before returning to wrestle against the human body pinned to the wall.

The two figures are crushed against each other on the pale grey stone, upright, half naked, locked together fighting to become one.

His father . . .

Giorgio

. . . impales her from behind with all his strength, his back moving, pumping with a fast, relentless rhythm, his eyes, in the brief moment they are visible, those of some crazed animal, a bull in agony, fighting for release.

Her face, half turned, glancing backwards from the rock, racked with a mix of ecstasy and pain, is familiar. A student from the class. Alessio remembers. That bright May day when he was left alone in the Palatino, for an hour, possibly more, wondering whether he would be claimed by Livia's ghost.

She was there afterwards, when Giorgio came to retrieve him, smiling in a strange, distanced way, inwardly to herself, he'd thought at the time. Like him: a little scared, yet excited too.

A detail rises in his mind: there was sweat on her brow then too.

And, in the half-light of the cave, her bright, crazed eyes are on them, some shame in her face, which is marked a little, bruised, blood at the corner of her mouth, growing, like a bubble of life, forced out of her by the brutal repetition of his lunging.

She screams.

No, no, no, no, no.

Infuriated, unfinished, Giorgio breaks free, turns to face them, a taut, bare figure of skin and hair, familiar yet foreign, screaming, his features contorted into an image from a nightmare, a demon, risen from the depths.

The child gapes at his father, ashamed, astonished by this sudden, physical presence he must witness, is unable to avoid. He recognizes this anger too. It is the same fury he, and his mother, have faced at home, in the seemingly perfect house overlooking the Circus Maximus. It is the violent rage that stems from an intrusion into his father's private world: of work, of books, of concentration, of himself.

There is an animal inside the man, a bull beneath the skin. There always was. There always will be.

Wide-eyed, furious, Alessio stares at their nakedness, remembering the rumours in school, through whispers and the small legends that children pass to their peers. Of that moment when the low, crude act between two people surpasses reason and something old rises in the blood.

It is the fury of the Minotaur, cornered in his labyrinth, of the false god, faced with his lies.

Of *Pater* failing his clan.

The rage encompasses them all. The sheep, who cower behind him, swearing they will never tell, never, though Ludo Torchia's voice is surely absent from these imprecations. It is there in the woman too, who has turned round to lean back against the rock, has picked up her torn clothing from the ground to clutch it to herself.

In the man, more than any.

And the boy . . .

. . . *the boy*, she calls, wild eyes staring at him, some sign of sympathy, some mutual shard of pain there that stops him hating her in an instant.

Nothing halts the man in his wrath, fists flailing, filling the air with menace. He is, the child understands, an elemental creature interrupted in some ancient private ceremony destined for the dark, and now doubly damned since it was both exposed and incomplete, like a sacrifice spoiled, a ritual ruined.

A rock sits in her hand. She lunges forward, dashes it to his father's head, not a powerful blow, a fairy's fist against the monster.

Stunned, Giorgio Bramante falls to the red earth, silent for a moment, eyes hazy, lacking vision.

The sheep flee, feet echoing into nothing down a corridor lit by the chain of dim yellow bulbs that lead from this grim and deadly place. Alessio wants to join them. Running in any direction provided it leaves this hidden tomb behind, forever.

Anywhere except home, a place to which Giorgio will return. A spoiled dream of lost memories and fanciful deceptions.

As his father writhes, half conscious, in the dust, the woman bends down, stares into Alessio's face, and for a moment his heart stops again. It is as if she knows his thoughts, as if nothing need be said at all, because in her eyes is a message they both understand: *We are the same. We are what he owns, what he uses.*

The blood is dry on her mouth now. She looks at him, pleading. For his forgiveness, perhaps, which he allows readily, since she is, he understands, a part of his father's damage too.

And for his hand, which joins hers, tight, the blood of Ludo Torchia's slaughtered offering joining them, and with that bond comes a promise of safety at last, perhaps, even, of release.

'Run,' she urges softly, and his eyes flicker towards his father, still barely conscious, but recovering quickly. 'Run to the Circus. Don't stop. Wait there. I will meet you.'

'And then?' the boy asks meekly, frightened and hopeful at the same time.

She kisses him on the cheek. Her lips are damp and welcome. A sudden rush of warmth falls down her cheek and enters his open mouth, a sacrament made of salt and pain and tears.

'Then I'll save you forever,' she whispers in his ear.

- 23 -

Remember . . .

The pain below, the delicious violence, the taste, the feel of blood that first time he took her, with brutal, rapid force, in a lonely dig down some desolate country lane in Puglia.

Judith Turnhouse lost her incurious virginity that day, in the remains of a dusty, unremarkable Dionysian temple while the other students worked with their trowels and their brushes, no more than fifty metres away, out in the sun, unknowing. The condition was taken from her in no more than three or four savage minutes, as if it were truly meaningless, a pathway to some brief moment of fruition on his own part, one that lay outside her own small individuality, dismissive even of its existence.

She was the simple vessel, the physical route to this conclusion, and somehow this made it all the more rewarding. In her humiliation and his animal fire lay a reality, so hard and wretched and alive that she could nurture it later, hold the feeling to herself on the cold lonely nights when she thought of him, nothing but him, over and over.

Here, now, in the Mithraeum beneath the Circus Maximus, in the place they'd agreed on all along, she could recall everything of the last fourteen years, every time they'd coupled after that first moment, every savage, bloody encounter, beneath the earth, against rough stone, fighting, fucking . . . It was all the same, and had been from the beginning.

That act was the closest she would ever achieve to ecstasy, a ritual that took her out of herself, sent bruised and battered angels flying through her head, then left her exhausted, praying for the next time.

Never again.

That's what he'd said, all those years ago, before the world turned.

It was a lie, on both their parts. She'd watched his son stare through the keyhole in Piranesi's piazza that morning, followed them furtively, as he led the child into the dig.

She'd caught his attention, drawn him away from the child. They had argued in near silence, away from the boy. They had fought again. And then, on the promise that this was the last time – no more hard, violent encounters in the dark, no more damp, mouldy soil in her hair – she'd won, proved victorious through the brute physicality of this condition that conjoined them.

Not love. That was too mundane a word, and there was scant affection inside it, much less respect.

This was *need* and, that last time, as he heaved so hard into her she could feel her skull cracking against the rock wall, she knew he *would* deprive her of this, her only delight, because that was Giorgio Bramante: hard and cold and supreme in his own mind, a man to rule over everything and everyone, to remove from them what they found most precious, simply because he could.

Even on that hot June day, feeling his power inside her, some mindless, ecstatic agony rising alongside every thrust, she understood that he would still take what he wanted, leave her there, walk out, with his strange little child, go home, to his miserable, battered wife, believing nothing had really changed, that he could return to his world of papers and study, the life of a successful, intellectual academic, and no one would know, not even when it happened again, with some other naive student this time, some vessel to take her place.

Giorgio Bramante was at war with everything: her, his family, the world. But most of all, she knew, he was at war with himself. And there lay his weakness . . .

*

He was scarcely conscious when the boy fled. He had barely recovered his senses when she scolded him for his fury and his threats, told him to stay inside, where none of his victims could see him.

When he came to, he scarcely thought about the fact she'd hit him, that they'd been seen, locked together against the wall, their secret captured, stolen.

'Alessio,' he groaned, eyes scanning the chamber anxiously.

It was all so easy.

'Those stupid students took him,' she said quickly. 'They're too afraid of you, Giorgio. Leave this to me. I'll talk to them. They'll keep quiet. I'll find Alessio. Stay here. Don't worry.'

She could find somewhere to keep the child for a day. Perhaps more. A lesson would be delivered. A bargain would be struck. It was too, though not the one either of them had expected. Giorgio's fury, and the way it sparked such an unpredictable chain of events, saw to that. But by the time Ludo Torchia was dead, everything had changed. Alessio could not be returned to the world, not without the destruction of everything she possessed. And Giorgio was gone, lost to her, through his own stupid arrogance, turning murderous and suicidal inside his own grief and guilt and overweening self-hatred.

There was no going back. Not when he asked, that first time in prison, for her help in tracking them down, one by bloody one. Not now, near the end, a conclusion he craved because only in that final act, the sacrifice of himself, would lie peace.

And in his place, she found another. As Giorgio Bramante grew more bitter, more insane, in jail, his son flourished under her tutelage, from boy to youth to man, ever closer over time until he was hers completely, as she had been his father's, bound together by the hard, brutal force of her character, a cold devotion that made captives of them all.

In her mind there was no hiatus in time between then and now, between the blood and sweat in a cave in Puglia and this end, the one he sought, the one she would deliver, in a way he had never expected, beneath the Roman earth. All was continuous, linked, cemented together by the same harsh inevitability born of the sinuous, brute passion that had once joined them.

She waved the weapon at them, the three men in black, the inspector, crouched, helpless on the floor, Giorgio, imploring, pathetic, hands outstretched.

'He failed you,' she said to his son, alarmed now, because there were more men arriving. Time was growing short. 'He failed me. He is old and useless and wasted. Do it!'

Judith Turnhouse allowed herself a single glance towards Alessio, tried to put the right emotions in her face: force, power, resolution. It was all, in the end, a matter of will.

'He came here to die,' she said quietly, with no emotion.

She watched his rifle raise. Giorgio didn't move. Then, from behind her, came a voice, distantly familiar.

Judith Turnhouse racked her racing mind to place it.

– 24 –

'She killed Elisabetta.'

Costa took two steps to place himself in front of Messina and Peroni, just an arm's length away from the young man who held the machine pistol chest-high, ready, as he'd been taught.

'Alessio?' he repeated. 'Did you hear me? She killed Elisabetta Giordano. She couldn't risk us finding out. You didn't know that, did you? *Alessio?*'

It was hard for Costa to suppress his shock. The figure in front of him looked so like Giorgio Bramante now: the same bold features, the same full head of dark hair. But there was a reluctance in him, an uncertainty, that his father had surely never possessed. Alessio Bramante had been raised by strangers, kidnapped into a world that was foreign to him. Then, when he became old enough, ensnared by the one who'd taken him in the first place, introduced, while entering a semblance of adulthood, to a slavery that hoped to pass itself off as love.

Giorgio Bramante fell to his knees. His hands came together in prayer. He stared up at his son, unable to speak, though some wordless plea for forgiveness seemed to shine out from his damp eyes.

Judith Turnhouse turned her weapon to the rock ceiling and let loose a burst of gunfire. Dust and rock and debris rained down on their heads. Bramante didn't cower. Nor did Costa.

'Look at the weak old man,' she yelled. 'Shoot him. *Shoot him!*'

Bramante's eyes couldn't leave his son. His lips moved as if mumbling some unheard prayer.

Then he said, simply, 'Forgive me.'

The woman swore. Her weapon turned to the figure on the ground. Gunfire ripped the cave, shells flying off the walls, ricocheting around them. Bramante's torso shook in a bloody fit as the bullets flew at him.

Costa was about to reach her when Alessio let loose with the pistol. The raking line of gunfire ripped her body, lifting it on unseen hands, pitching her across the dismal chamber, onto the bare rock floor where she lay in a messy heap, a still, broken sack of humanity, when the weapon finally fell silent.

A strange quiet descended on the cave. From the outside world came the sound of more men approaching. Lights flickered down the corridor, voices, some kind of reality.

Peroni was on Alessio Bramante in an instant, wrenching the gun from his hands. It was scarcely necessary.

Costa walked over and bent down to the woman. Judith Turn-house stared at the dusty ceiling with dead eyes, a gash the size of a child's fist in her forehead. He got up and went to Bramante. Falcone was there, and Peroni. They watched Alessio, down on his knees, holding Giorgio's hand.

– 25 –

A warm June day, in a world halfway between the living and the dead. Giorgio Bramante is the one crouching on bent knees at the door of the mansion of the Cavalieri di Malta, eyes tight against the keyhole, straining to see down the avenue of cypresses, to gaze out over the Tiber, on to Michelangelo's great dome, pale, magnificent, swimming in the morning mist, a perennial ghost, always present, sometimes invisible.

He takes a deep breath. This is difficult, painful.

'Can you see it?' asks a voice that seems to come from everywhere: above, below, inside. A voice that is familiar, no longer lost in the dark bitter depths of spent memories. A voice that is warm and near and comforting.

'Are you Alessio?' he asks, not recognizing the difficult cracked tones of his own voice.

'I am.'

He coughs. A warm salty liquid rises in his throat. A hand, strong, soft, grips his. He can discern little but shadows now, misty in the real world.

'I was a poor father,' he gasps, voice breaking, and tries to look beyond the pool of darkness spreading like an inky cloud through the dusty, miasmic air.

A distant shape is swimming in the mist ahead, beginning to take familiar form. He cannot see it fully yet. He feels no pain or any other sensation save the comfort of a young man's warm fingers gripping his.

'Are you *truly* Alessio?'

'I told you. Can you see it?'

'Yes,' Giorgio Bramante says, unsure whether he speaks these words or simply thinks them, 'I see it. *I see it. I see* . . .'

Out of the darkness it grows, a vision across the river, beyond the trees, white and glorious, beckoning, filling him with joy and dread, racing to fill his fading sight.

– Epilogue –

She lay in the bright white room in the hospital in Orvieto feeling a constant, deep ache in her side, the strange, nagging hurt of something missing. It was some time since she'd recovered consciousness from the operation. Every fifteen minutes a nurse visited to check her condition, measuring her blood pressure, placing an electronic thermometer in her ear. On the stroke of the hour – marked by the booming cathedral clock – the doctor, Anna, she could think of her by no other name now, entered alone, closing the door behind her, then walking to the window to bellow at the children in the street. There was a group of them playing football, even at this late hour, shouting happily as they kicked the ball from wall to wall, the way children must have done here for generations, and would for many to come.

Anna seemed younger than when they had first met that morning. Perhaps the operation had lifted something from her own shoulders. Perhaps it was simply the performance of medicine, the act of delivering some kind of remedy for a physical imperfection, that was a reward in itself.

They went through the post-op conversation. She didn't feel too bad at all. What was worst was the sense of guilt, of shameful relief. It felt as if something bad that lurked inside her had now been excised. Something that would, in a different set of circumstances, have become a child, one she and Nic had longed for. The juxtaposition of these two opposites would be difficult to shake from her head.

Then came the details. She'd scarcely listened when the doctor had outlined the possibilities before. Now there was no dismissing them. She had been subject to a procedure called a salpingectomy, the removal of one of her Fallopian tubes by laparoscopy. The remaining tube was unharmed. Her chances of a successful pregnancy in the future were now reduced to somewhere above 40 per cent.

'You won't appreciate this yet,' Anna continued, 'but you were very lucky. Had you not come to us when you did, it could have become very serious indeed. A few years ago this would have been a major abdominal operation, with some risk. We get a little better each year. Now, it is up to you.'

'To do what?' she asked puzzled.

'To learn to deal with what has happened. You've lost a child, and the fact it was an unborn one, with no possible hope of survival, does not make it any the less difficult to bear. That is how we are made. It is part of the process of trying to be a parent. Being a strong, young intelligent woman you will tell yourself this is really nothing at all. Just one of life's mishaps. You simply leave here, put it in the past, go back to your young man and start all over again. Which you will, I feel sure. But you will also feel anxiety and resentment and a general sense of bewilderment that such a cruel thing could happen, to you of all people. All of this is natural. Feel free to come here and talk to me if it helps. Any time. Orvieto isn't far from Rome. You can always phone.'

She smiled. There was something in the woman's manner – a simple, unspoken sentence, 'I understand' – that made Emily feel a little better already.

'You're getting married in the summer,' she added. 'That would be a good time to start thinking of trying again. Here's a suggestion from a stuffy, old-fashioned rural Catholic. Life is a journey, not a race, Emily. Be patient. Be a rebel for your generation. Try bearing a child out of matrimony. I suggest you discuss this with your uncle. He can't wait to come in. If that's all right with you.'

Emily shook her head.

'My uncle?'

Anna's bright eyes flared with sudden outrage.

'I knew that old goat lied! Messina said you were his niece! The daughter of some American relative of his. How else do you think you got a private room?'

'Ah,' she said quietly. 'My uncle. I'd love to see him.'

It was inevitable that, after the brief medical formalities – he already appeared to understand as much about her condition as she did – the conversation would turn inexorably to what had happened in Rome.

He explained what he knew – which seemed considerable – directly, with the precise, composed exactness she expected of a man of his background and experience. When he was done, Arturo Messina turned his face away from her and stared into the street outside, now dark, with just a single lamp to illuminate the old walls of the convent opposite, the night punctuated again by the continuing sound of ball against brick, and the distant laughter of the young.

'A woman's anger is different from a man's,' he said. 'We find ourselves gripped by a sudden fury. With a woman it can last. Grow sometimes. Had I discovered what had happened to that boy when I should, none of this would have occurred.'

She reached out and took his hand. He looked weary and old.

'You could say that about so many things, Arturo. If Bramante had been a better father, or capable of controlling his temper and his weaknesses. If this woman had come to her senses over the years, instead of letting her hatred grow alongside his.'

'None of these would have mattered if I'd found him,' he said immediately.

'No. But we're not perfect. You did what you thought best. What else is there?'

He nodded and said nothing, though she could sense his dissatisfaction.

'And Alessio?' she asked. 'What will happen to him?'

He shrugged, as if there were few options to be considered.

'The lawyers will run up some tidy bills about that. The best, I imagine, will be an accessory to attempted suicide. The dead woman could be construed as self-defence from what I'm told. He had nothing to do with the other killings, or so he says, and Leo seems to believe him so it must be true.'

Arturo paused and looked at her.

'What about the boy Giorgio first killed? Ludo Torchia?'

He grimaced.

'Torchia was no boy.'

'Then why didn't he tell you the truth? It would have been so simple.'

Arturo Messina laughed and squeezed her hand.

'You know, you really do belong in a police force somewhere,' he observed. 'You tell me.'

She considered the possibilities.

'Because he was still a boy. To himself. What Ludo was looking for was adulthood, and he believed the only way to find it was through some ritual. Perhaps any ritual. It was simply that Giorgio provided a convenient one. A ritual that bound them together, in some kind of implicit secrecy Torchia felt he couldn't break. Not even in circumstances like those.'

He nodded. There was some deep sadness in this man that affected her.

'*Especially* in circumstances like that, don't you think? When is a warrior most tested? In extremis. It makes no sense, not in our world. But it's not for us to appreciate what they believe. All that matters is that it was real to those concerned. Ludo was a meagre little creature. I imagine little else was real to him at all. He told Giorgio the truth. That he'd no idea what had happened to Alessio. Giorgio didn't believe him.'

Arturo Messina's face fell.

'Nor did I.'

'At least Leo wasn't hurt,' she said, hunting for some news with which to console him.

'More by luck than anything. I don't imagine Bramante cared much whether he was harmed or not. Principally, he simply wished to enrage the police sufficiently to engineer the end he wanted, once his labours – if I may describe them that way – were complete.'

He shook his large head.

'Lord knows, he struggled hard enough trying to drive my son to want him dead. Entering the Questura like that. Taking Leo. Doing what he did to that poor police officer.'

'They were insane. The Turnhouse woman and Bramante.'

'He was, perhaps,' he replied. 'If you count being simultaneously homicidal and suicidal as madness and there I'm not sure. In his own mind I imagine he felt himself to be as sane as the rest of us. As to the woman . . . no. She wished to inflict upon the man who had failed her the greatest pain imaginable. After all, she could have discouraged him in this pointless cycle of revenge when he was in jail, instead of becoming his accomplice. She certainly understood that if you condition a child, if you make it think there is only one possible view of the world, the one which you present to it, then the poor soul will do anything. *Anything.* Even kill its own natural father. You asked why Alessio would believe these stories. Because they came from her, and they were the only stories he had.'

'But she was wrong, Arturo,' Emily pointed out. 'In the end, he wouldn't.'

He leaned over to the bed and peered into her face.

'That is true. Nevertheless, I should tell you something. I was a good police officer for many a year, and a poor commissario only once. Consider the details. Judith Turnhouse did not simply want Alessio to shoot his father. She wanted Giorgio to understand two things before he died. That his son still lived, and would bring about his own end. And that she had taken him. Both as a child and as a man. As a lover, if one can call it that. Perhaps she treated him the way Giorgio had once treated her. Need I say more?'

'But . . .' she wanted to object, and found she lacked the words.

'We call this insanity only because we're afraid to see it for what it truly is,' he insisted. 'A perversion, a *monstrous* perversion, of the emotions we all feel and hope to suppress. Hatred and revenge. Loss and rejection. She was obsessive, cunning and fixated. But she was not insane. We should not allow ourselves that comfort.'

Arturo eyed the clock on the wall. It was now almost nine thirty.

'Your young man will be here very soon, I think. I would have brought flowers but I didn't want to steal his thunder. He will feel guilty. He will believe he neglected you at a time when you most needed him.'

'That's not true,' she answered. 'I never told Nic what was happening here. I didn't want to distract him from what he was doing. There was nothing he could do anyway. And plenty he could – and did – achieve in Rome.'

Arturo Messina seemed to approve of that answer.

'Listen to an old man. We are human. We are designed to think with the head *and* with the heart. Ignore one and the other fails you too. Talk to Nic. Listen to him. Make sure he does the same with you. It is at moments like these that families go wrong. I speak from experience. The fissures, the doubts, the guilty, unspoken fears . . . these enter our lives unseen only to surface years later, like old sore wounds we thought we'd forgotten. Be wary, my young friend. Both of you. Once you allow these creatures to breathe they can be hard to smother. After a time . . . impossible, perhaps. Raffaela and Leo Falcone must be thinking these same thoughts themselves. She is determined to see him, you know. However embarrassed he might be over that stupid phone call.'

'Of course she wants to see him. She loves him!'

'Well, love isn't everything,' he grumbled. 'Giorgio loved Alessio. That didn't make him a good father. Without a little more – work, application, intent – it is insufficient. Leo and that poor woman. I don't know . . .'

He had that reproachful look in his eyes she knew by now.

'You should call your son,' she said, interrupting him.

He emitted a short, dry laugh.

'I should. Perhaps he'll remember why we've been at war with one another all this time. For the life of me I can't. Also' – he raised a short stubby finger – 'we can share the experience of getting fired. Over a good meal and some wine, at his expense. The pay-offs they get these days . . .'

'Arturo?'

'No, don't push me. I should. I will. I promise.'

She leaned over the bed and kissed him once on his bristly cheek. Arturo Messina was, at heart, a lonely man, she thought. And loneliness was one human misfortune which could so easily be changed.

He cleared his throat and got up to go.

'We will stay in touch?' he asked. 'After you return to Rome?'

'There's a wedding in the summer. If you'd like to come.'

Arturo Messina's face brightened with sudden joy.

'A wedding!' he echoed, delighted. 'A wedding! I will raise a toast to that this evening. To you and your lucky young man.'

She surveyed the hospital room.

'Lucky?'

'You're alive, you're young, and you're in love. What's that against a few stupid medical statistics? Yes, I count you very fortunate indeed. They will be wonderful children when they come. I cannot wait to meet them.'

He took out an old blue beret, placed it on his head and grinned from ear to ear.

'Arturo is a noble name for a boy, you know,' he added. '*A domani*, Emily Deacon. I shall return – with flowers – in due course.'

He bobbed his beret and was gone. In the empty room she watched the minute hand on the clock lurch forward a cog: time passing. Lost moments, opportunities carried away on the wind, forever.

Soon there would be the sound of Nic's car. Soon there would be the touch of his hand.

She lay back on the soft white pillow and closed her eyes, listening. Outside the children played in the street under the moonlight, voices rising shapeless towards the black starlit sky, innocent and unknowing in their search for a word, a deed, an act, a thought . . . anything that might give their lives form.

– Author's Note –

Mithraism originated in Persia before the sixth century BC. From around AD 136 onwards, it was adopted as one of the most important cults among Roman and government officials. Subterranean Mithraic temples built by Imperial troops are common in all of the empire's military frontiers, from the Middle East to England. Three have been identified along Hadrian's Wall, in northern England, alone; more than a dozen, out of a suspected hundred or more, have been discovered in Rome itself.

At the heart of Mithraism lay several features which seem to have appealed to the military and bureaucratic mind. The cult was highly organized, secretive and confined to men. It demanded insistence on absolute hierarchical obedience, first to local, higher-ranking members of the cult, and ultimately to the emperor. It also used a series of different 'sacraments' to mark the passage of followers from one of its seven ranks to the next. Indeed the very word 'sacrament', while religious in nature today, stems from the original Latin term used for the oath of allegiance sworn by soldiers on joining the army. What those sacraments were, we can, in the main, only guess, but they appear to have involved a separate initiation ceremony, with a swearing of oaths and on occasion a sacrifice, for each of the specific ranks, from the most junior, Corax, to the leader, Pater.

Mithraism shared some similar ideas and features with early Christianity, though the idea that the Catholic Church copied deliberately from the cult is probably far-fetched. None of the Mithraic scriptures remain, however, since this was a religion fated to be wiped from the history books. On 28 October AD 312, at the conclusion of a civil war, Constantine won control of the empire at the Battle of the Milvian Bridge, a strategic point at which the Flaminian Way crossed the Tiber into Rome, and site of several other military engagements in subsequent centuries. Though a follower of pagan ways himself at the time, Constantine, probably for political reasons, decided to make Christianity the sole religion of the empire. As his troops sacked Rome, the repression of Mithraism began.

The most visible relic of Mithras in Rome today is the archaeological find uncovered in the nineteenth century by Irish Dominican monks excavating the basilica of San Clemente close to the Colosseum. Here, an entire underground temple has been revealed, with chambers for ceremonies, and the focal point of worship, the Mithraeum itself, where the ceremonial altar, with its image of Mithras slaying the bull, would have stood. San Clemente is open to the public; many more underground sites, including other Mithraeums, are open by appointment. The visits offered by the voluntary organization Roma Sotterranea (www.underome.com) offer the best way to explore the extensive hidden city which lies beneath modern Rome. Many sites are difficult, dangerous and illegal without expert assistance.

Since history is invariably written by the victors, we have no independent contemporary accounts of what happened on the day the victorious Constantine entered Rome. However, we know that he 'disbanded' the imperial elite troop of the Praetorian Guard, which had sided with his opponent, Maxentius, and destroyed entirely their headquarters, the Castra Praetoria, which possessed a Mithraeum in the vicinity for their private worship. A glimpse into the events of that day can be found in a less well-known Roman Mithraeum, on the Aventino hill, not far from the area where much of this book is set. Excavations beneath the small church of Santa Prisca in the 1950s revealed that the original Christian building had been built on the remains of a Mithraic temple. When the archaeologists made their way into the heart of the Mithraeum they discovered it had been desecrated, probably some time shortly after Constantine's victory, by the destruction of statues and wall paintings with axes. What happened to the temple followers during this turbulent period is unknown.